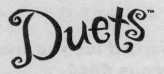

Duets™

**Two brand-new stories in every volume...
twice a month!**

Duets Vol. #63

Talented Lori Wilde will tickle your funny bone
with a very special Double Duets this month.
Lori "brilliantly weaves together lovable characters,
charming scenes and a humorous story line,"
say reviewers at *Romantic Times*.

Duets Vol. #64

Popular Bonnie Tucker kicks off the holiday season
with *A Rosey Little Christmas*. *RT* says this writer
always creates "wildly funny scenes and memorable
characters." Jennifer LaBrecque continues the fun
with *Jingle Bell Bride?*—which has more of her
trademark lively scenes and humorous dialogue.
Enjoy!

Be sure to pick up both Duets volumes today!

S0-AAZ-709

Bye, Bye Bachelorhood

"Jack warned me you were an outrageous flirt."

Jack gulped, uncertain what to do next. He opened his mouth to tell her that he wasn't his twin brother, Zack, but then without warning, he caught himself replying in a voice as provocative as CeeCee's own. "All bad, I trust."

"Jack tells me you're footloose and fancy-free." She sent him a coquettish, sidelong glance. "A no-strings-attached kind of guy."

As opposed to Jack, a forever kind of guy. The very kind of guy CeeCee's ridiculous family curse wouldn't allow her to date.

And then it hit him. A bolt from the blue.

Why not become Zack? Here was a primo opportunity to prove to CeeCee she could fall in love with a good, steady guy. Because he knew in his heart, curse or no curse, he and CeeCee were meant to be together.

"Yeah." Jack grinned wolfishly, playing the part to the hilt. "That's me. The happy wanderer."

For more, turn to page 9

Coaxing Cupid

"Is this your fort or can anyone play?" Greg quipped.

Then to Janet's complete dismay, he scooted underneath the table beside her.

"What are you doing?" she snapped.

"Keeping you company. I saw you slip under here, and curiosity got the better of me. Who are we hiding from?"

"Nobody. Now go away."

"Are you always this grouchy?"

"Only when I'm hiding under a table at an event thrown by my new bosses."

"Is your mom the problem? She's a real hoot. A little too obsessed with your love life, maybe. Or lack of one."

Janet frowned. Darn him for looking so adorable.

"You've got something on your chin," he murmured, leaning in close.

"Oh, for heaven's sake." She scrubbed vigorously at her face. "Is it gone now?"

"Nope. If you'd allow me..."

Then before she could react, he kissed her.

For more, turn to page 197

HARLEQUIN DUETS

ISBN 0-373-44129-0

Copyright in the collection:
Copyright © 2001 by Harlequin Books S.A.

The publisher acknowledges the copyright holder of the individual works as follows:

BYE, BYE BACHELORHOOD
Copyright © 2001 by Lori Wilde

COAXING CUPID
Copyright © 2001 by Lori Wilde

Bye, Bye Bachelorhood

Lori Wilde

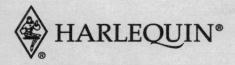

HARLEQUIN®

TORONTO • NEW YORK • LONDON
AMSTERDAM • PARIS • SYDNEY • HAMBURG
STOCKHOLM • ATHENS • TOKYO • MILAN • MADRID
PRAGUE • WARSAW • BUDAPEST • AUCKLAND

Dear Reader,

I'm delighted to share with you book number two in my medical trilogy about three best friends who've all been a little...well...jinxed when it comes to love. First there was Nurse Lacy Calder, the heroine of #50 *I Love Lacy* (Harlequin Duets, April 2001), who was struck by the "thunderbolt" and found her true love in the form of sexy surgeon Dr. Bennett Sheridan.

Now it's CeeCee's turn. Bubbly CeeCee Adams is a free-spirited, flame-haired therapist with a passion for healing and a heart as big as the world. But she lives under the shadow of a Gypsy curse. She's doomed never to find true love, so she dates adventuresome men who don't want to settle down. But her handsome next-door neighbor, Dr. Jack Travis—a forever kind of guy if there ever was one—is determined to prove that he's the man for her, even if he's got to let CeeCee think he's his wild twin brother, Zack, in order to do it.

But what happens when CeeCee discovers wild man Zack is really her best friend, Jack? You gotta turn the pages to find out. My greatest wish is that you'll smile a little, chuckle a lot and have a darned good time in the process.

Enjoy!

Lori Wilde

To LouAnn—
a wonderful person who sees the best in everyone.
Circumstances made us sisters,
love made us friends. I'm so proud of you
and everything you've accomplished.
You've come a long way, kid.

1

CeeCee Adams was cursed. Hexed. Jinxed. Doomed.

Forever unlucky in love, and destined to traipse the earth as a single woman, compliments of the Jessup family whammy.

How else to explain the numerous failed marriages and hapless love affairs among the women in her family? And how else could she account for the likes of Lars Vandergrin, a six-foot-four Neanderthal who wrestled for the WWF?

Lars had a grin to melt snow off mountain peaks, sheer blond hair cascading to his waist and hands as grabby as quadruplet two-year-olds at a shopping mall. The man also possessed the same rudimentary disregard for the word "no" as the aforementioned toddlers. For the last three hours she'd fended off his advances while sitting through the latest Tom Cruise flick and she was quickly running out of patience.

Thanks a million, Grandma Addie. As if dating in this new millennium when men are from Mars and women are from Venus isn't difficult enough.

Fifty years ago, her maternal grandmother, Addie Jessup had stolen a gypsy woman's lover. The gypsy, a rather vengeful sort it seems, not only zapped Addie with the evil eye, but damned every Jessup female for three generations. No woman in Addie's direct line—

age stayed married. Divorce was as commonplace as swapping cars.

Which was the very reason she never dated any guy for too long. She refused to fall into the same trap as her mother, aunts and older sister, Geena. No multiple marriages for her! No revolving charge account at Neiman-Marcus's bridal registry. No ugly child custody battles.

No siree. She was forever a free-spirit. Single and loving it.

Except for times like these.

She had met Lars when he had sought treatment in her physical therapy department for a torn rotator cuff. Over the past three weeks he had pestered her to go out with him. She had finally agreed, hoping to persuade him to appear in the wrestling regalia he wore as the Missing Link for St. Madeleine Hospital's charity bachelor auction held annually the third Friday in July. The auction raised healthcare funds for Houston's inner-city kids.

At the moment they were standing beneath the porch lamp on the front stoop of her apartment. Lars had her pinned against the door, his hot breath fanning the hairs along her forehead, fingers thick as kielbasa twisting the top button of her blouse. She cared deeply about the charity auction but not deeply enough to grant this slab of marble carte blanche access to her body.

"Stop it." She swatted his hand and her charm bracelet jangled. "I don't appreciate being pawed."

"Come on *bay-bee,* you owe me." He puckered his lips.

"Owe you? How do you figure?"

"Shrimp dinner, movie, popcorn."

"Hang on, I'll give you the cash."

"No cash." He shook his head and his hair swung like the artificial blond mane on the My Little Pony her first stepfather had given her for her seventh birthday. "The Missing Link wants kissy-kissy."

"If you don't remove your hands from my body this instant, you'll be singing the John Wayne Bobbitt blues."

He giggled and ground his hips against her. "You're feisty. Lars like that."

"You haven't seen feisty, buster. Hands off." She didn't intimidate easily, but a small splash of fear rippled through her. Lars was a very large man.

Immediately she thought of her good friend and next door neighbor, Dr. Jack Travis. Was Jack home?

She dodged Lars's attempt to kiss her, and shot a glance through the sweltering June darkness to the ground floor apartment across the courtyard. Light slanted through the blinds.

At that moment she would have given anything to be with good old dependable Jack, listening to jazz music, sharing a laugh. Jack had such a great laugh. A resonant sound that made her feel safe, secure and cared for. She valued their platonic relationship far more than he would ever know.

If things got really nasty, she would scream for Jack, but she wouldn't call unless she had no choice. She proudly fought her own battles. Besides, thanks to the curse, she'd had more than her share of run-ins with guys like Lars. Still, it was nice knowing she had Jack as backup.

"Come on, *bay-bee*." Lars cupped his palm against her nape. "Let's go inside."

Over my dead body!

"Listen here, Vandergrin." She splayed a palm across his chest and cocked her knee, ready to use it if necessary. "Things are moving too fast between us."

"You want me in your bachelor auction? I do a favor for you. You do a favor for me."

Blackmailer.

This time she wasn't quick enough. Lars captured her mouth and gave her a hard, insistent kiss. She was in trouble deep. Forget subtlety. No more Ms. Nice Girl. As for the charity auction, she'd just have to find another celebrity.

"Shove off!" CeeCee jerked her mouth away at the same moment Lars thrust out his tongue. Her forehead accidentally whacked into his chin.

"Yeow" he screamed, and pressed a hand to his mouth. "You made me bwite my tonwue!"

"THANK YOU FOR TAKING OUT my garbage." Miss Abbercrombe smiled at Jack.

The elderly lady, who had once been an exotic dancer and had numerous photographs displayed around her apartment to prove it, wore a chartreuse muumuu with a bright pink feather boa draped around her neck. She wobbled on three-inch mules and peered at him over the top of her soda-bottle-thick glasses. In her arms she held a snow-white poodle dubbed Muffin. The dog's curly coat was festooned with pink bows, her toenails painted to match.

"It's no problem." He picked up the trash bag and headed for the door. Miss Abbercrombe *clip-clomped* behind him.

Every Sunday night he wasn't on duty at the hospital, Jack took out the trash for the elderly single women at the River Run apartment complex. And for one other special lady as well. His next door neighbor and best friend, CeeCee Adams. At the thought of her, he smiled. Zany, bubbly, flame-haired CeeCee with her fearless zest for adventure and her unbridled lust for life. He admired everything about her, and wished he could be more like her.

Muffin whined from her owner's embrace.

"She wants to come with you," Miss Abbercrombe said. "Do you mind?"

The button-eyed mutt gazed longingly at him and wriggled from Miss Abbercrombe's grasp. Tail wagging, Muffin leaped to the ground and sniffed his ankle.

"I can't believe how much Muffin loves you. She usually hates men. Then again, you're not like most men. You're so sweet."

Yeah. So women kept telling him. But sweetness and a two-dollar bill wouldn't even buy him a cup of decaf latte at the coffee shop around the corner.

"Come on, Muff," Jack said, although he would have preferred not to have the dog snaking between his legs on his trek to the Dumpster.

He and the poodle stopped at the bottom of the stairs to pick up two other garbage sacks Jack had left behind before climbing the stairs to Miss Abbercrombe's apartment. Prince, the border collie who guarded apartment 112, jumped to his feet and trotted after them. As they rounded the corner, a roly-poly beagle/terrier cross waddled from the alley and joined the procession.

Terrific. Not only was he the neighborhood trash collector but he was now the official dog walker as well.

He caught his breath as they neared CeeCee's apartment and his pulse revved. He hadn't seen her for a couple of days and he missed her. A lot.

From the moment he'd first seen her sailing through the courtyard on in-line skates, a saucy, come-catch-me-big-boy smile on her oval face, her curly red hair streaking behind her like livid fire, he'd wanted her.

He'd known he wasn't her type, and he had never once rallied the courage to tell her how he felt. How could he? Dr. Jack was solid, responsible, dependable. Face it, he was boring.

He saw the men she dated. Scuba divers and rock climbers. Bungee jumpers and snowboarders. Guys with tattoos and pierced body parts, long hair and beard stubble. Men who stared danger in the face and laughed. Men like his twin brother, Zack.

For identical twins, their differences were amazing. Jack was cautious; Zack reckless. Jack methodical; Zack messy. Jack dedicated his life to medicine. Zack, a famous motocross champion, dedicated his life to wine, women and wheels. Most women considered Jack a great friend. Those same women considered Zack a great lover.

He wasn't jealous. Well, not much. Occasionally, however, he would have given anything to possess Zack's charm with the ladies. Like when CeeCee came over to his apartment, flopped on his sofa, tucked those pinup quality legs beneath her and filled his ears with another tale of a relationship gone bad.

If she had asked him, he could have told her where she was making her mistakes. The guys she picked were wrong for her. A spontaneous girl like CeeCee needed a steady guy to balance her out. Someone like himself. But he was too afraid of ruining their friendship to offer his unsolicited opinion.

He started up the staircase. A guttural scream from the direction of CeeCee's apartment stopped him cold. In an instant he sprang into action, sprinting the remaining steps to the second-floor landing. He spotted CeeCee standing on her doorstep grappling with a human rendition of King Kong's third cousin.

"Let go!" She tried to yank her arm from the big ape's grip.

The primate wore black leather motorcycle pants, hobnailed boots and chains. He towered at least six foot three and possessed the prominent brow of a Cro-Magnon. His platinum-blond hair dangled to his butt, and he had one hand clamped over his mouth.

Despite being four inches shorter and sixty pounds lighter, Jack never hesitated. His best friend was in trouble.

He slung the trash bags to the ground, lowered his head and plowed into the guy's abdomen at a dead run.

Jack hit hard.

The Missing Link's stomach muscles were solid as bone. The creature didn't even grunt.

Jack heard birds singing. *Tweet. Tweet. Tweet.* His knees slid to the cement.

Uh-oh.

Missing Link sort of growled, shook his head, grabbed Jack by the collar and pulled him to his feet. His long hair slapped Jack in the face, stung his eyes.

Jack's chin snapped up, and he looked into a kisser as deadly as a steel trap and he knew he'd met his Waterloo.

Fools rush in.

Which was the very reason he rarely acted heedlessly. He should have been smart and telephoned the cops.

But he hadn't thought. He'd seen CeeCee was in trouble and he had simply reacted.

A first for Jack Travis. In a weird way, in spite of the peril, he kind of enjoyed his automatic, yet foolhardy bravery.

"CeeCee," Jack managed to say, despite looking at the business end of a fist the size of a Virginia ham. "Are you all right?"

"Is she aw wright?" Missing Link howled. "She de one who made me bite my tongue."

"I'm sure you deserved it." Jack's gaze flicked to CeeCee. She looked gorgeous in skintight capri pants and a form-fitting, rainbow-colored tunic blouse.

"She's a real witch," Missing Link snarled.

"Apologize to her for your comment." Jack thrust out his chest, faced the guy down.

"What are you gonna do about it, twash boy." Missing Link planted a hand on Jack's chest and gave him a shove. Jack stumbled backward into the garbage sacks.

Calm fury overtook him. Never in his life had he been so determined. The creature was going to apologize to CeeCee if it was the last thing he ever did.

Jack picked up a trash bag, swung it at him. "I'm going to kick your backside around this apartment complex. That's what I'm going to do about it."

"Oh, yeah?"

"Yeah." Jack smacked him in the chest with the trash bag.

The bag split open, splattering garbage over the Missing Link's leather ensemble. He let out an angry whoop and lunged for Jack, trapping his neck in a stranglehold and squeezing like a starving boa constrictor.

"Don't you dare hurt him, Lars!" CeeCee commanded the iron giant. "Let him go."

Stars burst behind Jack's eyelids. Red. Yellow. White.

His head swam dizzily. He heard dogs yapping, but they sounded very far off.

If he didn't do something quickly, he was going to pass out, leaving CeeCee at the mercy of this cretin. Reaching out, he snatched a handful of long blond hair.

And jerked with all his might.

"Ow! Stwop pulling my hair," he howled.

Jack tugged harder.

Lars spun to the left, his elbow wrapped around Jack's neck. Both of his fists were entangled in Lars's mane.

CeeCee bound into action. Faster than Wonder Woman in a tailspin, she lunged onto Lars's back.

For one crazy, dizzy moment the three of them were locked in a bizarre tango. Lars staggered forward, then back, trying to maintain his balance with CeeCee above him, Jack beneath his feet.

"Let him go!" CeeCee shouted again.

"Make him wet go of me," Lars bawled.

Muffin, Prince and the beagle-terrier mix barked and chased them in a circle.

"Everybody let go of everybody," Jack managed to say in a throttled voice.

Throughout the apartment complex doors were opening. People shouted. An audience gathered in the courtyard. More dogs scaled the stairs and joined the fray.

Lars spun into the wall trying to dislodge CeeCee who still clung to his back. In the process, his grip on Jack's neck loosened.

Jack released Lars's hair and instead reached for his ankles, intending on tripping him.

"Jump off of him, CeeCee."

"He's the Missing Link."

"Tell me about it. He's a cross between King Kong and Mighty Joe Young."

"No, you don't understand. He's Lars Vandergrin, a professional wrestler, Jack."

"Now you tell me."

Lars growled.

"Jump. I swear he's going down," Jack urged her, determined to remain undaunted in spite of the fact he was tangling with a professional wrestler. He kept his hands locked like handcuffs around the man's ankles.

CeeCee cleared Lars's back at the same moment he tumbled like a felled redwood straight into the pile of trash sacks torn open during the fight.

Slam dunk!

Lars hit with a thud. The staircase shook. He lay lifeless in the debris.

Jack and CeeCee looked at each other.

"Is he breathing?" She squinted. "Oh my gosh, did we kill him?"

Pulse pounding at the thought he might have hurt a fellow human being, Jack hurried forward to investigate.

"*Oof,*" Lars groaned. He sat up and slowly shook his head with the lethargic motion of a hibernating bear rousing from a long winter's nap.

Jack backed away, his hands raised. "Let's have no more trouble."

Lars looked down. Peanut butter and coffee grounds hung in his hair. Something green and sticky oozed from his elbow. Eggshells decorated his lap. A banana peel dangled from one ear. Muffin licked the toe of his boot. The other dogs were sniffing hungrily at his clothes.

"My hair!" Lars burst into tears.

"Gee," CeeCee muttered, standing on tiptoes to peer over Jack's shoulder. "What a big baby."

Muffin looked up at Lars and growled.

"Poodles!" Lars cried. "I hate poodles." The huge man lumbered to his feet and took off.

The yelping dogs gave chase, nipping at the Missing Link's heels as he thundered down the stairs. *Woof, woof, woof.*

Jack and CeeCee leaned over the railing, watching the Missing Link screech away into the inky darkness, then turned to smile at each other.

The neighbors who had gathered during the altercation, applauded and cheered before finally ambling back to their apartments, shaking their heads in amusement.

CeeCee flung her arms around Jack's neck. Her gold charm bracelet jangled merrily in his ears. Her cheeks were flushed, her green eyes sparkling with excitement, her hair sexily mussed. Her well-rounded chest rose and fell heavily against his.

She smelled exquisite. Like rainbows and sunshine and moonbeams. Jack's stomach took a roller-coaster ride up to his throat and then plunged back down again. He realized he was holding his breath.

Waiting.

"My hero!" she exclaimed, then cupped his face in her hands and kissed him.

Rock my world, baby, yeah.

CeeCee couldn't say who was more stunned by her impromptu kiss. She or Jack.

She certainly hadn't planned on kissing him. A smart girl didn't go around kissing her best guy friend on the lips. Not if she intended to keep him as her friend, and she considered Jack's friendship one of her most prized possessions.

But what a Leonardo Dicaprio/Kate Winslet/Titanic sort of kiss it was!

CeeCee sank as hard and fast as the ill-fated ocean liner.

Jack's clean-shaven cheeks were smooth against her palms, a pleasing contrast to the scruffy-faced men she normally dated. Driven by spontaneous impulse, she pressed her mouth to his in the heat of the moment, intending nothing more than a quick peck to thank him for rescuing her from Lars.

Instead his mouth welcomed her warmly. She had allowed her eyelids to drift shut, her lips to part.

Blood strummed through her veins, pounded loudly in her ears. Her knees drooped like overcooked spaghetti. Her skin tingled as if she had sprinted a mile in under a minute flat.

Oh, she never wanted to stop.

In the course of the past five months she had touched Jack many times. She had brushed against his fingers reaching into the same popcorn bowl they shared while indulging in their mutual passion for Monty Python movies. She had patted his shoulder to comfort him when things had not gone well at the hospital. She had even taken his hand and helped him from his car into his apartment after he'd had eye surgery to correct his nearsightedness.

While touching him in the past had been a pleasant experience, it had never raised the kind of response in her that kissing him did.

She wanted to keep on kissing him until the earth stopped spinning. Until the sun stopped rising and setting. Until birds stopped migrating and the polar ice caps melted like Popsicles in Arizona.

Holy cow, what was wrong with her? She could not risk romantic involvement with Jack. Not now. Not ever. She was cursed. Any love affair could only end tragically, and she would never hurt him like that.

Ever.

He was too good.

CeeCee's eyes flew open and she found herself staring deeply into Jack's startled stare.

Instantly they broke apart and dropped their gazes, neither able to look at the other.

"Um…I'm sorry. I didn't mean…I got carried away." CeeCee lightly fingered her sizzling lips, both amazed and terrified at what had just transpired between them.

What had she done? Without intending to do so she'd caused a gigantic shift in their relationship.

"You took me by surprise," Jack admitted, a good-natured smile flitting across his lips. "But it was a very nice surprise."

"Whew." She focused her gaze on the garbage strewn across the upstairs landing. Her next words were very important. She had to treat the kiss casually, as if it meant absolutely nothing.

"Whew indeed."

"What a mess. I'll find fresh garbage bags and help you clean up."

He reached out a hand and lightly encircled her wrist with his fingers. "Forget the garbage for now. I think we should talk about what just happened."

Nervously she laughed and pushed her free hand through her hair. His fingers burned like a brand against her skin. "You want to talk about Lars?"

"No," he said firmly. "I want to talk about you and me and that kiss."

CeeCee swallowed hard. "Let's not make a mountain from a molehill. It was just a 'thank you' kiss."

"It felt like much more to me."

"Please, Jack," she begged.

She didn't want things to change between them. If she admitted she had experienced something monumental when their lips met then he would demand more. She knew Jack. Whenever he fixed his mind on something he wanted he never let go.

"Please, what, CeeCee?" His voice was husky, his body tense.

"Let's forget about the whole thing."

"I don't want to forget about it."

The expression in his dark brown eyes clearly said, "I want to be *waaay* more than friends with you". That look scared the bejesus out of her.

CeeCee cleared her throat. She couldn't have Jack believing they might have a romantic future together. Better to hurt his feelings a little now than to break his heart later.

Cruel to be kind, so the saying goes.

Opening her mouth, CeeCee told the biggest whopper of her life. "I'm sorry to disappoint you, Jack, but it was like kissing my brother."

2

LIKE KISSING HER BROTHER!

Jack fumed to himself twenty minutes later after he'd disposed of the garbage and taken a cocky Muffin, complete with a hank of long blond hair triumphantly plucked from the Missing Link's head, back to Miss Abbercrombe. Apparently the wrestler's poodle phobia had been well founded. Jack actually felt a little sorry for the guy. Muffin could be more vicious than a pit bull.

He washed up in his bathroom, and stared at himself in the mirror. How did CeeCee know what kissing a brother was like? She didn't even have a brother.

He studied his reflection. Okay, maybe he was a bit stodgy and maybe he didn't have the animal magnetism of the Missing Link, but to say kissing him was like kissing her brother.

Ouch! Low blow.

Plus, he knew she was lying. He had felt her willing response. Her breathing had quickened; her lips had softened; her arms had gone around his neck. She had murmured deep in her throat like a contented kitten. Then, when she had told him the kiss had not affected her in the same way it had affected him, her cheeks had flushed tomato-red and she'd been unable to look him in the eyes.

Yep. She'd fibbed. What he didn't know was why, but he was determined to find out.

He left his apartment, stalked across the courtyard and up the stairs to her place. His palms were sweating, the voice in the back of his head shouting that he would screw up his friendship with CeeCee if he wasn't careful.

Jack took a deep breath and told the voice to hit the road.

Pretend you're Zack. What would your twin brother do?

He plastered a bedroom grin on his face, cocked his hips forward and knocked on her door.

A long minute passed.

Do-do-do-do. Do-do-do-do. The theme song from final Jeopardy ran through his head as he waited, the emotional tension mounting.

He knocked again.

No answer.

Had she fallen asleep? He looked at his watch. Eleven o'clock. She had to be at work at seven in the morning. He couldn't blame her for going to bed. He should be considerate, head home and save the discussion for tomorrow. He had an early surgical case himself.

He turned to leave, but something stopped him.

No by God, he wasn't leaving this for tomorrow. He was tired of losing out on the good things in life.

Jack raised his hand to knock again and the door opened.

CeeCee peered out, hair turbaned in a towel. She was barefoot and wore a silky blue-green caftan that melded to her curves like cling wrap. His pulse skittered wildly at the sight of her.

"Sorry," she apologized and crinkled her cute little nose. "Just got out of the shower. I must look a fright."

"You look gorgeous."

Raising a hand to tuck a damp tendril of ginger-colored hair back up inside the turban, she snorted. "No makeup, hair in a towel. I don't think so."

She was a beautiful woman, yes, with a body that wouldn't quit. But he liked so many other wonderful things about her. He admired her inner fire, her lively spirit. Whenever he was near her, Jack felt like more of a man.

Tonight, he had reached a crossroads. He was sick of watching her date creeps. Sick of remaining silent waiting for her to notice him in a sexual way. His patience had run out.

A drop of water glistened on her cheek. He ached to reach out and whisk the droplet away.

Go ahead. Why not? It's what Zack would do.

And so he did.

CeeCee sucked in her breath at his touch and took a step backward. Instead of waiting for her to invite him inside as he normally would have, Jack breezed past her.

"Come on in," she said, closing the door behind them. "Have a seat. Would you like some iced tea?"

He nodded, not because he was thirsty but because he needed to have something to do with his hands. Hands hankering to caress her.

"Be right back." She headed for the kitchen, stopping long enough to turn on the CD player. Strains of Duke Ellington filled the room. They had discovered on the first day they'd met that they both loved Ellington's music.

Jack sank onto the couch. CeeCee returned a minute later, handed him a glass of iced tea, then curled up beside him, tucking her legs beneath her in an unconsciously sexy manner. He couldn't pry his eyes off her, his gaze tracking her every movement.

How to start the conversation?

Not yet ready for the direct "Zack Attack" approach, he took a sip of iced tea then asked, "How did you cause Lars to chomp his tongue?"

"I swear it was an accident." CeeCee chuckled. "But he shouldn't have been trying to shove the thing down my throat without my permission."

"Remind me never to get fresh with you."

"As if you would." She waved a hand, effectively dismissing him as any kind of threat. "You're much too honorable of a man to force yourself on any woman."

Her glibness bugged Jack. Did CeeCee actually consider him completely harmless and was she really so clueless about his feelings for her? Powerful sexual feelings he barely managed to camouflage.

He shifted on the couch, looked her in the eyes and asked her the question he'd been dying to ask her for five months. "All kidding aside, CeeCee, why do you keep going out with guys like Lars?"

"Lars wasn't a real date." She shrugged. "He's an ex-patient, and I was trying to convince him to appear at the hospital charity auction. Guess he's not gonna say yes."

"Probably not."

"Darn. I promised the director I would secure a celebrity to help sell tickets. Maybe someday I'll learn to stop shooting my mouth off."

Tilting her head back, CeeCee took a swallow from

her glass. Jack's gaze melded to her throat. He couldn't seem to peel his gaze from her slender, swanlike neck. His mouth watered; his stomach heated.

You shouldn't be having these lascivious feelings toward your best friend, his cautious voice urged. *Not if you want to keep her as your best friend.*

"Back on the subject," he said, ignoring his interfering conscience. Opportunity had knocked and he was flinging open the door. "I'll grant you that Lars wasn't your dream date and you weren't picturing settling down and making babies with him."

"Heaven forbid!"

"But you've definitely got a pattern going, CeeCee. What's the deal? Why do you keep picking emotionally immature men?"

"I'm just having fun." She shrugged.

"Why don't you go out with a nice, dependable guy?" Jack toyed with his glass.

A guy like me.

CeeCee rolled her eyes. "In a word? Nice guys are boring."

Her statement sliced his gut. She thought he was boring. He'd always suspected as much, but now he knew for sure.

"Present company excepted of course," she said quickly. But it was too late, he already knew what she thought of him. She wanted a wild, irresponsible good time. Something he didn't think he could provide.

"Jackie." She leaned over and touched his hand. White blistering sparks shot through him and it took every ounce of control he possessed to remain calm, cool and collected. "I appreciate your concern I really do, but you don't have to worry about me. I can fend for myself. Honest."

"Like with Lars tonight?"

She pursed her lips. "He was an exception. Most guys aren't *that* pushy."

"Cee, if you keep going out with bad boys how are you ever going to find a good husband? One who'll cherish and respect you the way you deserve to be cherished and respected."

"That's the whole idea, Jack. I don't intend on getting married."

"Ever?"

She shook her head.

Dumbstruck by her declaration, he could only stare. "But why not?"

"It's a long story." She sighed and waved a hand. He couldn't help admiring her long, shapely fingers.

"I've got two ears and all the time in the world. I want to know why a beautiful, vibrant young woman with so much to offer the right man never wants to marry."

"Swear you won't laugh at me?"

"Of course not."

"Okay. I suppose I do owe you an explanation, considering you've seen me through several miserable dates and rescued me from the Missing Link."

Nervously CeeCee took a deep breath and peeped at him through lowered lashes. Jack sat, not saying a word. Every time she peeked over at him she kept thinking about their kiss.

Darn it! Jack was her friend and nothing else. She could not, would not let their relationship become anything more than platonic. For both their sakes.

Her entire life she had trained herself not to expect

much from the male sex. She knew from experience they couldn't be counted on in the tough times.

"Have fun with men," Gramma Addie had told her, "but don't think you can escape the curse."

She had learned to make the most of fate. In high school she'd been dubbed the girl most likely to break hearts. In college, her roomies had razzed her about putting in a revolving door for all her boyfriends. At the hospital, her colleagues believed her to be light-hearted and freespirited and always up for a good time.

And essentially, she was all those things.

She'd striven to cultivate her adventuresome, no-holds-barred personality. She told jokes around the water cooler and regularly threw parties. She went out three or four nights a week, dancing, karaoke, hanging out with club bands. On weekends she liked to jet ski or go to martial arts tournaments or ride in bike-a-thons.

Yet no one ever guessed that deep down inside she longed for something more. Just once she'd like to be known as the quiet one or the smart one or the complex one. Not even her closest friends had the slightest clue she was secretly aching to be loved by a man who could promise her happily ever after.

But it wasn't going to happen and she knew that. No man could promise her a rosy romance. No point pining for things she couldn't have. Melancholia wasn't part of her nature. She was a "pull-yourself-up-by-the-bootstraps-and-get-on-with-it" kind of gal. She didn't waste much energy feeling sorry for herself.

"I'm listening," Jack prompted.

Except for her two best girlfriends, Lacy Calder

and Dr. Janet Hunter, she'd never discussed the curse with anyone outside the family. And she'd certainly never broached the subject with a man, but if anyone deserved an explanation it was Jack.

Besides, he wasn't like most guys. Jack was different. Quiet, strong, understanding.

And there in lay the problem. Jack was a forever kind of guy and CeeCee was *not* a forever kind of woman because of the curse.

"Remember when I told you my mother had been married and divorced four times?" she asked.

Jack nodded. "So?"

CeeCee squirmed. "Even though I had four fathers, I had no real male role models."

"Don't tell me your mother's bad experiences have soured you on the entire institution of marriage. You're not your mother, CeeCee."

She raised a hand. "That's not the whole of it. It's a lot more complicated."

"Go on."

"I'm cursed."

"Cursed?"

"My whole family is." Then in excruciating detail she told the story of Grandma Addie and the gypsy curse.

When she had finished, Jack stared at her incredulously. "You're such a smart woman, I can't believe you would buy into that ridiculous myth."

"It's not ridiculous," she denied, feeling a tad defensive that he thought she should be able to overcome a lifetime of indoctrination by a sheer effort of will. He had no idea what it was like to live with the Jessup family whammy.

"Okay, it's a *dangerous* myth."

"It's not a myth. See this?" She fingered the charms on the gold bracelet adorning her left wrist.

"Yes. You're always wearing it."

"The bracelet's a reminder."

"Of what?"

"To stay single. Each charm represents the occupation of all seventeen of my family members' ex-husbands."

"You're kidding."

"Nope. There's dice for my gambling grandfather. He's the one who left the gypsy for Grandma Addie, but she went through two more husbands before finally calling it quits. The saxophone is for my father. Haven't seen him in fifteen years. Last I heard he was playing in strip clubs in New Orleans."

She held out her wrist, picked another charm to hold up to the light. "A race car for Aunt Sophia's seventh husband. A wine bottle for Aunt Beverly's alcoholic second mate. A tennis racket for my sister Geena's cheating soon-to-be first ex-husband."

"That's bizarre, CeeCee."

"Tell me about it."

"All right, I'll grant you it's not a myth. It's a self-fulfilling prophesy. Somehow the gypsy scared your grandmother badly enough to believe in the evil eye. Your grandmother passed on her screwball values. Your mother and your aunts and you and your sister bought into them. Are you really going to allow your grandmother's fears to rule the rest of your life?"

"The gypsy vowed no male babies would be born into the Jessup family for three generations and guess what? None have been. How do you explain that, Mr. Skeptic?"

"Coincidence."

CeeCee shrugged. "Maybe. But I'm not taking any chances. I've seen enough divorce to last me two lifetimes. No need to make those same mistakes on my own."

"You wouldn't." Jack's brown eyes shone with certainty. She might believe in this nonsensical curse, but he believed in her. CeeCee could have anything she wanted, if she would only let herself. She was graceful and charming, friendly and fun to be around. She had strength of character and she could achieve anything she set her mind to and that included facing her family demons, if she would own up to her fears. He could see the truth so clearly, how could she not?

"Self-fulfilling prophesy or not, the Jessup family whammy is no laughing matter. It's very real. And I don't have a clue as to what makes a loving relationship work. I made up my mind a long time ago. The curse dies with me. I'll never marry and have children."

Jack made a choking noise. He hated to see her closing herself off this way. It was clear CeeCee bought into every word she was saying. If only he could convince her to go out with him, to allow their platonic relationship a chance to grow into something much more profound. He wasn't afraid of her "curse."

Setting his glass down on the coffee table, he leaned forward and took her hand in his. "Why don't you give me a chance to show you that you're wrong? Somewhere deep inside your heart you know exactly what it takes to love and be loved."

She shook her head.

"Go out with me, CeeCee. I know we would be great together."

"I can't," she whispered. A drop of moisture glimmered on her cheek, and this time it wasn't water.

"Why not?" He tapped his foot, impatient, antsy. He wanted so badly to break through her barrier, to tear down the family-induced emotional propaganda that kept CeeCee attached to bad boy types. "Let me prove to you not all men are like Lars. Let me show you I'm different."

"I can't take the chance of jeopardizing our friendship, Jack. I won't lose that."

He clenched his jaw, got to his feet. "You're turning me down."

Breaking my heart.

"Yes, but only for your own good."

"Friendship isn't enough for me anymore, CeeCee. I want you. I've wanted you from the first time I set eyes on you. I've helped you pick up the pieces every time one of those guys has dumped on you. I'm telling you I can't keep watching you hurt yourself."

CeeCee's eyes widened in alarm, her chin trembled. "What are you saying, Jack?"

"I'm saying..." He paused a moment, the words causing a sharp pang of regret. "I don't think we can continue being friends."

"SOMETHING'S WRONG WITH JACK," CeeCee told girlfriends Lacy and Janet. They were browsing a bridal shop in search of bridesmaids dresses they could agree on for Lacy's impending wedding. "He's acting really weird."

"What about these?" asked Lacy, a petite blond surgical nurse. She fingered pink, puffy-sleeved taffeta dresses with bustles.

"No!" CeeCee and Janet cried in unison.

"Come on," Lacy coaxed. "They'd go perfectly with the lime-green tuxes I've got picked out for the men."

Janet and CeeCee exchanged horrified glances.

"Forget it. I'm not dressing up like some bubble gum Southern belle, and standing next to some guy who looks like a toxic spill," Janet said adamantly. Janet, a tall, willowy brunette with indigo eyes, possessed a no-nonsense personality that counterbalanced Lacy's inherent sweetest and CeeCee's usual optimism.

"Gotcha." Lacy grinned. "I was just kidding."

"Thank heavens," CeeCee said. "I thought we were going to have to call in the fashion police and have you carted away for violation of the good taste code."

"Go ahead." Lacy waved a hand. "I didn't mean to joke in the middle of your problem. What happened with Jack?"

"Last night he told me he could no longer be my friend." CeeCee pushed a hand through her curls.

Jack's declaration caused a strange emptiness inside her chest, and she couldn't say why. As an outgoing, gregarious girl she had lots of friends. Why would the loss of one guy affect her so strongly, especially when she was accustomed to losing the men in her life on a regular basis?

"What?" Lacy asked. "But why would he do that? Bennett says Jack is about the nicest intern at St. Madeleine's."

"Jack is a great guy and he's a wonderful doctor. He interned under me during the fall, remember," Janet agreed. "What did you do to him, Cee?"

"It's the curse," CeeCee whispered.

Always a bridesmaid, never a bride.

"Oh, please." Janet rolled her eyes. "Not that excuse again."

"It's bad enough the darned curse keeps me from ever getting married, but now it's even causing trouble in my friendship with Jack," CeeCee said.

"Hogwash." Janet shook her head impatiently. "There's no such thing as a curse."

"I don't know about that. If there's such a thing as the Thunderbolt," Lacy said, referring to the incredible love-at-first-sight zap that had caused her and Dr. Bennett Sheridan to fall head over heels in love, "why can't CeeCee be a victim of the Jessup family whammy?"

"You're not helping," Janet told Lacy. "CeeCee needs for us to bolster her confidence, not perpetuate her belief in some superstitious mumbojumbo."

CeeCee turned her back on her friends and blinked away the tears gathering in her eyes. They didn't understand. No one understood what it was like to grow up in a fractured household where the men came and went like taxicabs.

She had spent a lifetime trying to make lemonade from lemons. Grinning and bearing it. Never getting too attached to any stepfather, stepuncle, stepgrandfather.

For the most part she maintained an optimistic attitude. She didn't want to marry knowing it could only end in disaster, but she did want Jack's friendship. More than she'd ever realized until the threat of losing him loomed.

"Start from the beginning." Janet placed a hand on CeeCee's shoulder and guided her to a table and chairs situated in the back of the shop for customer convenience. "Now exactly what happened?"

"Jack asked me out."

"The beast!" teased Lacy.

"What a brute! You want us to call the law on him?" Janet joined in.

"Ha-ha."

"Come on, Cee, is it so tragic that he asked you out?" Janet looked puzzled.

CeeCee gazed at her dark-eyed friend. "Yes. I like him too much to hurt him."

"Do you suppose he could be in love with you?"

She froze. Please, no, don't let it be so.

"Of course not." CeeCee forced a laugh. Then she remembered the kiss, and the way Jack had touched her, the look on his face. Groaning, she closed her eyes.

"Do you want to be more than friends?" Janet nudged her.

"It's not an option, Jan. I can never fall in love. Ever. And especially not with Jack. He's the kindest, most gentle man I know, and I will not hurt him by getting romantically involved with him."

3

THREE DAYS HAD PASSED and CeeCee was in the hospital swimming pool assisting a stroke victim with her aquatic exercises, when her assistant, Deirdre came over and told her that Dr. Travis wanted to see her.

She glanced over at the door, spotted Jack standing in the archway. He wore green hospital scrubs, white leather sneakers and had a black stethoscope tossed around his neck. His hair was sexily mussed, as if he'd been repeatedly threading his fingers through it. Her pulse hip-hopped. She hadn't seen him since that fateful night.

"Deirdre," she asked, surprised by the tremor in her voice. "Could you finish up with Mrs. Mathers?"

"Sure."

She and Deirdre switched places. CeeCee came up the ladder fully aware Jack's eyes were on her. She reached for a towel, wrapped it around her waist and slid her feet into a pair of flip-flops. Pasting a pleasant smile on her face, she sallied to the door.

"Hi!" She greeted him as if they'd never had an argument, as if everything was hunky-dory and she hadn't spent her nights tossing and turning and worrying that she had wounded his feelings by refusing to date him.

"Sorry to take you from your work."

"No problem. You want to go into my office?"

She indicated a door at the other end of the physical therapy room. A few patients ran on treadmills with monitors attached to their chests. Others lay on mats enduring range-of-motion exercises, or practiced crutch walking with attendants. Weights clanged. Voices echoed against the tall ceilings.

"We can talk here. It won't take long," he said.

Was he that afraid of being alone with her? CeeCee searched his face, unearthed no answers. Anxiously she ran her tongue over her lips. All right, all right, she was the one afraid of being alone with him. She feared her hormones would kidnap her brain and do something really insane—like throw Jack on her desk and kiss him until he begged for mercy.

"Okay. What's up?" She forced a carefree note into her voice. No renegade estrogen was gonna boss her around.

His gaze flicked over her. His pupils widened. Self-consciously, she unfurled the towel from her waist, held it to her chest.

"I've come to say goodbye."

"Goodbye?" Her heart dived to her tummy. *Plunk!* "You're leaving St. Madeleine's?"

"Not forever." The corners of his eyes softened, his smile deepened and her tummy, which was currently swimming somewhere around her ankles, turned to pure mush. "Just for a couple of months."

"B…but where are you going?" she asked, feeling strangely abandoned. It was a familiar sensation. She should be quite used to it by now.

Why Jack should be any different, she couldn't say, but her disappointment was as barbed as the day her real father had told her and Geena he was moving to Australia without them. Or their mother.

"Mexico. Remember, I told you I'd applied to volunteer for Dr. Blakemoore's surgical team."

Yes, she recalled. He had mentioned something about joining a group of doctors and nurses from St. Madeleine's who traveled to poverty-stricken countries every summer in order to provide free medical care to indigent children.

"I was placed on the alternate list," he continued, "and at the last minute one of the surgeons had to drop out, so I got bumped up. Since my internship is over and my orthopedic residency doesn't start until September, this opportunity came at a great time. It even saves me from having to teach a lab class in summer school."

"Oh." CeeCee cleared her throat. "Well, that's great, I suppose." It was terrific that he so willingly gave of himself to others, but on a selfish note, she was going to miss him something fierce.

"I also thought it might give us both some time to think things over."

She nodded.

"I brought you the key to my apartment." He passed the key over to her. "If you don't mind watering my plants for me."

"Of course not." She took the key in her hand. It was still warm from being clutched in his palm.

"And here's my beeper number, too. Just in case you need to get hold of me for any reason. There are no phones in the village we're going to. It might take me a while to hitch a ride into a bigger town so if I don't call back right away, don't worry."

"You go on to Mexico and don't fret about a thing here. Have a wonderful time. Help those children. Learn a lot."

"Thanks. I hope to."

He nodded, his gaze never leaving hers. He wanted to say more, she could see it in his eyes. But nothing he could say would soothe the bizarre sensation that he was leaving for good.

So what? the tiny voice in the back of her mind sniped. The defensive voice from her childhood that reared up whenever some man left. *Ta-ta. Bye-bye. So long chum. Been nice knowing ya. Don't let the door hit you on the way out. Who needs you anyway?*

"Is that it?" she asked.

"Oh, one other thing. My twin brother, Zack, might be dropping by. He's the motocross champion."

"Oh, right."

"Actually, you two will probably hit it off. He's a real mad man. He even goes by the moniker Wild Man Zack. Loves extreme adventure sports. Never dates any one girl for too long. Always on the move. Always looking for excitement. Your kind of guy."

CeeCee didn't know what to say. In a perfect world, Jack was exactly her type. But she couldn't have him. And Zack did sound like a lot of fun but only because he would have no expectations of her. No strings attached. How could she explain her fears to Jack so he could understand?

"Anyway, I percolated on your dilemma with the charity auction, and I phoned Zack and asked if he'd mind helping out. Zack wouldn't make any promises. He's not a promise-making kind of guy, but he said he'd try. I told him he could stay at my place."

"That's so sweet of you." She almost threw her arms around him but then the thought of what she might stir up held her back. Okay, so Jack was better than most.

He shrugged. ''It was the least I could do after chasing off your pro-wrestler.''

''You're so thoughtful.''

He shrugged. ''Thoughtfulness hasn't gotten me anywhere with you.''

''Oh, Jack.'' She reached out a hand, touched his cheek.

''I'm going to miss you.''

''I'll miss you, too.''

This was awful. Too bad Jack wasn't a self-centered, macho male who wanted nothing more than a casual fling. That, she could handle. Then again if he were a self-centered, macho male she wouldn't worry about hurting him.

In spite of her best intentions not to notice him in a sexual way, she found herself studying his strong profile, admiring the way his short hair lay against his head.

He was a very handsome man. Perhaps it was a good thing he was leaving town. By the time he returned, she'd have her attraction to him firmly under control.

He cleared his throat, and gestured toward the door. ''I've got to go. I've barely got enough time to round up my gear before the van leaves.''

''You're leaving right now?''

''Yes. May I ask another favor of you?''

''Of course, but I can't make any promises.''

He smiled ruefully. ''You sound just like Zack.''

''What is it?'' she asked softly.

''Will you think about me, about us, while I'm gone?''

"Jack…"

"It's okay." He eyed her regretfully. "Your tone of voice answered my question."

A MONTH LATER, JACK RATTLED north across the Texas/Mexico border in the bed of a 1952 Ford pickup truck. He was being driven home because one, he couldn't afford the flight on his intern's meager salary and two, because it was almost as far from the little Mexican village he'd been working in to the nearest Mexican airport, as it was to drive straight to Houston. His injured left knee, which he could barely bend, ached like the dickens, rivaling the chronic ache that had festered in his heart for four long weeks.

He took another slug off the tequila Pedro, the pickup driver, had given him to ease his discomfort during the twelve hour trip home. Jack found himself face to tongue with the worm.

He'd reached bottom.

"Ay-riba!" he sang to the darkness and swallowed the worm whole.

If CeeCee Adams could see him now. Drunk, knee busted, eating tequila-soaked worms. Very Zack-like. He hadn't shaven or cut his hair the entire time he'd been out of the country. His skin was bronzed to the color of whole wheat toast by the relentless Mexican sun.

Wild? CeeCee wanted wild? He'd show her wild.

Pedro slowed the truck as they approached the Houston city limits and stopped at a signal light. He stuck his head out the driver's side window. "You okay, amigo?"

"Mucho fino," Jack sang and wondered why the city lights kept fading in and out.

"You're going to have one helluva headache to-morrow."

"I know."

He needed some kind of crutch. He wasn't ready to see CeeCee again. He had planned on being away for eight weeks. In eight weeks he might have come up with a plan for winning her over. A plot to convince her that she wasn't cursed, that they could make a perfect couple and live happily ever after. But four weeks wasn't enough. For the last month, he'd done nothing except work and pine for CeeCee. When he wasn't in surgery or checking up on the kids in recovery, his mind had been on his best friend.

Correction. His ex-best friend.

Then he had dislocated his knee by stepping into a gopher hole while carrying an anesthetized child to the post-op tent. And bingo! Dr. Winstead had insisted he return to Houston for rest and physical therapy before starting his orthopedic residency. He was coming home four weeks early and completely unprepared for seeing CeeCee again.

"Is this the place?" Pedro asked several hours later.

Jack propped himself up on his elbow and peered over the bed of the pickup. He squinted at the entrance to his apartment complex, and spied a mass of haphazardly parked cars.

Patio lanterns had been lit. Sounds of conversation, laughter and splashing in the pool carried easily on the late night air.

"Yeah."

"Sounds like a party," Pedro observed.

Jack knew who was throwing the party. It had to

be the same gregarious girl who instigated all the River Run soirees.

CeeCee Adams.

Pedro parked, got out of the pickup and came around to let the tailgate down. Jack ran a hand through six-hundred miles of windblown hair, then scooted to the end of the truck bed.

"You want me to help you to your door before I go over to my girlfriend's house?" Pedro asked. "She only lives a few miles from here."

"Naw." Jack gestured in the direction of the cars. "My friends are here. They'll help me."

"You sure?"

Jack nodded. The truth was he didn't want his friends and colleagues to see him limping through the complex leaning on Pedro's shoulder. He had gone to Mexico to help children, not to bang up his knee and return a failure.

Pedro unloaded Jack's duffel bag. "I'll carry it for you."

"I can manage."

"Amigo, you can barely walk."

"Thanks, Pedro. I'll be fine." The slur in his voice denied his words.

Pedro shook his head. "You one proud dude, Dr. Travis."

Jack pulled a wad of bills from the pocket of his jeans and passed them to Pedro. "For gas money."

Pedro hesitated a moment, then took the cash. He clasped Jack on the shoulder. "I hope you win her," he said.

"Win who?"

"The *señorita* who has kept you so sad." Pedro

flashed a smile, then hopped in his truck and drove away.

Even Pedro had seen through him. He wasn't ready to face CeeCee when his heart was still so obviously flapping on his sleeve. Sighing, Jack shouldered his duffel bag and gingerly tested his knee.

Ow! Ouch!

Okay. Twelve hours of sitting in the back of the truck hadn't improved his circulation or his range of motion. He glanced around. If he could hop to the fence, he could use it to brace himself up to the sidewalk. Then, he could slip through the apartments, using the buildings themselves as support. And keep to the shadows so he wouldn't be spotted by the party goers.

Good plan except the tequila had affected his equilibrium. He commanded his head to stop spinning. By some miracle he made it to the fence. He clung a moment, getting his balance.

He inched forward one painful step at a time. At last, he came to the end of the fencing. From his vantage point, hidden in shadows, he could observe the pool area.

Most of his colleagues from the hospital, decked out in swimwear, were there. Rock music filled the air along with the smell of barbecue and watermelon.

CeeCee was throwing an all-out wingding, something she often did when she needed a pick-me-up. When she felt blue she didn't dress in sweats, hole up with sad movies and guzzle gallons of Butter Brickle ice cream. Not his girl. She threw parties, the bigger the better.

Was CeeCee depressed? he worried. Could she be longing for him the way he was longing for her? His heart leapfrogged at the possibility. Jack spotted CeeCee's friend, Lacy, sitting poolside kissing her fiancé, Dr. Bennett Sheridan. He recognized her other friend, Dr. Janet Hunter, serving drinks. He kept searching the crowd, and at last he found what he was looking for.

CeeCee.

Wearing the skimpiest aqua string bikini he'd ever seen. Her wet hair was slicked back off her face. She looked as fetching as a mermaid. With those honed curves the woman could have posed for the cover of *Sports Illustrated.*

She was leaning over a lawn chair talking to some man he didn't know. The guy's gaze was welded to her cleavage. Obviously she hadn't been pining away for him. He had misinterpreted the reason for her party.

What did you expect, nimrod?

Then a terrible thought occurred to him. What if the family curse story had just been an excuse to let him down easy?

The guy in the lawn chair moved closer to CeeCee and whispered something in her ear. She swatted friskily at him, then threw back her head and laughed.

Jack grit his teeth. Jealousy turned to battery acid in his throat. Damn! He didn't need to see that. He gulped and turned his head away.

He had to decamp to his apartment. Before he did something really stupid like limp over to the pool and punch the guy's lights out. Hand on the side of the building, he eased forward and stumbled over a hibachi. The thing clanged loudly.

"Shhh!" Jack cast a furtive glance back at the pool. No one noticed. Pushing the hibachi back in place with the toe of a charcoal-smeared sneaker, he struggled on.

He finally reached his apartment and dropped his duffel on the front stoop, only to realize when he went to open the front door that he had given his only key to CeeCee. He would rather break into his apartment than make an appearance in his current condition.

He managed to stay out of sight from the revelers while prying the screen off his window. Now came the hard part, smashing the glass without drawing attention.

"Pretty desperate, Travis," he muttered.

But he was desperate. He was also more than a little drunk, a lot jealous and rather teed-off at himself for not coming up with a better plan. Right now, however, he wanted nothing more than to collapse into the bed and sleep for twenty hours straight.

With that objective in mind, he peeled off his T-shirt, wrapped it around a fist and gave the window pane a quick, hard jab.

The glass fell inward onto his bedroom carpet with hardly a sound. Between the laughter, the splashing and a raucous updated version of "Wild Thing," he was sure no one in the pool area heard him. Tomorrow, he'd replace the pane, tonight his body thirsted for sleep.

Slipping a hand through the hole he'd made, he fumbled for the latch. And felt something hard and cold press into his back. Something suspiciously like the nose of a gun.

CEECEE'S KNEES SLAMMED together like a loose door in a hurricane. When she had gone upstairs to fetch a fresh bucket of ice, she'd caught sight of someone trying to break into Jack's apartment. Without thinking twice she'd grabbed the flashlight from the kitchen drawer and ran downstairs to confront the prowler.

She hadn't stopped to ponder whether the intruder could be dangerous. Only one thought dominated her mind. She'd promised Jack she'd keep an eye on his place and damn if she would allow a sneak thief to make off with his things.

Besides, half of St. Madeleine's doctors were swimming in her pool. If she needed help, she would throw back her head and scream bloody murder.

"Hold it right there, buster," she growled, pressing the butt of the flashlight into his bare back in hopes he'd believe she had a gun. "Put your hands over your head."

"And if I refuse?"

CeeCee gulped. She hadn't counted on that response. "I'll pull the trigger and blow you to kingdom come."

"I'd pay to see that trick," he drawled. "Since I've never heard of anyone getting shot by a flashlight."

The voice sounded familiar. Very familiar.

"Jack?"

Slowly, the man turned and CeeCee found herself staring into Jack's deep brown eyes. Except nothing else about the guy was familiar. He smelled of tequila and Jack only drank beer, and rarely that. His hair was long, his beard scraggly. His bare, muscled chest was darkly tanned, and he was favoring his left knee as if injured. The guy might look like Jack, but he was five pounds leaner and had a thrilling lawless quality about him.

The air of a very bad boy inviting her to a bedroom romp.

The quality stirred an instant response inside her. Their gazes locked. CeeCee found it hard to catch her breath.

Her pulse bounced like busted bedsprings—*boing, boing, boing*. In that moment she realized what she'd found

One hot, sexy, motocross champion.

CeeCee dropped the flashlight to her side and grinned. "Hey everyone," she shouted, waved to the crowd. "Come on over and meet Jack's twin brother Zack."

JACK HAD NEVER INTENDED ON LYING to CeeCee about his identity. She had simply assumed he was Zack, and before he could correct her, she'd tucked his arm in hers and leaned her lithe body into his bare chest.

Her breast swayed delicately against his nipple. Her skin was velvet on his. She smelled of coconuts and pineapples and sheer blue heaven.

A cold sweat popped out on his forehead. Suddenly, despite the tequila he'd consumed, Jack was stone sober.

"Hi, Zack," she whispered in a sweet, sexy voice he'd never heard her use. A delightful voice that raised goose bumps on his arms and sent a shaft of pure desire arrowing straight to his groin. "You're here way early for the charity auction."

"Uh-huh." Overwhelmed by his reaction to her, he barely mustered the sound.

CeeCee had never looked more beautiful. With that passion-red hair curling around her shoulders, her full lips tinted with a whisper of pink lip gloss, her damp swimsuit clinging to every curve, she resembled an ethereal water nymph.

Mythical, magical, enchanting.

Jack stared as if seeing her for the first. Through Zack's fresh eyes. He even heard his brother's vernacular tumble through his head.

Whew-ee, bro, she's the bomb! Long legs. Perky breasts. Hair like liquid fire. Cheeky dimples. You've got yourself a real hottie.

Except CeeCee wasn't his.

And she was so much more than a "hottie." She was fun and smart, a delight to be around. She cried at sad movies and threw pennies in wishing wells. She smiled often and rarely got mad. She cared about others and gave unselfishly of herself. She had hundreds of friends and not a single enemy.

Well, maybe except for Lars Vandergrin, but who cared about him?

She was perfection walking.

And he wanted her desperately. Not just for now. Not for a night. Not for a four-week affair, but for a lifetime.

"I'm CeeCee." She flashed him a winsome dimple. "It's wonderful to meet you at last. Your brother has told me so much about you."

Jack gulped, uncertain what to do next. He opened his mouth to tell her the truth, but then without warning, he caught himself replying in a voice as provocative as CeeCee's own, "All bad, I trust."

Where the hell had that come from?

She giggled. "Jack warned me you were an outrageous flirt."

"That's me, outrageous."

"Hey, Zack!"

The crowd from the pool had moved their way. Dr. Bennett Sheridan thrust out a hand in greeting. Bennett had been the resident overseeing Jack's internship during his rotation through cardiac surgery earlier in the year. Bennett had his other arm draped around Lacy's waist. "Great to meet you, buddy. Jack speaks of you often."

Awkwardly Jack shook Bennett's hand. Shame over his deception had him avoiding the gaze of the man who'd trained him for three months. Other party guests, most of them people he knew from the hospital or the apartment complex, welcomed him, too, increasing Jack's uneasiness. In her misconception, CeeCee had unwittingly partnered him in chicanery.

How could he extricate himself without embarrassing them both?

"Let's go sit by the pool," CeeCee suggested, pointing in the direction of the festivities.

He held back, feeling exposed walking around in nothing but his blue jeans, his bare chest on display for anyone who cared to ogle.

"My shirt." He gestured toward the shattered windowpane. "I used it to break the glass. I er…forgot that Jack said you had his key."

"Don't worry about going shirtless. It's a pool party. No one cares what you wear. We've got food and drink and a wide selection of music. Let me guess, I bet you're a rock and roll fan."

Silently Jack nodded. Although he didn't care a fig for rock and roll himself, Zack did.

"Janet," CeeCee hollered and waved at her friend across the courtyard who was manning the stereo system. "Put on some Stones."

Janet complied and "Start Me Up" oozed from the outdoor speakers placed strategically around the pool area, and the song expressed Jack's sentiments exactly. He wanted CeeCee to never stop hanging on to him, never stop gazing his way with adoring eyes.

"And I bet you could go for a margarita, right?" CeeCee beamed at him, her fingers wrapped possessively around his upper arm.

Actually he was thirsty for a tall drink of CeeCee. And the last thing he needed was more tequila clouding his brain, making him do dumb things like pretending he was his twin brother.

Speaking of which, this ruse wasn't right. He should come clean before things really got out of hand.

But excitement showed in every feature on CeeCee's delicate face and she was chattering so fast he could hardly make out what she was saying. He thought she might be lauding his motocross skills. Apparently she was quite thrilled to meet Zack.

Jealousy, the green-eyed beast, charged through him like an ambulance dispatched to the scene of a serious accident. Simultaneously his gut clenched in disappointment. As himself, he had never induced this kind of enthusiasm in CeeCee.

"Jack tells me you're footloose and fancy-free." She sent him a coquettish, sidelong glance. "A no-strings-attached kind of guy."

As opposed to Jack, a forever kind of guy. The very kind of guy CeeCee's ridiculous family curse wouldn't allow her date.

And then it hit him. A bolt from the blue.

The answer to his problem with CeeCee.

Why *not* become Zack? He wasn't due at the hospital for another month. Everyone thought he was still in Mexico. Here, dropped right into his lap, was a primo opportunity to prove to CeeCee she could fall in love with a good, steady guy. Even if he had to use his brother's persona to convince her. He might not be as interesting as his twin, but dammit, curse or no friggin' curse, he knew in his soul he and CeeCee were meant to be together. If the only way she would give him a chance was as a sexy motorcycle champion, then he would become that man. Anything to win her.

"Yeah." Jack grinned wolfishly, playing his part to the hilt. "That's me. The happy wanderer. Never in one place for too long. Fathers have been known to lock up their daughters when I stroll into town."

"You're scandalous." Grinning, she swatted him lightly on the shoulder, causing his blood to pump like a faucet.

"Don't ever forget it, sweetheart."

He forced himself to remain nonchalant. In actuality, he was about to split right out of his skin. She was so close and smelled so nice. He was acutely aware of her long bare limbs and her lovely cleavage threatening to overflow her skimpy bikini top. In fact, Jack realized, he was drilling a hole through her with his stare.

She blushed and ducked her head. Jack marveled. He'd managed to fluster the unflappable CeeCee. Amazing.

"Let's pour you a drink." She took his hand and led him toward the makeshift bar set up near the diving board.

"Hey." She stopped and peered at his leg. "You're limping."

"Don't worry. It's nothing."

"What happened?" Her eyes widened to the size of quarters. "A motorcycle crash?"

That certainly sounded more macho than the truth, but he was still uncomfortable out and out lying to her, so he simply nodded.

"Oooh," she said, clearly impressed with his supposed recklessness. "Was the crash scary?"

He shrugged, doing the strong, silent number.

"Does it hurt?"

"A little."

"Poor baby," she murmured, her tone filled with compassion.

He was torn, part of him wanted to act tough, another part of him wanted to milk her sympathy for all it was worth.

What would Zack do?

Zack wouldn't be standing here gaping at her like some tongue-tied simpleton. Zack would take full advantage of the situation. Somehow, Zack would have her in his apartment giving him a rubdown in five minutes flat.

A shudder knifed through Jack at the thought of CeeCee's fingers gliding over his skin.

"Well," he lowered his head until his cheek was almost touching hers. "If you promise not to tell anyone, my knee is aching a lot. I've been traveling all day, and I'm ready for bed."

At least that was the truth.

"Oh my goodness, I'll bet it is. You must be exhausted. And here I've been yammering my head off." She took a step away from him and he noticed her chest was rising and falling in a quick, heady rhythm unexpectedly matching his own. "Did Jack tell you I'm a physical therapist?"

"He might have mentioned it."

She nodded, her fiery red curls bouncing. "I could look at your knee if you like. Maybe massage it for you."

If he liked?

Not to seem overeager and frighten her away, Jack barely lifted one shoulder. "I don't want to take you away from your party."

She waved a hand. "Never mind. The party'll be breaking up soon. Most people have to work tomorrow and anyway my friends Janet and Lacy are sharing the hostess duties."

"Well...if you're sure. A massage does sound great."

His ease at manipulation both surprised and shamed him. But this was for CeeCee's own good, he told himself. If he didn't pull out the stops and pretend to be Zack, she would never allow herself to love her best friend, Jack.

Are you sure you're not just trying to rationalize less than honorable intentions, Travis?

No. He was doing this to liberate her from her self-imposed prison. If she fell for him, then wonderful. But even if she didn't, he wanted her to be free to love someone. He couldn't bear the thought of her living out the rest of her life alone simply because she'd been too indoctrinated in some family myth to gamble on love.

"You wait right here," CeeCee said. "I'll locate Jack's keys and let you into his apartment properly. Then we'll tuck you into bed, and massage your leg.

And in the morning we'll tell the superintendent the windowpane needs replacing."

Tuck him into bed? Damn the erotic images her words produced.

"That's really sweet of you, CeeCee." He covered his lascivious thoughts with a smile.

"Hey, Jack's my best friend in the whole world. I would do anything for him. And that includes taking care of his twin brother."

And I'd do anything in the world for you, CeeCee, my love. Anything at all. Even pretending to be my twin in order to keep you from taking up with the wrong guys.

"I won't be a second." She touched him briefly on the arm then took off upstairs.

His eyes followed her graceful movements. His stomach hitched a ride to his throat. She was captivating, stunning, absolutely breathtaking. If he played his cards right, before this month was out, he might have CeeCee for his very own.

And Dr. Jack Travis wanted nothing more in the entire world.

4

CEECEE'S HANDS TREMBLED as she fumbled in her junk drawer for the keys to Jack's apartment. Giddiness enveloped her.

Was Zack destined to be her scorching affair? In essence, Jack antivenin.

"Calm down," she chided herself after she dropped the keys for the third time on her way to the front door. "Chill. You're getting ahead of yourself."

Understatement of the year. Fifteen minutes with Zack and her libido was ready to stampede right off a cliff. For the first time since Jack had left, CeeCee realized how much her midnight sexual fantasies had taken their toll.

Was she so gosh-darned hungry for her best friend she was willing to vault into the sack with his lookalike twin simply to sate her appetite? It was a natural urge, but to act on those urges wouldn't be fair to either Zack or Jack.

"Look what you've done to me, Jack Travis," she muttered under her breath. "And all I ever did was bestow one little kiss on those killer lips. You've turned me into a nut case. Thank heavens things never went any further between us!"

She slipped out the door, keys clutched firmly in her hand, and found Zack sprawled in a lounge chair surrounded by a throng of women.

Giggling, cooing, beautiful women draped over him like tablecloths. One sat in his lap. Two others leaned on each shoulder.

Hmph.

She'd run slap-dab against the downside of setting one's sights on a sexy rogue—fierce competition. But a little rivalry was fine with her. She wasn't looking for a forever kind of guy. She wasn't jealous. Zack was a charming freebird, and that's what she liked about him. No strings tying down this twin.

CeeCee approached the group, dangling the keys at Zack. She wriggled her toes—painted Pretty-In-Pink just for the party—inside her strappy gold sandals and forced a casual smile.

"Ready, Romeo?" She couldn't resist the dig.

Zack studied her toes, a contented expression on his face. She could have sworn he murmured something like, "And this little piggy cried wee-wee-wee all the way over to Zack's place."

What an ego.

"Zack," she said sternly.

"Yes, ma'am?" He raised his gaze and gave her a lazy wink.

Oh! but he was a rounder.

"Your knee. The pain. You wanted to lie down. Remember?"

A flair of momentary irritation flashed through her. He was bold enough to flirt with her while three other women flanked him. She almost told him he could sweet-talk one of his new conquests into massaging his leg, but why let his behavior perturb her? It wasn't as if she cared. It wasn't as if he was Jack.

"Oh, yeah."

Grinning, he gently lifted the blushing young lady

from his lap and cautiously rose to his feet. He tried to disguise his discomfort but CeeCee detected his brief wince of pain and immediately her irritation vanished. He was her best friend's brother. He'd been hurt. She was a physical therapist. She'd give him that massage.

It didn't have to mean anything.

"Nice meeting you, ladies," Zack said to his admirers.

Ladies? CeeCee fumed. Apparently he threw the word around generously.

The women tittered and grinned.

"This way, Lothario." CeeCee ushered him back across the courtyard toward Jack's apartment.

"Hey," he said. "I'm not as bad as all that."

"That's not what Jack tells me."

"My brother has a tendency to exaggerate my reputation."

CeeCee tossed a glance over her shoulder at the women who were still giggling and waving at Zack. "Oh, no? Then how do you explain them?"

"Jealous?" He chuckled.

"Of those women? Over you? Get real." CeeCee stopped on Jack's stoop, eyed him up and down before jamming the key into the lock with more force than she'd intended.

"CeeCee?"

"What?" She snapped and turned to find him standing right behind her.

His eyes glimmered darkly, from tequila or lust, she couldn't be sure which, maybe both. "Not one of those women can hold a candle to you."

For a brief second there, he sounded just like Jack.

CeeCee caught her breath, then quickly expelled it. "Flatterer."

"I mean it."

"Yeah, right Casanova." She wagged a finger under his nose. "You don't fool me."

"I've had my share of women." His breath was warm against her nape. "Does that bother you?"

"Why should your sexual history bother me?"

He quirked a smile, reached out and traced a finger along her collarbone. "Because I was hoping…"

She knew what he was hoping. CeeCee turned away, lightning quick, before he spoke the words already on her mind. She nudged the door open.

"Ta-da," she exclaimed far too brightly, flicked on the light and scurried inside.

He ambled in behind her, pulling the duffel bag that had been resting on the porch after him.

"Hey, that looks exactly like Jack's duffel."

"Does it?" With one foot, he nudged the bag behind him.

"I saw a program on one of those news shows about identical twins," she chattered, anxious to fill the air with sound. Anything to lessen the reality that she was wearing nothing but a string bikini and standing beside one of the most sexually potent men she'd ever run across.

"Apparently these two identical twins were separated at birth," she continued, "and didn't meet until they were in their thirties. The similarities were uncanny."

"No kidding." He looked distracted, as if he was worried about something.

"They both had wives with the same name, and they drove the same make of car. They were both lawyers, and they liked the same foods. And when they bought each other a birthday gift for the first time, they gave the exact same shirt! Spooky, huh?''

''Spooky,'' he echoed.

''Is that how it is between you and Jack? You know, like telepathy? Obviously that must be the case to some degree. I mean you've both got the exact same duffel.'' She gestured at the bag again. ''Just like those twins and their shirts.'' She was rattling on endlessly and she knew it but she couldn't seem to stop.

''Jack and I really aren't that close. Despite being identical twins we don't have much in common.''

''Except for the duffel bag, of course.''

''Oh, yeah, well that.''

They stared at each other a long moment.

''Why don't you…um…head into the bedroom and shimmy out of those jeans?'' she suggested.

''Why, CeeCee, that's the best offer I've had in weeks,'' he teased.

''You know what I mean.'' She mentally cursed her peaches-and-cream complexion that blushed so easily when she was befuddled.

''I'm sorry.'' He touched her shoulder. ''I didn't mean to embarrass you.''

''I'm not embarrassed,'' she denied although she felt her face heat to the flaming crimson of American Beauty roses. Zack was an odd man. One minute teasing and outrageous, the next almost like Jack, thoughtful and apologetic.

He sent her a knowing grin, dispelling the notion he was the least bit like his brother.

She ducked her head, avoiding his eyes and opened the door to Jack's bedroom. Glass lay on the carpet beneath the window. A breeze blew through the hole, lifting the curtain and bringing in sounds from the party.

"Holler when you're out of those pants and ready for the massage."

Zack sauntered into the room. CeeCee closed the door behind him, sagged against it on the other side and waved a hand to fan herself. Whew, somebody flip the air conditioning to arctic blast.

A minute passed.

"CeeCee," Zack called.

"You ready?"

"Well...I'm having a problem."

She opened the door again, found him gazing sheepishly at her from the middle of the room. His jeans were unzipped, his rippling muscled chest still bare.

The sight was enough to make her eyes bug.

In the glow of the bedroom light he was thunderously breath-stealing. His tousled, collar-length hair and the beard covering his lean jaw gave him a knavish appearance. His skin was a burnished bronze, his grin devastating.

How had she ever thought this undisciplined man was anything like his kind, gentle twin? Jack and Zack were different as dusk and dawn. One heralded the coming of darkness, the other celebrated daylight.

As much as she might long to reside in the daylight, it was her fate to spend her life in the dark thrill of night. Best to embrace destiny, not fight it.

"I couldn't shuck my jeans past my knee," Zack explained. "It's too swollen. I need you."

"Oh." CeeCee wet her lips with the tip of her tongue.

He wriggled his pants down over his hips, giving her full view of his white cotton briefs, and sat on the edge of the bed. CeeCee stayed rooted to the spot, staring, mouth agape.

"Come here." He crooked a finger at her.

No way. Un-uh. She wasn't moving.

"CeeCee." His voice poured over her like warm brandy. "I need you."

How many times over the past four weeks had she imagined a scenario like this? Except in her fantasies it had been Jack on the bed calling her name—not his reprobate twin.

But since she couldn't have the man she wanted, was Zack the next best thing?

She was physically attracted to Zack, yes siree, but only because he reminded her so much of Jack.

She was confused. She had an overwhelming desire to kiss Zack, to see if he tasted like Jack. A good sign or a bad one? Was she trying to sublimate her feelings for Jack by taking up with his brother?

A dangerous, wicked, forbidden thrill electrified her.

Being with Zack would be like having her cake and eating it, too. She wouldn't have to fear breaking gadabout Zack's heart. And he was exactly what she needed at the moment. Sexual anesthesia to take her mind off Jack.

Clearing her throat, she squared her shoulders and stepped across the room toward him.

He sat on the edge of the bed, slipped the jeans down over his good right leg and extended his other leg toward her.

CeeCee knelt before him, her heart thudding so hard she feared it would explode in her chest. Grasping the denim material in both hands, she slowly began to work it over his swollen knee.

Winnowing his Levi's from around his ankle, she let the jeans drop to the floor then slid her hands up his leg. Her fingers skimmed his honed calf muscles, tangled in the woolly hair on his shins, came to rest on his knee. Gently she began to stroke him with soft, circular movements.

Zack hissed in his breath.

"Sore?"

"Uh-huh."

"Try and relax. You're very tense."

His laugh was hoarse. "Well now, who wouldn't be tense with a fine-looking woman like you rubbing his knee?"

"You need to spend twenty minutes a day in the whirlpool, for two to three weeks," she said briskly, ashamed to admit his compliment pleased her.

CeeCee was accustomed to men making passes at her. She fended off pickup lines on a daily basis. Zack's desire for her was nothing new. What was new was her corresponding passion.

"Yeah, that's what the doctor told me. But I don't have access to a whirlpool."

"Yes, you do." She still avoided his gaze. Avoided acknowledging that he was almost buck naked, that she was on her knees in front of him, that his nearness set her skin on fire. "We've got a whirlpool right here at the apartment complex, and I could give you a treatment every evening when I get home from work."

"Wow, that'd be great."

She finally caught his eye, beheld raw desire shimmering in the depths. He inhaled in rapid succession.

A fine sheen of perspiration glimmered off his one hundred percent fat free chest.

He possessed a devilishly sort of magic she couldn't ignore.

Trickery, witchery. I need help, she thought. *A talisman, a good luck charm, something, anything to ward off his fatal allure.*

Oh! She pressed her teeth into her bottom lip to draw her focus to the task at hand and away from Zack's amazing body.

Did Jack look the same underneath his clothes? she wondered. They were identical twins. The thought sent shivers capering up her spine like kids playing hopscotch.

"Stop doing that," he said hoarsely, causing CeeCee to lift her head and meet his gaze full on.

"Am I hurting you?" Alarmed, she let go of his leg and rocked back on her heels.

"Yeah, but not in the way you think."

"Excuse me?" Puzzled, she cocked her head.

"Stop biting your bottom lip. It's driving me crazy."

"Huh?"

"Seeing those pearly teeth sinking into that full, lush bottom lip of yours makes me so…" His strangled voice trailed off and then he whispered, "hot."

He reached out and ran his thumb along the bottom lip in question. A lip tingling with electrical impulses. "It makes me want to kiss you."

She groaned softly. "Stop it, Zack."

"Why?" he asked. "It's obvious there's a powerful chemistry between us. Why ignore it, sweetheart?"

Then, before she could hightail it out of there, Zack

hooked one arm around her waist, hauled her onto the bed with him, lowered his head and kissed her.

DRUNK ON THE CHARISMATIC power of Zack's identity, the vestiges of cheap tequila and the proximity of CeeCee's perfect little body—abracadabra!—Dr. Jack Travis was a man transformed.

She wore a string bikini. He was in his BVD's. Her dewy skin rubbed against his tanned hide. Her warm breath fanned the hairs on his forehead.

A sure recipe for disaster.

But Jack didn't care. He was no longer cautious, practical Dr. Travis. He was Wild Man Zack.

The desires he'd repressed for six months gushed forth like a geyser spewing hot, libidinous energy into his system. The proverbial Jack had been sprung from his box.

Pop goes the weasel.

He ate her up. Plunging heart and soul into that kiss.

His mouth absorbed her flavor. His tongue explored every corner of her warm, willing mouth. He kept his eyes wide-open. He marveled at her long feathery lashes, the sweet curve of her cheek, the way one bottom front tooth was just the slightest bit crooked. He was completely awed to have her in his bed.

He could scarcely believe she was here. He kept running his palms over the planes of her face to prove to himself she was real and he wasn't caught up in an elaborate dream.

Mine, he thought greedily. *Mine.*

In that moment he knew he had made the right decision by assuming his twin's persona. Anything. Whatever it took to win her. She was worth it.

CeeCee wriggled beneath him, mewling low in her throat.

Her feminine timbre, her dainty movements thrust him headlong into full-blown arousal. Passion gripped him and refused to let go. He was hard enough to punch holes in tin metal.

His blood surged through his veins, thundering in his ears louder than the ocean's surf. His temperature spiked as hot as Arizona in August. A whole blasted chorus of butterflies cavorted in his stomach, kicking like Vegas showgirls.

He reveled in her.

Silky lips. Satiny hair. Velvety fingertips. Downy nape.

Fuzzy. Fluffy. Plush and cuddly.

She was sweeter than the most heavenly dessert. Death By Chocolate, hell. Give him Death By CeeCee. What a way to go!

Down, down, down he fell into everything that was CeeCee. Her taste, her smell, her exquisite sounds. He couldn't stop his descent.

As if he wanted to!

For the first time in his life, he felt utter bliss. He closed his eyes, savoring the experience.

The moment lasted a good thirty seconds.

Then he screwed it up by saying, "I want you, CeeCee."

"Zack," CeeCee murmured, her mouth pressed to his, her small hands knotted into fists against his chest.

"Uh-huh." He drifted languidly in the pleasure, enjoying the way her whisper tickled his lips.

"We can't do this."

"Do what, babe?"

"Have sex."

Have sex? He wasn't having sex, he was making love.

No wait. Jack made love. Zack had sex. And CeeCee thought he was Zack.

He couldn't let her think he wanted to make love instead of simply having wild circus sex. If she had the slightest inkling that he was crazy for her—as either Jack or Zack—she would dash away faster than the Roadrunner zipping off from Wile E. Coyote.

Beep. Beep.

Nonchalant. Carefree. Tons of fish in the sea. That's the attitude.

Yeah, easy to say. Now if only he could convince his heart to stop reeling into his rib cage every time he looked at her.

He opened his eyes. "I'm on fire for you and I think you're hot for me, too. We're both consenting adults. What's the problem? Is it because I'm not looking for a long-term relationship?"

"Oh, no." She struggled to sit up. He moved aside, watched her prop herself against the headboard and give him a look that was part regret part longing. "It's not that. I'm not interested in a long-term relationship, either. In fact, I never plan on getting married."

"Why not? Beautiful woman like you?" He reached out to finger a curl. He asked because he wanted to know if she'd tell Zack the same fantastic tale she'd told him.

"It's a family curse." She waved a hand. "But I don't want to get into it right now. Suffice it to say, that because of my childhood, I don't believe in the institution of marriage."

"That's great, 'cause neither do I. Not that I had a

bad childhood. In fact, my family was a bit like *Father Knows Best*. But heck, maybe that's why I want something different.''

A thrill blasted through him. Yea! She hadn't made up that Jessup family whammy story simply to let him down easy.

"But," he continued, "I do believe in having a good time." It was hard knowing how to strike the right balance between Jack and Zack. He didn't want to come off egotistical, but on the other hand he didn't want her to think he cared too much. Insouciance was the only thing that would keep her interested. "So let the good times roll."

"No. Not tonight. We've both been drinking and after all, we just met." Her curls bobbed seductively across the top of her breast.

He had to glance at the ceiling for a second and compose himself, before turning his gaze back to those mesmerizing sea-green eyes.

"You're right." He took her hand, and ran his thumb across her palm. "And I apologize if I overstepped my boundaries, but you're so damned sexy, CeeCee, it's all I can do to keep my hands to myself."

"This isn't a forever no." She slanted him a coy, sideways glance that was almost his undoing. "Just a not-right-now no."

"So there's hope?"

She simply giggled.

"I pray that's a yes."

"I better go." She scooted off the bed. "My party guests are probably wondering where I've gotten off to."

Quick, do something, she's getting away.

"Are we still on for whirlpool treatments?" Jack

gingerly rubbed his knee, and sent her a hangdog expression, playing on her sympathy.

"Of course I'll still give you therapy. I'll see you Monday afternoon when I get off work."

"What about tomorrow?" he said. "On your day off."

"You're pretty persistent, aren't you?" She adjusted her swimsuit strap, smoothed down her mussed hair.

He angled her a grin. "Didn't Jack tell you? That's my middle name. Zack Persistent Travis."

"Until after you get a girl into bed and then I bet your middle name switches to Zack See-Ya-Around Travis."

He laughed. "You got my number."

She shook her head in amusement. "That's what I like about you. You might be an intractable rapscallion, but at least you're honest about it."

"I'm not into leaving a trail of broken hearts behind me. I tell it like it is. Only those with heavily armored chest protectors need apply."

She leaned over, giving him an superior view of her excellent cleavage and boldly chucked a finger under his chin. Jack just about swallowed his tongue.

"You don't have to worry about me. After my crazy childhood, I've developed a heart of titanium. You'll never burn through it."

"Good," he said, but what he thought was, *We'll see about that.*

"Until tomorrow." She turned away, wriggling her fingers behind her.

Until tomorrow my sweet, he thought and watched her walk out the door.

Tonight, he'd struck out. But that was okay. He

had a whole month to convince her. Eventually he'd get her where he wanted her—denying that damned family curse and saying "yes" to his proposal of marriage.

Now all he had to do was find out how to burn a hole through titanium.

"So?"

CeeCee blinked at Janet. She'd been daydreaming about kissing Zack. Remembering how his lips had felt on hers—strong and hungry. Thinking that he tasted exactly like Jack. And if it weren't for the scratchy beard she could almost pretend he was Jack.

"So?" Janet repeated.

She jerked her mind off Zack and back to the present. "So what?"

It was well after midnight, and the guests had departed. They were cleaning up the courtyard, stuffing plastic cups, aluminum cans and paper plates into different colored trash bags for recycling.

"So how was Jack's brother?"

"What do you mean how was he?"

"Come on, you were with him in Jack's apartment for almost an hour. Are you going to tell me your physical therapy session didn't turn a little more physical than a simple knee massage?"

"Janet! Why on earth would you even suggest such a thing?"

"You mean besides the hickey on your neck?"

"What!" Appalled, CeeCee slapped a hand to her throat.

"The other side," Janet pointed out.

"Oh gosh." She slumped into a nearby lawn chair. "Now everyone will know."

"CeeCee, you would have to be deaf, dumb and blind not to see the sexual chemistry snapping between the two of you. The air was practically electric."

Groaning, CeeCee plunked her head in her hands. "I don't want Jack to find out about this. It would break his heart to know that I made out with his twin brother."

"Hmm. Made out? Just how far did you go? Don't tell me Zack managed to hit a home run."

"Janet!" CeeCee lifted her head. "What you must think of me."

"I think you're a healthy, red-blooded American woman with no strings tying her down, who came across a man who really turned her on."

"We just kissed."

"That's it?" Janet sounded disappointed. She sat at the edge of the pool, and dipped her toes into the water.

"Well, I was in my bikini and he was in his underwear so of course there was body-to-body contact. Is that second base?"

"Any touching below the waist?"

"No."

Janet stuck her hand out straight, twisted it in a quasi wave. "First base, stealing for second."

"Am I horrible?"

"Not at all, honey." Janet leaned over and shook her foot. "You're wonderful."

"I bet Jack wouldn't think so if he knew."

"Why are you so worried about Jack? He's over six hundred miles away."

CeeCee shrugged. "I feel like I'm cheating on Jack. Sounds weird doesn't it?"

"Considering that you're nothing more than friends, yes."

"I know. But I'm wondering if I'm simply attracted to Zack because he reminds me of Jack."

"Could be."

Why couldn't she shake this feeling she was betraying Jack? And why, the entire time she'd been kissing Zack, had she kept wishing that he was his twin brother?

"You're thinking too much," Janet said. "Where's the lighthearted, carefree CeeCee we know and love? I'm supposed to be the gloomy cynic in the bunch, remember?"

CeeCee smiled. Thank heavens for her friend's clarity. She was obsessing over nothing. "You're right. There's not a problem. I'm making a mountain from a molehill. Jack is my friend. Zack is my patient. Neither one of them is my lover, and that's the way it's going to stay."

5

OKAY. THIS WAS THE PLAN. He had to find a way to convince CeeCee to become Zack's lover. Or rather *his* lover. Doggone it, but he was confusing himself with this identity shifting. It was getting so he didn't know where he ended and Zack began.

Last night, in his delight at having discovered a surefire plan to help CeeCee overcome her fear of that silly family curse, he'd moved too quickly, scaring her with his bold desires. Subtlety was the key. A slow, simmering, seduction.

He would use Zack's persona to get her into bed, but it would be he, Jack, who would keep her there. Once CeeCee realized that she could indeed fall in love, that they could share a wonderful life together, that he would never leave her come what may, he would have an unbreakable lock on her heart.

That was his only goal. To give her the love she deserved, the life she secretly craved but was so afraid to reach for. But in order to get her to the point where she could even consider that loving one man forever was a possibility for her, then he had to perpetuate this masquerade.

He had gotten off to a good start. He had awoken just before noon with his first hangover ever. Head throbbing, he had stumbled to the medicine cabinet for three aspirins. After washing back the pills with a gallon of water, he caught sight of his answering machine light blinking a message.

The minute he heard CeeCee's voice spinning into his room, he forgot his aching temples. She was going out to lunch with her friends, but she could supervise his whirlpool treatment at three-thirty. Would that be all right?

Spurred into action, he spent the next hour at the mall shopping for "Zack" clothes. Black leather pants, a leopard print Speedo, Harley-Davidson T-shirts. Although his beard was driving him crazy, he would not shave it, for he feared once the hair was gone the line between him and his twin would be irrevocably gone. He needed the hair as a crutch to separate himself from his brother, at least in his own mind.

Because the landlord had called and said he couldn't repair the window for two days and because he was bored, he detoured by the hardware store for a new pane of glass and repaired the window in record time. Still it was only two o'clock. He called Zack's house to tell him not to bother coming to the charity auction, that he'd act in his stead, but he got Zack's roommate who told him Zack was on a three-week motocross run. He made a mental note to call his brother again in three weeks. He didn't trust the roommate's message-relaying skills. He certainly couldn't have his twin showing up at an inopportune time and blowing his whole cover. He spent the remaining time pacing his apartment and practicing Zack's lower-pitched, slower-paced speech patterns.

Every time he heard a car engine, he popped over to the living-room window, lifted the curtain and studied the parking lot, anxious to catch a glimpse of CeeCee returning home.

After about the nine hundredth time of peeking from behind the curtain, the little lime-green late-model VW Bug slid into her parking space. Stomach in his throat, Jack watched her get out and toss her fiery mane over her shoulder in a familiar way that made his gut clutch.

She flowed up the stairs to her apartment, moving so gracefully it seemed her feet never touched the ground. She had on a lavender floral print dress with a matching beaded choker and cute little white ballet slippers.

Jack, realizing he'd been holding his breath, inhaled deeply, his gaze fixed on her trim athlete's hips. The door closed behind her, and he moved away from the window, perspiration beading his forehead.

She gives me a fever, he thought, delirious with need. *Break out the Tylenol STAT! Grab an ice pack or two. And while you're at it, wheel in a defibrillator in case my heart stops.*

The telephone rang.

Jack shot across the room, snagged the cordless receiver from its base. "'Lo" was all he could manage.

"Zack?" CeeCee's voice, rich and sweet. "You ready for your treatment?"

"Uh-huh."

"Meet you at the whirlpool in ten minutes. Do you know where it is?"

Jack knew, but Zack shouldn't. "No."

"Through the courtyard to the left, past the laundry room, behind the gym."

"See you there."

Pulse bumping with anticipation, he raced to the bedroom, jammed himself into his new Speedo and mentally reminded himself of his goal. *Win her over. But slowly. In fact, make her work for it.*

THE MINUTE ZACK SAUNTERED into the steamy, fern-filled whirlpool room favoring his left knee, CeeCee's jaw hit the floor and her eyes rounded wide.

Most men would look ridiculous in a leopard-print Speedo. Jack wouldn't be caught dead in such an outfit. But on Zack the tiny strip of material fit. Perfectly. He appeared wild and macho. With his washboard abs, and those wickedly delicious whiskers, he flat put Tarzan to shame.

From the time she was a small girl, she'd had a secret crush on Tarzan. A lingering jungle fantasy that included making love on a bed of banana tree leaves. But to heck with the King of the Apes. Zack Travis was the absolute sexiest thing she had ever clapped eyes on. She wanted him to pound his chest, throw back his head and do the Tarzan yell. Her toes curled at the notion. Last night had been no margarita-induced anomaly.

Bummeroo.

She'd hoped a good night's sleep and the stark light of day would help her see things clearly.

Apparently not.

Inwardly she groaned. It was official. Like it or not, she had the serious hots for Zack Travis.

Then again, what wasn't to like?

Great body, handsome face. Adventuresome, sexy, fun-loving, decidedly not marriage-minded, he was the perfect guy for her. They had a lot in common. Besides, what was so wrong with a red-hot fling?

It had been a long time since any man had moved her to this degree. The only one that even came close was the very one she refused to feel anything sexual toward. His twin brother, Jack.

Zack closed the door behind him, moved across the room to where she perched on the edge of the Jacuzzi, her feet dangling in the warm, bubbly water.

The closer he came, the harder she found it to draw breath. She peeked surreptitiously at him from lowered lashes. Despite his limp, he moved like a predatory cat on the hunt, lithe and graceful. He had a white towel, that contrasted sharply with his tanned skin, thrown over one shoulder.

She stared at the sinewy muscles bunched across his chest. Her pulse fluttered, as weightless and fast as hummingbird wings.

He stopped and peered down at her. CeeCee felt his gaze igniting the top of her head but she was too nervous to turn and meet his stare straight on.

The humidity in the room accentuated his scent. A fragrant masculine aroma, not cologne, she decided. Lighter, milder. Probably one of those zesty manly soaps.

His abdomen was chiseled; his belly button a provocative innie just begging to be tickled. His body hair swirled in a dark line that disappeared into the waist of the compact, low-slung swimsuit.

Her eyes grew even wider. The suit hid absolutely nothing.

Embarrassed, she spun her gaze across the room, focused on a ficus plant in the corner.

She was so aware of him. His broad-shouldered presence seemed to encompass the entire building. She found herself wishing that some other apartment dweller would pop inside to join them in the whirl-pool.

No such luck.

"How you doin'?" he drawled, his voice pushing through her like heated chocolate.

"Fine, fine."

"I had a great time last night."

"Me, too." She couldn't keep avoiding his eye. Bravely she raised her gaze, preparing herself for a head-on collision.

Whack!

Their eyes locked as they had the night before.

Steam rose around them in lazy, drifting curls. The water gurgled like smothered laughter. CeeCee felt flustered and girlish and completely out of her depth.

He was an unbelievably...virile male, no escaping it. Standing there in nothing but that skimpy spotted swimsuit proud as the King of the Jungle, he was extravagant eye candy.

Thank heavens for that! Eye candy she could handle. No danger of her falling in love with eye candy. Because she certainly wasn't falling in love. No siree. She might be riding the fast train to Lustland, but that was hunky-dory. Lust was fine.

Stop this, CeeCee. You're in charge here. You're the therapist. Take control.

She squared her shoulders. "Ease into the pool slowly," she commanded. "Hold onto the railing for support."

"Oooh. A forceful woman. I like that."

"We're here to heal your knee, Zack. Least you forget."

"Yes, ma'am," he said, not at all contritely and settled himself beside her.

Their legs touched. Bare thigh against bare thigh. Zip! Pop! Sizzle!

The heat that swamped her body had nothing to do with the humidity in the closed confines and everything to do with her body's spontaneous reaction to Zack.

She wanted him, oh, yeah, but the intensity of her desire scared the stuffing out of her. She'd never experienced anything like this raw, animal chemistry.

"What next?" he whispered.

"We get wet."

"Sounds good to me."

Good grief, the man could make the simplest statement sound like sexual innuendo.

CeeCee slid into the Jacuzzi and across to the other side away from Zack. Her heart pounded and her face felt flushed. She tried desperately to convince herself it was due to the water temperature and nothing else. Heaven forbid she could keep her libido under wraps for a mere twenty-minute session in the whirlpool.

"We'll start by just sitting here a couple of minutes, letting our muscles relax."

"Whatever you say." He was looking at her lips now instead of trying to catch her eye.

"Why don't you tell me about winning the moto-cross championship," she suggested.

He shrugged. "Not much to tell."

CeeCee frowned. That didn't sound like most of the guys she knew. Ordinarily men loved bragging about sports and cars and things like that. Funny, Zack certainly didn't strike her as the modest type.

"Come on, don't be humble. Jack's told me you've won tons of contests. What kind of bike do you have?"

"Ducati."

Boy, getting him to talk about himself was like pulling teeth. Plus, he just kept staring at her. As if she were a succulent piece of fruit ripe for the picking. The more he studied her mouth, the more disconcerted she became, flicking out the tip of her tongue to moisten her lips.

She ducked her head, wanting to hide from him.

"Feels like a tropical island in here," he said.

"Uh-huh."

Stop looking at me!

"Reminds me of Hawaii."

"You've been to Hawaii?" Her head came up at that, and she managed to focus on his bearded chin which lent such a lawless quality to his appearance. "Which island?"

"Maui, Oahu and Kauai. Never got around to the big island."

"You lucky dog," she breathed. "What was it? A motocross race?"

"Family vacation when we were kids."

"I've always wanted to go to Hawaii. It's a childhood dream of mine. In fact, Jack and I both entered a radio call-in contest on Q102. They're having a drawing to give away a free trip to Hawaii on the twenty-first."

"I'll keep my fingers crossed for you." He raised his crossed fingers.

"Thanks." She grinned. "I get goose bumps just thinking about going there."

"I'd love to be the one to take you there for the first time." The longing in his voice startled her. Was the longing for Hawaii or her or both? The thought of lying on the beach with Zack in Hawaii stacked goose bumps on top of goose bumps until she felt like a goose bump sandwich.

"What's *your* secret dream?" She changed the subject as she struggled to regain her equilibrium.

"I've always wanted to skydive, but I've never gotten around to it."

"Me, too!"

"No? Really? Imagine that."

"Maybe we could go together sometime."

"Uh, maybe," he replied. "But not until my knee heals of course."

Was it her imagination or did he pale visibly beneath his beard? As if he were scared of skydiving. Nah. Couldn't be. This guy wasn't afraid of anything.

"Time for a few gentle stretches," she said, buffeted on all sides by a myriad of feelings.

She wanted him and yet the power of her feelings unnerved her. It was only sexual chemistry. She knew that, but it had been a very long time—if ever—since she'd felt anything this forceful.

She was forced to move closer. Her hands encircled his ankle and she carefully flexed then extended his leg.

"How does that feel?"

"Fine," he murmured.

"You have great musculature." She ran a hand up the back of his calf and her fingers caught fire.

"Why, thank you. I work out often."

"I think it has more to do with genetics. Jack's got the same calf muscles."

"Oh really? You've noticed?"

"Only in passing." She shrugged.

Ticktock. Silence filled the room for a long moment, then Zack murmured, "You wouldn't have a secret thing for my brother, would you?"

"Gosh no." She wasn't fibbing. Not really. She could have a thing for Jack if she let herself, but where a forever kind of guy was concerned she kept her heart locked tight.

"Are you sure? Are we in competition for your affections, CeeCee?"

She shook her head. "No. Jack understands that we can never be more than good friends."

"Does he?" Zack gave her an enigmatic stare. "Really?"

"Of course. He tells me everything about his life, and I tell him everything about mine."

"Everything? Do you give him a play-by-play of your dates like you would with a girlfriend?"

"Well, yeah. That's the beauty of our relationship."

"I think it stinks," he said bluntly.

"Excuse me?" She blinked.

"My brother listens while you chatter away about your encounters with other men?" Zack wagged an index finger. "You're a cruel one, CeeCee Adams."

"What do you mean?" She frowned.

"Teasing Jack with tales of your sexual antics. Whether you know it or not, you're driving the man bonkers."

Startled, she reflected on Zack's statement. Had she been tormenting Jack? When she had needed a shoulder to cry on Jack was always there for her. She'd never given his availability much thought beyond friendship.

Zack was correct. She had not only been unintentionally cruel, but selfish and blind to her faults as well. The realization stunned her.

Poor Jack. No wonder he'd snapped and issued her an ultimatum.

"And," Zack continued, "he's too much of a schmuck to do anything about it."

"Hey! Don't talk about Jack like that." Indignation momentarily replaced her shame.

"Don't get me wrong. I mean it in the nicest possible way. He's my brother and I love him, but he's a schmuck. He's got a fabulous babe like you living next door and he's never made a move."

"Unlike you," she replied tartly, glaring at Zack. "Your brother is a perfect gentleman."

"In other words, he's *bor-ing*."

"No, he's not." Her emotions toggled from anger to regret to guilt and back again. "Jack is steady and dependable, tender and funny. He's a wonderful person."

"But you're the kind of girl who likes flashy cars, fancy parties and not-so-wonderful men."

Yes. No. Not exactly.

"What you'd really like," he continued huskily, "what you secretly long for, is a man to take charge. A man who'll let you know exactly what he wants. No ifs, ands, or buts about it."

"You don't know me well enough to say what I like."

"That's true." He narrowed his eyes, peered at her through half-lowered lids. "But I'd like to get to know you very well indeed. For instance, if I were to kiss you on the back of your neck would you wriggle with pleasure?"

"That's something you'll have to find out for yourself."

He was clay in her hands. Her fingers kneaded his knee, massaging away the stiffness while at the same time sending tingles of awareness barreling straight up his leg and bursting into his groin.

Kiss her, man, Zack's voice urged him.

But then Jack had a clearer, more rational thought. Wait. Let the tension escalate.

She raised her head. Her eyes shone brightly. Tendrils of hair cleaved like a vine to her forehead, her cheek. She looked moist and dewy and ready for anything.

He clenched his jaw to keep from groaning, knotted his hands into fists to keep from touching her. His gaze traced down her long neck to her slender collarbone and beyond.

Her peach-size breasts swelled against the practical one-piece navy-blue swimsuit. This sensible suit was in sharp contrast to the teeny-weeny string bikini she'd had on last night, but it made no difference. The garment couldn't blot out her attributes.

Breasts of a goddess. Not too large, not too small. Just right. High and firm and round.

How he wanted her!

A shimmering furnace of heat blasted up his nerve endings. His nostrils flared as he inhaled deeply of her sweet, sexy scent mingling so intriguingly with the smell of chlorine.

With a blink of the eye he could picture her naked and in picturing her completely bare, tortured himself beyond endurance. His groin tightened, turned thick and heavy.

What was happening to him? Normally he had excellent control over his more...er...baser instincts. If that wasn't the case, could he and CeeCee have remained just friends for so long? But playing the role of his twin brother was changing him in unexpected ways. He was becoming hungrier, less cautious, more willing to take a gamble to get what he wanted.

"Have you ever made love in a whirlpool?" She had stopped massaging him, although her hand was still at his knee.

Surprised, he could only stare. Of course he had never made love in a whirlpool. What was she suggesting? That they make love right here? Right now?

His pulse revved.

"Jack told me you've made love in exotic places all over the world."

Casually he shrugged, belying the pounding in his heart. "I don't like to brag about my...romantic conquests. I'm not the type to kiss and tell."

Ha! That was a good one. Zack not bragging about his sexploits? That would be the day the earth stopped spinning. His twin brother crowed about his women from the time he got up in the morning until he took some nubile young female to bed at night. But the gentleman in Jack wouldn't allow him to emulate Zack in this area. Talking about his romantic encounters around the locker room was not only crude but disrespectful to the lady in question.

"But have you made love in a hot tub?" CeeCee repeated. Obviously the subject intrigued her. "No need to name names."

"Sure. Hasn't everyone?"

"Not me," she whispered.

"Is this an invitation," he asked huskily, reaching out to brush a curl from the side of her face.

"No." She shivered lightly. A sharp sense of power surged through him knowing he had caused that response in her. "At least not yet."

"Not yet?" For one second, his heart stopped.

"I may not be interested in a permanent relationship with you, but believe it or not, I don't hop into bed with just any and everyone."

"And you think I do?" He placed a palm to his chest.

"Don't you?"

"No." He snorted.

"But Jack told me that you've had dozens and dozens of girlfriends."

"And he told me you've had dozens and dozens of boyfriends."

"Touché."

"Hey, lady, just because I like to have fun and go out on lots of dates doesn't mean I'm easy." He tossed her a teasingly offended expression.

"I know! Everyone thinks the same thing about me." CeeCee laughed. It was a rich, hearty sound that warmed him straight through his bones.

"You'd think people could see beyond stereotypes," he said, "myself included."

"Exactly. Same here. Guilty as charged."

They laughed together, and it was a wonderful moment. The tension had dissipated. They enjoyed an easy camaraderie. The water was warm, the company fantastic. His knee didn't even hurt. In that instant, Jack had an irresistible urge to come clean. To tell her the truth.

But before he could weigh the wisdom of such a move at this point, CeeCee flashed him a toothy grin.

She flicked out her tongue; ran it over her bottom lip. She was tormenting him and she knew it.

The little minx.

Overcome by an onslaught of erotic sensation, he realized he was going to have to kiss her. Angling his head, he leaned in so close their mouths were almost touching.

"Ahem."

The clearing of a voice pulled them apart and drew their attention to the doorway.

"Excuse me, am I interrupting something?" Miss Abbercrombe wore a high-cut gold lamé French swimsuit even though she no longer had the figure to pull it off. Her hair was piled up on her head, held in place by a myriad of colorful bows. Muffin, as always, was clutched in her arms.

"No, not at all," CeeCee said and sprang from the water. Before Jack could move, she'd already grabbed her robe and stuffed her feet into flip-flops.

Muffin barked.

"Shh," Miss Abbercrombe hushed her dog and squinted at them. "Is that you, CeeCee dear?"

"Yes, ma'am."

Muffin barked again, her eyes trained on Jack. She struggled to break free from Miss Abbercrombe, her yelps growing frantic.

"Is that Jack with you?" The elderly woman came closer. "Home from Mexico already, young man?"

"No." CeeCee pushed back her hair from her forehead with one hand in that carefree manner of hers that plucked at Jack's heartstrings. "This is Jack's identical twin brother, Zack. He's visiting for a few weeks while Jack is in Mexico. He…er, um…hurt his leg and I was giving him physical therapy."

Miss Abbercrombe grinned. "Oh, is that what you call it nowadays? In my time we used different terminology."

CeeCee's face flushed redder than her hair. Jack wanted to get out of the whirlpool, but he didn't want Miss Abbercrombe to see him in the Speedo.

Muffin whined and pawed at Miss Abbercrombe's arm.

"What's the matter with you, Muffin? That's not Jack," Miss Abbercrombe scolded, then raised her head to address him.

"Do you mind if she has a little sniff of you? Just to let her know you're not your twin brother."

He was trapped! One sniff from meddlesome Muffin and his cover was blown.

The poodle leaped to the ground, trotted over to the hot tub and hopped up on the edge beside Jack. Her little body trembled with excitement. She joyously licked his face.

"Will you look at that," Jack said, determined to plow his way through this. "She must think I'm Jack."

Miss Abbercrombe come closer still, she peered hard at him over the top of her glasses. "Muffin hates all men except Jack. Are you sure you're not Jack?"

He gulped and met the elderly lady's knowing stare. Laughing nervously, he cast a glance at CeeCee who was watching the whole episode with her hands cocked on her hips. Meanwhile, Muffin kept licking his earlobe like it was an ice-cream cone.

"Of course I'm not Jack, although people have mixed us up a time or two. I'm a good five pounds thinner than my brother and I tan easily. And hey, look, I wear a beard and have longer hair."

Even he had to give a mental eye roll at that last comment, but he was desperate, grasping at straws. He couldn't have CeeCee finding out the truth this way. He wasn't going to be bested by Detective Mutt.

"You two look exactly alike," Miss Abbercrombe commented.

He had the strangest feeling she was about to pry open his mouth and examine his teeth in her search for the truth. "We are identical twins."

"Well," CeeCee said, "I'll leave you two to discuss the miracle of Muffin liking two men. I've got things to do."

"Hey, wait!" Jack said, rising to get out of the hot tub.

But CeeCee just waved at him and headed for the door. "Meet you here tomorrow at six after I get off work. Is that okay?"

"Great," he muttered. This had not turned out the way he had planned.

The minute CeeCee left he found Miss Abbercrombe perusing his Tarzan getup with a suspicious eye.

"Uh, hi." He lifted a hand.

"Don't you hi me, Jack Travis. I want to know why you've got CeeCee convinced that you're your own twin brother and I want to know now."

There was no fooling Muffin or Miss Abbercrombe. He might as well come clean. In fact, Jack realized, it might do him a world of good to share his secret. It never hurt to have an ally.

He cast a glance to the door making sure CeeCee was gone, then lowered his voice. "Promise me you won't tell CeeCee."

Miss Abbercrombe looked skeptical. "I can't

promise that. Why are you trifling with the girl's affections? That's not like you, Jack.''

"Miss Abbercrombe, this is very important. I promise you the last thing I want to do is hurt her. In fact, I'm in love with her.''

"Well, why didn't you say so.'' Miss Abbercrombe smiled gleefully. The woman loved a good romance. "I'll even help play matchmaker. I always thought you two would be perfect together.''

6

FOR THE NEXT THREE WEEKS he and CeeCee bonded like hydrogen and oxygen. Coming together for those short, sweet twenty-minute intervals every evening where they teased and coaxed, massaged and stroked. Moving ever closer to a deeper intimacy.

But at times it was tough keeping up his ruse. On many occasions, Jack had to push through his natural reticence, and tap into his own wild side. He flirted outrageously with CeeCee and he touched her often. Before she went to bed every night, he called her on the phone and said uninhibited things that were just this side short of phone sex.

With each passing day, the tension mounted. He was wound tighter than a roll of surgical tape. Taut with anticipation. Hungry to consummate their love. Because whether CeeCee would admit it to herself or not, she was falling for him. He could tell by the way her eyes lit up when she saw him. She looked the way he felt inside. Like Christmas had come early every time she walked into a room.

His fantasies kept him awake at night, tossing and turning with sweat. Fantasies that made his heart swell with yearning. The only thing he'd ever wanted as much as he wanted CeeCee was to become a doctor.

Well, he was a doctor now.

But he'd yet to become CeeCee's lover.

He only had one more week to get her into his bed. One more week to convince her that she could fall in love and stay in love for a lifetime. One more week to prove to that ridiculous curse was nothing but a self-fulfilling prophesy.

The clock was ticking. Time for phase two of his "debunk the family whammy" plan. Time to accelerate this slow seduction. Time to consummate this simmering tension before they both exploded from raw need.

She'd called him last night and told him she would stop by after work to shore up last-minute instructions for the bachelor charity auction the following afternoon. He'd almost forgotten about the darned thing until she brought it up.

Meaning his Friday night and Saturday afternoon would be taken up by some socialite rich enough to outbid the others for the privilege of hanging out with Motocross Champion Zack "Wild Man" Travis on Galveston Island.

He called his twin again, but no one answered. He left a message on the answering machine telling Zack not to show up. The bachelor auction was taken care of. Still he worried. What if his brother didn't go home after his motocross race? What if he came straight to Houston?

You're obsessing, he assured himself. Zack will get the message.

At that moment he heard the distinctive noise of CeeCee car's engine pull into the parking lot. Jerking open his front door, he hurried out to greet her.

"Hey, beautiful," he called.

"Hi, handsome." She breezed over, carrying a garment bag. How he wished he could bottle that smile to carry in his pocket whenever he was away from her.

She looked so gorgeous he couldn't speak for a full sixty seconds. She gazed at him. The wind tossed her curls against the smooth curve of her cheek. Her green eyes held a hint of mischief.

"Here's your tuxedo for the bachelor auction tomorrow."

He just stared, taking her in, and thinking; I'm going to give you all the love I have to give. I'm going to convince you that your life is charmed, not cursed. I'm going to help you see that you can have your heart's desire.

"Zack?" She dangled the tux from its wooden coat hanger.

"Huh, oh, yeah." He took it from her. "Aren't you coming over to fill me in on the details?"

"Sure. Just let me go change first."

He jerked a thumb at his apartment. "You know I was about to throw a steak on the grill. Would you like to join me?"

Man, he was getting good at telling these white lies. He'd been marinating the steak, tossing a salad and baking potatoes for the last hour awaiting her arrival.

"Sounds great. I'm starved."

"You take your steak medium-well, right?"

"How did you know that?"

He went silent a moment, realizing he had slipped. Zack had no idea how CeeCee liked her steaks. "Um, you just seem like a medium well kind of woman."

"You read women pretty well, don't you, Zack?"

"It's a talent of mine." He gave her a little salute, one of Zack's trademarks.

"See you in a few," she said and went to her apartment.

Lord, the woman had the most perfect tush in the entire world, bar none. Tonight, he was going to kiss her again. Although there'd been a lot of caressing and deep eye gazing these past three weeks, he hadn't kissed her since the night he'd come back from Mexico.

He had wanted to wait, but he'd reached the end of his rope. He couldn't wait any longer. Tonight, he was going to kiss her silly and let nature take its course.

Slipping back into his apartment, he hung up the tux, then hurried to the kitchen to grab the steaks from the fridge. He stepped out onto the thumbnail-size patio and slapped the filet mignon on the grill. He felt keyed-up, twisted in knots. Perspiration beaded his brow; he swiped it away with a forearm. Closing his eyes, he took a deep breath.

Stop freaking out.

But his insides were syrup as he thought about kissing CeeCee again. And what might come after the kissing. His gut tightened. Would tonight be the night they made love?

"Need any help?"

At the sound of CeeCee's sexy voice, he jumped a foot and his eyes flew open. She lounged in the doorway between the kitchen and the patio, a vision of loveliness. Her hair, freshly brushed, cascaded over her shoulders like a red-hot lava flow. She wore a pair of well-worn, denim shorts, thin white sandals and a blue cotton sleeveless blouse.

She sauntered out onto the patio, smelling of the tropics. All pineapple and banana and coconut. She perched on the edge of the hip-high rock wall separating his pathetic patio from the apartment next door, and gently swung her so-fabulous-they-could-be-insured-by-Lloyd's-of-London legs.

Jack strategically held the empty steak platter in front of his lower anatomy, desperately trying to camouflage his very masculine response to her appearance.

Come on. Say something Zackish. Be bold. Take charge. Don't think. Act!

But he could only stare, dumbstruck by her beauty.

Before he could think of anything remotely interesting to say, from inside the kitchen, they heard the telephone ring.

"I'll get it," she said, seemingly relieved to have something to do. "I'll bring it out here and put it on speakerphone so you can talk while you tend the steaks."

She zipped into the kitchen and zipped back again. She settled the phone on the patio table and hit the speaker button.

"Hello," he said, tongs in hand.

"Hello!" replied a rapid-fire, enthusiastic voice. "This is Ron Tipman from Q102."

"You won! You won!" CeeCee squealed and bounced around the patio like a pogo stick. "Oh my gosh, they called!"

Jack grinned. He had won that trip to Hawaii for CeeCee. Her delight sent him straight over the moon. He couldn't wait to see her face when they stepped off the plane in Oahu. Volcanoes in the background, palm trees swaying in the foreground.

"If you can just tell me that your name is indeed Jack Travis of 198 River Run, you will have won an all-expense paid trip for two to Hawaii!"

"What?" His gut clenched.

"Sir," the disc jockey said, "are you Jack Travis?"

"Uh, well..."

Was he Jack Travis? He looked from CeeCee to the phone and back again.

"Remember, sir," the disc jockey prompted, "you must show valid proof of your identity in order to claim the prize."

CeeCee's face fell like a fractured plate.

He could prove he was Jack Travis all right. But not now. Not today. Oh hell, why had the radio station called when CeeCee just happened to be here and stick him on the speakerphone?

If he told a lie, he'd lose the trip.

If he told the truth, at least at this point, he would lose CeeCee.

And he couldn't let that happen. Not when he was so close to winning her heart.

Oh, what a tangled web we weave when first we practice to deceive.

"Sir?"

"No," Jack croaked at last, he could feel the heat of CeeCee's gaze on his face. "I'm not Jack Travis."

"That's too bad, sir. I'm sorry."

"But Jack's my brother. I could contact him, have him call you."

"I'm afraid not. The rules state he had to be home to get the qualifying call. But keep listening to Q102." the disc jockey said, then hung up.

"Rats!" CeeCee exclaimed. "Jack will be so disappointed."

He's only disappointed because he couldn't win the trip for you CeeCee, don't you realize that?

"Sorry, I couldn't fake it."

"It wasn't your fault."

"You deserve to go first-class to Hawaii."

"Oh, Zack, that's so nice of you."

"I'm not being nice," he growled. "I'm thinking of you wearing a grass skirt and coconut shells and swinging those awesome hips of yours in tempo to 'Tiny Bubbles'."

She boldly met his gaze. "Only if you wear those Tarzan swim trunks and swing from a Banyan tree."

"You've got yourself a deal, Lucille."

"Check the steaks." She laughed, not taking him the least bit seriously. "They look done."

His frustration over not winning the trip passed, but Jack still couldn't shake his nagging conscience. He'd seriously begun questioning the wisdom of the masquerade, even though Zack's Crock-Pot slow seduction had been progressing nicely with CeeCee. He felt pulled in two directions, and neither course was optimal.

"THE STEAKS WERE GREAT," CeeCee enthused as they sat at the patio table, surrounded by empty plates. "But you're not fooling me. You didn't just happen to have an extra filet mignon and baked potato lying around."

"You got me," he confessed. "I'd been wanting to do something for you, to say thanks for the physical therapy but I was afraid to ask you out on a date. I didn't want to be too pushy."

"I appreciate that." She grinned. "But if you'd have asked, I wouldn't have turned you down."

"Oh really? Then how about tomorrow night? We could grab a bite to eat, head out to the speedboat races."

"You can't."

"What?"

"Have you forgotten already? You'll be in Galveston with your charity auction date."

"Why don't you bid on me?" He leaned closer, gave her Zack's best grin.

"Well, first of all it's against the rules for the coordinator to bid in the auction, but mostly you're out of my price range."

"What are you talking about?"

"Wait and see." She winked in a way that sent a fissure of pure heaven sparkling through him. "You're a top draw. Advance ticket sales have skyrocketed since it was announced you were going on the auction block."

"No kidding?"

"Face it. You're hot stuff, Zack Travis." Then she began to hum a few bars from the Rolling Stone's song "Hot Stuff" and sway languidly in time to her own music.

He laughed.

She swung her leg back and forth under the table. She had kicked off her sandals earlier. Her foot grazed his shin. Her pupils widened. Although he thought the initial contact had been accidental, it was no accident when she took those toes and ran them from his knee to his ankle.

"CeeCee." He leaned in close and whispered softly into her ear. "What are you doing?"

"Who me?" She feigned an innocent expression.

"You're fooling with fire, lady."

"Am I?"

"You don't want to get me started."

"Why not."

"I might have a hard time stopping."

"Oh, yeah?" Her jaunty eyes glistened.

"Yeah."

He tugged her from her chair and pulled her into his lap. She squealed with delight.

"Oh." CeeCee inhaled deeply and stared into his face.

Her heart revved. She'd decided that three weeks was long enough. She was about to explode from the sexual chemistry seething between them. She'd come over here tonight hoping they would finally end up in bed together. Her choice of short shorts had been no accident. Nor had her cologne—*Forbidden Sin*— been a careless afterthought. "You're so bad."

She was ready for anything he could dish out. She'd gotten to know him well enough to realize they could indeed have a terrific time without either of them getting hurt.

He pressed his heated mouth to hers. His tongue…oh heavenly days…better than ambrosia and champagne and chocolate all rolled into one. He licked her lips with quick flicks of that incredible tongue, traced the outline of her teeth. He drew her bottom lip between his teeth and sucked gently.

Greedily she kissed him back with an overwhelming, ravenous desire. The strength of her passion almost bowling her over so unbelievable was the aching need growing inside her.

She leaned into him, cocked her head slightly to

grant him easier access to her mouth. She splayed her hands across his chest, thirstily drinking from his lips.

The tingling started in her breasts but it swiftly spread, heating her skin, skipping along synapses, ending up a tight ball of electrical impulses many inches below her waist.

He pulled away a moment, her lips bereft at his parting. He looked deeply into her eyes and threaded his fingers through the loose tendrils of hair trailing along her shoulder.

She reached out to stroke the silk of his beard. Their gazes stayed locked. She heard her pulse beating in her ears.

There was no mistaking the degree of his desire for her. His hardness was both flattering and exciting. He spanned her waist with his hands, then kissed her again.

His muscled chest crushed her breasts, but it wasn't unpleasant. Her nipples ached sweetly, raising up to press against him. When he shifted, his movements abraded her nipples through the thin material of her blouse, causing her to gasp out loud.

She inhaled him like oxygen. His tongue delved deeper. She moaned into his mouth, riding the crest of intoxicating sensation until CeeCee didn't think she could stand one minute more not being merged with him.

Tilt! Tilt!

His mouth was on her throat now, his tongue licking little swirls of heat that only served to send her over the edge, deeper and deeper into impending oblivion.

"Oh, Jack," she moaned.

And everything stopped.

Zack stopped moving, stopped kissing her, stopped stroking her skin with his fingers. She could have bitten off her tongue when she realized she'd called him by his twin brother's name.

"What?" he whispered. "What did you call me?"

CeeCee pulled back, expecting to see disappointment etched on his face, but oddly enough another emotion flickered in the depths of his chocolate-brown eyes.

Was that joyful surprise?

She must be mistaken. Besides the look was gone. Gently he settled her back into her own chair, their sudden passion dissipating like a spent balloon.

"I'm sorry, Zack, so sorry. It was a simple slip of the tongue. I'm just so used to Jack being around that I accidentally called his name."

"While you're kissing me? Sure it wasn't a Freudian slip?" Jack held his breath as he waited for her answer. "Would you rather be with my brother?"

"'Course not." Her voice rose slightly on the denial.

"You've got sexual feelings for Jack?" He finally dared to speak the words.

"No." She shook her head as if trying to convince herself as well as him.

"You're certain?"

"Don't worry, Zack." She knotted a fist over his chest, and sent rivers of heat shaking through him. "You're the one I'm attracted to. Not your brother."

Jack's hopes dropped. *Ker-splat!*

That's what he got for perpetuating this dangerous charade. This dungeon of his own construction. He was hearing the truth whether he liked it or not. But he and Zack were one and the same. If she loved one dimension of himself, she had to love the other.

Right?

"Zack...I really am sorry."

"There's nothing to apologize for." He forced cheerfulness into his voice and shrugged. "I've called out the wrong name at the wrong moment myself."

"It would probably be better if I went home." She started to rise to her feet.

"Wait." He reached out and wrapped his hand around her slender wrist and came into contact with her charm bracelet. The damn bracelet that reminded her why she would always have to pick guys like Zack over guys like him.

"Yes." Their eyes met again. She wanted him. No mistaking that sultry look.

Keep her on the hook. Keep her dangling. When she finally sleeps with you, it's going to be forever, bracelet or not, curse or not. She's just never seen or experienced unconditional love. When she realizes you'll do anything within your power for her, she'll be yours.

He could only hope he was right.

"Take this with you," he said, then kissed her within an inch of her life.

CeeCee tried not to stare but it was downright impossible what with Zack in that black tuxedo, red tie and matching cummerbund. Not to mention the blood-red rosebud tucked into his lapel.

They were standing in the hospital corridor that led to the auditorium where the bachelor auction was due to start in fifteen minutes. Zack looked completely different than he had for the past three weeks. Plus, his limp had almost vanished. At this moment, except for that beard, he looked exactly like Jack.

Her heart gave a strange hop. She asked herself not for the first time who she was really attracted to. Her wild, fling-waiting-to-happen or his steady twin.

CeeCee forced her gaze off Zack and onto the clipboard in her hand. She stifled a yawn. She had slept poorly, thanks to what had *not* happened in Jack's apartment the night before. Each time she had dozed off she would jerk awake a few minutes later, soaked in perspiration and tingling all over from the vestiges of a steamy dream where Zack was the starring attraction.

At dawn, she'd given up trying to sleep and had instead proceeded to worry herself sick about the auction. It was her first time hosting such an event and she was desperate for things to go smoothly.

Of course with Zack as the headliner, what could possibly go wrong?

Women fainting in a fervor over him?

Men getting jealous and busting his chops?

Kids chasing after him for an autograph?

Okay, tons of things could go wrong.

"Um, you've got something poking out of your dress," he said.

"What?" Distracted, she reached around to feel a price tag sticking up from her zipper.

"Hold on, sweetheart. I'll deal with that pesky tag."

And then his fingers were on her skin, burning a searing path straight to her groin.

Oh gosh, they were going to have to do something about this sexual tension. Before her thong panties spontaneously burst into flames. Before she melted into a puddle and evaporated.

The sooner they got their affair rolling, the sooner the sparks would sizzle then fizzle, the sooner things could get back to normal.

But she couldn't have Zack until Saturday evening. He would belong to the lucky lady who outbid all the others. In the meantime, she would have to put all sexy thoughts on hold.

"Got it." Zack tucked the errant tag into his pocket, his grin so endearing, she almost absconded with him back to her apartment.

What the heck was the matter with her? Yesterday, when she could have made love to him, she had chickened out and run away.

Why?

And why did the thought of those man-starved single society women bidding on him at the charity auction make her blood run cold?

Sheesh, she was losing it.

She didn't want him to strut his stuff before other women. She didn't want to hear them ooh and ah over him. She didn't want him to go off with anyone else.

But she couldn't bid on him, and she couldn't spirit him away from the event. The auction normally raised thousands of dollars in funds for health care programs to benefit inner city kids. She couldn't put her own selfish desires above children.

She'd have to tough it out.

And pray Zack didn't start a fling with the lady who paid big bucks for a date with him.

The bad thing was, tomorrow was her twenty-eighth birthday and she'd be spending it alone without either Jack or Zack.

"Here," she said, tucking her clipboard under her arm and giving Zack a last-minute once-over. "Your tie is a little crooked." She reached out to adjust it. He grinned down at her.

"Oh, my gawd!" a female voice shrieked "That's Zack Travis! Isn't he just the bomb?"

Another girl squealed in response. The next thing CeeCee knew they were knee-deep in teenage girls giggling and blushing and asking Zack to sign their T-shirts.

Tsk, tsk, what a spectacle.

I won't get jealous. I won't! It's just showbiz and the attention is good for the auction.

Besides, she had no call for jealousy. She had no claim on Zack, nor he on her. And that's exactly the way she wanted it.

Wasn't it?

"Sorry, ladies," she said, firmly taking Zack by the arm and detaching him from one leggy blonde with a skirt so small she could have used it as an eye patch. "I've got to get him backstage."

He shrugged helplessly at the teenagers, and one even had the audacity to hiss at CeeCee.

Brat!

She hustled him through the back door to the auditorium. "I've got a few things to take care of. You be good."

"Sweetheart," he murmured, leaning in close. So close the hairs on the back of her neck stood on end. "I'm always good. Just you wait and see."

"You're impossible," she said, torn between being irritated with him and being very turned on by his hand lingering at her waist.

"Oh, no. That's where you're wrong. I'm very,

very possible. Especially when it comes to you, my flame-haired vamp.''

"Quit it!" She moved away, unable to stop a warm flush from spreading up her neck. "I'll be back in a few to check on you."

"Bye." He gave her a goofy grin, and wriggled both his fingers and his eyebrows.

Why did she have the feeling she was going to come back to find half a dozen women feeding him grapes and fanning him with tree fronds?

Because that's the kind of guy he is, CeeCee. Face facts. Mr. Footloose and Fancy-Free may not come with strings attached, but for that very reason you can't expect him to have eyes for only you.

But dammit, that's exactly what she did expect!

She was confused about her feelings for Zack. Very confused.

7

COULD THINGS POSSIBLY GET any more snarled between he and CeeCee? Jack thought as he leaned against the wall. While his plan to impersonate his brother might have looked good at the onset, the deeper he slipped into the deception the harder he found it to look himself in the mirror.

Hang on. Not much longer. You're almost there.

"Mr. Travis?"

A soft, feminine voice brought his head up. Three young women sidled up to him, each clutching glossy eight-by-ten photographs of Zack.

"May we have your autograph?" The boldest one tentatively extended a picture and pen toward him.

All three looked so excited with awestruck gazes on their faces, he didn't have the heart to send them away.

"Sure, sure." He smiled. "What's your name?"

"Suzie."

He scribbled, "to Suzie of the amazing blue eyes" across the bottom of the photo, then added Zack's signature.

"Thank you so much," she breathed, blushed prettily and stepped back to let her friends come forward.

And the next thing he knew, he was surrounded by women. Tall ones, short ones, old ones, young ones. Blondes and brunettes, and redheads. All of them seeking to talk to him, touch him, flirt with him. They batted their eyes and asked him about himself. They offered to cook him dinner or take him for a ride in their cars. They oohed and ahed, cooed and simpered.

Jack had never received this kind of female adoration, and it disconcerted him. He felt claustrophobic and ached to bolt from the room. But how could he? These women would be bidding on him, supporting the auction. If he were rude, it would take money from CeeCee's worthy charity.

He forced himself to smile and joke, to say something nice to everyone of them, but it wasn't easy. He drew on everything he knew about his charming brother and used it to the hilt. The endearing grin, the lazy drawl, the flirtatious wink.

Zack might enjoy being the center of women's attention, but Jack found out rather quickly that he did not. There was only one woman he wanted fawning after him, only one woman he wanted to kiss for the rest of his natural days. Only one woman who made his heart beat faster and his breathing accelerate.

The one standing in the doorway, arms crossed over her chest, looking mad enough to chew nails.

''What's going on in here?'' CeeCee snapped, drilling Jack with a bone-chilling glare. ''No one's allowed backstage except employees and the bachelors. Shoo, ladies. Go on. You can bid on Mr. Travis to your heart's content when the auction begins.''

Jack watched the disappointed women file out the door, then he turned his smile on CeeCee. No point wasting the charm he'd gone to so much trouble to milk.

''Hey, babe.'' He winked.

''I thought I told you to be good,'' she chided.

"All I did was sign a few autographs. No harm done."

"Women follow you like a trail of ants to cookie crumbs." CeeCee shook her head, but she was smiling. He took that as a positive sign.

" I didn't invite them back here," he said. "They just sniffed me out."

"Must be your cologne. What is it? Eau d' Harem?"

"Nah, Scent of a Rebel."

"Gets 'em every time."

"You know that's right."

"Zack," she said at the very moment he said, "CeeCee."

They both chuckled.

"You go first," he said.

"No, you."

"I don't want you to think it means anything when I flirt with other women," he said. "Because it doesn't."

She shrugged. "Makes no never mind to me."

"You're not the least bit jealous?"

"Not a bit."

"Not even a teeny-weeny little bit." He marked off an inch with his thumb and index finger.''

"Not even a speck."

She laughed again and shook her head. He couldn't help tracing his gaze along her body. She looked fabulous in that sparkly blue dress with the cinched waist. Her three-inch heels made her almost as tall as he.

Dammit, he wanted her to be jealous. He wanted her to fight for him. Then before he realized what he was doing, Jack kissed her.

His arm snaked around that gorgeous twenty-four-inch waist.

Deny this!

He hauled her flush against his chest, caught her wrists with one hand. His mouth captured those red-hot lips.

Just try and pretend you don't want more, princess!

Jack kissed her hard and deep, with an urgency that vibrated up from the core of him. Her body heat penetrated his psyche on a primitive level, excited him beyond belief.

She sagged into him. Desire shot through his body like a heat-seeking missile. He reached up, traced a finger over her soft as silk cheek.

In just a few minutes a horde of hungry women would be bidding on him, vying for the honor of taking him to Galveston Island. But Jack didn't want any of them. He only wanted CeeCee.

He looked into her eyes, saw her staring up at him, alarm on her endearing features. Immediately she drew back.

"I got lipstick all over your face," she said huskily. "And here I am without a tissue."

From his pocket, he produced a handkerchief.

"You're just like Jack." She dabbed at his cheek and studiously avoiding his gaze. "Never without a clean hankie."

But I am Jack, he longed to tell her. *I'm the one giving you toe-curling kisses, not Zack.*

Go ahead, tell her.

He opened his mouth to speak the truth but at that moment five tuxedoed bachelors strolled through the door and the opportunity was lost.

NOW SHE KNEW WHY they called him Wild Man. You could never tell what he might do.

CeeCee fingered her lips. Truthfully, her knees were still a little shaky as the aftermath of Zack's kiss lingered in her system, rending her almost useless. The auditorium was packed, the attendees anxiously awaiting the bachelor auction.

She should be battling stage-fright butterflies. Instead, all she could think about was kissing Zack. What was going on here? She had kissed dozens and dozens of handsome men. She'd even had a fling or two. Jack was her only regret. But ever since Zack had come along, she'd gone all gooey headed over him.

Not a good sign.

Her pulse whirled like a helicopter blade whenever she chanced to look at him. In his form-fitting tux, he overshadowed every other bachelor behind the velvet curtain. But it wasn't the tuxedo that lent him his sexual attraction.

No siree.

Even if he'd been in a pair of cutoff blue jeans and a ratty T-shirt, he would have outshone every other man there. She knew exactly what he looked like under those fancy duds. She had been giving him physical therapy in the whirlpool. Except for his brother, in CeeCee's eyes, there was none finer than Zack Travis.

And apparently more than a hundred women in the audience chanting, "Wild Man, Wild Man, Wild Man," shared her opinion.

The jealousy she'd earlier denied stormed into her throat making it hard to breath. She couldn't believe that he would be leaving with some other woman this afternoon.

An irritating tic jumped in her left eye. This was crazy. She had to snap out of envy mode. She had a benefit to host. CeeCee clasped and unclasped her hands. Then she threw back her shoulders, held her head high and stalked onstage. She reached the podium, took the microphone in her hand and then began to tell the crowd about the charity.

The audience settled down, but only slightly. CeeCee introduced the auctioneer, then moved back into the wings to watch the proceedings.

They had saved the best for the end. Zack was the last bachelor on the program. When he strolled onstage and the auctioneer called his name and began describing his attributes, checkbooks flew open, ballpoint pens clicked.

From across the platform, Zack's eyes searched and found hers. He gave her a wink. A wink that snagged her heart.

Oh! CeeCee thought. *I'm getting into something I can't handle.*

"Let's start the bidding at five hundred dollars," the auctioneer said. "After all we are talkin' one mighty sexy motocross champ."

"Six hundred," a familiar voice rang out.

CeeCee shielded her eyes and peered into the crowd. Was that Janet's voice?

"Seven hundred!"

"Eight hundred."

"Nine hundred."

It *was* Janet! Her best girlfriend was bidding on the guy *she* wanted to have a fling with? CeeCee glowered. How could she do this to her? Janet knew how much she liked Zack. She gritted her teeth and slowly began to shred her copy of the program into tiny little pieces.

"One thousand dollars."

Shred.

Zack gave the audience a Cary Grant smile and tossed his head like a fashion model, working them up.

The rascal.

Shred. Shred.

"Eleven hundred." Janet again. CeeCee could see her statuesque friend standing up in the front row waving her hand. The eye tic was back jumping uncontrollably.

"Twelve hundred."

"Thirteen."

"Two thousand!" Janet shouted.

Shred. Shred. Shred. Too bad the paper wasn't Janet's throat.

"Twenty-one hundred."

The bids flew so fast the auctioneer could barely keep up. She had known Zack was popular, she just hadn't realized how many women would be willing to spend so much money simply to spend thirty-six hours with him at a cute bed-and-breakfast on Galveston Island.

The lucky dogs.

"Twenty-five hundred," Janet shouted.

Good grief! Did her friend have no shame? The highest any of the other bachelors had gone for was eighteen-hundred dollars. What was the matter with Janet? Why did she want Zack so badly? Hurt feelings replaced her resentment. Yes, she'd known she what she was up against from other women when it came to Zack, she just hadn't expected to compete with her friend.

Zack seemed delighted by the whole thing. He kept strutting around the stage like a prize peacock, preening and striking macho poses that had the crowd in gales of laughter. CeeCee was ready to trot over and kick him in the behind. His ego desperately needed downsizing.

And she was just the woman to do it. Unfortunately she'd have to wait until he returned from his date.

Argh!

Patience wasn't her strongest virtue.

Shred. Shred. Hey, she was out of paper.

CeeCee looked down at the snowstorm of paper flecks surrounding her. Pathetic! It was the sexual tension making her so crazed. That was all. If she'd slept with him and gotten him out of her system, she wouldn't give two hoots in the wind who was bidding on him.

"Sold for three thousand dollars to the leggy brunette in the front row!" the auctioneer shouted.

Janet bounced with joy.

CeeCee's stomach plummeted to her feet. Janet had won Zack. Then to her horror, her eyes went misty.

What was the matter with her? She didn't get weepy over men. Not ever. Well, except the tears she'd shed over losing Jack's friendship. But she shouldn't care about a short-term romance that had never even progressed beyond kissing.

She wanted to flee, get away before she had to face either Zack or Janet. But her assistant, Deirdre, appeared at her elbow, an excited look on her face. "We raised ten thousand dollars," she whispered.

Yes. Well, that was great. She had to go to the

podium and announce the details to the audience. It was the last thing she wanted to do, the last place she wanted to be, but CeeCee sucked up her disappointment and strode out to deliver the closing speech. The bachelors and their dates were lined up across the stage, eagerly waiting her news.

By some miracle she managed to come off sounding polished and professional. Finally she was able to escape only to be stopped in the hall by Janet's voice.

"CeeCee! Wait."

She tried to hurry outside. Tried hard to pretend she hadn't heard. She picked up the pace, threw the heavy exit door open. She burst out into the bright sunlight. She stood there blinking and then the damned door slammed on the tail of her dress.

Before she could jerk herself free, Janet tugged open the door and gaped at her. "Where are you rushing off to? Didn't you hear me calling you?"

"Uh, was that you?"

Great. Now Janet was going to rub her face in her victory. She turned to find Zack and Janet arm in arm and grinning like a pair of opossums.

"What is it?" CeeCee asked, feeling exceedingly tired.

They looked good together. Both tall and dark. If she were a bigger person, she'd give them her blessings. Instead she wanted to wring both their necks.

"Happy birthday to you," Janet began to sing and thrust Zack forward.

"It's not my birthday." CeeCee felt quarrelsome.

"It is tomorrow," Zack said.

"Happy birthday to you," Janet kept singing.

Zack reached out and took CeeCee's hand. "Pack your bags, lady, we're off to Galveston."

"I don't get it."

"Your birthday present." Janet waved at Zack with a flourish of her hand. *"Ta-da."*

CeeCee frowned. "Will you two please just tell me what's going on?"

"Since the foundation's rules prohibited the coordinator from bidding on the auction items, Janet and I cooked up this little scheme."

CeeCee stared at Zack. "You mean you rigged the auction?" She turned to Janet. "You weren't really bidding on him?"

"I was bidding on him for you, silly. Did you actually think I'd try to steal your guy?" Janet shook her head.

"Who's shelling out the three grand?" CeeCee asked.

"I am." Zack grinned. "It's for a good cause and hey, I needed the tax deduction."

"You mean you paid three thousand for a date with me?" She placed a hand to her chest, flattered, but suddenly very apprehensive.

"Yeah," he admitted, a certain glimmer in his eyes that looked far too much like the way Jack had looked at her the day he had given her the ultimatum.

Oh my gosh, what did that mean? If Zack was forking out three thousand dollars for her birthday present, he must be more serious about her than she thought.

And that scared CeeCee more than a million beautiful supermodels screaming, "Wild Man, Wild Man, Wild Man."

JACK AND CEECEE STROLLED arm in arm down the Galveston seawall at sunset. He in black jeans and a print silk shirt, she in a siren-red sheath dress that threatened to stop his pulse.

People passing by, most of them in swimsuits or shorts, gave them the once-over. Who could blame them for staring? He was with the most gorgeous creature on the face of the earth and he knew it.

Overhead, seagulls cawed and glided gently on the breeze. The air tasted salty and smelled of delicious aromas emanating from the restaurants lining the street. Couples and families pedaled surreys around them. The young and the young at heart whizzed by on in-line skates. Souvenir shops beckoned from the sidelines, offering seashells and brightly colored trinkets.

But Jack couldn't stop looking at CeeCee. She was chattering about anything and everything. The auction, the weather, how nice it had been of he and Janet to arrange this for her birthday. He hung on her every word but he was so dazzled by her beauty, he forgot what she had said. Occasionally she would turn toward him, tilt her head in that endearing way of hers and smile at him like he held the key to the universe.

It was a powerful feeling.

He couldn't believe he actually had her all to himself. No friends or co-workers around. No Muffin or Miss Abbercrombe to interrupt. For the next day and a half they would be alone together. They were staying at a turn-of-the-century Victorian style bed-and-breakfast on The Strand and even though they had separate rooms, there was an adjoining door.

Things were going so right he scarcely dared admit it. One false move could upset the delicate balance. He had to tread lightly while at the same time doing everything in his power to win her heart.

His hopes soared. He had the evening planned to the tiniest detail. An extravagant candlelight dinner at Guido's, a moonlight jaunt across the ferry, a horse-drawn carriage ride back to their bed-and-breakfast. He'd already arranged with inn owner to have rose petals sprinkled across CeeCee's bed, a bottle of champagne on ice and a tray of chocolate-covered strawberries. The whole thing had cost him a mint, but it didn't matter. Nothing was too good for his CeeCee.

"Oh, look, Zack, a po' boy stand." She stopped beside a six-by-six foot wooden hut, dispensing fried shrimp poor boy sandwiches and greasy curly fries. "I haven't had one of those since I was a kid and my third stepfather Ernie used to bring us here. Can we get one?"

"But what about dinner?"

She waved a hand. "Who wants to sit in some stuffy old restaurant when we can plunk down right here on the seawall and have a shrimp po' boy with lots of tartar sauce."

"We've got reservations." He glanced at his watch.

"Goodness," she said. "If you're that set on the restaurant then okay, but I gotta tell you, you're acting a whole lot like your brother and not a bit like the Wild Motorcycle Man."

"Am I?" he murmured.

"Oh, you know, Jack. He plans everything to the nth degree. Not that it's bad mind you, but he's not very spontaneous." She lowered her voice as if revealing a secret. "Like he'd never blow off dinner reservations for a curbside po' boy."

"Shrimp po' boy it is," Jack said firmly, her com-

ment stinging a little. Did she really consider him that
dull? But when CeeCee leaned into him, her breasts
crushed against his chest, he forgot about everything
except pleasing her.

Remember, lunkhead, act like Zack.

He stepped up to the vendor and ordered two sandwiches to go.

"Get us some fries and a couple of root beers, too.
No wait. Just get one big root beer with two straws.
We can share."

After he'd paid for the order, CeeCee took the bag
from him, pulled out a French fry and nibbled on it
gracefully.

"This way." She guided him to the edge of the
seawall, kind of dancing as she went, and away from
the bulk of foot traffic. She plunked down on the cement, kicked off her shoes and let them tumble to the
sand some three feet below.

He shook his head bewildered and bemused by her
ability to turn anything into a lark. Jack stood there
a moment, not sure what to do next, but when she
turned those inquiring green eyes on him, he followed
suit. He planted himself firmly beside her, then peeled
off his socks and shoes and carefully set them to one
side.

She giggled and fished another French fry from the
sack. "This is so much fun. I'm glad we decided to
skip the restaurant."

"Uh-huh." Skip the only four-star restaurant in
Galveston, skip the birthday cake he'd arranged for
the waiter to deliver to their table.

*Let it go, Jack. This is what she wants. Spontaneity,
a sense of the whimsical.*

"Open wide." She snuggled closer.

And the next thing he knew they were feeding each other French fries. Her fingertips lightly sweeping his lips. The easy way she touched him sent something hot and urgent gushing through his veins. He tasted salt and potato, but his tongue burned with the indefinable flavor of her skin.

They drank from the root beer together. Their heads touching as they simultaneously sucked on the straws. Next, she tackled the shrimp sandwich, moaning with such gusto he couldn't help but wonder what magnificent noises she made in bed. A shiver sliced through him at that vivid image.

"Oh, this is so good."

His gaze dropped to her mouth and he spotted a speck of tartar sauce clinging to her lush bottom lip. He sat mesmerized by that tiny droplet. Then her tongue darted out and whisked away the object of his fascination.

They sat eating and watching the sunset. After they finished, CeeCee gathered up the wrappers, padded to the trash can a few yards away, weaving through the throng on the seawall. Jack's gaze followed her slender frame. He loved to watch her walk. The way she bounced with so much verve, so much life.

In that moment, a dark thought hit him. Who was he kidding? He could never be right for CeeCee. She needed someone more like Zack than him. Someone who could match her exuberance.

His heart filled with longing.

How he wanted her!

But was he playing the fool? Acting out of character in a sad attempt to win a woman he could never have?

She returned smiling in the moonlight. She dropped

from the seawall to the sand. "Come on," she invited, reaching a hand to him. "Let's go wading in the surf."

He hesitated. From somewhere down the seawall came the sounds of a band warming up.

Arms outstretched, head thrown back, she twirled across the sand, her skirt spinning out from her like a glorious red flag. "Come catch me, Wild Man," she dared, then took off down the beach.

Rolling up his pant legs, he then followed her into the water, fighting his natural tendencies, trying his best to be carefree and reckless, just the way she liked.

8

ZACK WASN'T BEHAVING LIKE Zack tonight.

Gone was his teasing banter, his wolfish grin, his take-no-prisoners charm. He seemed quiet, subdued, contemplative even.

Like his brother Jack.

And that bothered CeeCee.

She didn't want to think about Jack. Not tonight. Not this weekend. All she wanted was a scorching affair with Zack. Nothing complicated. Nothing either of them would regret. Just have a darn good time and make lots of great memories.

Because memories were all she would ever have. She refused to tempt fate, to defy the Jessup family whammy by falling in love. She could never hurt the man she cared about by subjecting him to the curse. So she would collect her memories, remember the day and not dwell on what she couldn't have.

Jack.

She stopped walking, turned and saw Zack silhouetted in the moonlight, looking identical to his twin brother.

Uncertainty struck her. Maybe she shouldn't have a fling with him. Maybe, instead of making her feel better about not being able to have Jack, a casual affair with Zack would only make her feel worse.

Especially since Zack showed signs of liking her as much as Jack did. It was all too confusing.

What she needed was something to take her mind off the issue. They needed to do something wild and crazy and unexpected. CeeCee's gaze swept the sea-wall, searching for a diversion, searching for anything to distract her.

The purple-and-blue neon sign flashed from across the street.

Tattoos.

CeeCee's breath caught. She'd always wanted a little tattoo. Something discrete in a place where most people wouldn't see. Something to remind her that she was a free spirit and loving it. And Zack was the kind of guy game for such adventure. It would be something they could share. A memory to be made.

She ran back up the beach to Zack and jumped into his startled arms. She wrapped her legs around his waist, buried her face against the hollow of his neck. He smelled wonderful.

"Whoa," he said, latching onto her with both hands.

She mussed his hair. He looked into her face, the moonlight accentuating his masculine features.

"What's going on?" he asked.

"Are you up for something really crazy?"

"Er…I don't know. What have you got in mind?"

"Come on, where's the risk-taking maniac your brother is always bragging about? Mountain climbing and hang gliding. Alligator wrestling and bar brawling."

"What's going on in the wicked little mind of yours, CeeCee?"

Heavens above, she loved looking at him. His eyes

twinkled at her, the corners of his lips edged upward. She ran a finger along his cheek, felt his body tense beneath her.

"Just say yes." She slipped from his grasp and dropped to the sand.

"Say yes to what?"

She took his hand and tugged him toward the seawall to retrieve their shoes. "Say yes."

"Okay, okay." He laughed, perching on the edge of the wall to put his socks and shoes back on. It was a soothing laugh that warmed her to her toes.

"Jack?"

"What?" His eyes widened in alarm.

"Oh, I did it again." She slapped a hand across her mouth. "I'm so sorry I keep calling you by Jack's name. But when you laughed just now, you sounded exactly like him."

"It's all right."

"Well, tie your shoes and come along then."

"Where to?"

"You'll see."

"Tell me what you're up to, CeeCee," he demanded in a sexy, commanding, masculine way.

"Why, to get a tattoo. No self-respecting motorcycle man and his girl should be without one."

A tattoo?!

Jack balked, digging his heels into the sand. He didn't want a tattoo. He wanted to take CeeCee to supper at Guido's. He wanted to kiss her on the ferry ride. He wanted to whisper sweet nothings to her on the horsedrawn carriage. He wanted to draw a bath, fill it with peach-scented soaps and slosh around in it with her. He wanted to feed her champagne and chocolate-covered strawberries. He didn't want to eat po' boys from a paper sack or walk the beach barefoot and he certainly didn't want to get a tattoo.

"Why do you want a tattoo?"

"Because they're kinda sexy and besides, a tattoo represents freedom."

The woman certainly had skewed ideas of freedom. "How do you figure?"

"The freedom to do what I want, when I want, without anyone telling me no."

"You know what they say about freedom don't you?"

"No."

"It means you don't have anything to lose."

She got real quiet then, and her face went serious. "Maybe they're right. I don't have anything to lose."

Jack felt awful. He'd inadvertently reminded her of that stupid curse. He wanted to reach out to her, tell her that she *did* have something to lose. Something very precious; her ability to give and receive love.

CeeCee shook off her momentary gloom. "I'm considering a dove on my tushy. Small. Very tasteful. Or maybe a dolphin. What do you think?" she asked, still oblivious that she had disconcerted him when she mentioned getting a tattoo.

"Honestly? I think there's no need to elaborate on perfection."

"Oh you!" She tickled him lightly in the ribs. "What are you going to get? A big old Harley on your bicep? Maybe a lion or a tiger? Something ferocious? How about a Tasmanian devil?"

"I was thinking maybe a heart with 'CeeCee' running through it."

She stopped and stared at him. "You're kidding. Right?"

He shrugged. Uh-oh. Had he said something wrong? Cautious as a barefoot man walking on a carpet of glass shards, he studied her face.

"Why would you want my name on your arm?" Suddenly she looked panic-stricken and Jack realized his mistake. "You wouldn't want the name of some girl you barely knew for three weeks once upon a time, lingering on your arm forever, would you?"

"Relax. I'm kidding."

"Whew." She laughed shakily. "You certainly had me going there for a minute."

"And you had me going when you said we were getting tattoos."

"I wasn't kidding, though."

Jack looked up and realized they'd been moving steadily to this little place across the street from the seawall. The rubber had met the road. He was going to have to get a tattoo or tell CeeCee he wasn't Zack.

But if CeeCee learned his real identity before she made love to him, before she had a chance to fall in love with him she would be humming, "hit the pavement, Jack."

That thought was more terrifying than tattoos. And not just because his heart would be irreparably damaged, but because CeeCee would never have her happily-ever-after ending if she keep insisting on running after bad boys.

The neon sign flashed off and on. Tattoos, Tattoos, Tattoos.

He took in a deep breath, his gaze sweeping across the grungy building. Did he spill his guts? Or keep his mouth shut?

"CeeCee," he said. "There's something I have to tell you."

"Yes?"

Their eyes met.

"Er...uh..." He scrambled to come up with a good excuse, a way out of this.

She touched his arm, her eyes open, honest, trusting. "What's on your mind, Zack?"

He couldn't do it. He couldn't tell her the truth, couldn't stand to see the disappointment in her eyes.

"Do they take credit cards? 'Cause I'm low on cash." He jerked a thumb at the tattoo shop.

"It's on me. Come on." She pushed open the door plastered with bumper stickers advertising the shop owner's liberal politics. The bell over the door tinkled. Like a condemned man headed to the gallows, Zack followed.

Help! How was he going to get out of this?

This'll teach you to try to pull a fast one on the woman you love.

"Can I help you dudes?"

The man behind the counter wore a red bandanna wrapped around his head, a suede leather vest with fringe on the bottom, no shirt and faded holey blue jeans. Tattoos covered a good portion of his body, not to mention the numerous body piercings. From earlobes to nose to eyebrows and beyond.

Gulp.

"We want to get tattoos," CeeCee chirped.

"Are you sober, dudes?" He narrowed his eyes and studied them.

"As judges." CeeCee smiled.

"'Cause I can't tattoo you if you're drunk."

"We're not drunk," Jack assured him although he was beginning to wish for a tall bottle of Pedro's tequila.

"Sweet. Pick out which ones you want." Tattoo Dude waved a hand at all four walls covered floor to ceiling with thousands of tattoos. "They're in arranged in sections. Feminine stuff like butterflies and unicorns are over on the left, the masculine stuff on the right, unisex ones at the back."

CeeCee dragged Jack to the back wall. "Oh, look. You could get a mermaid."

"Nah."

"Stick of dynamite?"

"I don't think so." He made a face.

"A Tweety Bird?"

He shook his head.

"You're right. Too kiddish. We gotta find something that screams Zack! Let's check out the macho section."

Then he saw the caduceus. Before he even thought, he reached out a hand. "I'll have this one."

"A caduceus?" She frowned and belatedly he realized his mistake. He was supposed to be Motorcycle Zack, not Dr. Jack. "Why would you want a caduceus?"

"No, not the caduceus. This one." He let his finger slip to the section below the caduceus and tapped the first art square he came upon.

A grinning red devil.

Wonderful.

"That suits you to a tee." CeeCee chuckled, then added, "Now come help me pick out mine."

For the next half hour they browsed the shop. But while CeeCee looked at tattoos, Jack looked at CeeCee. His gaze caressed her creamy, flawless skin, and he cringed at the thought of her marring such exquisite beauty with a tattoo.

"You dudes ready?" the tattoo artist asked, when CeeCee finally managed to narrow her selection to a small, tasteful dolphin.

"Yes," CeeCee told him, then whispered to Jack, "I'm going to have it on my tushy."

He visualized her firm little fanny decorated with art and he hardened instantly. Then he realized that Tattoo Dude would get an eyeful of that fanny, too, and he clenched his jaw.

"You sure of your choices?" Tattoo Dude asked. "This stuff don't come off with soap and water."

"We're sure." CeeCee nodded.

"Then sign these waivers." He pushed two clipboards with the appropriate forms and ink pens at them.

"I'm so excited," she whispered to Jack, scrawling her name in her freewheeling, loopy script. "I've dreamed of doing this for years."

Damn, why did she have to be so happy when he was still racking his brain for a way out?

"Thanks so much for doing this with me." She squeezed his hand. "You're the greatest. I wouldn't have had the courage to go through with it without you."

Okay. He could do this. He had survived medical school. If he could survive that grueling schedule, he could survive this. Scarring himself for life with the devil's effigy was no biggie. If this was the sacrifice it took to win CeeCee then he would gladly accept a tattoo. Anyway, it was chic to decorate one's body with ink art. Lots of celebrities did it. So what if very few physicians sported them. He would start a new trend.

"You're so cool."

She squeezed his arm again and in that moment, Jack felt like the king of the world. All his life he'd wanted to be thought of as cool and hip and badass, just like Zack, but his cautious nature had prevented him from either following or leading the crowd when it wasn't prudent. Now, he finally had his chance to test his mettle. Did he have what it took to be a Wild Man?

"Who's up first?" Mr. Tattoo Dude asked.

Jack glanced at CeeCee. She looked nervous. She worried her bottom lip with her teeth, restlessly shifted her weight from side to side. He didn't think he could stand watching her go through the process. Maybe after he finished, he could talk her out of it. "I'll go first."

"Where you gonna put it?" Tattoo Dude asked.

Jack rolled up his left sleeve. "Upper arm."

"Have a seat in the chair."

Tattoo Dude gestured toward what looked like a massage chair situated behind the front desk. Swallowing hard, Jack sat.

The tattoo artist plunked down on a four-legged stool, unwrapped a packet of tattoo supplies and spread them out on a rolling tray. He then flicked on a bright gooseneck lamp and focused it on Jack's upper arm.

"Do you sterilize your equipment?" Jack eyed the needles suspiciously.

"Got my own autoclave, dude."

"Good to know." Jack raised his eyebrows.

"Can I watch?" CeeCee asked.

"Sure, pull up a chair," Tattoo Dude offered magnanimously.

CeeCee complied, arranging herself close enough to observe but out of the tattoo artist's way.

"You ready?" he asked Jack.

"As I'll ever be."

Tattoo Dude turned on the power. His tattoo gun made a buzzing noise.

Cringing, Jack closed his eyes and prayed the electricity would go out or that the guy's tattooing apparatus would short-circuit or a spur of the moment hurricane would kick up and blow in across the island to topple the tattoo hut.

He braced himself for the pain.

But it never came.

"Mick!" A woman's voice broke the silence.

Jack's eyes opened to see a very pregnant woman standing in the room, her eyes fixed on Tattoo Dude.

"Can't you see I'm busy, Carrie?"

"I'm having contractions, and they're only two minutes apart. You gotta take me to the hospital right now."

Mick turned pale. "Okay, okay, honey." He looked at Jack. "Sorry, dude, my wife's in labor, the tattoo'll have to wait."

Jack blew out a sigh of relief. Sometimes prayers were answered. "No sweat."

Carrie hollered and sank to the floor.

Oh, no!

Mick and Jack jumped up simultaneously and rushed to her side. Her face was contorted with pain, and she was holding her abdomen.

"How many pregnancies have you had?" Jack asked, automatically slipping into doctor mode without thinking twice.

"This is my third. Oh, gosh, I don't think I'm going to make it to the hospital."

"I'll call 911," CeeCee said and sprang to the desk.

You can't act like a doctor, you'll give yourself away, the voice that had kept him cautiously assuming Zack's identity for three weeks protested.

Forget that nonsense. Jack had no choice. He *was* a doctor and he had to help this woman. If he blew his charade, then he blew his charade. Under no circumstances would he risk a patient's well-being.

"Have you ever done Lamaze?" he asked Carrie.

"Uh-huh."

"Great, then practice your breathing."

She obeyed him, breathing in short panting he-he-he-he's.

He calmed her down and CeeCee joined them on the floor. She checked Carrie's pulse while Jack slipped a pillow under her head, and spoke soothingly to her.

Mick paced the tattoo parlor. Carrie had another contraction and screamed loud enough to raise the roof off the building.

Luckily the ambulance arrived before Jack ended up having to deliver the baby and whisked Carrie away. Mick went into the back of the shop where they apparently lived, gathered up his two older children and followed in the family car.

As a favor to Mick and Carrie, CeeCee and Jack locked up the shop for them and slipped the key under the door when they were finished.

"Wow." CeeCee turned to him.

"Some night, huh?"

She reached out and took his hand. "Let's walk."

They walked in silence for a while, CeeCee's shoes striking a lazy rhythm against the cement. Jack was dying to know what was going on inside her head. He angled her a couple of surreptitious glances but he couldn't tell what she was thinking.

"You were great with that woman," CeeCee said at last.

"Thanks."

"You were so calm."

He shrugged casually, but inside he was quaking. Had she figured out he wasn't Zack?

"I mean I'm a physical therapist and even I was flustered."

"You don't see a woman go into labor every day."

"Neither do you."

"True."

"You were as cool and calm and collected as your brother."

"I guess I must have picked up a few tips from Jack. Plus, I've taken first-aid classes. It's important to know first aid and CPR in my line of work."

"You're a multifaceted guy. Much deeper than Jack led me to believe."

You don't know the half of it.

"We didn't get our tattoos," she went on, "but we did have some excitement."

"Yes. But we're not done yet."

"What do you mean?"

He would show her he could be spontaneous, and it didn't require getting a tattoo or assisting a pregnant woman in labor. Without another word, he leaned over, scooped her into his arms and carried her down the seawall.

"What are you doing?"

"You want spontaneous. I deliver."

"But your knee," she protested.

"It's fine. I've been healed by the best."

He stalked toward the horse-drawn carriage stand, zigzagging through a throng of curious onlookers.

"Zack, put me down."

She sounded scandalized but looked pleased. Her head was thrown back exposing her pale neck glimmering in the moonlight. Her hair swished enticingly against his forearm.

"Hush, woman."

"Oh, my," she whispered, her green eyes snapping pure passion.

He hired the carriage, and gave the driver the address to their bed-and-breakfast. Settling her onto the seat, he climbed in beside her, then tucked her securely into the curve of his arm.

"Now," he said, "isn't this much more romantic than any tattoo?"

"Yes," she admitted and burrowed against his chest. The excitement had jazzed her and seeing Zack act so authoritative back there in the tattoo parlor got her juices flowing. He constantly amazed her.

They necked for the entire two-mile ride. Moist mouths joining. Tongues strumming. Eyelashes lowered. Teeth gently nipping.

Shod hooves clomped against cobblestones. The carriage's wooden wheels creaked as they rumbled past restaurants and nightclubs. Muffled strains of Dixieland jazz spilled into the night. The driver clicked his tongue, guiding the horse.

But CeeCee heard nothing except the strong, steady beating of Zack's heart.

A myriad of scents wafted on the breeze. Frying

shrimp from the seafood place in the middle of the block. Freshly popped popcorn from a street vendor. Robust garlic, tangy oregano and zesty onion from Mario's Pizza on the corner.

But CeeCee smelled nothing except Zack's heady, manly aroma.

The well-worn leather seat was smooth against her bottom. Gritty sand filled the soles of her shoes. Her charm bracelet lay cool against her wrist.

But CeeCee felt nothing except Zack's arm held tightly around her waist, and his firm lips pressing against hers with just the right amount of urgency.

The lights around them were bright. Beer signs flickered from O'Hara's pub. Old-fashioned, turn-of-the-twentieth-century street lamps lit the way past the regal mansions of a bygone era. Lights twinkled gaily from the tops of buildings as they approached the Strand.

But CeeCee saw nothing except Zack's deep, penetrating dark eyes staring at her in wonderment, as if she were the only woman in the world.

Everything else was peripheral and unimportant. Her focus was narrowed to one thing and one thing only.

Zack Travis.

The driver pulled up outside their inn. Zack paid him, then scooped her into his arms once more and laughing, carried her up the stoop and into the house.

CeeCee giggled, impressed by his impulsiveness. He was as impetuous as she. Seizing the moment. Enjoying the present. Not fretting about tomorrow and what the future might or might not bring.

It was the only way to live.

Happiness, she had once heard someone say, was

not getting what you wanted, but rather wanting what you got.

And for now she had gotten Zack.

It was enough.

Or so she kept telling herself.

9

_____

THIS WAY, MY LADY.'' He led her up the stairs, her hand tucked firmly in his.

The closer they got to the bedroom door, the louder CeeCee's heart knocked until she feared all the guests in the bed-and-breakfast would hear her. How embarrassing it would be if the inn owners caught her sneaking Zack into her bedroom.

Because she had made up her mind. Tonight, she was going to set a match to this power keg of sexual attraction that had been smoldering between them for two long weeks. She was not going to back down or run away.

She wanted him.

Desperately.

He stopped outside her bedroom door, took her room key from her and unlocked it. Then he drew her into his arms. She stared at him, her whole body trembling.

''May I come inside with you?''

''Do you really have to ask?''

He grinned.

She opened her door with one hand, grabbed him by the collar with the other and pulled him in after her. She was so busy kissing him and undoing the buttons on his shirt that she smelled the scented candles before she saw them.

Pulling back, she swept her gaze around the room. A dozen candles were strategically placed. The bed had been turned down, and rose petals had been strewn across the sheets. On the dresser sat a tray of chocolate-covered strawberries and a bucket of iced champagne.

Zack was busy planting kisses down her neck and softly kneading her buttocks.

"Wait. Stop."

"What is it?" He raised his head and peered at her, his eyes glassy with passion.

"What's all this?" She swept a hand over the room.

Trepidation flitted through her. Zack had gone to an awful lot of trouble to romance her. Suddenly she found it hard to breathe.

No. No. No. This couldn't be happening. He couldn't like her this much. Last night's filet mignon dinner had been bad enough, but she had accepted his explanation that it was a thank-you for the physical therapy treatments. This setup with the wine and the roses went far beyond thank-you.

"Do you like it?" He looked quite pleased with himself.

"You planned this," she said flatly.

"Well, yeah." He blinked, confusion on his face. "I thought you'd be delighted."

"You thought wrong."

"What have I done? I don't understand."

"I told you from the beginning I can't get serious about you. I can't get serious about any man. I just want to have fun, Zack."

"I still don't understand. It's a birthday surprise."

"But you shouldn't have planned anything." Her

voice held a desperate note. She had wanted so badly to have a red hot-fling with Zack. Had wanted only a physical relationship with a man who wanted nothing else from her.

"Sweetheart, you're overreacting."

"Jack's the one who plans," she whispered, her voice thick. The truth was deeper than she wanted to admit. Maybe her anxiety sprung from the fact that she was liking Zack too much and not the other way around. "You're supposed to be spontaneous, free-spirited. You should have made love to me on the beach, Zack, not orchestrated this elaborate seduction."

"It doesn't mean anything, CeeCee, I swear. I just thought you'd enjoy it."

"See. That's the problem. You were being thoughtful! You're supposed to be selfish."

"Easy, sweetheart, easy," he soothed. "I promise you're blowing this way out of proportion. I'm still leaving in a week and you'll probably never see me again."

"Really?" She slanted him a sideways glance.

"Really." He reached out and drew her to him once more.

She felt so conflicted. On the one hand, if she were a normal, noncursed woman, she would be flattered that he had gone to so much trouble to romance her. But as a hapless casualty of the Jessup family whammy, she was dismayed by his caring, his attention to detail.

What did this mean? That he thought she was special? CeeCee groaned inwardly. She couldn't be special. Not to Zack. Not to Jack. Not to anybody. She was hexed. Jinxed. Doomed. Any man who looked at her as a long-term love interest would be sorely disillusioned. With Zack, she had believed them both to be safe from heartbreak. Now, she wasn't sure about anything.

And maybe, just maybe, whispered a little voice in the back of her mind, you're afraid the perfect man wouldn't be so perfect if you had him for your very own.

"Let's enjoy the moment, CeeCee, it's all any of us has." He tucked a strand of hair behind her ear. His breath was warm on her skin.

"Promise you're not going to fall in love with me, Zack?"

"Sweetheart, I would promise you the moon to get you tucked under those covers with me."

"Ah," she said. "That's what I want to hear. A selfish man."

CeeCee surrendered to her physical urgings and curled into him, feeling his heat, his hardness. In an instant, his mouth was on hers, giving her another one of his mind-altering, body-shaking kisses. His breathing came in fast, uneven spurts. His hands were all over her at once but it wasn't enough.

Her insides felt ready to detonate. Her skin seemed too tight, her belly too heavy, her breasts too sensitive.

More. She needed so much more.

She tugged his shirt from his waistband, slipped her hands up under it and across his bare back. His hands roved over her hips, his mouth never left hers.

It was hot and sexy and she ached to her very toes for him.

He pulled her to the edge of the bed, and they collapsed down together on the plush roses. The lush scent wafted up to greet them. She luxuriated in the rich, erotic aroma.

And then, without any warning, an image of Jack's wonderful face popped into her head.

Zack was kissing her like there was no tomorrow. His mouth on her cheeks, her eyelids, her chin, her throat, but in a few moments he stopped, pulled back and looked down at her.

"What's the matter? You stopped responding. Just because I'm a selfish rogue, doesn't mean I don't please my women."

"It's not you," she said, wondering at the wall of tears building in her throat.

He snorted and rolled to one side. "What is it then? You keep claiming you can't have anything but a casual relationship yet every time things get hot and heavy you slow down. Why?"

"I was just thinking about Jack."

"Again!"

She nodded, miserable that she had upset him, worried why she couldn't stop thinking about Jack. Here she was having a wild old time, and he was down in Mexico giving of himself to help poor children. She should be ashamed.

"Have you noticed that every time we come close to making love you bring up Jack's name?"

"No? Yeah?"

"You use him as a barrier between us."

"Do I do that? Really?"

"You tell me."

"I guess I do," she mused.

"Face it, lady, you've got some serious issues with my brother."

"It's not that. I just don't want to hurt him."

Zack reached out and gently stroked her curls. "How would our making love hurt Jack?"

"He's jealous of your romantic conquests." CeeCee shrugged and turned her head, distracted by Zack's fingers running through her hair. She was aroused enough without him touching her.

"Is he?"

"Surely you knew?"

"And what about you, CeeCee?" He chucked a finger under her chin, raised her face to meet his. "This is between you and me. It's got nothing to do with Jack."

"You don't understand."

"So tell me." He draped his legs over hers, holding her down on the bed beside him.

"It's complicated. I'm not sure I understand it myself."

"Maybe I didn't go to medical school like Jack but I'm not stupid. Try me. I might see things more clearly than you think."

She raised a hand to push a sheaf of hair from her eyes. The charm bracelet at her wrist jangled.

"I think Jack has a crush on me," she said after a long pause.

"Yeah?" Jack held his breath, then asked. "But you keep saying you don't have sexual feelings for him."

"He's one of my best friends."

"And that's all?"

"Yes," she replied firmly. Then she shook her head. "No."

Jack raised an eyebrow, his spirits soared. "So what is it? Yes or no?"

"I don't know." She said mournfully and lifted one shoulder in a regretful half shrug.

"If Jack is the one you really want then why are you here in bed with me?"

"I can't have Jack. I told you about my family curse. You have no idea what it's like, knowing you can't trust any man. That any love affair I'm involved in is doomed to end in failure."

"You don't know that for certain."

"Yes, I do. There's not a man on the face of the earth who can defeat the curse."

"Well, if anyone could, it's Jack. He's very determined, and he doesn't love lightly. In fact, I don't think he's ever really been in love with anything except medicine. Unless he's in love with you. If that's the case he would fight for you tooth and nail. He's the most loyal guy I've ever known."

It felt weird talking about himself in such glowing terms but he had to make her see that he *was* different from any man she'd ever known. He wasn't a quitter and he wasn't a coward. He'd do anything for her. Even go so far as to perpetuate this accidental hoax.

"It's more than the curse," CeeCee admitted in a whisper. "Even if there wasn't a curse, I'd still be too terrified to ever get married."

"And why is that?"

At last! They were getting down to the nitty-gritty and he would find out exactly what scared her so much.

"I wouldn't begin to know how to have a successful marriage. Not a clue. I've only had bad examples. Everything starts out all champagne and roses and the next thing you know there's shouting and accusations being thrown and men walking out the door. It's not just the curse. Being lousy at relationships is my heritage. I don't know anything else.''

''Yes but, CeeCee, you're not your family. You're an intelligent woman with a lot going for her. You don't have to repeat toxic patterns.''

''But don't you see? I don't know what to replace those patterns with.''

He lay beside her, gently patting her arm, not knowing what else to say.

She took a deep breath. ''And then I keep thinking about Jack. About how unfair it is that's he's in Mexico working hard, probably not eating right or getting enough sleep and here I am this close to having sex with his twin brother.'' CeeCee measured off an inch. ''What kind of person does that make me?''

''Maybe Jack isn't as miserable as you think,'' he said, grasping at straws, searching for anything to make her feel better. ''Maybe he wouldn't even mind if the two of us got together.''

Propping herself up on her elbow, she looked him in the eyes. ''I'm not going to lie. I'm very attracted to you, Zack. But I think it'd be best if you went back to your own room. The moment's gone, and I don't think we're going to get it back.''

JACK WAS FRANTIC. Things weren't working out the way he'd planned. As Zack, he couldn't seem to close the deal with CeeCee. Couldn't get her to make love to him. Where was he making his mistakes? What could he do differently?

It was Saturday evening. When they'd arrived home from Galveston two hours earlier, CeeCee couldn't seem to get away from him fast enough. He couldn't figure her out. What did she want?

In desperation, he turned to Miss Abbercrombe for advice later that evening.

And found himself swallowed up by a bean bag chair in her flashback-to-the-sixties living room. The walls were painted a neon orange. Beaded curtains separated the rooms instead of doors. The couch was a paisley print. A lava lamp, mood ring and a statuette of the Beatles graced her knickknack shelf. She had Jefferson Airplane on the stereo and was urging him to drink ginseng tea and eat her homemade brownies. Frankly he was afraid to touch the stuff.

Miss Abbercrombe sat on the couch, Muffin perched in her lap. She adjusted her glasses and peered at him. "It's simple, young man."

"It's not simple at all, Miss A. In fact it's very complicated."

She shook her head. "What you know about women, son, could fill a thimble."

"But CeeCee's not like most women."

"Well, I admit, her problem is a little unique but her emotions aren't."

"Throw me a lifeline here. I'm not following you."

"You're going to have to drive her into Zack's arms. She's conflicted. Torn between two men. Before you can convince her to give herself to Zack she's got to know that Jack's isn't going to be heartbroken by her actions."

He shook his head.

"You've got to make her think Jack is off having as much fun in Mexico as she could be having right here with Zack."

He mulled over what Miss Abbercrombe was saying. It did make sense. If he could set CeeCee's mind at ease about him then she could let down her guard with Zack.

"Okay, so how do I accomplish that?"

Miss Abbercrombe leaned in close, a sassy smile on her elderly face. "Here's what we do."

"CEECEE, DARLING I WAS wondering if you could do me the tiniest favor." Miss Abbercrombe and Muffin stood on her doorstep.

"Won't you come in," CeeCee invited, ushering her guests into her living room. "How can I help you?"

Miss Abbercrombe stroked Muffin's fluffy head. "I need to speak with young Dr. Jack, and he told me that you knew how to get in touch with him."

"I do have his beeper number, but I think he meant for me to use it only in the case of an emergency."

The thought of talking to Jack turned her stomach to cranberry sauce and she couldn't really say why. She hadn't spoken to him in over seven weeks, and she worried what he would say.

"Well, this isn't exactly an emergency, but it is important. That obnoxious Missing Link person is claiming my Muffin bit him, and he's threatening to sue me."

"Oh, no!"

"Yes. I need Jack to give my lawyer a deposition saying that Muffin did not bite that man."

"Muffin most certainly did not bite him. I was there, too. I'll give the deposition for you."

"That's nice, dear, but I need Jack's statement, too. So could you just beep him for me, please?" Dramatically she laid a hand across her chest. "Tonight, if you please. The sooner I get this cleared up the better it will be for my poor aging heart.''

"Okay. Sure. I'll beep him and when he answers I'll have him call you.''

"That'd be wonderful.''

"It might take a while, though. Apparently there are no phones in the village where Jack's working. He'll have to hitch a ride to the nearest town. He might not be able to return my call until tomorrow.''

"That's all right.'' Miss Abbercrombe got to her feet. "Ta-ta, dear. Let me know when you hear something.''

"YOU CAN'T CALL HER BACK this soon,'' Miss Abbercrombe said. "And what if she has caller ID?''

"Don't worry. My beeper system shows up as an out-of-area call no matter where you're calling from,'' Jack told her. Twenty-five minutes earlier his beeper had gone off, listing CeeCee's number in flashing red digits.

His heart had stampeded into his throat and he'd almost grabbed the phone immediately but Miss Abbercrombe held him back. Her subterfuge had to work. Time was of the essence. This was his last chance to drive CeeCee into Zack's arms.

"I'll trust you on this,'' Miss Abbercrombe said. "I don't know anything about these new-fangled electronic gadgets.''

Jack paced Miss Abbercrombe's living room and repeatedly checked his watch. He couldn't stand much more waiting. "You've got the music ready?''

"Selina's greatest hits.'' She put the compact disc in question on to play.

"Let's hear your Spanish accent again.''

Miss Abbercrombe purred some seductive Spanish phrases. "Lucky for you I had several Latin lovers when I was a younger woman."

"Lucky me," he muttered and checked his wrist-watch again.

"You're about to crawl out of your skin. Go ahead and call her before your burst wide-open."

Jack grabbed the telephone. With trembling fingers he dialed the routing number through his beeper and then punched in CeeCee's number.

"Hello."

He almost dropped the receiver at the sound of her voice. He took a deep breath, tried his best to sound casual. "Hey, CeeCee."

"Jack? Is that you?"

"Uh-huh."

"You sound different."

"Probably because I'm so far away."

"And I haven't talked to you in seven weeks. I'd almost forgotten what your voice sounded like."

"I've been busy."

"It's really great to hear from you."

"You, too."

"I...I've missed you."

His heart skipped at the catch in her voice. He wanted to tell her how much he had missed her, too. He had missed being himself, missed being CeeCee's best friend, missed their intimate conversations about anything and nothing.

Miss Abbercrombe was standing in front of him mouthing "now?"

He shook his head. The plan suddenly seemed very stupid. He didn't care about tricking CeeCee. He just wanted to talk to her, to tell her the truth. That he loved her. Had loved her for many months now. Would love her for the rest of his life.

"Oooh, *señor,* you're *muy muy macho. Por favor,* do that again," Miss Abbercrombe moaned in a surprisingly sexy voice.

Jack glared at his neighbor and made slashing motions across his throat. Cut! Cut!

But Miss Abbercrombe was giving the performance of a lifetime, and she wasn't about to let up. She cooed Spanish words of love.

Jack frowned, violently shook his head and mouthed "stop it". But Miss Abbercrombe ignored him. Instead she tuned up for more, moaning and groaning and putting her face close to the receiver to make sure CeeCee got an earful.

"Er…Jack…" CeeCee's voice raised an octave. "You're not alone, are you?"

Miss Abbercrombe kept talking in fractured Spanish and wriggling around on the couch. Jack was ready to throttle her.

"CeeCee, I…it's not what you think."

"Oh," she said quickly. "You don't owe me any kind of an explanation. Everyone is entitled to a little R & R. You just have a good time."

"I'm not having a good time," he growled, completely frustrated by the way things were turning out.

"Maybe you should tell that to your lady friend. Sounds like she's having a ball."

"It's not what you think, Cee."

"Every man is entitled to his er…diversions."

"No. No I'm not entitled. Listen to me, CeeCee. I've got something to tell you."

Muffin barked, enlivened by her mistress's antics.

"That dog sounds exactly like Miss Abbercrombe's Muffin," CeeCee commented.

"Really? Probably the Chihuahua from next door. These walls are pretty thin."

"I've really got to hang up now, Jack," she said with false cheerfulness but he could hear the pain in her voice. "Could you please call Miss Abbercrombe? She needs to talk to you."

"But, CeeCee…"

"Gotta go," she said and hung up on him.

He sat staring at the phone. He'd certainly upset her. And he felt horrible about it. But wasn't that what he wanted? To upset her enough to send her flying into Zack's arms?

"So?" Miss Abbercrombe asked, grinning brightly. "Did she fall for it?"

"She fell all right."

"Then why do you look so sad?"

"Because I just hurt my very best friend in the whole entire world."

10

WHY ARE YOU CRYING? You've got nothing to cry about. So Jack has a woman down in Mexico. So what? You should be happy for him, you selfish girl.

She should be happy but instead she was more miserable than the time when she was ten and had eaten fifteen green apples on a dare from one of her stepbrothers. Come to think of it, her mother had thrown out stepfather number two over that bellyache incident.

The truth is, she was shattered. Last night in Galveston, Zack had come very close to convincing her that Jack was different from most men. She'd found out the hard way that he was not. He had feet of clay just like the rest of them.

Why was she so disappointed? She'd told Jack they could never be more than friends. It was pure selfishness on her part to think he shouldn't get on with his life.

"I do want him to get on with his life," she argued out loud, and stared glumly at her bedroom wall. "I wanted him to find someone to love. Just not so soon."

Liar, you want him to love you.

The thought sprang unbidden from the ether.

She clasped her pillow to her chest, and curled into fetal position, tears still dampening her cheeks.

''No,'' she whispered. ''It's not true. I don't want him to love me. I would only hurt him.''

Besides, there was her confounded attraction to Zack. What did that mean?

The doorbell pealed.

''Go away,'' CeeCee mumbled.

It rang again.

She didn't want company, but she wasn't the type to let the doorbell go unanswered.

Sighing, she sat up and ran a hand through her tangled curls. ''Coming, coming,'' she called out. ''Rein in them horses, cowboy.''

She padded to the door in her pajamas, threw it open and found Zack leaning nonchalantly against the jamb.

He looked delicious and more than a little lawless in black jeans, a black Harley muscle shirt and black boots. His hair was pulled back in a tiny ponytail. She suddenly wondered why she hadn't made love to him at the bed-and-breakfast last night. Some misguided sense of responsibility to Jack. What had she been thinking? Jack had gotten on with his life, she should be getting on with hers.

''I'm through playing around, CeeCee,'' Zack said gruffly.

''Wh…what?''

''I've given it time. I've been understanding, but the truth is, I can't wait anymore. I want to make love to you. Here. Now. This minute. Say yes, CeeCee,'' he pleaded, ''say yes.''

Her knees turned to peanut butter.

''If you're not interested. Or if you can't get over Jack, then tell me and I'll walk away. I'll leave town. I'll leave you alone. I'll…''

Before he could finish his sentence, she grabbed him by the front of his shirt, pulled him into her apartment and slammed the door closed behind them. She wrapped her arms around his neck, tugged his mouth down to hers and told herself, *This is all I can have. Jack is not only off limits, he's found someone else. Zack is here and he wants you. You want him. That's all there is to it. And it is enough.*

Zack responded with a passion to equal hers. He scrunched her curls in his hand. His gaze burned into hers. He molded his mouth on hers, kissing her like a brand. He tasted incredible. Tart yet sweet, exotic and fresh and startlingly real. She feasted on him, a most sumptuous buffet.

He pulled away a moment, breathing heavily. "I don't want you to have regrets."

"I won't."

"No turning back this time," Zack said hoarsely. "Take me as I am CeeCee, for what I can give you now."

"Just hush and kiss me again."

This was exactly what she wanted. Heat and passion, no promises of undying love, no whispers of forever. Just Zack, hard and hot and filled with masculine energy.

Then he took her into his arms and carried her into the bedroom. CeeCee did not protest. She let herself go, falling into the steamy vortex that had been drawing at her from the moment she'd met Zack. The sexual chemistry between them was undeniable and anything beyond that did not matter.

He laid her down carefully on the mattress, then stood back to admire her. CeeCee raised a hand to her chest, embarrassed by her comfy but faded pajamas and fluffy pink house slippers.

"Sorry I'm not dressed for the occasion," she apologized, kicking off the slippers.

"You couldn't be sexier in black lace and garters, babe."

"I had no idea shabby pj's were a turn-on," she whispered.

"Oh, yeah. Holey underwear, baggy sweatsuits, anything or nothing. You could make a hospital gown look like designer duds."

She felt herself blush at his compliment. He made her feel beautiful and special, even if she knew deep down it was only a line. Guys like Zack instinctively knew how to charm. But that was okay with CeeCee. She would take what she could have.

He settled himself beside her, slipped one arm underneath her, then gently kissed her forehead.

He reached for the top button on her shirt and she realized in surprise that the womanizing Wild Man's hands were trembling. When he undid the last button to reveal her breasts, his breath caught in his lungs with an audible gasp.

"Fair's fair," she said gruffly, touched by the admiration in his eyes. "Off with your shirt as well."

She reached over, pulled his shirt from his waistband and rolled the soft cottony material up to his chest. Swiftly he jerked the shirt over his head, tossed it to the floor.

For a moment she simply stared in wonder at that firm, muscled chest, those chiseled biceps. This was all about sexual pleasure, and she drank in the sight of him.

He crooked a devilish grin that sent an icy hot shaft

of longing through her heart, and he slid her top off her shoulders.

CeeCee was absolutely incredible. Far more compelling than his most fantastic dreams, Jack thought as he cupped her breasts, teased her nipples with his thumbs. They grew rock-hard under his caress, delighting him. It delighted him even more when she raised her head and met his mouth.

She inhaled in erotic little gasps; a combination of surprise and arousal. She flowed like the athlete she was, all grace and coordination and strength. Her tongue dueled with his. Her teeth nipped his bottom lip. He could barely hang on to his control. It took his entire concentration not to take her that very second.

Not yet. This was important. Their lovemaking had to be perfect. And he knew it would be. For he loved her more deeply than he'd ever known it was possible to love another human being.

The hungry way she kissed him only solidified his resolve to take things slowly. They had all night. He would torture her the way she was tormenting him with that wicked tongue of hers, the lusty vixen— relentlessly.

He helped her wriggle out of her pajama bottoms and revised his previous thoughts. At this rate he wouldn't last two minutes.

And that wouldn't do. After all, he had Zack's reputation to uphold.

From his point of view, she was the quintessential woman. Perfect breasts, firm and high, the size of late-summer peaches. Her stomach was flat with the tiniest curve at the apex of her womanhood. Her waist was slender, her hips shapely. And those legs! She put all pinup queens ever to decorate a GI's locker to shame.

Jack was a doctor yes, but he'd never seen an anatomy like this one. And to think she was his at long last.

Lovingly he trailed a hand down her body, lingering at every trigger point that caused her to writhe with pleasure.

"Enough," she whispered huskily, her eyes burning as brightly as if she had a fever. "My turn."

She reached for his waistband. Jack gulped at her boldness, but then again, that was his CeeCee. She never held back from a challenge. She met life head-on.

Her breath still came in heavy, heated spurts, but she did not let that deter her. He leaned back against the pillows, enjoying the moment, relishing her desire.

Unsnapping the button of his jeans, she then went for the zipper, easing it down inch by inch. Occasionally she glanced over at him, flicked out her tongue and sent him a naughty grin. Raising his hips, he helped her shuck his pants free and toss them in the corner.

He was reminded of the night he returned from Mexico, the night he'd inadvertently started this whole deception.

For a brief second, his passion began to dissipate as he thought about what he was doing. Making love to her under false pretenses. It wasn't the honest thing to do and for his entire life Jack had been the honest, reliable twin.

But as his doubts reared up in his conscience, CeeCee went to work on him with her tongue, strumming it back and forth against one of his nipples, jettisoning him straight into outer space.

He was wearing the briefest of briefs, CeeCee noted. More leopard print. Tarzan in all his manliness.

And there was no hiding his arousal, barely covered by the thin material.

Oh my! The room was hotter than a sauna and twice as steamy.

She kissed him everywhere. His chest, his arms, his legs. He groaned and flailed and twisted his fingers through her hair.

"Come 'ere, red," he gasped and hauled her to his chest.

He kissed her sweetly, then deeply and finally ravenously. CeeCee melted into him. Spun dizzily into a place she'd never been before. Hung there like a kite in the wind. How she wanted this to go on and on and on forever. If she and Zack could just stay in bed maybe they could thwart the Jessup family whammy. Maybe the curse only worked when you were out of bed.

What a fantasy. What a dream.

"Focus on me," he said, as if reading her mind. "On us. On now. Forget about everything else."

And so she let go of all conscious thought, simply let her body experience what the night held in store.

"I gotta have you," she whispered into his ear. Jack's name was on the tip of her tongue but at the last minute she managed to bite it back. She wasn't going to make that mistake again. She was with Zack, the temporary twin who made her blood race but that was all.

"I gotta have you, too, babe."

"I can't take it anymore."

"Me, either."

He whisked off his briefs and they disappeared over the edge of the bed.

Holy Tarzan!

She had no idea he was so...so...magnificently endowed.

Now she knew why he had such a reputation with the ladies.

He laughed at her expression. "Surprised? Pleased? Perplexed?"

"Yikes."

He nuzzled her neck. "Don't worry, I'll be gentle."

She felt his heart pounding through his chest, matching the rhythm of her own erratic heartbeat. They pressed their palms together, stared into each other's eyes. He kissed her again, his fingers dancing over her back, causing her to melt.

"Protection?" she whispered.

"Got it covered." He laughed. "No pun intended."

His sheathed hardness throbbed against her thigh, pressing into her soft flesh. A searing moisture flowed through her. She felt on fire, alive with yearning to be one with him. He cuddled her into him and she arched her hips.

Fever swept her body, clouded her brain. There was no reasoning, no rational thought left. She acted on pure instinct. She lifted her legs and curled them around his waist.

"Come to me," she murmured.

With a groan he surged forward. Her body filled to overflowing with him.

"CeeCee," he cried and to her shock she saw a

single tear glisten on his cheek. She reached out and brushed it away with her fingertips. Their lovemaking had moved him to tears? It seemed so out of character for cocky Zack.

He moved deeper into her, taking it slowly at first then upping the tempo. Stroke after stroke, building the fire, escalating the sweet torture.

She clutched his shoulders, begged him for more.

He complied, bringing her to the edge of oblivion.

Her head reeled. Her stomach contracted. She'd never experienced such physical intensity. Two weeks of sexual teasing had taken its toll.

She hung suspended, staring up at him. At his dark eyes, the curve of his cheek, his scruffy beard. She stared at the face that looked so much like her dear Jack's but wasn't.

Why couldn't he be Jack?

A stabbing loneliness knifed through her at what she could never have, at what she had lost through no fault of her own.

In that awful moment, just before she exploded with an earth-shattering release, she realized she had just made love with one twin when she was in love with his brother.

JACK STARED AT THE CEILING. CeeCee was curled in a ball on the bed beside him sleeping soundly, her legs entangled with his under the sheet. Her hair spread out across his pillow.

His deepest dreams had finally come true.

Part of him was happy, euphoric.

Another part was filled with impending doom.

He'd finally made love to CeeCee, and it had been every bit as wonderful as he'd imagined.

But he had made love to her in the guise of his twin brother and that wasn't right, even though he had been forced to pose as Zack because her belief in the curse left him no option. His plan, which had once seemed so foolproof, now seemed very foolhardy. What if the whole thing blew up in his face? What if she ended up falling in love with Zack and not him? What if she ended up hating him for his duplicity?

His gut wrenched.

What if he lost not only his lover but his best friend as well?

Jack drew in a deep breath. It was time to tell her the truth. But how? And when? And where?

Closing his eyes, he remembered the intimacy they'd shared. Several times in fact. Even now, just thinking about making love to her had his body responding in a very unruly manner.

She'd been perfect in every way. Her sexual hunger matched his own. She'd known exactly where to touch, exactly what to do to send him spiraling into the stratosphere. She was without a doubt the best lover he'd ever had, not that he had anywhere near Zack's level of experience.

He could only hope and pray he hadn't screwed things up. That she'd forgive him for his charade.

Gulping, Jack opened his eyes and looked over at her. The covers rode low, exposing her silky bare skin. In repose her normally animated face was calm and serene. She looked like an angel.

His heart flapped raggedly against his rib cage.

"I never meant to hurt you, angel," he whispered.

"I just didn't know any other way to get you into my arms."

Should he wake her now and tell her what he must? He reached out a hand to stroke his fingers through her curls. No. Not yet. He had to find the right time, the right place. He had to make certain she'd fallen in love with him first.

THE PHONE WAS RINGING.

Groggily CeeCee reached for the telephone on the bedside stand. "Hello," she muttered.

She heard a dial tone but the phone kept ringing.

Huh? She dragged herself to a sitting position, looked over and saw a man-size lump in her bed. Her pulse skittered like a lizard up a brick wall as it all came back to her.

She'd made love to Zack last night after finding out Jack had another woman.

She froze.

The phone rang again.

Leaning over the edge of the bed, she searched for the insistent sound.

Hmm, Zack's pants seemed to be ringing.

"Zack," she said, nudging him with her toe. "I think you're getting a call on your cell phone."

Zack was sound asleep, not moving a muscle. She poked him again. Nothing. Just like his brother. At the hospital, Jack was notorious for being difficult to awaken when he got a chance to nap on his thirty-six-hour shifts. Apparently the Travis twins could sleep through a bomb. The phone chirped a fourth time.

"Okay, okay, I'll answer it." CeeCee leaned over the bed, hooked Zack's pants with a finger and hauled them onto the covers with her. She grappled in the pockets, finally found the tiny cell phone and silenced the damn thing.

"Hello."

"Why, hello," purred a smooth, male drawl that sounded a lot like Zack's. "My what a sexy voice you have."

"Please don't tell me this is an obscene phone call." CeeCee rolled her eyes to the ceiling.

"No, no, not at all. I'm just not accustomed to women answering my brother's phone. Then again, maybe I have a wrong number."

His brother? CeeCee frowned. What was this guy talking about? He wasn't Jack and she was sleeping with Zack and they didn't have any other brothers. Obviously it was a wrong number.

"Who's your brother?" she asked.

"Jack Travis. He called and left a message on my machine on Thursday telling me not to worry about showing up for the bachelor auction. But I just got home. I had a spill on my bike. Nothing major, a slight concussion but they kept me in the hospital for observation. His message was kind of garbled and I'm not sure I understood. I thought he was in Mexico."

"Wait a minute. Hold on. I'm confused. Is this Zack?"

"Wild man Zack Travis Motocross Champion 2000," he said proudly.

"Excuse me?" Stunned, CeeCee stared at the man beside her. If this was Zack on the other end of the telephone, then who in the heck was in her bed!

Who had she made love to last night like a crazed nymphet?

"Indeed. Guess what? I had no idea Jack had returned from Mexico,'' she said. ''In fact, I thought you were staying at Jack's place and that you'd already appeared in the auction on Friday afternoon.''

''What? I'm not following you.'' Then from the other end of the line she heard him say, ''Aha. I get it. Jack's been running the old switcheroo on you.''

''Come again?'' She gritted her teeth and clenched one hand into a fist barely keeping her anger in check. Anger that sprang from hurt. She felt confused, betrayed and duped. How could she have been so gullible? All along it had been Jack she'd given therapy to in the hot tub. Jack she'd kissed. Jack she'd just spent the night with.

But if that was the case then who was the *señorita* on the phone last night? And the anonymous Chihuahua? In an instant, she knew the answer. Miss Abbercrombe and Muffin. The Missing Link wasn't suing the elderly lady. She and Muffin were in on Jack's scheme.

''Aw, when we were kids we used to switch places,'' the real Zack told her. ''When I had a test I couldn't pass, Jack would take it for me. When he had a girl he wanted to ask out, I would do it for him. It's kinda underhanded but most identical twins pull that sort of thing at least a few times growing up.''

''Really,'' she said dryly.

''But I was always the instigator of the switch,'' Zack said. ''I can't believe Jack pulled this on his own.''

''Well,'' CeeCee said, trying to be fair despite having the strongest urge to kick Jack out of bed. ''To his credit, I was the one who assumed he was you. But he went along with it.''

''He must really care about you,'' Zack interjected.

"How do you figure?"

"Jack's as honest as the day is long. He would never pretend to be me in order to win a woman unless he thought he had absolutely no chance on his own."

"How did he think he was going to get away with this?" CeeCee sighed, exasperated now.

Zack was right. She would never have gone to bed with Jack. He was her best friend and she would have done anything to avoid hurting him. She was shocked by what he'd done. Shocked and guiltily pleased to discover that he had cared enough to pull such a stunt.

Still, no matter his motivation, the bottom line was they were both going to be hurt.

Looking over at him, she shook her head. *Oh, Jack, what have you done?*

"Would you like to know an underhanded way to wring a confession out of him?" Zack asked, a chuckle in his voice.

"Yes," she said. "I want him to have to explain why he risked our friendship."

"Then listen up. I've got a plan that'll take the starch out of Jack's socks and get you the answers you need. We'll teach that son of gun to try the old switcheroo with us."

"WAKE UP, ZACK, WE'RE GOING skydiving."

"Huh?" Jack blinked at CeeCee.

She was standing over him dressed in a denim jumpsuit and knee-length, black leather boots, looking all the world like a dominatrix. Give her a few props, like a whip and handcuffs and she'd be set.

"Remember when you told me that you've always wanted to go skydiving? Well, surprise! I've already called the local parachuting operation and they've got a class starting in an hour. If the weather's right, we can jump this afternoon.''

"But my knee," Jack had the presence of mind to complain. The thought of skydiving struck terror in his heart. What in the world had gotten into CeeCee? She seemed a woman possessed, tugging on the covers with a determined thrust to her chin and a scary gleam in her eyes.

"Your knee is healed. With your athletic skills, I'm sure you won't have a bit of trouble landing smoothly," she said glibly, and he thought, a little heartlessly. "Now get up and get dressed."

He tried to come up with another excuse but CeeCee didn't give him time.

She clapped her hands. "Chop, chop. Get moving. The sky awaits."

What was he going to do?

Turn on the old Zack charm. He gave her a seductive wink, purposely ran a hand across his bare chest and flicked his tongue over his bottom lip.

"Hey, babe, you look good enough to eat. Come 'ere." He reached out to grab her wrist but she danced away.

"What's the matter, Zack? I thought you were the Wild Man," she taunted. "Nothing you won't try. Isn't that right?"

Her angry tone of voice confused him. What was she mad about? Had he done something wrong last night? Had she been disappointed in his lovemaking?

"Uh...that's right."

Just tell her the truth, Jack. You're not Zack. You're terrified of heights and you can't go jumping out of airplanes. You've got to tell her sometime.

But was now the right time? Especially when she was acting so weird? What had happened to her? He had expected them to cuddle in bed until noon, then go out for lunch in a quiet restaurant. He had wanted handholding and stolen kisses and deep passionate sighs. He had expected her to fall in love with him.

Instead CeeCee was revved on superspeed, talking quickly with a hard inflection on the last word of her sentences. She barked out orders like a senior surgeon heading a dicey operation. She drilled him with looks that would make the bravest medical student quake.

Was she always like this after sex? No wonder her other boyfriends never hung around. Her fear of the Jessup family whammy ran deeper than he had imagined.

"Why don't you call and cancel the class." He tried soothing her. He gave her what he hoped was an endearing grin and patted the mattress. "So we can spend the rest of the morning in bed. We can always go skydiving another day."

"Need I remind you," she said. "Jack will be coming home next week and you'll be leaving town. We'll probably never see each other again. Come on, Wild Man, get out of bed. The time has come to put your money where your mouth is and prove you're as daring as everyone claims."

"Last night wasn't proof enough?"

"Sex doesn't count as fearless."

"It does with you." He wriggled his eyebrows suggestively.

"I'm beginning to have my doubts about your supposed fearlessness. Maybe we should change your name from Wild Man to Child Man."

"CeeCee," he protested.

"I'll wait for you in the car." She turned on her heels and walked to the door, then stopped, red hair atumble and looked at him over her shoulder with an expression that threatened to stop his heart. "Don't disappoint me, Zack."

THE PLANE VIBRATED WITH SOUND. Was the damned thing supposed to be so noisy? And did it have to be so old? He could have sworn the plane was manufactured during World War II. His fears were chomping on him like T-cells on a virus.

Jack huddled beside CeeCee, parachutes harnessed to their backs. They'd spent the last six hours in ground school training, learning far more than he'd ever wanted to know about skydiving.

He'd tried several times to find a way to tell her he wasn't Zack, but they'd been surrounded by instructors and other students all day. The opportunity had never arisen.

And then there was that part of him that whispered that he could be a guy like his twin brother.

Maybe he could jump out of the plane. If he could ignore the giant boulder in his throat that is. If he could unglue his butt from the seat.

Chicken.

Maybe this was exactly what he needed to prove to himself that he was brave and strong and tough. That his fear of losing her was much greater than his fear of heights.

Then again maybe he needed a straitjacket and a heavy-duty antipsychotic. They were going to shove him out of a plane and into the empty atmosphere, for pity's sake. Had he lost his ever-loving marbles?

He looked over at CeeCee. She met his gaze with a stony stare. She'd been like that all day. Edgy, fierce. He still couldn't figure out where he had gone wrong. Instead of their lovemaking binding CeeCee to him as he'd imagined it would, their passionate night together seemed to have agitated her and pushed them farther apart. His plan was unraveling like a ball of yarn in a roomful of kittens.

The plane climbed higher. His stomach roiled. Good thing he'd passed on lunch.

Aw hell. What was he going to do? He couldn't parachute from the plane. He was supposed to be fearless Wild Man Zack. The guy who would try anything once.

Hell, he couldn't even handle a tandem jump with the burly, exparatrooper jump master inappropriately named Tiny, sitting calmly on the bench across from them. Beside Tiny sat the other jump master, his exact physical opposite, a fidgety string bean of a man called Moose. Whomever nicknamed these guys had a warped sense of humor.

And he wasn't fearless Zack. He was terrified-of-heights Jack. He had been acrophobic since Zack pushed him out of the chinaberry tree in their backyard when they were nine years old and he had broken his collarbone.

Nothing but nothing could possess Jack to free fall out into the wide blue yonder, hurtling one hundred and ten miles an hour to the ground below. He blanched at the mere notion.

Nothing that is, except CeeCee.

He had to do this. For her.

If he behaved in a wild, crazy, spontaneous manner that would prove to her that if he could let go of his fears and change, then so could she. Nothing less dramatic would work.

In that moment, he knew he was going to have to jump. No lucky weaseling out of it like at the tattoo hut. Not even divine intervention could stop him from his mission.

He tapped his foot restlessly against the floor. Okay, so he wasn't tapping it restlessly. His leg muscles were jumping beyond his control. He couldn't have stopped his knee from bobbing up and down like a jackhammer any more than he could stop breathing.

"Getting excited?" CeeCee asked, eyebrows raised.

"Yep." His grin was faint.

CeeCee's heart thudded. Inside she felt as trembly as Jack's knee. She was surprised he'd let things go this far. Zack had assured her he would back out long before they got to the airplane. She was more than a little apprehensive about skydiving herself. But if he could keep playing his ridiculous game, then so could she.

Who would cry "uncle" first?

She had endured six hours of ground school simply to see how far he would take his masquerade before admitting he really wasn't Zack. Apparently he was taking it to the limit. When was he going to own up to the fact he would rather be sealed in a locked cellar with a hundred rats than challenge his fear of heights? Zack had told her Jack had acrophobia. Why didn't he just come clean? He was stubborn as a mule.

But she was stubborn, too. Stubborn and mad and hurt. Did he realize exactly how much he had wounded her? He had been the only man in the world she had trusted completely, and he had shattered that trust by lying to her.

And for three weeks!

Her heart ached. Plus, he'd tricked her into making love to him. Oh, Jack, why?

Was it because he realized she would never have gone to bed with him if she had known he wasn't Zack? Had she forced his hand? Was she actually in some ways responsible for his deception? And, she remembered, he'd never actually told her he was Zack on the night of her pool party. She'd simply assumed it.

Or was it more than that? Had she simply *wanted* to believe in Jack's flimsy ruse?

Still, it was no excuse. He could have corrected her.

"Eleven thousand feet," the pilot announced. "We're over the drop zone."

CeeCee rested a hand on his overactive knee. "This is it, Zack." She placed extra emphasis on his name.

"CeeCee, I..."

Her stomach squeezed and she looked deeply into his dark eyes. Was he about to tell the truth? "Yes?"

"You first," Tiny, the jump master who looked not unlike the Michelin man said, flicking a finger at Jack. Tiny got to his feet, ducking his head in the cramped confines and opened the side hatch. Moose rose to stand beside him.

Cold air blasted into the cabin. The hair poking out from CeeCee's helmet whipped around her neck. Even in that macho gear she looked impossibly beautiful.

He felt like a World War II soldier leaving his girl

at the train station while heading out on a suicide mission.

"Are you ready?" Tiny asked.

According to their ground school instructor, Jack was supposed to respond with an enthusiastic "Yes!"

He leaned forward, stared out the door at the blue sky and clouds and the tiny scenery far, far below and swallowed hard. His knee bobbed with the rigor of a hound dog scratching an ear with a back leg. "No."

"No?" Tiny blinked.

"I've got something to say to her first." Jack stared at CeeCee and mentally begged her to understand.

Her eyes were on his face, her hands clenched in her lap. "What is it?" she asked.

He met her gaze and held it firm, sweat slicked his palms. "I'm Jack," he said simply.

"I know." She clenched her jaw. He saw the muscles work beneath her skin. "You've been pulling the old switcheroo."

"You knew?" Dread seized him and refused to let go.

Silently she nodded, her green eyes filled with so much hurt his gut lurched. To think he'd put that expression on her dear, sweet face. He was a royal bastard.

"But how?" he asked. "Since when?"

"Since this morning. Zack called your cell phone while you were still sleeping."

Ah. So his brother was the impetus behind the impromptu skydiving expedition. He might have known. He felt lower than a snake's belly. It wasn't supposed to turn out like this. The last thing he'd ever wanted was to disillusion her like all the other men in her life.

"I can explain," he began.

"I don't want an explanation."

"I did it for you."

"Ha!"

"I did it for us."

"There is no us," she said flatly. "Not anymore."

"You've got to listen to me, CeeCee."

"Save your breath. I don't want to hear it. You're just like every other man I've ever known, Jack. I'm not going to feel the least bit badly if you get your heart bruised over this. I tried to warn you."

"You're wrong. I'm not like the others."

She fingered her charm bracelet and frowned. "No. You're not like all these guys. You're worse. At least with them I knew where I stood. I never believed in them. Never put my trust in them."

"I just wanted to prove to you that you could fall in love."

"Oh, Jack, I already knew I could fall in love with you. Why do you think I told you we could never be more than friends? I knew it wouldn't take much to push me over the edge and now you've gone and ruined everything."

"You're in love with me?" He stared, not sure he'd heard correctly in the noise from the wind.

She shook her head. "I don't even know who you are anymore. I was afraid I might be falling in love with Zack except I couldn't stop thinking about you. I was so confused. But either way, it doesn't matter. Even if I am in love with you, I can't marry you. There can be no happily ever after for me. Didn't I make that clear enough? Love's got nothing to do with it. I'm cursed, dammit, don't you get it?"

"You're just afraid," Jack said quietly. "Afraid

that maybe you aren't cursed and you'll have to assume responsibility for your own happiness. Afraid you'll no longer have something to blame for your failures.''

''You're nuts.''

''Am I? You're as afraid of marriage as I am of heights. Admit it.''

''Okay. All right. Yes. I'm afraid.''

''What's going on here?'' Tiny, asked, clearly irritated with them. ''Are you two goin' to jump or make love or what?''

Moose just loomed tall and skinny like a silent lodgepole pine.

''Should I kill the engine?'' the pilot asked over his shoulder. ''Are they jumping?''

''No,'' CeeCee said at the same time Jack said, ''yes.''

The pilot shut off the engine. The silence was almost deafening. Only the sound of their breathing filled the small plane. Jack scooted to the open portal.

''What are you doing?'' she shrieked.

''I'm ready to face my fears, sweetheart. I'm trying to prove that there's nothing in this world I wouldn't do for you. Even jump from a perfectly good airplane if that's what it takes.''

''Get back over here, Jack, you're not jumping.''

''I love you, CeeCee. I want you. For now and always. Curse or no curse. Can't you understand that?''

''Jack, no, please don't do this. I never meant for you to skydive. It was just a ploy Zack and I cooked up to get you to confess. We never thought you'd go through with it.''

"It was an effective plan." He reached out and took hold of the strut as he'd been taught.

"You're still going?"

"I can't prove anything to you from inside this plane."

"But what about your knee?"

He shrugged. "I'm ready to accept the consequences of my love. Are you?"

"Are you ready?" Tiny boomed.

"Yes!" Jack shouted.

"Please don't do it," CeeCee cried and reached out to him.

But it was too late.

He'd already jumped.

JACK LOVED HER.

Of that she had no doubt. Who could overlook such a grand gesture? He'd faced his greatest fear by leaping from a plane eleven thousand feet in the air just to provide to her how much he cared.

The least she could do was follow suit.

"Dammit, he didn't wait for me," Moose finally spoke, "he could get hurt." Then Moose bailed headlong from the plane after Jack.

"Oh my gosh." CeeCee's hand went to her throat. "Is he going to be okay?"

"He'll be fine. Moose is the best." Tiny crooked a beckoning finger at her. "You're next."

CeeCee inched toward the door. She peeked out, saw Jack falling like a stone, Moose right behind.

Terror struck her heart. If anything happened to him, it was all her fault.

What had she done?

At that moment, Jack's parachute opened. Thank God.

"Are you ready?" Tiny shouted to her. "To take a gamble on the most incredible experience of your life?"

Tiny was talking about skydiving, but that wasn't why CeeCee answered, "Yes!"

At Tiny's signal, she climbed out onto the strut, held on with all her might in the eighty-mile-per-hour wind. Her pulse was racing as fast as it had the night before when she and Jack had made love. Memories of the previous night danced in her head, mingled with the adrenaline spiking through her veins. She thought of Jack. Of how he'd showed her with tender kisses, gentle caresses and soft hugs just how much she meant to him.

"Check in," Tiny called, snapping her back to the present.

She performed the maneuvers she'd been taught, then she let go the strut and started her free fall.

Tiny followed behind her. Once he was in the air beside her, he tapped on his altimeter to remind her to watch her altitude.

Ten thousand feet.

Good thing Tiny was there. She was so terrified she could barely get her body in the correct position, arching her back, putting her arms and legs out, spread-eagle.

Nine thousand feet.

Falling, falling, hurtling toward the ground at an incredible speed. The fear was intense. She forced herself to smile, to give Tiny a thumbs-up.

Eight thousand.

What if her chute didn't open? Dear God, what if

she was killed before she had a chance to tell Jack that she loved him? That she forgave him. Everything passed in a blinding rush.

Seven thousand feet.

Nothing was more important than Jack. Nothing.

Five thousand.

She pulled the cord on her chute. It billowed out in an puffy orange rectangle, slowing her descent.

Once the fear of her chute not opening passed, her adventuresome nature roared to life and she began to enjoy the experience.

Floating suspended. Tranquil. Other than the flapping of her chute in the wind, she heard only silence.

A deep, thoughtful silence.

She'd leaped into the arms of emptiness, trusting that the parachute would open, trusting she would be okay. Why did she have the courage to do something most people would never dream of doing but she didn't have the courage to do something that almost everyone did—fall in love and get married? Why couldn't she let herself jump into love with Jack? Why couldn't she trust that together, they could break the curse?

Down, down, down she drifted, while her spirit soared at the possibilities. Maybe Jack had been right all along. Maybe the Jessup family whammy was nothing more than self-fulfilling prophecy.

Did she dare hope?

She hit the ground in a landing so soft a two-year-old could have made it. Grinning, she spun around, looking for Jack. Where was he?

She took a deep breath and spied Tiny. He trotted over and gave her a high-five. "Great jump."

"Thanks." She felt her face flush with happiness,

but she didn't care about what she had accomplished. She just wanted to see Jack, and make sure that he was all right. Stripping off her helmet, she then tucked it under her arm.

They were in a large open field, no one else around. She had to find him, had to tell him what revelations had occurred to her up there in the air.

She had to tell him that she loved him. That she forgave him his deception. That she understood why he'd pretended to be his twin brother.

For he was right. She would never have allowed herself to get intimate with Jack. He'd done what he had to do to achieve his goal and she could not fault him for that.

Jack was nothing if not determined.

But where was he?

She started to panic, and turned to Tiny. "Where's my friend?" she asked. *My friend, my lover, my mate, my everything.* "Did you see where he came down?"

"Isn't that him right over there?" Tiny pointed and she saw a Drop Zone van parked on the side of the road, with Jack and Moose leaning nonchalantly against the hood.

She ran to Jack, laughing and crying and breathing hard. "Hi."

"Hey you," he said, catching her as she hurled herself headlong into his arms.

Jack pulled her to his chest, gazed at her with a sultry expression that was pure bad boy. A look that told her he was remembering last night and hoping for many more such nights to come. Good thing he was holding her tight because her legs were so rubbery she would have slid straight to the ground.

"What did you think of the dive?"

"It was wonderful, exhilarating, terrifying, fabulous, fantastic," she enthused, then lowered her voice. "It changed my life."

"Mine, too," he whispered and pressed his lips to the top of her head. "I'm so glad we did it together."

"You jumped out of an airplane for me."

"Sweetheart, that isn't the half of it. I would walk across hot coals for you, I'd swim with sharks. I would even get a tattoo, and that's saying a lot."

She didn't care that the skydiving instructors were gawking at them. She didn't care that her cheeks were windblown, or that her hair was a disheveled mess. She raised her chin and brushed her lips against his.

Jack kissed her back. Hard. Fierce. Hungry.

He grasped her slender shoulders in both hands, touching her, caressing her, making sure she was all right. His blood boiled liked candy syrup, thick and hot. He felt free, weightless, invincible. He'd faced his fear and survived. Survived the jump, survived telling CeeCee the truth, survived his own adventure. He'd done something even his twin brother had never done.

He had tumbled eleven thousand feet from the sky for CeeCee's love.

He held the moment close to his heart, creating a cherished memory.

Their audience applauded.

They didn't care.

"Am I forgiven?" He pulled back, his eyes searching hers.

"Absolutely." She kissed him again.

Someone, he thought it might have been the massive Tiny, snickered.

"I love you, CeeCee."

She fingered his lips. "I love you, too, Jack. So much it scares me."

"Don't be scared. I don't love lightly but when I do, I'm in it for the long haul. Saying that, I've got to ask you something important." He was afraid to ask the question but if he'd learned nothing this afternoon, he'd learned to meet his fears head-on.

"Okay."

"Are you sure it's me you love, and not Zack?"

"I never even met Zack! How could I love him?"

"He's funnier than I am, wilder, more adventuresome. He's sexier, too."

"Oh, I don't know about that," she murmured low in her throat. "You're pretty darned sexy, Dr. Travis. And don't forget romantic. Rose petals and champagne and carriage rides and chocolate-covered strawberries."

"But I thought you didn't like my romantic gestures."

"I liked them! Too much. That was the problem. I was trying to keep up my guard, but you kept slipping in under my radar. You're a tough one to thwart, Jack."

"And you're a tough cookie to romance, sweetheart." He leaned his forehead against hers and peered deeply into her eyes. She saw her future in those dark depths, warm, welcoming, accepting. The intensity of his feelings blew her away. "I promise, CeeCee, I'm here for you. I'll always be here. You don't ever have to worry about me leaving. Face it. I'm a forever kind of guy."

"Oh, Jack," she whispered, tears of joy springing to her eyes.

In that moment, CeeCee Adams knew the truth.

She was not cursed, jinxed, hexed or doomed. She was charmed, enchanted, blessed and redeemed by the love of a wonderful man who'd risked everything to prove to her life was what you made it. There was no such thing as curses. No whammies, no spells, no magic except the power of love.

"Come on," he said and took her hand. "Let's go home."

THIS TIME, SHE WAS GOING to make love to Jack. Really, truly make love with the man of her dreams. And indulge her naughty, secret fantasy.

They were sitting in the whirlpool, warm bubbles surrounding them, a glass of champagne in their hands, toasting themselves and their bravery. They had posted a bogus Out of Order sign on the door and locked it tight against the other apartment dwellers. Jack had shaved off his beard, and he looked breathtakingly handsome. They were laughing and giddy, still high on their new experiences, their fresh expressions of love.

And they were completely naked, their clothes in a heap beside the hot tub.

CeeCee ran her hands over his smooth chin, happy to have her clean-shaven man back. His tan had started to fade, and he'd gained back the five pounds he'd lost, nicely filling out his muscular frame. He was Dr. Travis again.

Except for that lingering gleam in his dark eyes. Somewhere between playacting his twin and jumping out of that plane, he had developed his own wild streak. He was no longer afraid of adventure, and she was no longer afraid to love. Together, because of each other, they had conquered their fears and won.

At long last she had found true love, but best of all, she knew she would be able to keep it forever.

"I'm so happy it's you I'm in love with and not Zack," she whispered.

"Me, too." His voice was husky with emotion.

"And I can't believe I'm about to make love in a hot tub."

"It's my first time, too," he smiled at her. "But first, there's something we have to do."

"What's that?"

"Give me your hand." She extended her arm across the tub.

"No, the other one."

She switched out. He unclasped the charm bracelet from around her wrist and tossed it beside their towels. "You won't be needing that anymore."

"Satisfied?" She grinned.

"Not totally satisfied. Not yet." Resting in the soothing water, watching CeeCee through half-lidded eyes, sent Jack's thoughts tumbling back to the night before and whet his appetite for more of the same.

Water glistened on her smooth, bare skin. Her damp hair lay draped over her shoulders, framing the tops of her breasts. He grew hard. So hard he felt it straight to his brain.

Lord, she was incredible.

Steam rose up around them. He stretched his foot across the length of the tub and ran his big toe along the bottom of her foot. She giggled.

"What are you doing way over there?"

He was light-headed. High on champagne and CeeCee's intoxicating presence. She smiled that bouncy, flirty smile of hers then coyly stuck out her tongue before ducking her head and denying him access to his favorite part of her. The window to her soul, the mirror of her heart, those stupendous ocean-green eyes.

"Would you like for me to come closer?" She peered at him from lowered lashes.

"Oh, yeah." *In the worst way!*

Laughing lightly, she inched toward him, her champagne flute raised to avoid the churning bubbles. Her laughter sent him into a sensory overload. He loved that laugh. Wanted to hear it ringing in his head for the rest of his life.

"How about here?" she asked. "Is this near enough?"

"Closer," he murmured, feeling very, very lusty.

She scooted nearer. "Here?"

"Closer."

"You sound dangerous." Her eyes twinkled, enjoying the game they were playing. He liked the game, too. Jack hadn't felt this free, this lighthearted since he was a teenager.

He crooked a finger at her. "All the better to eat you with, my dear."

She giggled again and covered her mouth with a delicate hand.

"I think you've had too much champagne," he diagnosed.

"Only one glass." She smiled smugly and raised a finger.

"You're a cheap date if one glass of champagne does you in."

"Not drunk," she proclaimed. "A little tipsy maybe, but definitely not drunk."

"You're an incredible woman."

"How so?" She arched an eyebrow.

"You're a dream come true."

"So are you."

He slid his tongue past her lips. Her laughter dissipated.

She tasted so good! Like champagne and honey and heat. He kissed her. Hard and long and thoroughly.

"Wow," she murmured, when he broke the kiss. "Wow."

"Just call me Dr. Love."

"Well, medicine man." She reached out for his hand and tucked it between her legs. Jack's heart leapfrogged. "I've got this ache. Right here. Have you got a remedy?"

"Have I got a remedy!" He pulled her smack dab onto his lap. Her thighs straddled his. "You tell me," his voice grew husky. "Do I have the cure for what ails you, sweetheart?"

"Oh my!" Her fingers searched for his arousal, and wrapped around him.

"Uh." Jack's grunted at the intensity of the sensation. He cupped the soft curves of her bottom in both hands and tugged her closer.

Her breasts bobbed above the water, shimmering with wetness, her nipples sweetly puckered. Jack lowered his head, placed his mouth over first one pink straining nipple and then the other. Her hands went to his shoulders, her fingernails digging lightly into his flesh as she moaned with pleasure.

She bumped against him with her pelvis. "My ache, Dr. Love, it's getting worse. You better do something. Quick."

"I'm a doctor who likes to take my time."

He watched a trail of perspiration trickle between her breasts. He licked it, savoring the saltiness of her heated skin. He lowered his hand, came up behind her bottom and slowly began to stroke her between her firm, supple thighs.

She made soft keening noises that told him she was winding up to something incredible.

"Make love to me, Jack. Now. Right now," she pleaded.

Happy to oblige, he got a condom from the pocket of his discarded jeans and slipped it on. He lifted her higher in the water and up onto his bludgeoning erection, sliding deep into her sweetness. She hissed in her breath. Jack closed his eyes, relishing the glory of their joining, relishing CeeCee.

"Kiss me," she commanded.

He roamed his mouth over hers, sucking, licking, reveling in her warm moistness. He slipped his tongue inside, feeling the rough edges of her teeth, tasting the wine's tart sweetness.

She moaned, then leaned back, breaking their kiss. He held onto her with both hands wrapped securely around her waist. She moved over him, using her knees as a fulcrum to deepen his penetration.

They soared together on the wildest of roller-coaster rides, lurching steadily higher and higher, anticipating what was coming next, knowing there would be a frantic plunge, hurtling down into ecstasy as they climaxed together in one powerful shudder. Jack finally floated down from the nether reaches of passion, his breathing hard, his mind scrambled.

She lay draped over him, her face buried against his neck, her wet hair sticking to her face. From the waist up they were drenched in sweat. From the waist down, they were drained.

"I love you, CeeCee Adams." Jack hitched in a breath, amazed at what he'd managed to accomplish in spite of himself. He'd won this woman over, freed her from her past, made it okay for her to love. He was so proud of her.

"And I love you, Jack."

He kissed her once, twice, three times. Her eyes drifted closed. The pulse beating at the hollow of her throat perfectly matched the rhythm of his heart.

She wanted him. He, Jack Travis, and not his twin brother. No more pretenses, no more deception.

He kissed that supple neck, ran his tongue along that pounding pulse.

"I love your hair. It's wild and free, spilling over your shoulders like a waterfall of fireworks. Wild and free like you." A terrifying thought suddenly occurred to him. "I don't want my love to change you, to pin you down."

"You won't," she said fiercely, wrapping her arms around his neck. "I only acted wild and free because I thought that's all I could ever have. I never thought I'd be lucky enough to find my anchor. A man who isn't buffeted off course by life's storms."

"But anchors can drag people down."

"Jack, darling, listen to me. I've spent my whole life longing for someone to ground me, and that's exactly what you do. We balance each other. I'm air, you're earth. You keep me steady, I lift you up."

She was right. So very right.

She inspired him to greater heights, to try things he would never undertake on his own. She lifted his heart, his soul, his mind. He peered into those laughing green eyes. She completed him and made him whole in the way nothing else ever had. He was her harbor, and she was indeed the wind beneath his wings.

And at long last, they'd both found their way home.

Epilogue

"I FOUND A WAY TO REVERSE the gypsy curse," Jack said. They were walking hand in hand on a secluded stretch of beach in Galveston, the evening sun sliding its way west, a full moon rising in the east. "Guaranteed."

"But you said there was no such thing as the Jessup family whammy, remember?"

The last six months together had been perfect, idyllic. She trusted Jack, with all her heart and soul, but what if something happened that was their control? Giving up a lifetime indoctrination was difficult and she was still working her head around the reality that she was living a fairy tale and all her dreams were coming to pass.

"Yes, sweetheart, but you've believed in the whammy for so long I figured a little exorcism ritual was in order."

How did he know exactly what to say? She did need some sort of ritual, some sense of closure in order to shut the door on the past forever.

"So where did you get your information?" She slanted him a coy glance.

"I have my sources."

"This wouldn't have anything to do with the Romanian woman whose baby you delivered last week during your obstetrical rotation, would it?'' she teased.

''It might.'' His grin widened.

He stopped on a rock pier and pulled her into his arms just as the sun plunked down on the horizon. The wind ruffled their hair, the air smelled crisp and sharp. They were all alone, no one else in sight.

''So what's involved?''

''It's a two-step process.''

''It is?''

''Yep.''

''So what's step number one?''

''I'm way ahead of you on that one. First, you take a negative talisman.''

''A what?''

''You know, something that represents the negative experience. In this case, your anticharm bracelet.''

''Oh.'' CeeCee wrapped a hand around her bare wrist. She hadn't missed the bracelet since Jack had taken in from her that day they made love in the hot tub.

''Anyway, you take the negative talisman and use it to make a positive one.''

''I'm not following you.''

Jack's eyes twinkled and he pulled something from his pocket. A small black box. He cracked it open, and CeeCee stared down at an exquisite two-carat diamond ring.

''I had your bracelet melted down and used the gold to make the setting for your engagement ring. The diamond came from my grandmother. She and Grandpa were married sixty years. My parents have been married thirty-five. Long and happy marriages run in my family, CeeCee, so my history cancels out yours. This ring symbolized the death of old super-stitions and the beginning of our new life together.''

She raised a hand to her throat, her heart galloping a thousand miles a minute. ''Oh, Jack.''

He knelt on the rock beside her, took her left hand in his. ''CeeCee Adams will you do me the honor of becoming my wife?''

''Are you sure?'' she whispered. ''That it's really me you want?''

''None other, sweetheart. Until death do us part. Please, say yes.'' He looked so earnestly endearing, so full of hope and promise.

The sun had disappeared but the moon had risen higher. Her stomach clutched. She wavered there in moonlight, the surf crashing into the rocks. She could choose fear or she could choose freedom. All it took was one little word.

How could she say no to this man? The one who'd loved her enough to pretend to be his twin in order to win her. The one who'd jumped from a plane to prove his love. The one who promised to stand by her through thick and thin, no matter what came. The one who'd so thoughtfully gone to all this trouble to fashion a very special engagement ring for her.

And how could she say no when saying yes felt so incredibly right?

''Yes,'' she said. ''Yes, Jack, I'll marry you.''

''Oh, CeeCee.'' He gathered her closer, rained kisses on her face. ''I'm going to spend the rest of my life showing you how much I love you.''

For a long moment, they simply kissed, enjoying the moment, enjoying each other, then CeeCee pulled away and angled her head up at him.

"Wait a minute. You said breaking the curse was a two-step process. What's number two?"

"It's going to be a sacrifice on my part." He laughed. "It requires me to be adventuresome, free-spirited and spontaneous."

"What is it!" she demanded.

"You sure you want to know?"

"The curse won't be lifted until we do this thing, right?"

"That's correct." He grinned.

"So give it up, Dr. Travis, and stop with all the mystery. What must we do?"

"We must make wild, passionate love on the beach under a full moon and say bye, bye to my bachelorhood."

"Really?" she purred.

"Really," he said. "We could start tonight and finish on our honeymoon in Hawaii."

"What!" she squealed.

He pulled two tickets from his shirt pockets and grinning, passed them over to her.

"You were pretty sure of yourself," she said, lovingly fingering the tickets to paradise.

"Sure enough to count on you, sweetheart."

"Well then, what are we waiting for?"

And so they made love under the full moon on the deserted beach, once and for all putting an end to the Jessup family whammy and in the process, ensuring themselves a very long and happy future.

Play The Lucky Hearts Game

and get...
FREE BOOKS & a FREE GIFT...
YOURS to KEEP!

Yes! I have scratched off the silver card. Please send me my **2 FREE BOOKS** and **FREE MYSTERY GIFT**. I understand that I am under no obligation to purchase any books as explained on the back of this card.

Scratch Here!
then look below to see
what your cards get you.

311 HDL DC5X   **111 HDL DC5P**

NAME   (PLEASE PRINT CLEARLY)

ADDRESS

APT.#   CITY

STATE/PROV.   ZIP/POSTAL CODE

Twenty-one gets you
2 FREE BOOKS and a
FREE MYSTERY GIFT!

Twenty gets you
2 FREE BOOKS!

Nineteen gets you
1 FREE BOOK!

TRY AGAIN!

Offer limited to one per household and not valid to current Harlequin Duets™ subscribers. All orders subject to approval.

Visit us online at
www.eHarlequin.com

(H-D-OS-11/01)   **DETACH AND MAIL CARD TODAY!**

The Harlequin Reader Service® — Here's how it works:

Accepting your 2 free books and gift places you under no obligation to buy anything. You may keep the books and gift and return the shipping statement marked "cancel." If you do not cancel, about a month later we'll send you 2 additional novels and bill you just $5.14 each in the U.S., or $6.14 each in Canada, plus 50¢ shipping & handling per book and applicable taxes if any.* That's the complete price and — compared to cover prices of $5.99 each in the U.S. and $6.99 each in Canada — it's quite a bargain! You may cancel at any time, but if you choose to continue, every month we'll send you 2 more books, which you may either purchase at the discount price or return to us and cancel your subscription.

*Terms and prices subject to change without notice. Sales tax applicable in N.Y. Canadian residents will be charged applicable provincial taxes and GST.

If offer card is missing write to: Harlequin Reader Service, 3010 Walden Ave., P.O. Box 1867, Buffalo NY 14240-1867

BUSINESS REPLY MAIL
FIRST-CLASS MAIL   PERMIT NO. 717-003   BUFFALO, NY

POSTAGE WILL BE PAID BY ADDRESSEE

HARLEQUIN READER SERVICE
3010 WALDEN AVE
PO BOX 1867
BUFFALO NY 14240-9952

NO POSTAGE
NECESSARY
IF MAILED
IN THE
UNITED STATES

Coaxing Cupid

Lori Wilde

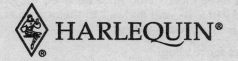

TORONTO • NEW YORK • LONDON
AMSTERDAM • PARIS • SYDNEY • HAMBURG
STOCKHOLM • ATHENS • TOKYO • MILAN • MADRID
PRAGUE • WARSAW • BUDAPEST • AUCKLAND

Dear Reader,

What's a doctor to do?

Prim and proper Dr. Janet Hunter's meddlesome, matchmaking mother has been listening to her wacky astrologer again! Mom's convinced that if she's not a grandmother within the next eighteen months she'll never be one, so she's throwing one inappropriate guy after another in her daughter's path. Add to that, Janet's best friends, Lacy and CeeCee, are getting married, and they keep yammering on about true love when Janet's convinced she'll never fall for such romantic hooey. Then, on the morning she's running late for her very first day on the job as a full-fledged pediatrician, she finds a very handsome, very naked man on her terrace!

It's all too much. Could things possibly get any worse?

You bet they can! Janet discovers to her dismay that her sexy visitor is none other than her colleague, Dr. Gage Gregory. And they've got to share an office together for the next seven months! How will Janet survive?

Coaxing Cupid is the last book in my medical trilogy about three friends who once believed they were unlucky in love, and find out to their complete delight they are very lucky indeed.

Thanks for reading!

Lori Wilde

1

THERE WAS a naked man on her terrace.

Dr. Janet Hunter froze in midstride, her medical bag, purse and a small flat briefcase tucked underneath one arm. Keys in hand, she had been on her way out the front door for her first day on the job as a junior member of the Blanton Street Group—Houston's most prestigious pediatric practice.

She blinked in disbelief.

Yep. No mirage. Indeed, a buck-naked man was lurking among her wrought iron patio furniture.

"Mother, this time you've gone too far," Janet muttered under her breath and took a third look.

Okay, so the guy wasn't totally nude. He was strategically clutching an empty charcoal bag—presumably pilfered from the trash can beside her outdoor grill—in front of his manly appendages. But everything else was open for perusal.

And peruse she did.

It could have been much worse. The guy could have been built like a sumo wrestler. Instead, she found herself treated to a very pleasing view. Mom's tastes were definitely improving. She had to give her credit.

"Any other day, Mother, I could handle this. But today of all days, your timing really stinks."

Janet set her medical bag and briefcase down on the kitchen table and slipped a can of Mace from her purse. She stalked to the sliding glass door and yanked it open.

"Hey buddy!" she hollered, keeping the Mace hidden in her palm.

The man had his back to her and leaped a good foot off the ground at her appearance. He spun around, the empty sack of briquettes barely camouflaging his lower anatomy.

He had nice biceps, a classic washboard stomach and legs to shame a racehorse. Dark stubble encroached the chiseled terrain of his masculine jaw. He possessed sand-colored hair, piercing cocoa-brown eyes and strong features.

Utterly gorgeous. Beyond perfect. Well, except for that panic stricken expression on his too-handsome-for-his-own-good face. If she had a testosterone meter mounted on the wall beside her outdoor thermometer, the mercury would most certainly have been erupting through the top.

What was the matter with her? Why was she admiring this guy's body? That's exactly what her mother wanted her to do, but Janet wasn't going to play into her hands. No ma'am.

"Are you speaking to me?" he asked as casually as if they were companionable shoppers in the A&P

produce aisle, squeezing cantaloupes and comparing their findings.

"You see any other nude reprobates hanging around? How much is she paying you?"

"P-p-pardon me," he stammered.

"How much is she shelling out? It can't possibly be worth this kind of humiliation."

It had been bad enough when Gracie Hunter had sent over an exterminator last week to spray Janet's totally bug free condo. Or when she'd called the fire department with a tall tale about a kitten caught in a tree. Or the time she had taken out a lonely hearts ad in Janet's name. But depositing a bare buns male on her terrace was beyond the pale.

Ever since Gracie's astrologer, Nadine Maronga, had told her mother that if she wasn't a grandmother by the age of fifty-two then she never would be, Gracie had gone completely around the bend when it came to finding her only child a husband.

Unfortunately for Janet, Nadine's predictions were uncannily accurate. Gracie, who had been having her chart done twice a week for the last thirty years believed every word the woman told her. Nadine had correctly predicted that Janet's father would take a powder, that Gracie would need a gallbladder operation and that she would win two thousand dollars in a lottery scratch-card game. Gracie never let Janet forget these things.

The clock was ticking. In eighteen months Gracie would be fifty-two, and she was hell-bent on having a grandchild. Half in jest, Janet had started thinking of her mother's self-delusional affirmation as the Baby Predicate, because Gracie's determination to see her only daughter hitched and pregnant was strong enough to affirm a baby.

"Excuse me?" the guy said, jerking her back to the present. "What are you talking about?"

"The jig's up. You're not fooling anyone. I know you and my mother are in cahoots. Now shoo!" She waved both hands at him like she was scaring crows from a cornfield, one thumb remaining wrapped around the Mace, just in case.

He looked at her as if she'd hopped the fence at a mental facility. "Sorry lady, but I think you're mixing me up with someone else."

"You think so?" Janet arched an eyebrow.

"Could I please come inside for this discussion?"

She considered him a moment. "I'm not sure that's such a good idea. Mom finagled you into this situation, let her get you out of it."

"Ah, come on," he begged. "I don't know what you're talking about. I swear it."

"Then would you care to explain this scenario?" She sent a critical gaze over his body.

Zowie! It oughta be illegal to look that good.

A strange shocking heat more forceful than a rain swollen river flowed through her body. Her reaction was inexcusable. She had to stop feeling so...so... darned impressed with him.

"It's a long story that has nothing to do with your

mother, whomever she might be.'' He gave her a shaky grin. ''And I'm feeling a little vulnerable at the moment.''

Janet bit the inside of her cheek to bolster her resolve. She kept her eyes trained on his face and avoided looking down. ''Obviously.''

''Let me inside and I'll fill you in on all the gory details.''

''I might be mistaken, but didn't the Big Bad Wolf hand Little Red Riding Hood a similar line?''

''Could be, it's been a while since I've read nursery rhymes.'' He had really amazing brown eyes that held her gaze like a thumbtack.

''Grimm's fairy tales.''

''What?''

''The Big Bad Wolf is not a nursery rhyme. The story first appeared in a collection of Grimm's fairy tales.''

''Gee, thanks for the literary lesson. That's exactly what I needed at the moment.'' His sexy disc-jockey voice held more than a dollop of sarcasm.

''Would you rather discuss the cautionary tale of Hans Christian Andersen's *The Emperor's New Clothes?*'' she asked dryly. ''It seems more apropos under the circumstances.''

''I think we can skip the fairy tales all together. How 'bout you just let me come inside?'' He turned up the wattage on the grin, doing his best to look suave and debonair despite the awkward state of affairs, and going all Cary Grant on her. Janet had to admire his aplomb. Maybe her mother wasn't behind this after all.

"I'm still not convinced that letting you into my house is such a smart idea."

"I'm not a deviant or a raving lunatic or anything like that," he said. "And your mother didn't hire me. I promise. I would show you my ID, but unfortunately I don't have it on me."

He had a sense of humor, she had to give him credit for that. She sighed and stood to one side. "Come on in."

"Thanks." He edged past her, struggling to maintain his dignity while keeping his backside turned away and his front side obscured by the charcoal bag. "Perhaps your husband has something I could borrow to cover my er…bareness?"

"I don't have a husband."

Now why had she told him that? She should have said something like, oh no, my six-foot-seven, two-hundred-and-fifty-pound professional boxer husband's clothes are way too big for you.

"Live-in lover?" he asked.

"No."

"Perhaps an old boyfriend left a pair of Skivvies laying around?"

"If he had, I would have torched them long ago."

"Hmm, just my luck you're not the sentimental type. Do you have an apron, or a towel, or anything like that?" His voice rose a little. "I'm not picky. Throw me a bone, lady. I'm desperate here."

"I can loan you one of my bathrobes," Janet said, trying to hide her amusement at his discomfort. He was in something of a pickle and now that she realized he wasn't part of her mother's marry-off-Janet plot, she felt more sympathetic to his plight.

"Okay. Anything will do. I just need some coverage to get back upstairs to my place."

"You live upstairs?" Janet couldn't help but sneak a quick peek at his chest sprinkled with a nice number of curly dark sprigs. As her good friend CeeCee Adams would say: He's a hunk among hunks, who wants a chunk?

"I just moved in," he said.

"Me, too."

"I'd shake your hand, neighbor, but under the circumstances..." He shrugged.

"Let me get you that robe." With the canister of Mace still clutched in her palm, she hurried to the bedroom. Janet hated leaving him alone, but the guy was a neighbor. Surely he wouldn't try anything funny.

She pulled her bathrobe from the closet and scurried back to the living room. He was lucky she was tall and preferred plain terry cloth to fluffy chenille.

With a grateful smile, he snatched the robe from her hand. "Thanks a million. You're a life saver."

She stood there feeling awkward. The sensation was an odd one. Janet was a professional, a doctor. She was accustomed to being in control. Having a naked man in her house should not rattle her. Especially now that she knew he wasn't being paid to seduce her.

But she felt more shaken than a James Bond martini.

"Do you mind?" he asked.

"Huh?" Janet realized that she had been staring at him as intently as a germ under a microscope.

He made a twirling motion with his index finger. "Turn around."

"Oh. Yeah. Excuse me." If she were the type to blush, her face would be flaming crimson. As it was, she pressed her lips firmly together and turned her back to him.

Is this smart? her rational voice queried. *Turning your back on a naked stranger? What if he attacks you? What if he's casing the joint to come back and rob you later? What if he's lying about being your neighbor? Just because he's cute doesn't mean he's harmless.*

"Okay," he said. "You can turn back around now."

She did. He looked silly in her purple robe. The hem hit him midthigh and the sleeves, which were long on her, fell to his elbows.

In his hands he held the wadded up charcoal bag. Sheepishly, he shook his head and a lock of sunburnished hair flopped over his forehead making him appear years younger than his age, which she guessed was probably four or five years older than her own thirty years.

"So you got down here..." Janet crossed her arms over her chest and tossed her head in the direction of her patio. "How?"

"Gravity."

"Har, har. No kidding. Gravity sucked you right through your shower and onto my terrace?"

He grinned. "Witty. I like that in a woman."

"Clothes. I like them on a man."

"All the time?"

"Don't go there." She fingered the Mace and his eyes followed her movements.

"Ooo," he teased. "Armed and dangerous. I like that in a woman, too."

"I'm waiting for an explanation," she replied. "A good reason why I shouldn't call the police and tell them I found a naked lunatic lurking outside my condo."

"I doubt you'll believe me."

"Give it a try."

"I'd just gotten out of the shower," he began, "when I heard these mockingbirds squawking. They have a nest in the oak tree outside my terrace."

"Uh-huh."

"I had a towel knotted around my waist, so I stepped outside to chase away a big white cat hell-bent on getting to those baby birds. Apparently, he had a poultry breakfast on his mind. Anyway, I leaned over the edge of the patio wall to scare him out of the tree and the mama bird dive-bombed me and pecked the top of my head.'' He reached up to finger his scalp. ''And I was only trying to help.''

''That's what you get for being a good Samaritan.''

''Tell me about it.'' He winced. ''I lost my balance and fell. My towel got hung in the tree, and I landed on your terrace sans coverage. I swear, it was never my intention to moon you.''

She eyed the stranger critically, and tried to decide if he was telling the truth or not.

''Go ahead, check the tree for my towel if you don't believe me.''

She shook her head. ''I don't have time. I'm going to be late for work. Just go to your own place. You can return my bathrobe later and please feel free to throw that charcoal sack away.''

''Okay. Thanks again.''

''You're welcome.''

''I'm sorry to have intruded.''

''We'll forget this little incident ever happened.'' Janet ushered him toward the door, her heart thudding strangely. ''You keep quiet and so will I.''

''Nice meeting you,'' he said after stepping into the hallway. ''Maybe I'll see you around sometime.''

I certainly hope not, her rational voice sniffed.

''Bye.'' She closed the door in his face, vowing to avoid her new neighbor at all cost.

FEELING LIKE forty shades of fool dressed in a woman's purple terry cloth bathrobe, Gage Gregory slunk up the back stairwell to his condo. So much for keeping a low profile. He had moved to Houston to escape the limelight, not to end up on his exceptionally lovely neighbor's backyard terrace in his birthday suit.

Lunkhead.

He raised a hand to push fingers through his hair and caught a whiff of her scent from the robe. A piquant blend of oriental spices enveloped him.

And intrigued him.

The woman was fascinating. A frank-talking, raven-haired beauty with patrician features and a challenging, look-but-don't-dare-touch aura. When they had been eye-to-eye, he'd had the strongest urge to reach out a hand and trace her full, rich lips to see if they felt as soft as they looked.

Just his luck. He'd met the sexiest woman he had come across in months while in the throes of a very embarrassing situation. It was unlikely she would even speak to him again. And he couldn't blame her.

Thank God, she was the sensible sort and hadn't called the police. Gage cringed at the thought. The tabloids would have had a field day with that tidbit.

If a regular Joe Schmoe had saved Senator McConelly's son from drowning on that California beach five weeks ago, it wouldn't have caused more than a minor ripple of media attention. But let an ex-child actor turned plastic surgeon to Hollywood's elite turned Houston pediatrician do something altruistic and the paparazzi couldn't shut up about it.

He shuddered to think of the headlines if they got

wind of this incident. *Personalities Magazine*'s Hunkiest Bachelor Alive Caught With His Pants Down In Texas, or, Child Star Gage Gregory Starts New Career On A Low Note, or, Has Hollywood's Favorite Doctor Hero Gone Nudist?

He'd dodged a bullet with this one. He'd come to Houston for a clean break, a fresh start. The less people here who knew of his celebrity the better. He wanted nothing more than a normal life.

A thriving medical practice, a loving wife, healthy kids, house with a white picket fence, dog in the yard, vacations twice a year…yada, yada, yada.

"No more sticking your nose in where it doesn't belong, Gregory, you got that?" he muttered. "No more damsels in distress. No more diving in without testing the waters."

And no more turning up on his sumptuous neighbor's terrace. In fact, if he was smart, he would avoid her all together. Why that last thought should disturb him, Gage had no idea.

But it did.

ON THE DRIVE to work Janet couldn't stop thinking about the stranger. He hadn't told her his name, she realized, and she still harbored niggling doubts about the veracity of his story. Although the minute he'd left her condo, she *had* checked the tree and seen a Batman beach towel flapping from the branches, confirming his claim.

Face it, she was Gracie shy. Two months of evading unwanted male attention, courtesy of the Baby Predicate, confirmed her lowly opinion of men in general and romance in particular.

Janet would never be swept off her feet. If and when she ever did get married, she would go into it with her eyes wide open and her heart firmly anchored in her chest. She didn't believe in love at first sight like her friend, Lacy Calder, or that best friends make the best lovers like CeeCee. Neither did she believe marriage was for the sole purpose of producing offspring as her mother apparently believed.

The truth was, when it came to love, Janet wasn't sure what she believed. She'd spent twelve years striving to become a pediatrician. She'd never had time for romance. Nor even the inclination.

There was only one man whose respect and admiration she courted. The one man who never showed his emotions, never told her he loved her. Her father, Dr. Niles Hunter. The most renowned plastic surgeon in the Southwest. The same man who'd divorced Gracie when Janet was three years old and sick with scarlet fever. The same man who'd shunned her medical school graduation and refused to give her a recommendation for her pediatric fellowship.

Janet shook her head and hurried through the physicians' entrance and down the hallway to the conference room. She smiled at the other eight doctors seated around the table. There were two empty chairs. Good. She wasn't the last to arrive.

"Am I late?" she asked.

"Not at all." Dr. Peter Jackson, the facility director, said. "We're still waiting for Dr. Gregory."

Dr. Gage Gregory. The other new doctor.

Janet had never met Dr. Gregory, and while she wasn't greatly impressed with the Hollywood connections she'd heard he had through the hospital grapevine, she did admire the tremendous contributions he'd made to medicine at such a young age by pioneering some revolutionary technique. Anyone with that kind of work ethic should be applauded.

"There is something we've been meaning to discuss with you." Dr. Jackson nodded at her.

"Yes?" She leaned forward.

"We just found out our expansion has been approved by the city zoning committee. During the next seven to eight months the construction crew will be tearing out the south wall, leaving us short an office and three exam rooms. As a result, Dr. Hunter, you and Dr. Gregory, being our newest members, will share an office."

Share an office? For seven or eight months? Janet cringed. She liked her privacy and her space. But what choice did she have? She wanted to be a team player.

"No problem," she said.

"I'm glad to hear you say that. Your temporary quarters may be cramped, but I'm certain you're going to love working with Dr. Gregory. He's very energetic and full of innovative ideas."

"I'm sure he is," she enthused.

"Sorry I'm late. I had an unavoidable delay. It won't happen again," a rich masculine voice interrupted from the doorway.

Stunned, Janet could only stare at the tall, muscular man who sauntered confidently into the conference room as if he owned the entire world.

Under his white lab jacket, he was dressed in a wild Hawaiian print shirt, chinos and a pair of black motorcycle boots. He didn't seem to care one fig that it wasn't proper business attire. His sandy hair curled attractively around his ears. He could just as easily have been on a tropical beach as in a pediatric practice. He looked cooler than cool and sexier than any midnight fantasy. A man at ease in his own skin.

Then recognition struck fierce as hot lightning. Dumbfounded she could only stare.

Her new office mate, the renowned Dr. Gage Gregory and her new neighbor, the very strange Naked Terrace Guy, were one and the same.

2

"WELL," GAGE SAID, some ten minutes later when the meeting had adjourned. He and Ms. Doctor Gorgeous Tushy were standing alone in the office they would be sharing for the next several months. "This is a bit awkward."

"A bit?" She crossed her arms over her chest, leaned back against one of the two oak desks jammed into the room and raised one perfectly arched eyebrow at him.

Damn. What was it about the woman that made him want to take her into his arms and kiss her into next week?

"Okay." He admitted and gave her a grin he hoped was both contrite and captivatingly boyish. The grin that had charmed the pants off more than one willing female. "A lot awkward."

She leveled him a measured stare, sizing him up in one cool glance. She didn't return his smile. Didn't give an inch. He had a sinking feeling she did not like what she saw. So much for his infamous, fool-proof smile.

Darn it, but he wanted her to like him. Why her opinion mattered, he could not say. But he wished he had opted for a traditional black suit, white button-down shirt, and conservative tie.

Except he didn't own any clothing that fit the bill.

"Listen," he said, extending his hand and walking toward her. "We got off on the wrong foot, and I would love to start over."

She slid along the edge of the desk, backing away from him. The soft material of her tailored gray dress made a gentle whispering noise that caused a curious tightening in his solar plexus.

"I respect your reputation, Dr. Gregory. I'm certain you're a fine doctor, but just because I've seen you without your pants on doesn't mean I'm interested in being pals or friends or buddies. This is a work environment. We are colleagues. We will perform together as a team. We will be pleasant to each other but that's it."

"Ouch." Gage retracted his extended palm. "Think I got a barb."

"I don't mean to be harsh." Her tone lightened a little. "But this is my first position, and I want to make a good impression. I've worked my entire life for this goal, and I can't afford any missteps that might jeopardize my future."

"I understand completely. You would prefer not to mix business with pleasure."

"Exactly." She rewarded him with a smile. The smile did amazing things to her face. "I'm glad we got that out of the way."

"How do you feel about carpooling?"

''What?''

''We do live in the same complex, work in the same office. Wouldn't it make sense to share a car?''

Vehemently, she shook her head. Boy, she sure didn't want to get stuck alone with him.

''No, that won't work. What if one of us had to work late? What if one of us has to go to the hospital to see patients? What if there's an emergency call?''

''I wouldn't mind waiting, or even helping you out.''

''It's a bad idea.''

Okay. Fine, if that's the way she wanted it, so much the better. Hadn't he just given himself a lecture on the dangers of getting too involved with people? Maybe Dr. Hunter had it right. Keep everyone at arm's length, and don't depend on anyone but yourself.

''You think I'm a hard egg, don't you?''

He shrugged. ''No. Not at all.''

''Don't take this the wrong way, but I believe in projecting a professional image. I don't want you to think me uncaring, but I feel people should keep their business and personal lives separate. Don't you?''

''You're right. Simply because we're neighbors and we're going to be working very closely together is no reason for us to become friends or to even carpool.''

''That's correct.'' She straightened. ''I'm happy that you see things my way.''

Whew! Clearly she did not care for his style. Probably their rocky beginning hadn't elevated him in her estimation, either. Still, it grated on his nerves that she didn't like him. Gage was accustomed to being liked, and he was determined to get on her good side.

"Despite what happened this morning, there's no reason you should feel vulnerable around me," he said.

"I don't feel vulnerable," she denied, but the look in her indigo eyes belied the words.

He scared the hell out of her, Gage realized and grinned inwardly. Now he knew the reason she was erecting road blocks to their friendship. Not because she didn't like him, but precisely because she did. What he didn't know was why he scared her.

"That's great. We'll forget all about what happened this morning on your terrace."

"Yes." She nodded. "No one here need ever know about it."

Gage dusted his palms together. "Now that we've settled that, do you want first dibs on a desk?"

"I'll take this one. If that's all right with you." She fingered the desk she was standing beside.

Bizarrely enough, Gage found himself wishing he was that slab of hard wood, wishing those long, tapered fingers were strumming over his skin.

He glanced innocently at her fingernails—painted a subtle shade of pearl pink—then not so innocently, his gaze traveled up the curve of her arm to her shoulder, down that long neck, to where the clinging fabric of her dress cleaved to the soft swell of her breasts.

Crash! Bam! Boom! Wayward thoughts collided in his head, piling up like patients in the waiting room during flu season.

Knock it off, Gregory. The lady's obviously not interested in you for whatever reason, and besides, you've got a practice to establish. She's right to lay down ground rules. It would be disastrous to get involved with your colleague.

Silence stretched between them for a long moment, then Janet spoke. "May I ask you a personal question?"

"Sure."

"How come you gave up practicing plastic surgery in Hollywood—which I assume was incredibly lucrative, not to mention glitzy—to become a pediatrician in Texas?"

Gage shrugged. He'd grown accustomed to the question. Hardly anyone understood why he'd eschewed Hollywood and the prestige of his plastic surgery practice. "It's not as glamorous as it sounds. Staying 'on' can get to be a real hassle."

"Oh right. Limousines and lobsters, beautiful babes in bikinis, courtside tickets to Lakers games... Sounds really heinous."

"You want to know the real reason?"

She nodded.

"I was bored. All that stuff might sound great, and I suppose it is. At first. It gets old quick. I discovered I really liked working with kids. They're so real, you know. Nothing false or flashy about them."

"Yes. I know exactly what you mean. I feel the same way. Children keep us grounded in a way nothing else can."

The sound of a throat being cleared drew their attention to the door. A UPS delivery man stood in the archway, a small brown package under one arm, a clipboard under the other.

"Dr. Hunter?" He looked from Janet to Gage and back again.

"That's me." She stepped forward and signed for the package.

The UPS man departed. Janet took a seat behind the desk and stared suspiciously at the package.

"Aren't you going to open it?" Gage ventured.

"I'm not sure."

"You're looking at it like you expect the thing to explode."

"It's from my mother."

"The mother you suspected of sending a naked man to your terrace?"

"She's the only mother I've got," Janet sighed. "Unfortunately."

"What about your father? Can't he corral your mother's matchmaking?"

"My parents are divorced. Have been since I was three. My father has never been a big part of my life. It's basically been just Mom and me. I feel obligated to tolerate her little eccentricities."

"You'd think after a rocky marriage herself she wouldn't be so determined to see you married off."

"You'd think," Janet echoed. "But Gracie is an eternal optimist. Nothing keeps her down for long. Guess that's why I'm more the half-empty type. Someone has to balance her out."

"Would you like me to open the package for you?" he teasingly offered. "Just in case good old Mom shrinkwrapped some poor schmuck and mailed him to you?"

"No!" She tried to look scandalized, but he could tell she was struggling hard to keep from laughing.

Ah, now that's the way he liked to see her.

"I'm just going to go over here and sit at my desk and review patient charts. If you find you do need help, just give a holler."

"Whatever," Janet muttered, turning her attention to the package and frowning darkly at it.

What now Mother?

Was it a ticket to her favorite play? If she went, would she find herself seated next to some dorky guy with Coke bottle glasses, a master's degree in computer science and a plethora of food allergies?

Maybe it would be a membership in a singles club where the members drank too much, touched too freely and whined about how there were "no good ones left."

Was it an invitation to another How-to-Get-Married-in-a-Month seminar stuffed to the rafters with desperate, man-hungry single women?

She groaned and laid her head on her desk. This shouldn't be happening. Not today.

"Just open it." Gage tossed his Swiss Army knife on her desk. "The suspense is killing me."

Much as she hated to admit it, he was right. Might as well get this over with. Janet sat up straight, unsheathed the knife blade and clipped the string. She peeled back the brown paper wrapping to reveal a small white box. Hands trembling, she removed the lid.

A small gold pin winked up at her. She lifted it out and held it to the light.

"What have you got there?" Gage squinted and leaned across his desk for a closer look.

"Saint Jude."

"Ah, what a thoughtful gift. The patron saint of hospitals."

And lost causes.

Her mother considered her a lost cause. Was that what this was all about? How encouraging. She searched the box, found a small piece of paper. She unfolded the note. It smelled like lavender. Like her mother. Sweet, flowery, romantic.

Dearest Darling Daughter,

I'm sending you this pin to wear to your charity event next Friday night. Nadine told me that if you wear this you'll meet the man of your dreams within the week. Please, darling. Wear it. I want nothing more than to see you happily married with a family of your own.

Love,

Grandma-to-be, your Mom

Disappointment hit like a splash of cold water. No congratulations on her first day as a pediatrician. No words of praise for Janet's choice of career. No recognition for her hard-won accomplishments.

Instead, her mother was taking her to task for the things she hadn't achieved. No husband. No family. For crying out loud, this was the new millennium. When would her mother realize women weren't defined solely by their reproductive abilities?

She groaned. If Gracie's astrologer had been in the room, Janet would have cheerfully strangled her. Why her mother chose to believe that woman's ridiculous predictions, she had no idea. Especially considering how Gracie's own marriage had ended in disaster. You would think being married to Niles Hunter would have soured her mother on matrimony for good.

Alas, such was not the case.

Her mother possessed a starry-eyed belief in fairy book quality happily-ever-after endings and nothing could shake her faith.

Janet did not share her mother's hopefulness. In fact, she often doubted whether she would ever marry at all. Her career meant everything to her. Physicians didn't work a normal nine-to-five, forty-hour work week. How could she adequately raise a child, please a husband, keep a home and meet her job expectations?

It wasn't that she didn't want children of her own.

She did. Maybe. Some day. Then again, maybe her life would be better served helping thousands of children over the course of her career, versus creating one or two of her own.

Her mother would say it didn't have to be an either-or proposition. That she could have kids now and throw herself fully into her practice when they went to school. But Janet wasn't so sure about that. Look at her father. He'd been unable to stand the pressure of marriage, medical school and a sick child, and had bailed. And he was a guy. How much harder would it be for a female doctor to juggle all those demands and still be a good mother?

"Dr. Hunter...Janet?"

"Huh?" Janet blinked at Gage and realized she'd been woolgathering. The note and Saint Jude pin were still clutched in her hand.

"Are you all right?" Gage asked, concern for her etched on his handsome features. "You seem upset."

"I'm fine," she replied brusquely.

Okay, maybe she was a little too brusque but the last thing she needed was for him to feel sorry for her. Especially when she had this inexplicable urge to rest her head on those broad shoulders and tell him her darkest secrets, confide in him her deepest fears.

What in the heck was that about?

She shoved the pin and note back into the box, avoiding the tender expression in his eyes. She softened her tone a bit. No point taking her frustrations out on him. He wasn't the cause. "You don't have to worry about me."

At some point he had come from behind his desk to stand beside hers. He reached over to pat her hand. "If you ever need to talk about anything, I'm here."

Janet jerked her hand away, stunned by the heat she felt at his touch, shocked by her desire for more. "Thanks, that's nice of you to offer but I've got plenty of friends I can talk to."

He shrugged. "The offer stands."

She forced a smile, wondered why her heart thudded and her palms grew sweaty.

Don't get involved with a man at work. You can't get involved with a man at work. It's out of the question. Forget it. No, no, no, rational voice scolded.

He was giving her this sultry, brown-eyed stare that seared a path straight through her stomach. In that moment she flashed back to her condo when that charcoal bag had been the only solid thing between them. Mentally, she embellished on the vision, imagined herself peeling back the charcoal bag and taking a peek at what lay beneath.

Hubba-hubba-hubba.

Yikes! Was she nuts?

Panicked at her reaction, she pushed back her chair and jumped to her feet. "Well, I better get to work. I've got patients to see."

She had to squeeze past him on her way out the door. Her breasts brushed oh-so-briefly against his shoulder.

"Sorry."

"'Scuse me."

Flustered, she tried to move away at the same time he also sidestepped, and they ended up crushing even closer together. Was it her imagination or did he inhale sharply as if injured by contact with her? Janet didn't wait around to find out. Head down, she darted into the corridor.

What was happening? Her nice orderly life was falling apart. She'd finally achieved everything she had ever dreamed of and yet, she had never felt more out of control. Between her mother's relentless matchmaking, laying down the foundation of her budding career and being sandwiched into that office with Gage Gregory, how in the world was she going to survive the next seven or eight months?

FOR THE PAST two weeks the tension in the office had been pretty dicey with Gage trying his damnedest to charm her and Janet doing her level best to resist. There was no denying that a certain spark existed between she and Gage, but it was only physical. And Janet never acted on her physical instincts.

By the time the Friday night charity event that was doubling as a welcome reception for she and Gage rolled around, Janet had come to terms with the fact that she found the man attractive.

So what? Big deal. She thought George Clooney was hot, and she had a minor crush on Tom Cruise. *But you don't share an office with Tom Cruise or*

George Clooney, impish voice taunted. *And Gage is every bit as dishy as those two guys. Come on, admit it, you'd like to take a big ole bite of him.*

She'll admit no such thing! It's not true. Janet has never given in to your urgings. Thank heavens, rational voice replied.

Half of Saint Madeleine's Hospital had shown up for the fancy shindig. Janet had been there for only twenty minutes and she was ready to leave. Parties had never been her thing. She found them forced and artificial, unless you were tipsy, which she certainly was not. Thankfully, CeeCee and Lacy were also in attendance.

"So tell us more about the naked guy you found on your terrace." Red-haired CeeCee, a bubbly physical therapist, was getting married in December to her best friend, Dr. Jack Travis in a dual wedding ceremony with Lacy and her fiancé, Dr. Bennett Sheridan. "How come sexy things like that never happened to me when I was unattached?"

"You didn't need a Naked Terrace Guy," blond, petite Lacy, a scrub nurse at Saint Madeleine's, quipped. "You had Jack."

"Yeah." CeeCee blushed prettily under her freckles. "Jack is worth a thousand Naked Terrace guys."

"Trust me, it wasn't the least bit sexy finding a nude man on my patio."

"Why? Did he look like Quasimodo or something equally grim?" CeeCee grinned.

"Not exactly," Janet hedged. She usually told her

best friends almost everything, but something kept her from revealing the identity of her terrace visitor.

The three of them stood clustered around the canapé table. Janet kept surveying the crowd, looking to see who had arrived. But each time the front door opened, she was disappointed. The one person she had hoped to see hadn't yet shown up.

Her father.

Disappointment settled low in her belly. Why did she keep expecting more from him? After thirty years of disappointment you would think she would learn not to get her hopes up. Determined to keep her mind off unpleasant thoughts, she delicately nibbled a shrimp in puff pastry and glanced around the room.

A string quartet played on the raised dais. People in formal attire milled around them. Waiters moved through the crowd carrying trays of champagne. A brightly colored banner hanging over the door proclaimed: Welcome To The Group, Gage And Janet.

She should have been enjoying this crowning toast to her achievement. Instead, she was anxious.

Gage stood in one corner talking to some of the other doctors. Unlike the rest of the men who were conservatively dressed in tuxedoes or dark suits, Gage stood out like a glorious gladiola in a field of ragweed. He wore an electric blue pinstriped suit, a neon red shirt and wingtip shoes. He resembled either a twenties gangster or new age pimp.

But if anybody could carry off the outlandish getup

with style it was Gage Gregory. Women had been bird dogging him all evening.

As if she cared.

Every now and then he would raise his head, meet her gaze and wink as if they shared some secret. Which they most assuredly did not.

What made her feel like a cat running across hot coals however was the fact that her mother was busily working the crowd on Janet's behalf, introducing herself to every eligible bachelor in the place.

Nervously fingering the Saint Jude pin she had reluctantly worn to please her mother, Janet scanned the room for Gracie, and spotted her talking to Max Crispin, the head of radiology.

Max was chronically single, forty, bald as a bumper hitch and stood maybe five foot six with lifts in his shoes. He was into stamp collecting, worm farming and playing the piccolo. If Gracie tried to foist him off on her, Janet would have to disown her mother on the spot.

Gracie grabbed Max's hand and started dragging him through the throng.

"Hide me, quick," Janet begged her friends. "Mom's on the warpath, and she's got Max Crispin in tow."

Her friends tried to form a human shield around her but at five-ten Janet towered over both of them. She crouched down, ducking behind CeeCee's shoulders.

"Eek!" Lacy said. "Max is dull as dishwater. Your Mom has terrible taste in men."

"Tell me about it. She married my father, didn't she?" Janet mumbled and swiveled her head, searching for an escape route. She didn't have much time. Gracie and Max were rapidly closing in.

CeeCee lifted the corner of floor length linen cloth covering the canapé table. "How about darting under here?"

Janet frowned. Completely undignified. And what if she got caught? How embarrassing would that be?

"Yoo-hoo, CeeCee, Lacy, have you seen Janet?" Her mother called. "I've got someone very special for her to meet."

That settled it. Janet dived under the table and CeeCee dropped the cloth.

Heedless of her dress, Janet sat on the floor and drew her knees to her chest. She was a doctor, a professional, a mature adult woman and yet her mother's obsession with the infernal Baby Predicate had reduced her to cowering under tables at swanky events.

"Why me?" she moaned softly under her breath and dropped her head to her knees.

Janet listened as Gracie and Max chatted with Lacy and CeeCee about the intricacies of worm farming.

Go away, Janet mentally willed her mother and Max from the vicinity. *Leave on the horse you rode in on. Good night, Irene. So long, Sam.*

More voices joined Gracie, Max, CeeCee and Lacy. It sounded like Dr. Jackson and some of her other colleagues. Apparently everyone had gotten hungry at once and descended upon the hors d'oeuvre table.

Peachy, just peachy. She would never get out of here now.

Patent leather toed shoes poked underneath the table. Someone's knee made an indention in the table-cloth. Janet edged to the opposite side, desperate to avoid being accidentally kicked and discovered.

"Has anyone seen Janet?" Gracie asked.

"I think she went outside for some fresh air," someone said.

Someone with a deep, midnight voice. Gage?

And he was deflecting her mother. Why? Had he seen her duck under the table?

Worried, Janet gnawed her bottom lip. She hated that he was trying to help her. She didn't like being beholden to people. Especially to men. And most especially not to Gage.

He was too cheerful. Too laid back. Too concerned about defenseless baby birds. Just too darned attractive by far. He made her feel things she'd never felt before. Troubling, distracting things.

And who needed that?

Certainly not her.

Besides, she had to work very closely with the guy. She didn't fancy owing him any favors.

The voices drifted off. Shoes disappeared. Janet breathed a sigh of relief. Perhaps the rush on the canapé table was over for the moment.

"Spptt," Janet whispered softly, hoping to get CeeCee's attention.

No answer.

"Spptt." She tried again.

From the other side of the table, the cloth swayed.

Janet put her mouth to the edge of the tablecloth and whispered, "CeeCee, is the coast clear?"

The cloth flipped up. A face peered down.

But it wasn't CeeCee's smiling countenance that greeted her.

"Hi." Gage grinned. "Is this just your fort or can anyone play?" Then to Janet's complete dismay, he plunked down on the floor, ducked his head and scooted underneath the table beside her.

"What are you doing?" she snapped.

"Keeping you company. I saw you slip under here, and curiosity got the better of me. I had to find out what was going on."

He drew his legs up. Both their heads were pressed against the top of the table. Their knees touched. His trousers brushed against her black fishnet stockings sparking a strange electricity. Disconcerted, Janet shifted away.

"Who are we hiding from?" he whispered, casting exaggerated furtive glances first left then right as if they were spies on a mission.

"Nobody. Now go on. Get out of here. Leave me alone. Scoot," she hissed.

"Are you always this grouchy?"

"Only when I'm hiding under a table at an event thrown by my new bosses."

"Is your mom the problem? She's a real hoot. I met her and some guy named Max Crispin."

Janet rolled her eyes. "Great."

"She seems like a very sweet lady."

"She is sweet, she's just nuts."

"I wouldn't say nuts, exactly. A little too obsessed with your love life, maybe."

Janet groaned. "She actually told you about my love life?"

"Or rather your lack of one. But don't worry. Somehow I already suspected that about you."

"What's that suppose to mean?"

She frowned. Darn him for looking so adorable. She wanted to dislike him. She really did, but he made it impossible with his knowing grin and that naughty twinkle in his eyes. As a kid he must have been hell on wheels. She felt sorry for his mother. Undoubtedly, he'd run the poor woman ragged. And now here he was tormenting her with those manly good looks, his intriguing clothing, that intoxicating cologne.

"All work and no play…"

"Hush up. You don't know anything about me."

"I saw the inside of your condominium, remember. It's pretty plain and unadorned. Not a lot of domestication going on there." He nodded, grinning as if he knew all her dirty secrets.

Janet bit down hard on her bottom lip to keep from

smiling back at him. The last thing he needed was encouragement. Sternly, she pointed a finger. "Out."

His I-gotta-have-ya grin widened, and he shot her with a dose of those warm puppy-dog eyes. "Come on, Jan-Jan. Don't be like that."

"Don't call me Jan-Jan and I've already told you, I'm not interested in being friends."

"Neither am I." A suggestive gleam glimmered in his eyes as provocative as dark hot fudge dribbled over homemade vanilla ice cream.

"I'm not interested in *that,* either."

"No wonder your mother is worried about you," he murmured, leaning in close.

"Back off, buster."

She could feel his warm minty breath on her skin. It felt nice. Friendly. She didn't like her response to the disturbing sensation. Her body heated from her toes and spread upward until she felt as if she was sitting in a simmering soup pot.

"You've got something on your chin. I was just going to dab it away for you."

"I clean up my own messes, thank you very much." She swiped at her chin with the back of a hand.

"No, not there." He pointed. "A little higher, just below the corner of your mouth."

"Oh, for heaven's sake." She scrubbed vigorously at her face. "Is it gone now?"

"Nope. If you'd allow me..."

Then before she could react, he kissed her.

3

GAGE HADN'T PLANNED on kissing her. At least not here, not yet. Impromptu canoodling had never been his intention when he'd crossed the room and joined her under the table. But there was something incredibly arousing about hiding with her. As if they were mischievous children sneaking off behind the barn to play doctor.

And there was something incredibly erotic about seeing this principled young physician caught in a compromising position.

Over the past two weeks, he had discovered Janet was independent, serious-minded and dedicated to the point of obsession. She refused to let him help her with anything. No carrying heavy medical tomes for her, no letting him volunteer to see her patients when she was overloaded, no fetching her a sandwich when she was forced to work through lunch. She insisted on performing every task as if she were being graded on her degree of autonomy. Apparently she believed she had to do everything for herself or fail miserably and she got kinda crabby when he suggested otherwise.

Her normal attire reflected her commitment to her

work. In the office, she wore crisp, conservative styles. Long skirts, tailored jackets, high-necked blouses, sensible shoes. Nothing revealing, nothing that hinted at the fine body that lay beneath her clothing.

But tonight was different. Tonight she looked more sizzling than Demi Moore in those, I'm-so-hot-for-you-handsome, three-inch, black, spaghetti-strap stilettos. This softer, sexier side both touched and fascinated him. He wanted to see more.

Her dark hair, normally pinned up on her head, was atumble about her shoulders. The dress, a slithery silk number, hugged her curves and called to him like a siren's song. Her lips, usually lipstick free, were painted an enticing shade of red.

Gage knew he had seriously jumped the gun the minute his mouth settled on Janet's lips. This was not a woman who leaped lightly into romantic adventures.

Not only had he jumped the gun, but he was back to making the same old mistakes. Trying to rescue helpless damsels. Except there was nothing helpless about Dr. Janet Hunter, and she most certainly did not need him to rescue her.

He was nuts. He was insane. Face it, he was being led around by his hormones.

Her lips hardened to cement against his. She didn't close her eyes. In fact, she was glaring. Those twin indigo orbs drilled holes straight through him.

Yulp.

Okay, so it wasn't the kiss of romantic stories. No

pounding hearts, no fireworks, no birds singing, no bells ringing. But that was just because she was stone-walling. The chemistry was there. No denying the hot rush of pleasure surging through his bones.

Stunned by Gage's impromptu kiss, Janet sat frozen for a moment. What in the heck was he doing? Did he have any idea the havoc he was causing inside her? She would not respond to his kiss. They were colleagues for crying out loud. They had to work together. Hadn't she made that clear?

To prevent herself from dissolving into his arms as much as anything else, Janet placed both palms against his chest and shoved.

Gage's head slapped into the table. "Ow."

"Get off me," she whispered and struggled to smooth down her dress which had somehow ridden halfway up her thighs.

"Listen." He lightly fingered his tender scalp. "I'm sorry. I didn't mean to kiss you. I don't know what got into me. Please accept my apology."

The last thing he wanted was for Janet to think he was the kind of creep who went around pawing women in vulnerable situations. He had never done anything like this. Ever. And he wondered what it was about her that so effectively caused him to lose his cool.

"If you really are sorry, then you'll go away and leave me in peace."

"I'm going, I'm going." He rolled to one side,

intending to slide from under the table when a stab of pain shot through his backside.

"Yeow!" he cried out in pain, forgetting for the moment where he was at.

"Shh!" Janet looked appalled.

Gage reached behind him and pulled something from his flesh. A pin. Saint Jude. Patron saint of lost causes.

"I believe this belongs to you." He dropped the pin into her palm.

At that moment the tablecloth was flipped up, and Gage and Janet found themselves staring at Dr. Jackson and a half-dozen other people marshaled around the table.

"Dr. Gregory!" Peter exclaimed. "Dr. Hunter! What's going on here?"

Gage peered up, gave his boss a beatific smile and lied through his teeth. "Hello, Peter. Janet was just helping me look for my contact lens."

WHEN JANET walked into the office the following Monday morning determined to confront Gage about his behavior at the party on Friday night, she found him playing peek-a-boo with a toothy seven-month-old. He held his lab jacket up between him and the baby who was sitting in his lap, then pulled the coat down and cried, "a-boo" in a startled voice.

The baby shrieked with laughter.

For no good reason whatsoever, goose bumps did the cha-cha up Janet's arm.

What would it be like, she wondered, to have a baby as cute as this one? To have a husband who knew how to play peek-a-boo?

Banish the thought! She didn't want a husband.

Or a baby?

Egads! Gracie was slowly but surely getting to her. She had no time for a husband or babies. Not for years and years to come.

If ever.

And yet she was irresistibly drawn to watching him interact with the child. The contrast was compelling. Gage, big and strong and sandy-haired. The baby girl, tiny and sweet with curly raven tresses. The way he held her tucked securely into the crook of his arm made Janet's heart feel too big for her chest. He dropped a kiss on top of the baby's head, and lightly tickled her belly.

Her own father had never played with her like this. She wasn't really sure men did that sort of thing. Especially with children who weren't even theirs.

"Who's your friend?" Janet asked casually, struggling to deny the unexpected feelings churning inside her. She dropped her purse and medical bag onto her desk.

"This is Miranda." Gage circled the baby's tiny wrist with a thumb and forefinger and waved at Janet. "Say hi to Dr. Hunter, Miranda."

The baby cooed, blinked her big brown eyes and blew a spit bubble.

"Isn't she a heartbreaker?" Gage gave them both

a loopy grin. He seemed completely besotted with the child. "I bet you were a heartbreaker when you were this age."

Janet ignored that last comment, but a treacherous fissure of pleasure pushed through her at his words.

"You probably had your daddy wrapped securely around your pinky."

Ha! Shows what he knew. Enough of this nonsense. Time to put a stop to *Romper Room*.

"She's a very pretty baby, but what's she doing here?"

"I'm baby-sitting."

"Baby-sitting! You've got patients to see, a practice to run."

"Settle down, oh Great Task Master. Miranda is one of my patients. Her mother forgot her purse at home and went back to get it. Miranda just had her shots, and I'm watching her for fifteen minutes to make sure she doesn't have an adverse reaction to the vaccine. I hope that's not going to cramp your style."

Good grief, he made her sound like Cinderella's cruel stepmother and that wasn't how she wanted him to think of her. Flustered, Janet pushed a hand through her hair and plunked down behind her desk.

"I'm sorry," she muttered. "You're right. I was overreacting."

The truth was she had arrived at work aiming to confront Gage about that kiss. She had a speech prepared, and a myriad of reasons why he must keep both his hands and his sultry looks to himself. Instead of finding him alone, she had found him with a baby. He had completely disarmed her without even trying.

"Excuse me?" Gage cupped a hand behind his ear. "What's that? Did I hear an apology?"

"Don't push your luck," she threatened but inside she was fighting not to be bowled over by his charm.

"Imagine that. The Ice Princess does have a pulse after all," he teased, bouncing little Miranda on his knee.

"Please, don't call me that." Janet inhaled sharply.

In med school her classmates had teased her with taunts of Ice Princess because she was always studying and had no time for parties or practical jokes. It hurt to think they had so misunderstood her. She had a sense of humor. She could have had a good time if she wanted. But she had been so determined to earn the best grades possible, so resolved to make her father notice her, that peer acceptance hadn't factored into the equation.

But despite the hard work, her efforts had been in vain. She had ended up sacrificing friendship and popularity for a 4.0 grade average and a father who had never given a hoot about her achievements.

"You're right," Gage said contritely, pulling Janet back to the present. "I shouldn't call you names. Not even in jest."

"Thank you." His apology soothed her ruffled feathers.

"Come on," he coaxed. "Why don't you give us a smile?"

She shot him a sideways glance. Both he and Miranda were grinning bigger than Dallas. Who could resist that? Grudgingly, she lifted her lips at the corners.

"You call that a smile? You can do better. Pretend you just gave your mother and her newest find the slip."

It was scary how much he already knew about her. Defeated, Janet allowed a smile wash over her face. She had to admit it felt good to let down her guard for a moment.

Gage ducked his head to Miranda's ear. "Will you look at that! Isn't that the most beautiful smile you've ever seen in the whole wide world?"

"Goo!" Miranda proclaimed in agreement.

"It's unanimous." Gage raised his head, met Janet's gaze. "You simply must smile more often."

She wanted so much to dislike the man but it was next to impossible. She had to keep her mind on her goal—to reiterate that he was not to kiss her again, or even flirt with her. They were partners in a pediatric practice. That and nothing more.

Janet cleared her throat, sat up straighter in her chair, and drummed her fingers on the desk. "I need to speak to you. Alone. Schedule permitting, can we meet for lunch at Donovan's?"

HOT DOG, but she was sexy when she glared at him.

From the moment Janet had walked into the office that morning Gage knew she had a bone to pick with him. And he suspicioned it had something to do with that kiss under the canapé table on Friday night.

If he hadn't been in the middle of rescuing two damsels in distress—little Miranda and her harried mother—Janet would have lit into him first thing. As it was, he got to watch her stew for a good three hours.

No one looked prettier in a snit than Dr. Hunter and nothing pleased him more than trying to turn that frown into a smile. He had done it once, with a little help from cooing Miranda, but now the baby was gone and he was left to his own devices.

They were sitting across from each other in a booth at the down-home-cooking restaurant across the street from Saint Madeleine's. Voices buzzed loudly around them. Silverware clinked. Delicious aromas filled the air, but apparently Janet didn't notice any of these things. Her stern gaze was riveted on him, and he found the attention disconcerting.

She had waited until they'd placed their lunch orders before straightening her shoulders, clearing her throat and saying those four dreadful words men the world over shudder to hear.

"We have to talk."

Time to turn up the heat on his charisma. Over the years, his aw-shucks-ma'am grin had gotten him an invitation into a lot of beds. Janet, however, seemed immune.

He nodded and tried not to notice how her tailored

kelly green coat dress molded to her curves. "Fire away."

Janet drummed manicured nails restlessly against the white Formica tabletop. A few tendrils of dark hair had sprung loose from her elegant chignon, framing her face and softening her features.

"I get the impression that you're very accustomed to having your way with women."

"Can't argue with that," he said lightly, his eyes never leaving her face, not for a minute.

"I'm sure it makes for a very exciting romantic life."

"I'm not complaining."

"That being the case, Dr. Gregory, may I suggest that from now on you do your skirt chasing far away from our office."

"Skirt chasing?" Gage tried not to smirk, honestly he did, but the serious look on her face, the stiffness of her vernacular was more than he could handle.

"This isn't funny! We can't have a repeat of what happened on Friday night. Such incidents could irreparably damage our reputations. And I don't know about you, Dr. Gregory..."

"Gage," he interrupted.

"Dr. Gregory," she reiterated firmly. "My career means more to me than anything else in the world. I've worked hard for what I've achieved, and I won't allow you or anyone else to jeopardize it."

She let out her breath. Her skin had reddened as she spoke, her eyes glowing with somber intent. This was a woman who took life far too earnestly. Idealism was one thing, inflexibility was quite another. Gage, however, was prudent enough to hold his tongue.

"Simmer down, Janet. I totally agree with you."

"You do?" She stopped drumming the table, and stared at him in suspicious disbelief.

Yes. No. Hell, he knew they weren't a good match. He had to stop rescuing women and she needed to lighten up. Getting involved with her was lunacy. They worked together and as she had pointed out, they were both starting their careers, a daunting task in and of itself.

But Gage wanted her as much as he had ever wanted any woman, and while he might have a tendency to fall for damsels in distress no one could accuse Janet Hunter of being a helpless flower.

She was a strong woman who stood up for what she believed in. A woman who challenged not only herself, but those around her to achieve their very best. Was this, after all, the kind of woman he needed? Hadn't he learned the hard way he couldn't rescue the world?

Maybe he was the one who required rescuing.

It was a novel thought.

Gage glanced up to see Gracie Hunter come through the door of the restaurant, a Mr.-Universe-Wannabe looming behind her.

"Don't look now," he said, "but isn't that your mother? She's got some guy with her."

"What?" She paled.

"Yoo-hoo, Janet dear." Her mother waved and made a beeline for their booth.

"Here you are!" Gracie exclaimed, stopping beside them. "I dropped by your office, and the receptionist told me you'd popped over here for lunch. Hi, Dr. Gregory."

Gage nodded and returned her smile.

"Mother." Janet clenched her fists. "What are you doing here?"

"I wanted to introduce you to Oscar. He's my personal trainer." Gracie waved with a flourish at the tower of a man beside her.

Oscar was dressed in black Lycra gym shorts and a muscle shirt, proudly displaying his buffed physique. Gage felt like the proverbial ninety-pound weakling, and he was glad they weren't at the beach. He wasn't crazy about having sand kicked in his face.

"See there, Oscar, didn't I tell you that my little Jan-Jan was beautiful." Gracie clasped her hands together and gazed adoringly at her daughter.

"Since when do you need a personal trainer, Mother?" Janet asked.

"Everyone needs a trainer," said Oscar in an oddly high-pitched voice. He raked his gaze over Janet like he was peeling a peach. He stuck out his tongue and licked his lips. Gage had to grit his teeth to keep from saying something. "Stand up and turn around."

"Excuse me?"

"Come on dear," Gracie took Janet's hand tugged her to her feet. "Let Oscar assess you."

"Mother! This is ridiculous."

"Yes, Gracie," he said. "Your daughter is very beautiful but it wouldn't · kill her to do extra crunches." Oscar angled his head and eyed Janet's tush. "Lunges and squats are in order, too. Looks like someone's gotten lax in their fitness routine."

Anger, quick and unexpected shot through Gage. How dare this overinflated baboon barge over and start criticizing Janet, who happened to possess the most exquisite body he had ever laid eyes on. He would certainly never kick her out of bed for not possessing buns of steel.

"So mother, is there any particular reason you and Oscar dropped by to humiliate me?" Janet plunked back down in her seat and glared at the duo.

"Don't feel ashamed, dear. I just got to thinking that maybe the reason you couldn't get a man was because you needed a little extra toning. Oscar volunteered to give you some pointers."

"Perhaps we could discuss this at a later time," Oscar, the-slab-of-beef, offered.

"Yes, later, that'd be much better." Janet wearily shook her head.

"Say tonight, over dinner at a healthy restaurant." Oscar glanced around Donovan's and turned up his nose at the chicken-fried steak on the platter of a nearby customer. "How about Tofu's? It's a new vegetarian restaurant on Summit."

"No. That's not good for me. I've got a jogging date with Lacy and CeeCee this evening." Janet shoved an escaping tendril of dark hair behind one ear.

"Honey, don't you get it?" Gracie interrupted. "Oscar isn't here just as trainer. He wants to date you."

Date! Gracie wanted her intelligent, gifted daughter to go out with this Neanderthal? The woman was so completely misguided. She had no idea what kind of man her daughter needed. Gage clenched his hands to refrain from telling her.

"Mother, please don't put me in the position of being rude to your trainer."

"Oscar," Gracie laid a hand on the big man's shoulder. "Why don't you wait outside in the car for me?"

Oscar hesitated a minute, then nodded and went back through the restaurant.

Janet looked desperate. She was frowning, and her lips were puckered in displeasure. More than anything, Gage wanted to ease that frown. He wanted to get Gracie off her back.

"Now, sweetheart, if you would just give Oscar a chance, I'm sure he's a wonderful man with..."

"I'm not going out with him," Janet interrupted. "And that's final."

Yea! Hip, hip, hooray! Stand up against your mother's matchmaking. You deserve so much better than some muscle bound jock who would monitor every fat gram you ate.

"Honey, please. We simply haven't got much

time." Gracie even looked at her watch as if each second was important. "I went to see Nadine yesterday."

"Not again," Janet groaned.

"Don't close your mind so fast, Missy. Nadine said if you haven't already met the man of your dreams, you will meet him very soon. Romance is in your stars. But, she said your stubbornness will blind you to his true identity. We can't let that happen."

"That's Nadine just covering her backside in case this mystery man never appears."

"Ahem." Gracie cleared her throat. "Nadine predicted you would be a girl, didn't she?"

"Fifty-fifty chance on that one."

"Will you just listen to me a minute Miss Hardhead and stop interrupting? In eighteen months I will be fifty-two. It will kill me never to have grandchildren. I so hated that you were an only child. Please, give Oscar a whirl. You never know darling, he might be the one."

"Believe me Mom, I know Oscar isn't The One. Actually, I don't believe there's any such thing as The One."

"Tisk, tisk, so stubborn."

"I don't understand why you believe this astrologer. Why are you trying to arrange our lives to fit into her predictions?"

"You know she's been the family astrologer for over three decades. Your grandmother used her and your Aunt Rhonda, too. That has to count for something, doesn't it? And Nadine has never failed me.''

Janet gave her mother a skeptical look.

''Well, okay, she told me not to buy cell phone stock because she thought they were only a passing fad and maybe she did make a mistake when she told me that Hamilton Mint commemorative gold-plated Elvis Presley toilet scrub brushes would triple in value. I admit financial predictions are not her long suit but she's never been wrong about matters of the heart. Please listen to her. I love you and I want to see you happy.''

''I am happy.''

''You don't look it.''

Janet glanced over at Gage, and shot him a ''help me'' expression.

Superman's theme song played in his head. Janet needed him. Gage to the rescue!

He rose to his feet. ''Mrs. Hunter.''

Gracie blinked. ''Yes, dear.''

''Janet can't go out with Oscar. Not tonight or any other time.''

The relief gleaming in Janet's eyes galvanized him. He felt like a million bucks. She *had* needed his help.

''And for that matter,'' he continued warming to the subject, ''she won't be going out with anyone.''

''Oh?'' Gracie's eyes rounded in surprise. ''And why is that?''

''Because we happen to be dating. Exclusively.''

4

WAS THE MAN out of his friggin' tree?

Dumbfounded, Janet's jaw dropped.

Dating exclusively? What? *What!*

Gage shot her a humble, Lone-Ranger-after-a-daring-rescue grin as if he had done something praiseworthy and not just upset the world's biggest apple cart.

Janet pressed a hand to her chest and tried to breathe. She was almost certain her face was a lovely shade of livid purple.

Gracie, however, was beside herself with joy. Squealing gleefully, she flung her arms around Gage's neck. "Oh my goodness. This is so wonderful."

She let him go, then spun around to face Janet. "See, see, I told you! Nadine was right. The Saint Jude pin worked. Why didn't you two say something before now?"

"Yes." Janet glared at him. Did the man have any clue what he'd just unleashed on them? Gracie at full throttle was an awesome force of nature. "Why didn't we?"

"Um..." His grin was more sheepish now than heroic. "Because I just now asked you to go steady."

Go steady? Was this guy for real?

Gracie clapped her hands and giggled like a school-girl. "And Janet said yes? You actually won my daughter over? Oh my, you do have your charms, Dr. Gregory."

"Call me Gage," he invited, then sat down beside Janet and slung an arm around her shoulder, suggesting an intimacy they did not share. Her heart started beating double time for absolutely no good reason at all. "She's not as testy as she seems."

Gracie peered at him over the top of her glasses and grinned. "I think she's finally met her match."

Janet shook her head in disbelief and tried to wriggle out from under his disconcerting arm, but he kept an ironclad grip on her. It wasn't fair that her body was suddenly swamped in shimmering heat, responding treacherously to his touch.

Not fair at all.

"You'll have to watch her. She's always been a little stubborn, a little too serious, a little too independent for her own good, but I can tell you'll balance her out just fine on that score."

"Absolutely." Gage trailed a finger along the back of Janet's neck raising goose bumps the size of the World Trade Center. She wanted to knock his hand away and tell him to cut it out, but something warm and pliant and treacherous inside her actually liked the sensations his touch stirred.

Blue skies above! Gracie, Gage and her own perfidious body were ganging up on her. What had she done to deserve this?

Then again, as much as she would like to solely blame Gage for this mess, how could she? To be fair, she had mentally telegraphed him a plea for help and he had characteristically leaped to her rescue. Yes, she had wanted to put a stop to her mother's meddlesome matchmaking, but not by perpetuating a white lie.

Be careful what you wish for, you just might get it.

Would it be so bad, she wondered idly, her brain befuddled by his fingers kneading her neck, pretending she and Gage were dating? Maybe it really would get Gracie off her back for a while. She could use a respite. Besides, Gage was a good-looking guy with a great sense of humor.

Not to mention that he's a world-class kisser, the long dormant, impish voice in the back of her head prodded.

She could definitely do worse. Like getting hooked up with Oscar and enduring a running lecture on the evils of flabby thighs.

But Gage is also your colleague, her ever-present rational voice crowded out the impish one. *This could be very dangerous indeed.*

Especially since Gracie had a dreamy, gooey-eyed, grandbaby-on-the-way expression on her face.

She should say something, put a stop to this nonsense before it really got out of hand. "Listen, mother…"

Then before she could complete the sentence, Gracie leaned over to hug her, gently kissed Janet's cheek and murmured, ''Darling, you've made me the happiest mother in the entire world.''

Oh cripes. What could she say to that?

''Mother,'' she whispered, appalled at her own lack of courage, ''it's not as if we're getting married or anything like that.''

''Maybe not yet. But a mother can hope, can't she?'' Gracie gave her attention to Gage. ''Can you come to dinner on Saturday at my house? If you don't have to work that is. Say one o'clock.''

''Neither of us are on call this weekend and yes, I would be honored to come to dinner.'' He nodded.

''And if she's good, you can bring her along with you.'' Gracie jerked a thumb at Janet.

Great. Now these two were bosom buddies. Her worst nightmare come to pass.

''We'll be there.'' Gage pulled Janet close against his side. ''Isn't that right, sweetheart?''

Janet glared at him. Oh, he was going to pay for this.

''I better go break the news to Oscar that you're not interested. I wonder if this means he's going to charge me his hourly rate for dragging him over here on a wild-goose chase,'' Gracie mused.

''If he does, I'll pay his fee,'' Gage gallantly offered.

''Aren't you the sweetest thing.'' Gracie pinched

one of his cheeks. "Where have you been all her life?"

"Floundering helplessly." He winked.

Janet rolled her eyes.

They were nuts. Both of them.

"And I can't wait to tell your Aunt Rhonda the wonderful news, and Nadine of course, and that snotty Mrs. Tattersol who bet me twenty bucks that you would never find anyone to marry you. I'm certainly going to make her pay up."

"Wait a minute. Hold it. Stop right there."

Janet felt the color drain from her face. Even though Gage had made his declaration at a diner frequented by hospital staff, it had been too noisy for anyone to overhear their conversation. But Gracie and Mrs. Tattersol were both hospital volunteers. If her mother told the other lady about Gage and her then it would only be a matter of time before the whole ridiculous story was rampaging throughout Saint Madeleine's grapevine. The last thing she needed was for anyone at the Blanton Street Group to believe she and Gage were going out.

Gracie blinked. "Why, what's wrong dear?"

"You can't tell anyone that Gage and I are... er...dating."

"Why not?"

"Because it's an office romance," Gage interjected.

"Oh." Gracie lowered her voice. "I see. You haven't told your colleagues yet."

"That's right." Janet laid a finger against her lips. "Shhh. Mum's the word."

"Darn. Can I at least tell Nadine?"

"No one." Janet frowned.

"All right," Gracie sighed. "But you'll let me know as soon as I can tell my friends."

"Mom, this whole thing between Gage and I is so new. Please don't get your hopes up." She flashed Gage a dirty look. He had started this whole fiasco. "It probably won't last a week."

Gage arched one eyebrow, pursed his lips and pretended to look offended. "Honey, say you don't mean it."

"Fiddlesticks." Gracie shook her head vehemently. "This man's your soul mate. Anyone can see that."

Janet groaned inwardly. "Please promise me you won't breathe a word of this to anyone."

Gracie said nothing.

"Mother."

"Oh all right. I promise."

"Thank you."

"I best be on my way." Gracie waved. "Ta-ta for now and I'll see you both on Saturday."

The minute her mother disappeared, Janet shook off Gage's arm, and turned in the booth to face him eye-to-eye.

"Excuse me, but what was that all about?"

He shrugged and had the good sense to look embarrassed. "It was a spur-of-the-moment decision. I know I was out of line, but I thought I was helping."

"Helping? You call that helping? Sheesh, you have no idea what you've done."

"Pardon?"

"Within days my mother will be consulting a wedding planner. She'll drop by a travel agency and get brochures on honeymoon destinations. She'll start thinking up baby names. She'll invite us to dinner every weekend, just you wait and see. She'll start asking you to fix things around the house. She'll want to meet your family." Janet smacked her forehead with an open palm. "It's going to be a disaster."

He smiled indulgently. "Surely you're exaggerating."

"Surely you're clueless about her grandmotherly biological clock."

"I'm sorry."

"Sorry? Is that all you have to say for yourself? Because of you, I just told a whopper to my mother. And I am not in the habit of telling lies, Dr. Gregory."

"Gage," he corrected in that oh-so-smooth voice of his. "And it doesn't have to be a lie."

"What are you talking about?"

She crossed her arms over her chest and inched away from him, trying to erect some kind of barrier between them. Suddenly the crowded restaurant was too small, too intimate. He was sitting too close. He was just too darned distracting by far.

"We could be dating each other exclusively. Go

out a few times. Catch a movie. Have dinner. Would that be so awful?''

She shook her head. ''No way. We can't date. It's unprofessional, and I don't even like you!''

''Oops! Better watch it, you're lying again.'' He gave her that loopy boyish grin that she imagined dissolved most women into pools of melted butter.

But not her. She refused to let him affect her. ''I'm not lying. I don't like you. You're egotistical and high-handed and...and...'' At a loss for words, she inhaled sharply.

He scooted across the seat toward her, quickly closing the distance she'd eked out. They were almost nose-to-nose. ''And when you've got that little glare thing going on—flashing your eyes fiercely and crinkling your nose—you're too cute for words.''

''Cute? Cute?'' Janet sputtered.

She was five foot ten in her stocking feet and weighed a hundred and thirty-five pounds. No tiny thing. No shrinking violet. She was a doctor, a respected professional. No one ever called her cute. Striking, yes. Commanding, many times. But cute? Never.

''Uh-huh,'' Gage murmured, leaning closer still until she teetered on the edge of the booth, millimeters from tumbling onto the floor. He repeated the word ''cute'' like he was dropping the gauntlet, and just daring her to contradict him.

Damn, why did it have to feel so nice for him to call her cute?

The next thing she knew he had his arm around her shoulder again. "If we're going to be dating exclusively, then you're going to have to admit you like me. That's all there is to it."

"I don't like you," she insisted again through clenched teeth, but she couldn't stop looking at his lips, which hovered above hers.

"You do like me," he said. "And I'm going to prove it."

She knew what was coming. Rational voice screamed for her to pull away, to tell him off but good. But self-indulgent impish voice, the voice she had pretty well managed to ignore for the past thirty years, was murmuring something very different.

Go ahead. Live a little. Let him kiss you.

Gage lowered his head, his eyes turned murky with desire.

Stop! good old rational voice roared.

Go, bad new impish voice whispered softer still.

Since when did a whisper trump a roar?

Since now. Ever since she'd met Gage, impish voice had been popping out of her mental box far too often. It was a little scary knowing she had this wild impulsive side that was aching to break free from the constraints of convention.

Rational voice's bluster collapsed like a house of cards, surrendering helplessly to the undercurrent of impish voice gently urging her into Gage's arms.

Janet whimpered. Helplessly, her lips parted, encouraging the kiss, through no conscious fault of her own. It was all impish voice's doing.

His mouth glided over hers. Slowly, sweetly, seductively.

Like water drops and honey and the finest Oriental silk.

He deepened the kiss, tentatively exploring her mouth. Her stomach flipped. Her knees turned to soup. She felt as if she were falling helplessly into serious lust.

His tongue set her ablaze. Sliding, slipping, shifting. Pressure and heat. Tension and fire. Rousing, enticing, exciting.

He was kissing her. Thoroughly, completely. In the middle of a crowded restaurant not two blocks from the office. Onlookers snickered. Someone murmured, "Ahh, ain't love grand." But they were wrong, this wasn't love. This was...what?

Nothing but a silly kiss.

No big deal. Not a thing to freak out about. Men kissed women all the time. It didn't have to mean anything or lead anywhere. Plus, it wasn't like she was a novice. She'd been kissed before. Lots of times. Just not recently. Okay, so it had been more than three years. Why was she making a federal case of it?

Why? Because the awful thing was, she was kissing him right back. As if she didn't have one brain cell in her head.

Her world narrowed. Her attention focused on one thing and one thing only. The flavor of Gage Gregory.

Tangy, crisp, delicious. Like nothing she had ever tasted. Ambrosia, manna, food of the gods.

Pure, raw, doctor man.

Gage kissed her with a delicious languor, as if he had all the time in the world to indulge himself in pleasure. She'd never experienced anything quite like this instant hunger and the sensation flummoxed her.

He moved infinitesimally closer. His body was pressed against hers. There was no denying his physical response to their kiss. Obviously, whether she liked him or not made no difference. He liked her.

He had been trying to make some kind of point with this kiss, but for the life of her she couldn't remember what it was. Her breasts tightened and ached. Heated desire coiled like a snake in her belly. Her mind swam fuzzy, dazed, flustered.

Wait a minute. Janet Hunter didn't get flustered. And most especially not from some guy simply kissing her. She was immune to such nonsense. She didn't believe in romance and she certainly didn't cave in to runaway lust. Not her. No sir. She was strong. She was in control. All she had to do was stop kissing him and pull away.

Nah-Nah! Rational voice crowed triumphantly and resumed control, shoving impish voice roughly back into her corner. Take that you shameless hussy.

Janet wrenched her mouth from his and stared him right in the eyes. The expression on his face was one of awestruck wonder.

Peachy. Just peachy.

The last thing she needed was to be responsible for that look in his eyes. Like he had stumbled onto a gold mine.

I don't wanna go, impish voice whimpered in one last protest.

Too bad. You're outta here. Rational voice gave her the boot.

"Wow," Gage said softly. "Wow."

Janet dropped her gaze, her mouth still stinging from the pressure of his lips, her head still spinning, her thoughts a crazy jumble. What was she going to say to him now?

The arrival of their lunch solved her problem.

"Who had the tuna melt?" the waitress asked, holding plates in her outstretched hands. "Or would you rather I left you two alone for a little while longer?"

"Here!" Janet raised her hand. "I had the tuna." The waitress plunked down their food and promised to bring drink refills before turning away.

"Get on your side of the booth." She pushed his club sandwich to the opposite end of the table.

"I'm not going until you admit you like me."

"Don't hold your breath."

"Stubborn." Gage shook his head. "Don't tell me I'm going to have to kiss you again."

"Don't even think about." She brandished her fork. His kiss, no matter how mind altering, was not going to change her attitude about their relationship.

She wasn't getting romantically involved with him. No way, no shape, no how.

"But we're going steady," he teased.

"Just eat your sandwich."

"Okay." He winked. "But don't think you're getting off the hook that easy."

STUPID. STUPID. STUPID. Gage felt like bashing his head against his desk.

He had gone and done it again. Rushed to save someone without a single thought to the consequences.

When was he ever going to learn?

Gage blinked at the stack of patient charts in front of him and tried to focus on the task at hand. Janet had left to orchestrate inoculations at the Well Baby clinic in a poor section of Houston and she would be out of the office for the remainder of the week promoting her preventive medical care programs. Thank heavens she had gone, taking her killer body, her spellbinding blue eyes and her intoxicating scent with her.

But no matter how hard he tried to concentrate, his mind kept wandering back to lunch when he had inadvertently become Janet's steady beau.

Okay, all right, it hadn't been so inadvertent. Secretly, maybe he wanted to go out with her and he had known she would shoot him down if he had simply asked for a date. But obviously, he had goofed up. Royally. In hindsight telling Mrs. Hunter that he and Janet were dating probably hadn't been one of his better ideas.

And kissing Janet in the restaurant had definitely been a mistake. He had kissed her just to prove a point but in the end, he had forgotten what in the heck that point had been and found himself swept away by the chemistry surging between them.

Not to mention her powerful response. And what a response it had been! Even now, Gage ran a hand along his mouth, remembering.

Oh, yeah. Whether the headstrong lady wanted to admit it or not, she did like him.

At least in a sexual way, if no other. His blood heated at the thought of making love to her.

Heated and boiled over.

Groaning, Gage kneaded his forehead with two fingers. Having a tête-à-tête with one's coworker was not a bright idea. What had he been thinking anyway?

The truth? He hadn't thought things through. He had simply acted on instinct.

Again.

As he had when he'd married his ex-wife.

In college, he and Pauline had been study partners, nothing more. When Pauline had gotten pregnant and the baby's father had run out on her, she had turned to Gage for a shoulder to cry on. He had been there for her and it felt good to help.

Then, her parents had kicked her out. She had nowhere to stay, no money to finish college on. Her

despair had cut him like a blade. The next thing he
knew, he was asking her to marry him.

For seven weeks, he had been prouder than proud.
He had done a good thing. He moved Pauline into his
little one-bedroom apartment just off campus. He had
been a thoughtful husband—cooking, cleaning, taking
care of the household chores. And he was going to
be a daddy, a prospect that thrilled him like nothing
else ever had. If he and Pauline weren't in love, well,
was that really so important in the big scheme of
things?

Once, he'd thought not.

Now he knew better.

Pauline had miscarried and Gage had quickly discovered that love was very important indeed. Without
the baby gluing them together, the loveless marriage
crumbled.

After that sad experience Gage swore that nothing
short of true love would lead him down the aisle
again.

It didn't take a Freudian psychiatrist to pinpoint
where he had derived his caretaking tendencies. His
mother had been sick during a large part of his childhood. In fact, her illness was the reason he'd given
up acting in commercials. Not that Gage regretted his
lost career. He'd loved looking after his mother. His
father, a brilliant Hollywood plastic surgeon, had
loved his wife deeply, but he had been buried beneath
his burgeoning medical practice.

Although there had been a succession of private-duty nurses, Gage had felt it was mainly his responsibility to help take care of his mother. After many years, she had finally made a full recovery and she bragged to anyone who would listen about how she could never have survived those dark days without her son by her side.

The satisfying feeling of helping to ease another's suffering led him to medical school. But he made the mistake of following in his father's footsteps. He was successful. Amazingly so. In fact, he had even pioneered a revolutionary new rhinoplasty technique called the Gregory technique that made him a multimillionaire by the time he was thirty.

But it wasn't enough. In spite of his early achievements he had the nagging sensation that something was missing from his life. Something very important.

His strong desire to help others in need, to do something more useful and satisfying than rearrange some starlet's already perfect nose, led him to complete a second residency in pediatrics.

It had been the right choice and he thought that he had put his celebrated past behind him. The kids knew him simply as Doctor Gage, the man who brought them little gifts and read them stories and told them jokes.

And that's the way he liked it. He reveled in obscurity.

Then, not two months ago, while walking on the beach not far from his parents' home, he had seen a young boy floundering in the surf, clearly in distress.

Without a second thought, he'd leaped into the powerful tide and pulled him ashore. Unfortunately for Gage, the young man had been the son of a United States senator.

The media had been mad for the story, dubbing him Doctor Hero. His picture had appeared on the front of countless publications, all his past accomplishments had been trotted out for public consumption. He had been invited to the White House, had even met the president. Strange women showed up on his doorstep wanting to marry him. The paparazzi followed him around as if he were Mel Gibson.

What an embarrassment.

The crazy, overblown hype underscored his decision to leave California at the end of his residency and accept Dr. Jackson's job offer. He needed to remember that he'd come to Houston for a fresh start. A fresh start that did not include trying to help his beautiful office mate when she so obviously did not want his assistance.

Face it, Gregory, you overstepped your boundaries. Apologize to her. You can go to Saturday dinner with her mother to keep from being rude, but after that, butt out of Janet's life for good. Got it?

5

"I WANT YOU to break off this ridiculous engagement in front of my mother," Janet outlined her plan. "Pick a fight with me, tell her you're gay, tell her you're already married. Anything, just do something."

They were in his 1965, fully restored, ice blue Mustang convertible with the top up—Janet's request, although he would have loved to have seen her wind-blown and tousled—on the way to Gracie's house for Saturday afternoon dinner. She was dressed in a cream-colored business suit with a red silk blouse and sensible beige flats.

Cruising to a stop at a traffic signal, he glanced over at her, wondering what kind of lingerie she had on beneath that oh-so-proper attire.

Red satin thong? A purple silk teddy? Black lace garters?

He imagined those mile-long legs wrapped around his waist. He visualized her firm, high breasts encased in a sheer bra. He fantasized she wore belly jewelry. Maybe a braided gold chain that showed off her fabulous waist.

"Did you hear me?"

"Huh?"

"You have this sappy, glazed expression on your face. What were you thinking about?"

"Uh...nothing."

"Men." She shook her head.

He was teasing himself with impossible daydreams. She probably had on high-waisted white cotton underpants and one of those Gestapo-style underwire bras. And belly jewelry? As his second cousin Nick, the nightclub owner from Jersey, would say, *Fuggediboutit.*

"I want you to break up with me in front of my mother," she repeated.

"I heard you."

"So why didn't you say something?"

Duh, because I was busy envisioning you naked, you repressed sex goddess you. Geez, how I'd love to unrepress you.

He shrugged. "I dunno. Maybe because I'm not crazy about the idea of being the bad guy. Why don't you break up with me?"

"Much as that would please me, I can't. If I break it off with you, my mother will think I'm just being difficult. According to Nadine I'm refusing to see the treasure that's right under my own nose. That's why I have to keep wearing this stupid pin to please Gracie." She fingered the Saint Jude pin on her lapel. "To remind me that I'm not a lost cause."

"Maybe you are." He winked.

"What, a lost cause?" Her voice rose slightly.

"No, no." Gage shook his head. The light turned green and he zoomed on down the road. "Maybe you're refusing to see the treasure right underneath your nose."

"Meaning you?"

He shrugged. "All I'm saying is that maybe if you weren't so picky you might find someone to love."

"Picky? I'm not picky. What do you mean picky?"

"*Pul-lease,* you've got an emotional barrier thick as a med school textbook surrounding you."

"I do not. Do I?"

"You erected the darn wall, you tell me."

That gave her pause.

"Okay," she admitted after a moment. Did he really see her as emotionally closed off and inaccessible? The thought stung. Was he right? Was she afraid to trust her feelings? "Maybe I do tend to keep my emotions in reserve, but it's because I don't believe in romantic love."

"You don't?"

"No. Do you?"

"Sure."

His confession surprised her. She had pegged him for the kind of guy who flitted happily from one woman to another, not someone's Prince Charming in the making.

"Romantic love is such a load of hooey. Pure fairy tale hogwash. You find someone you're compatible with, someone that shares your common interests and goals. Then, when you're both ready, you get married. That's all there is to it.''

''You're so clinical about the whole thing. What about romance? What about getting swept off your feet? What about feeling your heart pound, and your stomach swoon and your knees go weak?''

''Sounds like the flu to me. Wait it out and it'll pass.''

He looked at her as if she were an uneducated child. ''You poor thing.''

''Stop pitying me.''

''How can I not? You don't believe in true love.'' He clicked his tongue in dismay.

''So if you're such an expert, where's your Miss Right?''

''I haven't met her yet.''

''Come on, you expect me to believe that out of six-billion people in the world you think there's one right person for you?''

''Yep.''

She shook her head. ''You sound just like my friend, Lacy.''

''Has she found her Mr. Right?''

''Well, he's Dr. Right and yes she did. They're getting married in December.''

''See there.''

''In my opinion Lacy and Bennett's love affair was coincidence, not some weird bolt from the blue.''

''I agree with your friend, Lacy. Guess I'm just a romantic at heart.''

"Whatever." She rolled her eyes. "Either way I want you to break up with me."

"But why would I do that? You're smart, independent, accomplished and gorgeous. Even if you don't believe in true love."

"Gorgeous?" She blinked, totally taken aback by the word. "You think I'm gorgeous?"

Gage snorted. "Get a mirror, woman, will you. You're incredible."

"Really?" She straightened and met his gaze, the faintest hint of a smile hovering at her lips.

"Come on, you're trying to tell me that tons of men haven't told you how attractive you are?"

Janet shook her head. "Not unless you count being whistled at by construction workers, which I don't. They'll whistle at anybody."

"You've got to be kidding."

"No, really. Once, when I was a little girl, my grandmother and I walked past a construction site and they whistled their heads off at her. She must have been all of sixty at the time."

"I'm not talking about the construction workers, Janet. I'm wondering why men don't appreciate you. What kind of weirdos do you date?"

"Actually, I haven't dated much since college. In high school they called me Giraffe Legs. Doesn't do a lot for a girl's self-image."

"What about those college boys, didn't they know a good thing when they saw one?"

"I had a few boyfriends. Nothing serious. They

weren't the 'whisper-sweet-nothings' sort of relation-ships.''

''What about now?''

Janet shrugged. ''I think I intimidate most men.''

''You don't intimidate me,'' he said.

''No?''

''Not a bit.''

''Why not?''

''Because I can see through that hard-as-nails ex-terior of yours. You're just protecting a tender heart. I've observed you with your patients. No one's more gentle with those kids than you are.''

Suddenly feeling very exposed, Janet whipped her head around and stared out the passenger window. She was breathless, apprehensive and she didn't know why.

''So you see,'' Gage replied, ''if I'm going to break things off with you, I need a strong motivation for throwing back such a great—if somewhat unroman-tic—catch. Something your mother will buy into but doesn't cast you in a bad light.''

''You found out I eat crackers in bed,'' she said.

He shook his head. ''Sorry, so do I.''

''I drink milk straight from the carton.''

''Really? Me, too.''

''I squeeze the toothpaste in the middle.''

''Not gonna wash. We could just buy his and hers tubes.''

''Okay smart guy, you got any bright ideas?''

''Hmm, I know. You want kids and I don't.''

"You don't want kids?" She blinked at him.

"We're pretending here, remember."

"So you do want kids."

"Sure. Three or four. Don't you?"

Janet shrugged and glanced away when he looked at her. "I don't know. I have mixed feelings."

"Concerned about the pressures of juggling motherhood and a high-powered medical career."

"You got it." That, among other things. "But let's not bring up the kid issue." she said. "It's a sore spot between Mom and me."

"Good enough."

Silence fell as they both considered the options.

"Why don't we just go with the truth?" Gage said after a few minutes. "Our first priority is to our pediatric practice, and our love relationship threatens to adversely affect it."

"But we don't have a love relationship."

"Your mother thinks we do."

"Only because you told her we were dating exclusively."

"Hey, I apologized for sticking my nose in where it didn't belong and I'm working on repairing the damage, so cut me some slack."

"You're right. I do appreciate what you tried to do for me. At least I escaped dating Oscar."

"So we're square?" He grinned.

"We're square."

She couldn't resist smiling back. He really was a

nice guy. A little off center perhaps, but he meant well. She couldn't hold a grudge.

"Oh, look, here we are." Janet pointed. "It's the third house on your right."

Gage pulled up to the curb, cut the engine and climbed out. He intended on going around the car to open the door for her and help her with the pecan pie they'd brought for dessert but she was halfway up the sidewalk, the white bakery box tucked under her arm, before he could even round the bumper.

He sprinted after her. "Here, let me carry that for you."

She looked at him as if he'd sprouted wings. "Come on. The box doesn't weight half a pound."

"Just let me do something for you."

"Hey, dude, this isn't feudal France. I lift thirty-pound kids every day. This may come as a shock to you but I'm not some shrinking violet. I change the oil in my car, I repair my own plumbing and I'm not afraid of insects. I don't need some big strong man to lean on. I can take care of myself."

"Sorry." He backed off.

She was so damned independent. Couldn't stand to have anyone do anything for her. Maybe that was why she didn't have a boyfriend. She made a guy feel as useful as a third thumb.

He joined her on the front porch. Janet knocked and the door was immediately flung open as if her mother had been waiting on the other side with her eye pressed to the peephole.

"Come in, come in," Gracie called out gaily and escorted them inside the tidy house.

The minute he stepped over the threshold, Gage felt as if he'd come home. Gracie ushered them through the living room, chattering a mile a minute. She had dressed for the occasion, wearing an apron over what appeared to be a new outfit. The air smelled wonderful, reminding him of his mother's home cooking.

The living room walls were adorned with pictures of Janet. Playing at a birthday party, running through a sprinkler in her bathing suit, graduating from college. He lingered to examine them.

There were photographs of Janet with her mother and a few with other women. Grandmothers, aunts, neighbors and friends, he figured. But the male of the species was clearly absent. No men. No father.

"That's her first-grade picture." Gracie came up behind him. "Doesn't she look adorable with her front tooth missing?"

"Adorable," he echoed.

"And this is her first baby photo. She was just three months old. That little fuzz of hair on her head was soft as duck down," Gracie sighed wistfully. "They grow up so fast."

This was how their daughter would look if they had a child together, Gage thought. Seriously cute.

What a minute! What was he thinking? A daughter with Janet? Hell, as independent as she was, she probably wouldn't even need him there for the conception, much less the birth or the eighteen years afterward.

He had to stop creating these fanciful scenarios about her. She was most definitely not his true love.

He wanted an equal partnership from marriage. A symbiotic give and take. With Janet, no matter how much he tried to give, she simply wouldn't take from him. How could he ever achieve the intimacy he craved with a woman like that?

And yet, he was so damned attracted to her.

"What's that wonderful smell coming from the kitchen?" Gage asked Gracie, determined to rein in his internal musing about love and marriage.

"My specialty." Gracie beamed. "Beef Stroganoff."

"You're kidding," Gage exclaimed. "It's my favorite."

Gracie tittered.

"I've got a feeling you're a fabulous cook."

"I do my best." Gracie blushed and patted her hair into place.

"Can I see you in the kitchen for a minute, Gage?" Janet asked through gritted teeth.

"Can't it wait, snuggle bunny?" He knew he was irritating her but he couldn't help it. Ruffling her oh-so-controlled feathers seemed like a step in the right direction.

Snuggle bunny? she mouthed silently, frowned then said, "No, it can't wait."

"Go on, Gage, I bet she just wants to sneak a kiss." Gracie laughed and waved. "I know what it's like to be young and in love."

"We're not going to be kissing," Janet exclaimed, taking Gage's arm and dragging him into the kitchen behind her.

"Stop endearing yourself to my mother," she muttered, the minute they were alone.

He leaned insouciantly against the counter and leveled her one of his irritating grins. "I'm not."

"You are."

"I'm just being myself."

"And beef Stroganoff just happens to be your favorite meal." She sank her hands on her hips and narrowed her eyes at him.

"It is." He jutted his chin forward. "Just because I'm from L.A., doesn't mean I'm insincere when I give compliments."

"Fine. Okay. All right. Let's assume you're the real McCoy. You adore everything about my mother. Now cut it out."

"Why?" He seemed genuinely puzzled.

"Because you're supposed to be breaking up with me, that's why."

"I've been giving that some thought. Do you really think it's such a good idea to break up now? I mean if I ditch you she's only going to go fetch Oscar and bring him around again. Or maybe she'll even recycle Max Crispin."

Janet shuddered. He had a good point. But never mind. She couldn't go around masquerading as Gage Gregory's girlfriend.

"Look, as annoying as I find her matchmaking, it's

better than what's going to befall us if we keep up this charade. The longer we say we're going out the more likely she is to think this is a permanent relationship. I'm not kidding, Gage. She's hot for a wedding and even hotter for a grandchild. So break up with me. Now.''

"Can't it wait until after dinner.'' He sniffed the air. "That stroganoff smells heavenly.''

"Oh, all right.'' She shook a finger. "But then you pick a fight with me.''

"Fine.''

"Knock, knock, kids. Don't let me interrupt. I've got to check on those homemade yeast rolls.''

Gracie popped through the swinging double doors and into the kitchen. She bustled over to the stove, shoved her hand into red oven mitts shaped like lobsters, took a dozen rolls from the oven and set them on a trivet to cool.

"You're a woman after my own heart, Mrs. Hunter.'' Gage smiled at her.

"Didn't I tell you to call me Gracie? Mrs. Hunter makes me feel so old.''

"Forgive me, Gracie.''

"Apology accepted.''

The man could charm plaster off the walls, Janet thought with a mental eye roll.

"Here, let me butter one for you.'' Gracie retrieved a stick of butter from the fridge and slathered some across a roll. She wrapped the roll in a paper towel and passed it over to Gage.

He took an enthusiastic bite. "Incredible," he pronounced.

Double eye roll. If she hung around these two much longer her eyes would get stuck to the ceiling. What was Gage plotting? Why was he buttering up her mother like a Thanksgiving turkey?

"You like them?" Gracie grinned from ear to ear. "I'll give Janet the recipe when you two set up housekeeping together."

Janet shot Gage an I-told-you-so expression and crossed her arms over her chest.

"I have to warn you, though. She was never much of a cook," Gracie leaned in close and whispered to Gage as if Janet wasn't standing right there in the room with them. "Can't boil water in a microwave, poor thing, if you know what I mean."

Gage grinned at Janet and smugly took another mouthful of bread. "Do tell."

"Mother, I can hear you."

"Well sweetie, you were never much interested in cooking."

"And that's not likely to change any time soon."

"Of course it will. When you and Gage have children you'll want to bake cookies and make brownies and all sorts of nice things."

She groaned. "Mom! I've only known him three weeks. Aren't you putting the cart before the horse?"

"You're not getting any younger, dear."

Argh! She might as well bash her head against the wall as talk sense to her mother.

"Don't worry about the cooking thing," Gracie said to Gage. "She's got other talents."

From the speculative look on Gage's face, Janet knew he was contemplating bedroom talents.

"Not *those* kind of talents!" she snapped at him. "Get your mind out of the gutter."

"What?" Gage shrugged, feigning innocence, as if he hadn't been mentally picturing her swinging naked from a trapeze in his bedroom.

Actually, he was kind of enjoying putting Doctor "Ice-wouldn't-melt-on-her-tongue" in the hot seat. Whenever she got flustered, which granted only seemed to be around her mother, her deep indigo eyes took on a sexy sheen and twin spots of color rose high on her patrician cheekbones.

Gage had the strongest urge to reach over and muss her perfect hair, to smudge her flawlessly applied lipstick. Hell, who was he kidding? He wanted to kiss her again and hold her against the length of his body. He wanted to nibble on that long swanlike neck and strum his tongue back and forth across her earlobe.

She was such a challenge with her sharp cynical wit and that keep-your-distance facade. He knew she would never go out with him for real. Especially now. He had mucked things up when he'd told Gracie they were dating and he had only been trying to help.

The Good Samaritan was not always rewarded.

Gracie clapped her hands, bringing him back to reality. "You two are just so cute together."

"You're not burning something are you?" Janet

asked her mother, but her flinty-eyed stare remained fixed accusingly on him.

"What?" That distracted Gracie, which had obviously been Janet's intent. She scurried to the stove and began to lift lids and poke at the contents with a fork. The hearty smell of burgundy, sour cream and beef burst forth and mingled with the earthy, yeasty bread aroma.

His stomach rumbled. But he wasn't ready to eat. Not yet, because after dinner he was going to have to break up with Janet. And he sorta liked being her boyfriend.

What's the problem, pal? You're not really dating her.

"Darling would you mind pouring the iced tea into glasses?" Gracie asked Janet.

"I'll do it," Gage volunteered, pulling open the freezer compartment of the fridge and getting out ice trays.

That earned him another dirty look from Janet.

"Aren't you sweet." Gracie beamed. "And very handy. Your young man is quite a find. You've done much better hooking a mate on your own than I was ever able to do for you."

"Remember that, Mother. Okay? From now on, there will be no more matchmaking."

"Don't worry. Now that I know you're with Gage, there's no need. I can rest easy." Gracie patted one of his biceps. "He's got great genes. Your babies are going to be so gorgeous."

"Mother! Stop. You'll chase him off."

"I don't mean to embarrass. Did I embarrass you, Gage?"

"Not a bit, ma'am."

"See there, he's not embarrassed."

Janet sighed and shook her head. Truthfully, he felt sorry for her. It couldn't be easy having your mother constantly flinging guys in your path. Getting to know Gracie was helping him understand Janet better. That wall she kept around her heart was as much to ward off Gracie's unwanted suitors as to protect herself.

Well, he wasn't one of Gracie's suitors, and Janet didn't need to protect herself from him. He meant her no harm.

"We're almost ready. Janet, you bring the salad to the dining room." Gracie shoved the salad bowl in her daughter's hands, and Janet pushed backward through the swinging kitchen doors. "Gage, we're going to need one more glass of iced tea," Gracie said to him.

"One more?"

"Please."

"Mother, why are there four place settings at the table?" Janet came storming back into the kitchen, wearing a frown.

"Oh, didn't I tell you? We're having company."

"Wait a minute! I specifically asked you not to tell anyone that Gage and I were dating. Give it up, Gracie. Whom did you tell? Aunt Rhonda? That flake

Nadine? And please don't tell me that our mystery guest is gossipy Mrs. Tattersol.''

''No dear. I kept your secret.''

''Totally?''

''Well...''

''Who's coming to dinner and why?'' Janet sank her hands on her hips.

''Okay, so I told one person.''

''What one person?''

Why was Janet getting so upset? So what if Gracie spilled the beans to a close relative. No harm done.

Right?

Apparently not.

''Don't get mad, sweetie. He was really happy for you. In fact, it's been a long time since I've seen him this excited about anything. It just so happens he's heard of Gage, knows his reputation in the medical community and he's very impressed.''

Janet blanched. She began to tremble. Gage set the glasses of tea he had clutched in his hands on the counter and hurried to her side.

''Are you all right?'' he asked.

She reached out to him and gripped his hand for support. He liked that she was leaning on him, but he was confused by her reaction. What was going on here?

''Whom did you invite, Mother?'' she whimpered, almost like a lost little girl.

The sound jerked on his heartstrings. This wasn't the proud, independent young doctor he knew. What man could cause this kind of change in her? Was it an old boyfriend? he wondered in a momentary flare of jealousy. Was a bad heartbreak the reason she didn't believe in love?

"Don't ask me why I told him. I suppose I wanted to impress him. After all these years, I guess I'm still trying to win that man's approval."

"Who are you talking about?" Janet's eyes were wide as saucers. Her hold on Gage tightened. "Who's coming to dinner?"

Gracie looked chagrined. "Why dear, your father of course."

6

At that fortuitous moment the doorbell chimed.

All three of them stared at each other. Janet's heart leaped. Her father was at the front door. The man she had spent a lifetime trying in vain to impress.

Old childhood memories flashed through her head. Infrequent memories when Father would come by the house to pick her up for that occasional birthday excursion or Christmas outing.

If she had tried to kiss him, he would tell her that her face was sticky. If she ran to him, he would scold her unladylike behavior. If she tried to hold his hand, he'd tell her to quit draping herself over him like kudzu vine.

"Men despise clinging, dependent females," he'd told her frequently. "Nobody likes to be smothered."

She'd understood because Gracie had a tendency to smother. Was that why he'd left? she'd wondered a million times. Because her mother had been one of those viney women? Or was she the clingy one? Janet had spent her childhood trying to prove that she was anything but clingy.

Even now, knowing he was standing in the foyer

made her feel like that awkward little girl who repeatedly failed to please him.

Janet knew why her mother had let the cat out of the bag about her relationship with Gage—except that she had no relationship with Gage beyond colleague and neighbor. Gracie held a trump card in her ongoing emotional tug-of-war with Niles Hunter and she had played it. Janet knew her mother far too well. Her motive in asking him to dinner was twofold.

One, to triumphantly scoop her ex-husband. Two, to turn up the pressure on her daughter to get married and have babies. What better way to accomplish her goals than to tell Niles that Janet was dating one of the few men in the world her father could respect? Gracie knew how much Janet craved his approval, and she was using it against her.

Queen Machiavelli.

Gracie had effectively ensnared her. And at this very instant, her mother looked quite pleased with herself. That nutty Nadine had probably instigated the whole deal.

"I'll get the door," Gracie said when she saw Janet glowering at her, and darted from the kitchen.

"What's going on?" Gage asked.

Janet turned to him and wrapped her fingers around his upper arm. "I've got a tremendous favor to ask of you."

"Sure. Whatever you need."

"The breakup is off."

"What?"

"Don't break up with me in front of my father. Please."

"I'm right beside you," Gage whispered, his mouth close enough that she could feel his warm breath on her skin. "Backing you up. Whatever you need me to do."

She flashed him a grateful smile and her knees went weak with relief. Squaring her shoulders, she took a deep breath, swallowed her fear and followed Gracie from the kitchen. Gage walked right beside her as he had promised.

She shouldn't count on his support. She didn't like depending on him, but this was an emergency and his hand at her elbow felt so darned reassuring. Besides, Gage didn't seem to mind.

Her father had stepped over the threshold, his tall, broad-shouldered frame almost filling the foyer. He wore a dark blue suit and black dress shoes polished to a high sheen. Janet had never seen him in jeans or shorts or a pair of chinos. He was always impeccably dressed, no matter the occasion.

He presented a sharp contrast to Gage who at this very moment wore faded denim jeans, a garish Hawaiian print shirt and brown sandals. When he'd shown up at her door she'd marveled at how relaxed and casual he looked, how easy it was for him to be himself. Janet had spent many happy childhood hours watching reruns of old beach movies with Gracie, and she had developed a certain fondness for beachcombers and surfer dudes.

But now she could only imagine what her father must be thinking about his unconventional attire. Moon Doggy meets Prince Charles. She suppressed a shudder and wished she had a spare Armani suit tucked in her purse for Gage to slip into.

Stop trying to make Gage over. His unconventionality is what you like about him.

Gracie nervously wiped her hands on her apron. She looked so incongruous beside her ex-husband. Janet couldn't help wondering for the millionth time how the two of them had ever gotten together. They were as different from each other as leaded crystal and soft plastic.

When her father saw Gage, he broke into a smile and extended his hand. "Dr. Gregory, I presume." He didn't say it as a joke, a takeoff on the classic, "Dr Livingston I presume." That formal greeting was simply the way he spoke. "I understand you're dating my daughter."

Gage shook his hand. "How do you do, Mr. Hunter. I'm very pleased to meet you, sir."

Janet cringed. Oh no! She had forgotten to brief Gage on one very crucial essential. Her father was one of the most renowned plastic surgeons in Texas.

"Mister?" Her father swiveled his head in Janet's direction, drilled her with a hard-eyed glare. "You didn't bother to tell your friend that I'm a surgeon?"

"I...I..." Janet stuttered.

"The mistake is all mine, Dr. Hunter," Gage said

smoothly. "Please forgive me. Janet told me you were a physician but the fact slipped my mind."

I owe you big-time, Janet mentally telegraphed Gage.

He must have caught her vibes—by sharing an office with him she'd already discovered he was good at picking up on her moods—for his eyes met hers and he gave her a reassuring wink.

"That's all right," her father said magnanimously. "I'm sure you must be very busy setting up your practice here in Houston to worry about incidental details like my credentials."

It frustrated her how easily her father forgave a complete stranger. Where his forgiveness was concerned, Janet never felt absolved. Sometimes it seemed her greatest transgression had been being born female, and there was nothing she could do to correct that mistake, short of a sex-change operation.

"Setting up a practice," Gage echoed and dropped an admiring gaze on Janet that warmed her to the core. "And dating your lovely daughter."

She studied Gage intently, observing his lively intelligent eyes that were the focal point of his face. Those chocolate-brown eyes could easily sucker you in, make you feel special and cared for.

Be careful, rational voice warned. *Don't mistake gratitude for more than it is. Don't start buying into Gracie's fantasy. You could never have anything permanent with Gage. You're both too different. And besides, there's your career to consider.*

"How on earth did my daughter manage to attract an accomplished surgeon like yourself?" her father asked and placed a hand on Gage's shoulder. "You should have seen the riffraff she used to bring home to meet me when she was in college."

"Perhaps she was just going through an experimental phase," Gage offered.

He was only trying to help. She appreciated that, but why did she feel as if he was overstepping his boundaries, taking liberties and assuming things he had no right to assume?

Make up your mind, Janet. You can't have it both ways. Either you want his help or you don't.

"Experimental?" Her father replied, the displeasure in his tone unmistakable. "Rebellious is more like it. She was simply trying to make me angry."

It was true. In college she'd purposely dated ne'er-do-wells merely to irritate her father. At that stage in their relationship she had abandoned seeking his approval and gone straight to driving him crazy. After all, negative attention was better than no attention. Right?

"Um…" Gracie spoke up for the first time since Janet's father had entered the house. "Dinner's ready, why don't we all go into the dining room?"

"So, tell me about how you developed the Gregory technique," her father encouraged Gage as they entered the dining room. "I've heard all about you. Your story is amazing and an inspiration to young surgeons around the country. Plus, I also heard you were once a child actor. You know I appeared in a few plays myself back in college. Seems we have a lot in common. And to think you're dating my daughter.''

He glanced at Janet as if he couldn't possibly imagine what a man like Gage could see in her.

She should be accustomed to her father's cavalier treatment by now. A leopard couldn't change his spots. But still it hurt. On some foolish level she kept secretly hoping that one day he would accept her for who she was and be proud of her.

Good thing you're not holding your breath on that one. You'd have had a cerebral hemorrhage decades ago.

Janet helped Gracie set food on the table, then slipped into her chair next to Gage. He and her father were discussing the finer points of plastic surgery. It had been a long time, if ever, since she had seen her father so animated.

Why couldn't she be responsible for putting that excited expression on his face? Why couldn't he be as proud of her as he was of a man he didn't even know?

And she felt something else. An ugly green-eyed emotion that made her ashamed of herself. Envy. Yes. She was jealous over a man who'd done in five minutes what she hadn't been able to do in thirty years. Win her father's respect.

''So why did you leave plastic surgery, Dr. Gregory, if you don't mind my asking? Why the switch to pediatrics?''

Gage probably hadn't picked up on it, but Janet clearly heard the disdain in her father's voice when he said the word ''pediatrics.'' She knew he was uncomfortable around children. All through medical school she had tried to rally an interest in plastic surgery in order to please him, but she had excelled in working with children and more than one instructor had urged her to become a pediatrician.

Still, she had been determined to pursue plastic surgery, until her father had refused to give her a recommendation for the internship program.

''Stop being so needy,'' he'd snapped. ''Stand on your own two feet. Be independent.''

After that, she'd joyfully embraced pediatrics even though he turned his nose up at her chosen specialty.

Gage hesitated for a moment, weighing his words carefully. He was aware he was treading on eggshells. ''After I invented the Gregory technique I felt as if I'd accomplished as much as I could in cosmetic surgery.''

Janet's father shook his head. ''It's such a shame. A man of your talents wasting it on chicken pox and croup and bedwetters.''

Gage had to clench his fists to stay his anger. The man had insulted him. He thought of a smart retort but bit it back. What good would it do to make an enemy of Niles Hunter? Even though he considered the man a pompous windbag who obviously did not deserve a daughter as fine as Janet.

"The Stroganoff is excellent," Gage told Gracie to change the subject. "The best I've ever eaten."

"Then you've never been to the Russian Tea Room in New York City," Janet's father said. "Now that's beef Stroganoff."

What a snob. Gage wondered what was wrong with the man that he couldn't pay his ex-wife a simple compliment. He was also beginning to understand what made Janet such a perfectionist and why she sometimes acted defensively without much provocation. Trying to please this uncompromising man couldn't have been easy.

A new tenderness for her swept through him. After putting up with Niles Hunter for her entire life, she deserved a little extra T.L.C. whether she recognized it or not.

And Gage would love to be the man to give her that tender loving care if he could.

If she were his woman, he would indulge her with warm bubble baths and he'd gently scrub her lush body with sweet smelling soaps. Afterwards he would wrap her in a towel warmed in the clothes dryer, then massage scented lotion into her silky skin.

He would surprise her with thoughtful tokens of his affection, from a fragrant bouquet of wildflowers, to sexy notes tucked into her briefcase, to a box of sinful chocolates left on her bed.

If she had a cold, he would plump up her pillows

and serve her chicken soup in bed. He'd feed her ice chips from a spoon for her fever, buy her the softest tissues he could find and put a humidifier in her room.

He would wash her car and keep the gas tank filled. He would grind her favorite coffee beans and program the coffeemaker to start just before she woke up every morning. He would rub her feet when she'd had a hard day at work. He would either help cook supper or dial for takeout.

If she were indeed his, he would give her those things and so much more.

But she wasn't his. And probably never would be. They were too different. They were both consumed with establishing their careers. Besides, he'd sworn never to get married again unless he knew for sure they were both in love. Equally. No lopsided unrequited mess for him. No getting married for all the wrong reasons.

His gaze flicked over her features, his eyes drinking in her soft dark hair, her flawless complexion, her round indigo eyes. That perfectly shaped mouth.

Ripe. Pink. So kissable.

Here we go, Gregory. It's Pauline all over again. Admit it. You just want to take care of her.

Belatedly, he realized he had been staring intently at Janet's lips; ignoring both his meal and the elder Dr. Hunter, who had apparently asked him a question.

"Sir?" he blinked, feeling oddly groggy, as if he had been enchanted by some magical spell. "I'm sorry, could you repeat that?"

"I was saying how much I respect your work and how I wish I had a son like you."

"Thank you, I appreciate the compliment. But you've got a very accomplished daughter of your own," Gage pointed out, tactfully restraining himself from wringing the man's neck. Did he have any idea how cold and unfeeling his statement sounded? His heart broke for Janet.

"Ah well, I suppose so."

"Were you aware that in just her third week of practice Janet has single-handedly initiated a city-wide preventative health program for underprivileged children?"

"Are you seriously comparing that to developing something as cutting-edge as the Gregory technique?"

"Niles," Gracie spoke up. "That's not fair."

"I'll get the dessert." Janet leaped up, her face pale and drawn, and rushed from the room.

Gage glared at Niles Hunter and pushed back his chair. The man was as sensitive as a slug. "I'll go see if she needs any help."

Janet pushed through the swinging doors into the kitchen, anger, hurt and disappointment shoving her blood through her veins, quickening her pulse, making it hard to breathe.

She braced her elbows against the counter, lowered her head and took long, slow cleansing breaths.

"Janet, sweetheart?" Gage slipped an arm around her shoulder. "Are you all right?"

She shrugged off his touch. The last thing she wanted was to be comforted by the almighty inventor of the celebrated Gregory technique.

"Excuse me for saying so, but your father is a real ass," Gage said.

"Oh, like you aren't."

"What?"

"You were acting so smug, so superior," she said.

"Excuse me?"

He had been trying to rescue her again. Imagine. The nerve!

"It's damned egotistical of you to think you can analyze my relationship with my father and try to fix it over a twenty minute meal." She kept her head down, staring at the stick of butter her mother had forgotten to put back into the fridge. It had begun to melt and the butter bulged against the sides of the wax paper wrapping.

"Egotistical? Me?"

"You bet your sweet bippy."

"I was only trying to help." He sounded downright confused and a little hurt. "Isn't that what you wanted me to do?"

Yes, No, I don't know.

"The great Gage Gregory to the rescue," she said sarcastically even though she had no real reason to be mean to him. He'd helped her and now she was holding it against him. What was the poor guy supposed to think? What was the matter with her?

"Janet," he said, his voice suddenly very quiet. "I

know you're just lashing out at the one who's handy. You're displacing your anger toward your father onto me.''

''Gee, sounds like someone took Psych 101.''

''Look at me,'' he commanded.

She didn't want to.

But he wasn't the kind of guy who easily accepted no for an answer. Gage leaned over, cupped her chin in his palm and tilted her head up to meet his unwavering gaze.

She straightened. Their eyes locked.

He looked sad and a little bewildered. In that moment she knew she'd been wrong about him. He hadn't been seeing himself as her savior. He had simply been feeling sorry for her. She didn't know which was worse. His pity or his patronage.

Her mother had placed her in a precarious situation and her father had hurt her, yes, but the last thing she wanted was Gage's sympathy.

The kitchen filled with tension and embarrassment. Silence stretched. No sounds came from the dining room. A drop of water from the faucet plunked into the stainless steel sink.

Janet inhaled sharply.

He wanted to kiss her, she could tell. He moved closer, his gaze never leaving hers, his fingers still curled around her chin. He wanted to kiss her and make it all better.

If only it were that easy.

Her heart did an involuntary somersault, her stomach contracted, her toes curled in anticipation.

Well, a kiss might not make everything all better, but it certainly couldn't hurt.

Could it?

Apparently, she was about to find out.

Gage's mouth closed over hers but it wasn't a demanding kiss. Nor was it hot and heavy. His lips were light, his touch gentle—calming, mild, pampering—a balm to her irritated nerves, a salve to her battered ego.

He didn't use his tongue. He didn't hurry. His lips performed all the magic. No pressure, no expectations, no agenda except to comfort.

She sank against his chest and let him do what he wanted.

His touch eased her sorrow. His lips washed away her pain. His sweet caress dissolved her disappointment. He pressed his palm against her back and rubbed in a soothing circle.

Who cared if her father would rather have him for a son instead of her for a daughter? It wasn't Gage's fault that he was a brilliant, medically inventive, multimillionaire, ex-child actor with good looks and charms a plenty. He was on her side.

So it was okay for her to cling to his shoulders, right? It was okay if she enjoyed the taste of his mouth. Wasn't it?

Heavens above but the man could communicate so many emotions with those lips!

Sympathy, concern, compassion. Lust.

Suddenly, it was way too hot in that kitchen and what they were doing with her parents in the very next room was really stupid. Her eyes flew open.

His eyes were closed. Watching him was unbelievably romantic. Too darned romantic by half.

It isn't a good idea to let him keep kissing you, no matter how good it feels, rational voice piped up. *Remember, you're starting a new career. You don't have room in your life for this…this…whatever this is. Especially since your father likes him better than he likes you.*

"Do you two need some help with that dessert? It's taking a long time." Her father came through the swinging doors, then stopped cold.

Janet sprang away from Gage, her face heating with embarrassment. "Father…I…I…" she stammered.

Her father frowned, and held up a palm. His jaw muscle jumped. "No need to explain anything to me. You're a grown woman. A doctor even. If you feel the need to debase yourself in your mother's kitchen with a man you barely know it's no concern of mine."

Her heart raced, her palms grew slick. It was almost as bad as that time in college when her father had caught her making out with Ace Mulgrew in a hammock in the backyard. He'd called her a tramp and much worse. He didn't say those ugly words now, but he was thinking them. She could tell by the cold, hard look in his stony eyes.

Janet cleared her throat, drew herself up tall and stared him right in the face. "Father, you're wrong. It's not like that at all."

"Oh no?" His tone could have frozen molten lava. "What is it like then?"

Why was he always so disappointed in her? Why was he making a big deal out of something as simple as a kiss? Why was he so harsh and unbending? For the love of Pete, she was thirty years old! What on earth did he expect from her? If she lassoed down the moon and deposited it at his feet he would berate her for leaving a hole in the sky.

"Well?" he demanded.

Before she even considered what she intended to say, Gage blurted out, "Dr. Hunter, Janet and I are engaged."

Stunned, she could only stare at him.

"Really?" Her father broke into the most beatific smile she'd ever seen on his face.

Her gut wrenched. How many years had she struggled to put such a smile on his lips and how many times had she failed miserably? And now she had finally achieved her goal but only because her father thought her engaged to Gage.

"Uh…" was all she managed.

"Well, why didn't you say so before? This is absolutely the smartest thing you've ever done, Janet."

"What? What's this?" Gracie popped into the kitchen, too, bumping her father in the backside with the door. He was so pleased he didn't even chide

Gracie for jarring him. "Did I hear right? You and Gage are getting married?"

"You heard correctly Grace, but don't start with your usual antics," Janet's father warned.

Wait, whoa, stop, rational voice screamed. *Do something, Janet. Deny this. Right now.*

But the proud expression on her father's face stayed her tongue. She said nothing.

"My baby's getting married!" Gracie threw her arms around Janet and squeezed hard. "Darling, you've made me the happiest woman on the face of the earth."

Janet searched Gage's eyes. He tossed her an I-can't-believe-I-just-did-that look of apology.

"The ring! Let me see the engagement ring." Gracie snatched Janet's left hand in her own. "There's no ring. Where's the ring?"

"Um...er..." She stammered. Oh, she was a terrible liar.

"You're having the ring sized, aren't you," Gracie said, providing her with an excuse.

Janet nodded.

Gracie started humming Wagner's wedding march and pirouetting around the kitchen like a ballerina on amphetamines. Her father, as preposterous as it seemed, was spouting his ideal guest list for the engagement party he was planning on throwing for them at Garden Green Acres, Houston's oldest and most exclusive country club.

"Feel free to invite any of your Hollywood friends

and of course, your family,'' her father told Gage and waved his hand expansively. ''Your engagement party will be the event of the year.''

Holy cow! What had Gage wrought? Her father, or so he thought, was finally getting the son he'd always wanted. While her Baby Predicate obsessed mother was looking forward to wedding bells and lullabies, bridal gowns and cradles.

Everybody was happy.

Except for her.

''Could I see you outside for a moment, Gage?'' she asked, trying to keep her voice at an even pitch, belying the demented thoughts sprinting through her brain.

''We'll serve coq au vin, crepe ramekins, bulgar pilaf with green peppercorns, creamy fennel puree and maple hazelnut mousse for dessert. I'll hire Gil Chaney's orchestra,'' her father was saying, sounding as if this would be an over-the-top, designed-to-impress soiree.

''You can register at Harrisons, and we'll hire Reverend Newton to officiate and let's look into releasing doves. Mrs. Tattersol's daughter did that at her wedding last year, and it was beautiful. No wait, I forgot about the dove poop. What a mess that was. On second thought how do you feel about butterflies?'' her mother blathered, speaking at the same time as her father so that everything came out in a jarring cacophony.

"Butterflies are ridiculous, Grace, do you have any idea how much they cost?" her father interjected.

Omigod, look what those two little words—we're engaged—had done. Running into Frankenstein, Dracula and the Wolfman on a three-day drinking binge in a deserted alley in Bangkok at midnight wouldn't have been as scary as this.

"Don't be such a tightwad, Niles. Your only daughter doesn't get married every day."

"Especially not to Dr. Gage Gregory." Her father stroked his chin with his thumb and index finger.

Give it a rest, Father. We know, we know. You think the sun shines out of Gage's...

She crooked her finger at Gage in a come-with-me gesture and opened the back door. He seemed more than happy to flee to the privacy of the backyard, leaving her parents arguing over the—unbeknownst to them—never-gonna-happen wedding festivities.

Her whole body shook as she closed the door firmly behind them. Was she angry or upset or just the teeniest bit thankful? She didn't even know what she felt. But she did know one thing. No man had ever done anything so gallant for her.

Without a word, Gage took her arm and guided her to the wooden porch swing set up under the shelter shade of an old red oak tree.

"Sit," he commanded.

She sat, the intense scent of honeysuckle and jasmine vibrating the air around them. Spring. The best time of year in Houston. She should be enjoying the pleasant weather but her mind was muddled, her world turned upside down.

"I know what you're going to say," he began.

"Oh yeah? Now you're a mind reader on top of everything else?"

"I'm sorry but I couldn't stand there and let your father degrade you. I had to do something to shut him up."

"And declaring us engaged was the best solution that came to mind?" She still couldn't believe what he had done. Telling her mother they were dating was one thing, but pretending to be engaged? Preposterous.

Yet the news had made her father so happy. Miserably, she pushed her hand through her hair.

"I thought it was better than decking him flat-out. But you're right, I shouldn't have told your parents we were engaged."

"No kidding. What was your first clue? My father preparing the menu for our engagement party, or my mother wanting to let pooping doves loose at the ceremony?"

He grinned at that. "So you're not mad?"

"I'm both furious and confused and..."

"And what?"

"Grateful."

"Grateful?"

"My father has never been proud of me. Not once in my entire life. And now, because of you, he is."

Gage eased down beside her. The chain supporting

the porch swing creaked rustily beneath their combined weight. Sympathy for her surged through him. He wanted to take her in his arms, hold her close and make it all better.

Uh-oh, a bad sign. The last thing he needed was to feel sorry for her.

Have you flipped your ever-loving gourd, Gregory? Warning! Warning! Danger! Danger! Get out while you can.

The thought of being engaged to Janet for real stirred him in inexplicable ways. He'd traveled down a similar road in the past with disastrous results. Although pretending to be Janet's fiancé was a far cry from marrying Pauline for all the wrong reasons, it raised in him the same feelings—tenderness, pride, gallantry.

Those very emotions gave him pause. Was he truly attracted to Janet or was he just attracted to the fact that for once she had needed him?

7

"WHAT ARE WE going to do now?" she whispered as he reached out and took one of her hands in his. Her palm was cold despite the warmth of the late spring afternoon. Gently, he rubbed her knuckles with a thumb. "I mean we can't go around pretending to be engaged." She paused a moment then asked, "Can we?"

Before Gage could answer, the back door popped open and her father strode out. "I have reserved the country club for three weeks from next Saturday for your engagement party," he said, joining them beneath the tree. "Does that sound agreeable? And I've hired Henri Dubois, the head chef at Café Continental to cater the event."

"You didn't."

"I did!" he exclaimed, as if he'd just single-handedly organized a third-world coup.

Janet sighed inwardly. Her father hadn't let any grass grow under his feet. She had to put a stop to this deception. Now. She opened her mouth to tell him to call the whole thing off and then he said, "I'm so proud of you, darling. Marrying a man like Gage."

"Uh."

You've gotta tell him, rational voice intruded. *No matter how proud he is of you.*

But he's never been proud of her before, impish voice interjected. *Can't you just chill and let her have her moment in the sun?*

She's just going to get third degree sunburns and you're hiding the sunscreen, rational voice argued. *Better to come clean now and get it over with, than stretch out the torture.*

Party pooper, impish voice pouted.

Janet looked over at Gage. He cocked his head expectantly, waiting to see what she would do.

"I can't believe I'm finally going to have a son," her father enthused and pounded Gage on the back.

Her hopes dived like a submarine. There it was again. He wanted Gage, not her. All her jangled emotions—hurt, betrayal, sadness, loss—wadded into a tight ball and lodged uncomfortably in her chest.

Gee, Father, thanks for all your loving support.

"Monday evening I'm ordering the invitations and having them engraved. Would like to go with me to select them, Janet?" he invited.

The lump grew, glazed over by a silly, inexplicable happiness. Her father didn't ask her out on excursions. Ever. And now, because of this faux engagement, he wanted to be with her.

"Sure," she said in spite of herself. "I'd love that."

"I'll pick you up around five-thirty. We'll have

dinner first. My treat. Let me know if you get busy and can't make it.''

"That sounds great. It's a date.''

A date with her father. Her heart thumped heavily. If he didn't leave soon, she was going to burst into tears.

"I interrupted something here, didn't I?'' Her father glanced from her to Gage.

"Yes, sir,'' Gage said.

"I'll go back to the house. You two come in whenever you're ready.''

"Thanks, Dad.''

It was only after her father had gone back inside that Janet realized for the first time in her life she had called her father "Dad.''

"What's it going to be, sweetheart? Do we confess now or later?'' Gage asked. "Either way it's all right with me. If you need a fiancé for a while to improve your relationship with your father, then I'm your man. Just say the word.''

Her eyes met his. It was a dangerous game he was proposing. But if it helped mend years of tension with her father, wasn't it worth the risk?

"Yes,'' she said, her voice shaky. "I want to be your fiancée.''

"WHY IS THERE a man on your roof with a camera?'' CeeCee asked. She and Lacy had trooped inside Janet's condo carrying a bag of bagels and three tall coffees. "And why are a gaggle of reporters hanging around your front door?"

"What?" Janet, who still wore her pajamas, stared at her friends. It was just after nine o'clock on Sunday morning, not even twenty-four hours since she had become "engaged" to Gage Gregory. "What are you talking about?"

"Look out the window." CeeCee pushed aside the kitchen curtains and Janet peered below. Sure enough a bevy of people with notebooks and microphones and cameras milled around the courtyard.

"Why would reporters camp out in front of my building?" she mused.

"Personally," Lacy said, unfurling the newspaper she'd had folded under her arm. "I think it might have something to do with this."

"What?" Janet ran a hand through her mussed hair and stifled a yawn. Lacy passed the newspaper over to her.

On page one of the society section of the *Houston Chronicle* was a huge beefcake photograph of Gage with the headline: Local Physician To Wed Ex-Child Actor, Dr. Gage Gregory.

The lead paragraph read:

HOUSTON—Famous not only for his work in television commercials as a child but for developing a revolutionary medical technique as an adult, skilled Hollywood plastic surgeon turned pediatrician, Gage Gregory is engaged to the daughter of Houston's own illustrious Dr. Niles Hunter.

"Oh no." Janet groaned and sank into a kitchen chair. The whole city had seen this paper. She could just imagine Dr. Jackson having his Sunday brunch and finding out the sleazy way that his two newest doctors had gone off and gotten engaged to each other.

"You've been holding out on us," CeeCee said. "You naughty girl. When did you and Gage decide to get married?"

"Oh, Janet," Lacy said. "Wouldn't it be wonderful if all three of us were married at the same time? We could have a triple wedding. Wouldn't that be romantic and fun?"

"Sorry to burst your bubble, Lace, but Gage and I are not getting married."

"Huh?" CeeCee and Lacy plunked down in chairs on either side of her. "Are you engaged or not?"

"Kinda, sorta, not really. We have no intention of going through with it. We were just pretending to be engaged to make my father happy. But why did Gage leak the story to the media? I could kill him with my bare hands."

"According to the article, it wasn't Gage who broke the story, but your father." Lacy tapped the newspaper with a finger.

Father. Oh well, it all made sense now. He was big buddies with the *Chronicle's* managing editor. She should have known. It also did not escape her notice that it was Gage's name and photograph that appeared in the headline, not hers.

"Did you know Gage once saved Senator McConelly's son from drowning?" Lacy asked.

"So I heard."

"And he used to date A-list actresses." Lacy read aloud and then murmured under her breath, "Oh my goodness, he went out with *her?*"

"Why does that not surprise me?" What did surprise her was why Gage was interested in her when he could have his pick of the world's most beautiful women.

He's not interested in you, rational voice scoffed. *He just loves rescuing people. Don't go off on an ego trip.*

Janet snatched the paper from Lacy's hand. "Please. Enough already. The whole thing is turning into the media snowball from hell."

The phone rang.

Wearily, she picked it up. "Hello?"

"Is this Dr. Janet Hunter?"

"Yes it is."

"Hi, I'm Amanda Jacobs with *Gazing at Stars* magazine and I was wondering if I might ask you a few questions about your relationship with Dr. Gage Gregory."

"No comment," Janet said and hung up.

The phone rang again a few seconds later.

"Let the machine pick up," she told her friends.

They sat sipping coffee, eating bagels and listening to another reporter ask the answering machine for an interview. Another reporter called and then another.

"This is insanity," Janet muttered.

The doorbell chimed.

"Fabulous, now they've muscled past building security." Janet got up, stomped to the foyer, ready to give someone a piece of her mind. The last thing she wanted was to talk to tabloid tattletales about her impending nuptials to the sainted Dr. Hero. She peered through the peephole.

It wasn't a reporter, but rather the sainted Dr. Hero in question.

Big as life and twice as handsome. A lock of sandy brown hair had fallen rakishly over his forehead. He wore navy shorts and a Rice University T-shirt. He looked more like a college student than a doctor with two specialties.

At the sight of him, her heart gave such a strange hop. Janet wondered if she should have an electrocardiogram to make sure all four valves were firing properly. It wasn't normal to experience erratic palpitations simply from looking at a guy. Nothing in the medical textbooks described that phenomenon.

He rang the bell a second time, and Janet realized she must look like the rough end of an industrial mop.

Yikes! She couldn't let him get an eyeful of her dressed like this. Her hair was mussed, and she knew she had sheet creases on her cheek. Not to mention she had yet to brush her teeth this morning.

"CeeCee," she said and darted back through the kitchen. "It's Gage. Let him in while I get dressed."

"Hmm," Lacy mused out loud. "She's worried about how she looks in front of him. Methinks she's got it bad."

"I heard that!" Janet shouted, stripping her pajama top over her head as she ran for the bedroom. "And I do not have it bad."

"Yeah, honey," CeeCee teased. "You got it good."

"Just hush and let him in, will you." Janet was in the bedroom kicking off her pajama bottoms and wriggling into a pair of jeans.

She slipped on a form fitting, V-neck, crimson silk shell, jammed her feet into loafers and dashed into the bathroom. She heard a deep, masculine voice emanating from the living room and CeeCee's bouncy laughter in response to something he'd said.

In the bathroom, she scrubbed her teeth then gargled with mint-flavored mouthwash. She ran a brush thorough her hair, spritzed herself with anise cologne and rolled on Native Sunset—her favorite shade of lipstick.

Stunned, Janet stared into the mirror and realized Lacy was right. She wanted to look good for Gage.

What did that mean?

"Janet," CeeCee called from the living room. "Gage is here."

"Be right there," she called back but not before dragging blush over her cheeks. Then to her reflection she muttered, "You only want to look good for him because he's being so nice. It doesn't mean anything. Really."

Good one, Janet, rational voice said. *Tell us another fairy tale.*

Ignore her, impish voice interjected. *You go, girl!*

Leaving the bathroom, she squelched her divergent impulses and hurried to the living room to find Lacy and CeeCee perched on the couch beside Gage telling him embarrassing personal anecdotes about her.

"And there was the time she got up to give a lecture and she had a pair of panty hose stuck to her wool skirt. Lacy and I tried to signal her but when Janet is in professional mode she doesn't let anything break her concentration." CeeCee chuckled.

"The audience kept laughing," Lacy said. "The louder they laughed, the more professional Janet became. She never let them throw her."

"You guys! Don't tell him all that stuff," Janet protested from the doorway, her face heating at the memory.

To the outside observer she might have appeared controlled and professional at that lecture but inside her confidence level hovered below zero. She had been relieved to discover a pair of panty hose had been the butt of the joke and not her performance. But the truly awful part had been that her father had put in one of his rare appearances. Afterward he had harped on her "shameful display," declaring she had so thoroughly disgraced him that he wouldn't be able to hold his head up at the next American Medical Association meeting.

As if anybody but her father cared about a silly panty hose and static electricity mishap.

Gage's eyes met her. She saw nothing but sympathy reflected there. "It must have been very embarrassing for you."

She shrugged, not wanting him to know how deeply the silly incident had affected her. "I'd forgotten all about it."

CeeCee looked from Janet to Gage, then bounced off the couch. "We were just leaving, weren't we, Lacy."

"But I thought since Jack and Bennett were working we had planned a girls' day out. A trip to the art museum, lunch at Carshon's deli, the latest Sandra Bullock movie." Lacy shook her head and looked bewildered.

CeeCee took Lacy by the arm and tugged her to her feet. "Say goodbye, Lacy."

"Bye-bye." Lacy wriggled her fingers and let CeeCee drag her to the door. "Catch ya later."

When her friends had departed, Janet expelled a deep sigh. "So we've got paparazzi camped outside our building."

Gage smiled apologetically. "'Fraid so. The penalty of getting engaged to Dr. Hero. Instant celebrity."

"Did you know all this would happen?"

"I'd hoped it wouldn't."

''You could have warned me.''

''You could have told me your father was going to call every newspaper in the tristate area.''

''I didn't know,'' she said. ''But I should have realized. My father loves being the center of attention.''

''Then he's going to love this.''

''So what are we going to do?'' She waved a hand as the answer machine picked up on another call.

''We have four choices. One, break down and give them an interview.''

''Oh, please, no. I can't tell a bald-faced lie to reporters.''

''Fair enough.'' Gage nodded. ''I understand that. Or we could simply tell the truth.''

Janet winced. She wasn't ready to do that, either. ''I have to break the news to my father first.''

''Okay.''

''What are the other two options?''

''We could hole up here and cower on a beautiful spring morning.''

''Not my style.''

''Mine, either.''

''Or?''

''We could put on disguises and give them the slip.'' He grinned. ''We could make a day of it. You and I on the town. What do you say?''

THEY STROLLED incognito through the park. Gage wore a felt fedora pulled low over his forehead, sunshades and a lightweight jacket with the collar turned up. He looked like a third-rate P.I. from some Dashiell Hammett novel. She simply had to laugh.

Janet wore a Houston Astros baseball cap and cheap drugstore sunglasses. She felt a little foolish and a lot excited. Impish voice was thrilled with the adventure but rational voice was miffed that her sensible advice to publicly call off the whole engagement hadn't been heeded.

They had left their building separately, each departing through a back entrance, leaving their cars in the lot, and meeting up twenty minutes later on the river walk. The park was filled with joggers and picnicking families. People walked their dogs or tossed them Frisbees. Children threw bread crumbs to the pond ducks. Dappled sunlight sifted through the newly leafed oak trees lining the main walkway. Janet dared to relax in the peaceful environment.

That is until Gage reached over and took her hand. He held on loosely, giving her the option to pull away if she chose.

But she didn't choose. Surprisingly, it felt good to hold hands and he didn't seem to think she was the least bit clingy. So there, Father.

"You look really beautiful today," he said. "I like seeing you like this. Casual, mellow. Happy even."

It was true, she thought. She was happy.

She glanced over at him. He had taken off his sunglasses and was studying her with gentle thoughtfulness. She smiled and ducked her head, feeling strangely shy at his scrutiny. She worried that if he searched long enough he would find something to displease him.

His hand was warm in hers. Warm and firm and comforting. No judgment there. No condemnation. Just simple acceptance.

Gage squeezed her hand. Her pulse throbbed. She raised her head, met his gaze.

"You okay?" he asked.

"Fine." She nodded. She was *way* more than okay and that's what made her nervous. She liked being with him. Liked holding his hand. Liked seeing that sexy smile on his face.

"Was it always so invasive growing up?" she asked. "Reporters hanging around? Paparazzi snapping your picture?"

Gage shrugged. "Only during my heyday as the Grabble Cereal kid. Then again later when I invented the Gregory technique of course. And when I saved Senator McConelly's son from drowning."

He had mixed feelings about being a celebrity. On the one hand it had afforded him opportunities he wouldn't otherwise have possessed. But on the other hand, it was often a shallow life. He preferred medicine to acting, Houston to Hollywood, Janet to the sexiest starlet.

The last thought, and the strong feelings behind it, startled him.

She stopped walking and pulled him gently back to where she stood rooted on the sidewalk beside a tall hedge of red tipped photinias. She reached out and touched his brow between his eyes. "When you concentrate hard you get this little furrow right here."

Her fingers sent a river of fire surging through him. Her nearness damn near made him shiver.

His eyes gobbled her up. From the tasseled loafers on her feet to the faded blue jeans molding to her lithe body to the soft red blouse skimming her breasts to the cute little baseball cap cocked on her head, the bill turned backward. Would he ever get used to looking at her? If he stared at her for a thousand hours, he imagined he would still find something fascinating to see. Reaching over, he slipped off her sunglasses, folded them and stuck them in her shirt pocket.

"What are you doing?" she asked.

"I wanted to see your eyes."

"Why?" Alarmed, she raised a hand to her face. "Is something wrong? Is my makeup smeared?"

"Nothing's wrong." Damn Niles Hunter for making her doubt herself as a woman. "I just needed to see those beautiful eyes the color of velvet twilight."

She gifted him with an ear-to-ear grin that heated Gage's belly straight to his center. God, he loved to make her light up like Christmas.

Whoa! Wait a minute, buddy. Slow this pony down. This is not a real engagement. She doesn't want to be your wife. She doesn't love you and you don't love her. She's not your soul mate, or your other half. You're just helping out a friend. Get your head out of those clouds and your libido back on its leash. Pronto. In fact, may I suggest using the Ultratron titanium double-locking system that even Harry Houdini—at least according to the commercials—couldn't have opened.

Okay. So this wasn't going to be a forever thing. But what was wrong with enjoying the moment?

Hmm, what was wrong with that? Oh, about a hundred million things. Least of which was getting hurt again.

He opened his mouth to lay down the ground rules, to tell her they were walking a dangerous tightrope. One wrong move and they were both going to tumble. His mouth opened but no words came out.

Inches separated them. Her breasts were almost level with his chest. Her chin was just below his.

And her eyes. Oh man, those eyes. Drilling right into his. Sharp and intelligent, independent and strong, unflinching and principled. Something odd inside his chest pinged.

He couldn't be falling for her. No, not he. He was just thrown a little off balance, his perspective knocked askew by those indigo eyes. He just needed something temporary to hold on to until he regained his composure.

Gage reached out and touched her hand.

She made a small startled noise at the contact.

His blood surged. The sudden tenderness in her face, shining through all those defenses floored him.

So what if they weren't soul mates? So what if they weren't going to get married? So what if this was all a sham for the benefit of her parents?

It felt right to run his hands up her arms, over her shoulders and past her throat to cup that sweet-but-disconcerted chin in his palms.

What felt even more right was to push his fedora back, dip his head and capture those lips. To glide his mouth lightly over hers again and again with just enough pressure to make her sigh for more.

When he finally let go and stepped back, her eyelashes fluttered open. He found himself lost once more in those beguiling depths.

"You don't have to kiss me," she whispered. "When there's no one around to see. I don't want us to pretend with each other. It'll make things too confusing. You know. For later. When we break up."

As if he wasn't already confused enough. As if he wasn't already regretting the break up of their fictional engagement.

He had come to Texas to start a new life and instead he found himself repeating the same old patterns, running from the same old paparazzi, helping some beautiful damsel in distress.

Same old Dr. Hero.

But despite all rational arguments to the contrary, he couldn't stop himself from kissing her again. And she didn't put up one protest. Her arms went around his neck, her lips sought his just as eagerly as he sought hers. He could feel her heart thrumming against his chest they were so close.

What was going on here? Why this intense sparking between them? Was it merely the sense of adventure, or was there something more? Something strongly elemental drawing them into each other's arms.

Then without warning a man with several cameras around his neck, leaped from the bushes and started trying to take pictures. Behind him tumbled an attractive woman dressed in four-inch heels and a purple suit with a very short skirt. She had a tape recorder on a strap around her shoulder and a microphone in her hand.

"Amanda Jacobs, *Gazing at Stars* magazine," she said. "Dr. Gregory, can you give us a few minutes of your time?"

Gage winced. He hated putting Janet through this invasion of her privacy. Instinctively, he snatched her hand in his. One concern was paramount in his head. Protect her. At all costs.

"Run," he said, "we can outpace them."

They took off across the grass, sprinting around park benches. Dust-gray pigeons flew up before them. Amanda Jacobs's heels clattered against the pavement, but soon both she and her middle-aged, out-of-shape cameraman fell behind.

They zigzagged around the pond, snaking past hot dog vendors, dashing by a group of startled sunbathers.

Gage looked back. The cameraman had doubled over to catch his breath and Amanda Jacobs was busy berating him, but he and Janet didn't stop.

Hand-in-hand they ran. Their palms forged. She

kept up with him step for step. She wasn't even breathing hard. Her whole body tingled. She felt her cheeks flush with color. She felt positively radiant.

Fleeing from paparazzi must agree with her, Janet realized. She felt as if she were a kid again, streaking through the playground, no worries except not getting tagged. Her laughter bubbled up loud and clear, filling the air. Joy fizzed through her. When was the last time she had felt this free? Never.

Was it the silly game they were playing? Was it the fact she'd gained her father's respect at last?

Or was it Gage?

She glanced over at him, found he was watching her. He squeezed her hand, winked. Her feelings of goodwill grew, and filled her chest to bursting. He laughed with her. A beautiful sound. They were laughing together. Laughing and looking and longing for something inexplicable.

Gage was so busy staring at her, he didn't see the wooden mile marker on the jogging trail up ahead.

"Gage, look out!" she cried.

But it was too late.

Ooph!

The post caught him low in the belly. Her hand broke away from his at the impact. His fedora flew off. He somersaulted in the air and ended up on his back in the grass staring up at the cloudless sky and her worried face.

Great.

Sprawled out on the soft ground as he was, Gage

knew he must look like some hapless cartoon character. Now he knew how Charlie Brown felt when Lucy kept pulling the football out from under him.

"Are you all right?" Janet gently patted his cheek, first one side and then the other. "Gage, speak to me."

Way to impress the lady, Gregory.

The breath had been knocked from his lungs. He couldn't say a word. But he could look. He searched her eyes, telegraphing his feelings, telling her he was okay.

She bent lower over him, her hair falling against the side of his face. It tickled his nose in a nice way.

"I'm so sorry."

"Don't," he managed to wheeze and propped himself up on his elbows. "Don't you dare."

Her lips were inches from his now. One lone tear slid from her cheek and dropped to his mouth. The salty flavor of that bitter tear gave him strength. This was very important. He had to let her know exactly how wonderful she was.

"But..."

"Shhh. Stop blaming yourself for everything. You've been taking responsibility for things beyond your control for too many years."

"I...am I that transparent?" Her confused expression tugged at his gut.

"You're a terrific person, Janet. Beautiful, kind, understanding. A brilliant doctor. If your father can't see that, then he's a blind fool who doesn't deserve your love.''

"You really think so?'' She blinked back the tears and gave him a smile so sweet his heart jumped to his throat.

"I know so.''

He ached to taste those lips again. Gently, he pulled her down. She placed one knee on either side of his prostrate body and lowered her chest to his.

They were pressed hip to hip against the earth, held together by their gazes. The pressure of her body drove him wild with desire. He forgot everything. In that moment he was simply a man and she was simply the woman he wanted.

"Now where were we?'' he murmured. "Before we were so rudely interrupted.''

She lowered her mouth to his. Her tongue was both wicked and pure at the same time, her breath warm, her taste heavenly. All sorts of tumultuous thoughts tumbled through his head. Hot, sexy thoughts that included some long-held fantasies.

Snap. Click. Whirl.

"What the hell?''

In unison, they turned their heads and looked over at the grinning cameraman taking shot after shot of their compromised position.

Amanda Jacobs was on her knees in the dirt beside them. She thrust the microphone in Janet's face. "So tell the whole world, honey, just how good in bed is the hunkiest bachelor alive?''

8

JANET GLANCED down at the ring Gage had placed on her finger that afternoon in the shopping mall. It was a cubic zirconia in a cheap setting purchased for appearance's sake. It meant nothing. Nothing at all.

So why couldn't she stop holding her left hand out in front of her and staring at the stupid thing?

For that matter, why couldn't she stop having so much fun with him? After their run-in with the overzealous Amanda Jacobs, they'd had lunch at a local pizza hangout. It had been the best darned pizza she had ever eaten. Then they'd played video games in an arcade as if they were twelve. They had also had their photo taken in one of those booths with the cheesy black curtains. Janet had the snapshot—they were both sticking out their tongues—tucked into her front pocket.

In the picture, she looked totally unlike herself. Silly and carefree and girlish.

"Our official engagement photo," Gage had said when he handed it to her and she'd experienced this weird, sappy sensation in the pit of her stomach. A serious "what if?" scenario started playing in her brain until rational voice quickly shut it down. She was not going to indulge those ridiculous fantasies.

"So this is what it's like being engaged to Gage Gregory," she said lightly.

"For better or worse, yes. I guess it is."

They were walking toward their building, the afternoon almost gone, when they spied the contingency of reporters still camped out on the front stoop.

"They're more persistent than flies," Gage muttered.

"This is nuts." She shook her head.

"Gotta face 'em sometime. You ready?"

She nodded. Hand in hand, they ran the gauntlet. Gage shielded her with his arm as they pushed their way through the throng. Once inside, the door firmly locked behind them, Janet turned to view the tumult through the window.

"Aren't you glad we're not really getting married? Can you imagine the actual wedding bedlam?"

"No," she said in all honesty. "I can't."

Then through the miniblinds she saw something on the street that struck terror into her heart. She plucked at Gage's sleeve. "Oh, no, here comes my own bit of insanity."

From a white sedan parked at the curb, Gracie and a smiling, round-faced man Janet didn't know, emerged carrying boxes in their arms. Blithely they made their way toward the crowd.

The reporters fell upon Gracie and her companion like mosquitoes on beachgoers.

''We've got to stop her from talking. Once she gets wound up, she'll never quit,'' Janet said.

Determined to muzzle her mother before she could start in on her Baby Predicate spiel and Nadine's amazing powers of prognostication, Janet flung open the door.

''Mother, in here. Quick!''

Gracie beamed at her. ''Oh my dear, isn't this exciting. Everyone wants to ask me about you.''

The reporters were hurtling questions fast and furious. Janet dragged her mother and her male friend inside while Gage slammed the security door behind them. He hustled everyone toward the elevator and relieved Gracie of the heavy box in her arms.

''Janet, Gage,'' Gracie said, as the four of them entered Janet's condo. ''This is Sam Pinkerton.'' She flashed the man beside her a smile. He grinned back.

''How do you do, Dr. Hunter, it's a great pleasure to meet you. You too, Dr. Gregory.'' He sat his box on the floor then shook their hands.

''And you are…?'' Janet said, raising an eyebrow. She didn't like the way Gracie kept glancing at the man. As if she couldn't get enough of looking at him.

''Well, sweetie, it's a surprising story.'' Gracie blushed. ''Sam and I used to know each other in high school, but his family moved away and we lost touch. Imagine my surprise when I'm looking in the phone book last night for a wedding planner and lo and behold there was Sam's name. So I called him up to see if he was indeed my Sam Pinkerton and *ta-da*. Turns out Sam's a widower with three daughters of his own. He took over his wife's wedding planning business after she died. His oldest, Jenny, is due to deliver her first baby around Christmas.'' She clapped her hands and finally took a breath. ''Isn't this fantastic?''

Sam was Gracie's high school sweetheart? Her mother hadn't said as much, but the fact that Sam couldn't take his eyes off Gracie gave their secret away.

''We've brought along samples of his work.'' Grace indicated the boxes with a flourish. ''You wouldn't believe the choices. You can have a Renaissance wedding where everyone comes in costume and speaks Old English. Or you can get married in a hot air balloon over the ocean. Or you can tie the knot on a carousel in an amusement park.''

''Mother, I don't mean to be rude to Mr. Pinkerton, but this isn't the time or the place. We're not getting married in 17th century England, nor in a hot air balloon nor on a ride at Six Flags.''

''I think in your enthusiasm you've overwhelmed the young people, Gracie,'' Sam Pinkerton said. ''Perhaps they need more time.''

''You're right, Sam.'' Gracie blushed prettily. ''I do have a tendency to get carried away with a project.''

Understatement of the century.

Janet could only stare, openmouthed. She'd never seen her mother curbed so easily. What was going on here?

Sam smiled. "Your wedding can be as simple or as elaborate as you wish. Obviously, with all the goings-on downstairs you're not in the mood to talk wedding arrangements right now. I'll just leave my boxes and you can look through them at your convenience."

"Can't we just show them the fabulous honeymoon suite at that resort in Australia?" Gracie asked.

"All in good time." Sam touched her arm tenderly.

Janet noticed how similar they looked. Both short of stature, both with red hair and identical smiles. Like matching bookends.

Amazing.

What was the world coming to? Paparazzi chasing her in the park. Her father asking her to dinner. Her mother reunited with an old...*flame?* And then there was Gage who kept kissing her as if he really meant it.

Her world had skittered helter-skelter out of check and she didn't know how to regain control. It was all too much to absorb.

"Everybody," she said. "Please. I need to be alone."

DURING THE freak show that followed the broadcasting of their "engagement," work was Janet's only salvation. She kept busy, offering to take on extra duties just to keep her mind occupied and her body out of the cramped office she shared with Gage.

On Monday, she had gone to dinner with her father,

then on to pick out invitations to the engagement party. She tried to work up the courage to tell him the truth about the engagement but for the first time in her life he'd spoken to her as an equal. It was a heady experience and she'd been unable to break the bad news.

On Tuesday, the crowd of reporters grew, eager for a glimpse of the woman who'd stolen Gage Gregory's heart. She wore dark glasses, kept her head down and repeatedly muttered, "no comment," whenever someone thrust a microphone in her face. If this was fame, give her anonymity any old day. No wonder Gage had bolted from Hollywood.

"Morning, Dr. Hunter," Annie, the receptionist, greeted her on Wednesday morning when she stopped by the front desk to pick up her messages.

"Umm, thanks."

"You've broken all the nurses' hearts, dontcha know. Snapping up the sexiest bachelor doctor to ever grace these hallways."

Yeah, well tell them to dry their weeping eyes, he'll be back on the market soon enough.

Why did that idea strike her as dismal? She didn't want a real engagement with Gage.

Did she?

Perish the thought, rational voice said.

Why? impish voice asked. *Can you think of anyone more sumptuous to be engaged to?*

She'd rather not be engaged to anyone, rational voice responded in a condescending manner. *She's a smart, independent doctor. She doesn't need a man to complete her, you ninny.*

Hey, there's no reason to call me names just because she listens to you more than she does me.

Not lately she doesn't.

Maybe that's because she's beginning to realize you're no fun.

Janet shook her head to clear her mind of her internal warring factions and held out her palm to Annie. "Messages?"

"Oh, you've got a bucket load of them." Annie reached under her desk and produced a fat manila envelope stuffed to the bursting with scraps of paper.

"Are these messages all from patients?"

Annie shook her head. "Nope."

"The media," she sighed.

"Yep. And one message from your mother. She's got a special tea she wants you to try. Apparently it helps with fertility."

Mother! For pity's sake.

"If she calls again, tell her I'm too busy to talk."

"What about these others?"

Janet sighed. "I don't want this media frenzy to affect our work. Only forward me information dealing with patient care." She waved a hand at the pile. "You can throw the rest of those away."

Annie dug in the envelope and pulled out a piece of paper. "You mean you don't want to give *Entertainment Tonight* an interview?"

"No."

"How 'bout *People* magazine."

"No, Annie."

"I guess this offer to pose for *Playboy* is out of the question."

"What! Give me that." Janet snatched the message from the receptionist's hand and stared at it. "Oh, for the love of Pete."

She crumpled the paper and tossed it in the trash can. "Only information dealing with patients. Got it?"

"Yes, ma'am. I mean doctor."

Shaking her head, Janet hurried down the hall for the safety of her office. She had no notion of what she was getting herself into when she'd decided to pretend to be Gage's fiancée. All she had wanted was to make her father proud of her and what she had gotten was a three-ring circus without a ringmaster.

Engagement parties and engraved invitations. Fertility teas and batty wannabe grandmas. Paparazzi stalking her. If she wasn't so worried, she would have to laugh.

The Ice Princess in demand as a pinup queen. Ludicrous.

And yet, a small fissure of pleasure careened through her. For the first time in her life she was in demand as something other than a doctor. Oddly enough, she felt feminine and wanted.

But it was only because of Gage.

On Thursday morning she arrived in the office to find Gage standing at the window staring out at the parking lot. She caught her breath at the sight of him and placed a hand to her stomach to still the butterflies dancing there. His shoulders were silhouetted by the morning light pouring through the half-open blinds.

He was so unbelievably handsome. No wonder he attracted the attention of the paparazzi. What wasn't to like? He'd even captured the heart and imagination of her father and that was no easy feat.

She closed the door behind her. Gage turned to meet her gaze.

"Hi," he said softly. "How you holding up amidst the craziness?"

"Me?" It touched her that he was concerned about her welfare. "What about you? I'm so sorry for all this."

He shrugged casually but his eyes looked weary. She had the strangest urge to wrap her arms around him. "There you go again, accepting responsibility for something that isn't your fault."

"Part of this is my fault."

"It's got nothing to do with you. I can't escape my celebrity. No matter how hard I try." He inhaled deeply. "I just want to be a good doctor but this brouhaha gets in the way."

"You're an excellent doctor."

"I got asked to do an interview for *Playgirl*." Gage changed the subject. "Can you believe that?"

"I can go you one better." She flashed him a smile. "*Playboy* wants me to pose."

"You're pulling my leg," he said. "You wouldn't really pose. Would you?"

"Would that bother you?"

"I'm your fiancé," he growled but his eyes teased. "What do you think?"

Before she could respond to his question, Gage's intercom buzzed.

He leaned over the desk and flipped the switch. "Yes."

"Gage, good morning." Dr. Peter Jackson's voice filtered over the speaker. "Is Dr. Hunter in there with you?"

"Yes, sir."

"Splendid. May I see you both in my office?"

"We'll be right there." Gage switched the intercom off.

"We're in trouble," she said.

"Hey, slow down. Don't jump to conclusions. Maybe he just wants to congratulate us on our impending nuptials."

"Yeah, and maybe there really is a Santa Claus, Virginia. I think he's ticked off about the persistent mob in the parking lot."

Gage took her hand. "No point speculating. Let's go find out."

They found Peter lounging in his leather chair. He gave them a tight smile when they walked through the door. "Have a seat." He motioned them to two chairs positioned in front of his desk.

They sat.

"I think it's wonderful that you two have found love with each other," Peter said. "But I hope your relationship is not going to cause a problem for the clinic, or that you'll have any problems working as a team."

"No, sir," Janet said. "I can assure you that our relationship won't affect our work."

Gage knew fibbing to Peter was killing her. Letting her father believe they were engaged was one thing but perpetuating the masquerade was taking its toll. He understood her conflict. On the one hand she was a scrupulously honest woman with the highest moral standards, but on the other hand she was still a little girl, willing to do anything possible to gain her father's love and attention even if it mean violating her own values.

"That's good to hear." Dr. Jackson steepled his fingers and leaned forward. "However, I'm afraid the media chaos is already creating a disturbance. Our patients are finding it difficult getting past those reporters."

"The media circus is entirely my fault," Gage apologized. "If it wasn't for my past celebrity, they wouldn't be the least bit interested in my marriage plans."

Marriage plans.

It felt weird to think of himself as a groom again. Except he wasn't getting married. He was simply helping a friend in need.

Like Pauline?

No, not like Pauline, this was different.

How was it different?

This was Janet.

And?

You're not really going to marry her.

"I think you two should take a few days off until this blows over," Dr. Jackson said.

"What?" Janet's voice rose and her brow furrowed.

"For the good of our patients."

"But what about our practice?" Gage asked.

Dr. Jackson waved a hand. "Not to worry. Phil and I will take calls for you this weekend. He pulled a key from his drawer and tossed it across the desk to Gage. "I have a houseboat on Lake Travis. It's at your disposal. Take the rest of the week off starting now. Consider it an early wedding present."

"Sir, this is far too generous, we can't accept." Gage pushed the key back to his boss, not because he didn't relish the thought of spending a long weekend alone on the lake with Janet, but because he did.

"My reasons are selfish." Peter nudged the key back in his direction. "Getting you two out of town is in the best interest of the clinic. I can't take no for an answer. The houseboat is being stocked with food and supplies as I speak. Have a good time."

Gage took a deep breath. Here it was all over again. Running from the media, playing silly hide-and-seek games. All the things he thought he'd escaped. It wasn't fair to put Janet under this kind of pressure.

She didn't deserve to be hounded away from the one thing she loved above all else—her job.

He glanced over at her. Her knuckles were bone white from gripping the chair arms. Obviously, she didn't want to do this any more than he did. "Really, Dr. Jackson, we can't accept," Gage said.

"I'm sorry, Gage, Janet," their boss replied. "I'm not able to give you the option of refusing. To protect the clinic and your careers, you've got to get out of town until things cool off. I really must insist."

WE'RE GONNA BE *alone with Gagey-pooh for three whole days and nights,* impish voice sang to the tune of some boppy oldies number as Janet packed for the weekend.

Will you knock it off, you're giving me a headache, rational voice grumbled.

Janet felt as if she were being pulled in opposite directions. Her old self on one side of a giant fault line, this new unexpected self manifesting on the other. What was happening to her?

"This is so great, you and Doctor Handsome going away for the weekend," CeeCee stuck her head in the bedroom door. She and Lacy had dropped by to ask nosy questions about her trip. She loved her friends, but sometimes they could be annoying.

"Do you think he could be The One?" Lacy asked, coming to stand beside CeeCee.

"How many times do I have to tell you Lacy, I

don't believe in all that thunderbolt nonsense,'' Janet sighed, exasperated.

"Don't believe or won't believe?'' Lacy nodded knowingly.

"What's the difference?'' She shrugged.

"You'll find out.''

"Look, I haven't been struck by a bolt of lightning or cursed by a gypsy or succumbed to an astrologer's prediction or anything like that. Gage is a nice guy. End of story.''

"And you're going to be spending three days alone with him.'' CeeCee plopped down on the bed.

"If Gage isn't special then why are you acting so different?'' Lacy asked.

"I'm not acting different,'' Janet denied.

"Oh yes you are,'' CeeCee and Lacy cried in unison.

She looked at them as if they'd lost their minds. "In what way?''

"Humming love songs under your breath,'' Lacy said.

"I don't do that!''

"Oh no? I could have sworn you were in here singing *Can't Help Myself*.''

"You're imagining things.''

"And,'' CeeCee pointed out. "You've started wearing more makeup.''

"And sexier clothes,'' Lacy chimed in.

They were enjoying teasing her, Janet realized and secretly, she admitted the truth. Lately, despite the craziness of the paparazzi surrounding their "engagement," she was feeling lighter, freer...happier.

But it wasn't because of Gage, she assured herself. It was because she had gained her father's approval at long last.

CeeCee leaned over and rifled through Janet's suitcase. "Let's see. Bathing suit, check. Shorts, check. Skimpy tops, check. Oh, yeah. You've changed."

"Get out of there." Janet tried to close the suitcase.

"Wait! What's this?" CeeCee shrieked gleefully and pulled out a pair of thong panties Janet had purchased that afternoon. The darn things had been an impulse buy. She'd never worn a thong in her life—they weren't her style—and she couldn't explain why she had picked them up, except she'd obviously been possessed by impish voice. "Omigosh, you in a thong. Who'd have thunk it? That's so great."

"Gimme those." Janet snatched the scarlet underwear from CeeCee's hand and stuffed them back into the suitcase.

CeeCee struggled to keep a straight face. "I trust you're packing condoms along with that thong. Gage gets one look at you in that thing and you're done for."

Janet's face flamed. Dammit, she did not blush.

"Janet's gonna have sex." CeeCee giggled.

She wasn't planning on having sex with Gage. Not at all. The thought had never entered her head.

Liar, liar, thong on a four-alarm fire.

Okay, the thought had entered her head, but she'd squelched it. "Go home," she told CeeCee and Lacy.

It was bad enough having impish voice in her head echoing CeeCee's sentiments without having her best friends in on the conspiracy.

"We'll see you when you get back," Lacy said, tugging CeeCee off the bed. "Have a great time and don't do anything we wouldn't do."

Heaven forbid.

She walked her friends to the door, feeling oddly disconcerted, then went back to her packing.

Maybe you should pick up some condoms, impish voice whispered. *Just in case.*

Janet glanced at her watch. Gage would be down to pick her up in less than thirty minutes. She didn't have much time to make it to the drugstore and back. She stepped to the dresser and picked up her car keys.

As she turned and headed for the door, Janet heard rational voice's whine of despair. *What in the world has come over you?*

9

GAGE HAD a single goal in mind.

Show Janet a good time. Clearly, the woman worked too hard and she desperately needed a little R&R. If he could just get her to relax, as she had last Sunday, he knew they would find a satisfactory solution to their dilemma.

Fact of the matter, he liked the thought of Janet as his fiancée. Probably too much.

Also, he very much liked the notion of making love to her.

Definitely, he liked that idea too much. Making love to her was all he could think about. Sharing an office with her had become downright painful.

So how did he expect to survive this extended weekend with just the two of them. All alone.

How? By keeping a rigorous schedule and showing her a good time. He'd already made the reservations. They would go jetskiing and swimming and canoeing. They would hike nature trails and go fishing and build a campfire. After dark, they would lie on their backs in the cool grass and gaze up at the stars.

Busy, busy, busy. Anything to keep his mind off the sensuous feel of her soft skin, the delightful taste of her tender lips, the melodic sound of her sweet laughter.

On Saturday night, they would drive into town, go two-stepping at a local country-and-western nightclub. He would show her a great time, by gum, or die trying.

But as it turned out, all his plans came to naught.

The rain started the moment they pulled up to the dock beside Peter's houseboat on Thursday evening. It took them only twenty minutes to unpack and explore the boat.

They quickly discovered there was no television, which left them with nothing to do but gaze into each other's eyes.

A bad, bad thing.

Because gazing into those incredible indigo depths made him want to take her to bed on the spot.

Janet seemed as nervous as he felt, circling the houseboat repeatedly. She snapped on the radio, then turned it right back off again. She drummed her fingernails on the kitchen cabinet, then inhaled deeply and glanced over at him. "Well, here we are."

"Yeah."

She peered out the picture window that would have given a beautiful view of the lake if not for the downpour. "It's raining harder."

"Yes."

"Let's hope it lets up by tomorrow," she said.

"I'm sure it will."

He was so aware of her. The delicious scent of her

cologne filled his nostrils. The way she threaded her fingers through her hair drove spikes of desire clean through him. The manner in which she kept slanting him furtive glances made him ache to take her into his arms and satisfy the lurking question in her eyes.

He stepped across the kitchen toward her.

She hovered in the doorway, an uncertain expression on her face. "Gage, I..."

He was standing so close he could smell her shampoo. "Yes?" he hadn't meant to growl in a low, sexy tone, it just came out that way.

The next thing he knew she forcefully took his face in both her hands and kissed him.

Oh, how she kissed him.

Like she wanted so much more than kisses.

After a moment, he pulled back, gasping raggedly and gaping at her in disbelief. "Janet, I don't want you to think that just because we're isolated here together for three days that this has to lead to anything."

"Shut up," she said, "and kiss me."

So kiss her he did. He was not one to refuse a lady's heartfelt request.

Janet was like a woman possessed. She wanted him. Had to have him. And she had no idea where this unbridled passion had come from.

Oh, this...this loss of control was what she feared from the moment she had learned they would be sharing an office together.

Lust, lust, lust, lust, lust, impish voice cried. *What a wonderful force of nature it is.*

Her whole body tingled with shivery awareness. Her mind was completely numb, all blood supply being used to support her sweating palms and her pounding heart and her heavy loins.

Is this smart? Is this prudent? rational voice protested.

Ignore her. Surrender to the moment.

Gage pulled back again. "Janet," he croaked, "what are you doing?"

"What does it feel like I'm doing?"

"Are you sure?" He looked at once, both startled and pleased.

"Gage, I want you and I think you want me. No big deal, right."

"Honey, I do want you. So badly I can taste it, but this is a very big deal for me."

"Really?" She blinked. She was kind of surprised. She figured Gage had had lots of sexual encounters and she'd just supposed he took them rather lightly.

"Really."

Lightning flashed. Thunder rolled. Now was the time to back out.

Helplessly, she traced a finger down his jaw. He had done so much for her. He'd helped her to lighten up, to take herself and life less seriously. She wanted to be near him. She wanted him to stroke her hair, to kiss her lips again.

Who was she kidding? She wanted him to do a

whole lot more than that. Did such blatant desires make her weak?

Surreptitiously, she watched him. His face was tense, worried even. Not at all his usual confident, carefree self. She'd misjudged him from the start, thinking him superficial, but instead she'd discovered he was a man who cared deeply about people. And he cared enough about her to pretend to be her fiancé, even when he'd known the complications that would ensue.

Her heart swelled to bursting. No man had ever made such sacrifices for her.

Doubt clouded her thinking. Was he simply Dudley Do Right determined to untie Nell from the railroad tracks and thwart Snidely Whiplash? After they made love would he flash Nell a glistening white smile, climb aboard his trusty steed and gallop away into the mountains? Was that why he wanted her to be sure? Or would he swing Nell into his arms and kiss her within an inch of her life and tell her just how special she was to him? Honestly, which scenario was the most frightening?

Frankly, happily ever after scared her much more than a three-night stand.

Stop thinking, impish voice said. *Stop thinking and just go with the flow. Feel.*

Feel. Ah, yes. Luxuriate in the sensation of Gage's tongue strumming ribbons of pleasure throughout her body. Every touch was magical, sparking fires of awareness deep inside her soul.

"I'm so hungry for you," she whimpered when he stopped kissing her for a moment to catch his breath. Her fingers fiddled with the buttons on his shirt.

"Babe, I'm starved for you. Famished, malnourished, underfed." He threaded his fingers through her hair, cupped the back of her head in his palm. His brown eyes glistened with a searing heat so powerful, Janet gasped and placed a hand to her stomach.

"More," she whimpered. "More."

He eagerly complied.

Flesh fused with flesh. Tongues danced. Strong hands skimmed down the curve of her spine, setting her neuro sensors ablaze as his fingers burned a trail to her waist, then lower still to gently knead her buttocks.

She could feel his erection throbbing through the denim of his white shorts, straining hard against the zipper.

He groaned. She moaned.

They never made it to the bedroom.

When impish voice broke through and shouted right out loud, "Make love to me, Gage, right here, right now," he lowered her to the floor and they clung together in a mad frenzy of need.

Clothing flew across the room. Shoes bounced off the wall. Thunder shook the houseboat, but they were oblivious. They took no notice of anything except each other.

His finger skipped down her skin, from her shoulder, past her bare breasts, to the curve of her belly and beyond.

"What do you know." He hooked one finger around the strap of her red lace thong. "You do wear sexy undies."

"What did you think I wore? Prison warden underpants?"

"Yeah." He grinned. "Kinda."

"Oh you!" She tickled him lightly in the ribs.

The next thing she knew Gage was wearing her panties on his head. They were laughing and gasping and kissing and nuzzling.

"Janet," he murmured, his eyes glazed as he stared at her body mesmerized. "You're incredible."

"So are you," she said and meant every word. He was everything she'd never dared dream of. Everything and so much more. Nothing had ever felt so great.

And things quickly got a whole lot better.

She emitted a low cry of pleasure when Gage lowered his head and touched his hot, wet tongue to her moist, feminine heat. He suckled, tasted, feasted then drove her madly, wildly into a soul-screaming orgasm.

Limply, she panted and crooned his name like a mantra. Methodically, he kissed his way back up her belly, not missing a single spot on his journey to her nipples.

Once there, he laved the tender flesh with the tip of his raspy tongue, abrading her gently with a firm, steady pressure that had her crying out once more and grabbing fistfuls of his hair in her hands.

She quivered and a fresh heat coiled in the pit of her belly. The coil built and grew until she was wound tight as a new watch, her entire body thrumming with energy.

She wanted him inside her. Filling her up.

And she told him so.

"Wait," he panted. "We can't."

"Why not?" Startled, and aching with a sharp need, she raised up on her elbows.

"No condom."

"Check the pocket of my pants."

He grinned. "You sly vixen you."

They made love on the kitchen floor. Below her, the tile pressed cool against her naked back. Above her, Gage's hard muscled flesh sizzled hot against her naked front.

From the kitchen they moved to the living room, changing positions and doing awesome things in a chair that made Janet yell with unbridled enjoyment.

Couch pillows flew. Gage pulled her into his lap, and lowered her onto his burgeoning erection.

Ride 'em cowgirl.

The houseboat swayed in its moorings. The thick ropes holding the boat in place creaked.

Perspiration slicked their bodies. The musky scent of their lovemaking filled the air. Their kisses were furious, hard, wonderful. In all his thirty-five years, Gage had never experienced the like.

He wanted to push himself deeper inside her until they were merged forever. No longer two separate people, but one.

Harder, faster. Their passion for each other escalated, pushing them over the edge into uncharted territory.

Yearning, burning, they couldn't get enough.

He'd never known lovemaking could be like this. Never realized just how complex his Janet was.

Goddess, pagan, angel, devil.

She'd been holding herself in reserve for so long, keeping her emotions at bay. Was it any wonder that when the woman finally let loose, she let go in a big way?

And he'd been the one to release her passion. His heart swelled with pride.

Incredible.

He felt as if he'd received a treasure more precious than French truffles.

She was his every fantasy come to life. This was what he had been missing, yet secretly longing for. An equal, a partner, a woman whose sexual appetites matched his own.

Pure heaven.

They went through one condom, two, three and all the rooms in the houseboat. If the rain outside had been sprinkles instead of a deluge, he had no doubt they would have made love on the outside deck, too.

As it was, they finally ended up in the bedroom two hours later exhausted and spent.

Gage pulled her snugly against him, her bottom pressed into his hips. He wrapped one strong arm around her waist and curled his body around her like a protective shell.

No man had ever cherished her, revered her, treasured her this way, Janet realized. Sated, she lay there listening to the soft sounds of his breathing and reveling in their closeness.

Just before she drifted off to sleep she came to one stunning conclusion.

Never, had she ever, been so happy.

FOR TWO DAYS it rained and for those days and nights they made love. At times it was romantic—a sweet seduction in the bathtub complete with bubbles and candles and expensive champagne. At other times, like the first night, it was fierce—or scientific.

And it was playful—a romp in a tent set up on the living room floor. First they role-played island girl and sailor. Then later, head cheerleader and quarterback lost in the wilderness. Later still, it was plain old cowboy and Indian princess.

They showered together, sponging each other's bodies. They rifled through Dr. Jackson's extensive CD collection and ending up dancing to everything from Sinatra to Tommy Dorsey to the Rolling Stones.

They played strip poker and strip Go Fish and strip Old Maid. Giggling like teenagers they hand-fed each other. Strawberries and cream. Oysters and olives.

Chocolate and honey. Whatever sexy things they could find in the refrigerator.

Shades of *9 1/2 Weeks*.

Janet simply could not get enough of him. They made love, ate, slept and made love some more.

Gage painted her toenails and then they made love. Gage gave her a massage and then they made love. Gage brushed her hair and then they made love.

And she let him.

"I want to pamper you, Janet," he murmured. "You've been deprived too long and you deserve it."

At first, it was difficult, letting herself relax and feel comfortable with Gage tending to her every whim. It was hard for her to fathom a man who actually wanted to meet her needs. But as his fingers rubbed her skin, as he industriously applied Luminescent Red to her toenails, as he gently slid the brush over her scalp, she slowly gave way to the splendid indulgence of being spoiled.

Thirty years of repressed sexuality erupted from her like fireworks on the Fourth of July. Hot, spectacular, blisteringly bright. Nothing in her experience had ever compared to this weekend. It was like her birthday, Christmas, a trip to Disney World all rolled into one. It was even better than the day she aced the MCAT.

She was having so much fun!

And the whole time, rational voice did not once rear her ugly head to spoil the party.

In fact, Janet was beginning to worry. What had happened to her conscience? Where was that stern, practical voice that had followed her throughout her life, constantly telling her why hard work was good and fun was bad? Had impish voice bound and gagged rational voice and left her for dead in the basement of Janet's id?

But she wasn't worried enough to actually try to excavate rational voice. She was kind of enjoying the respite.

She awoke on Sunday morning to bright sunlight spilling through the window of the houseboat, and the glorious smell of Gage on her skin. She stretched in total happiness, then turned her head and spied the clock. No wait, it was Sunday afternoon! She hadn't slept past noon since she'd worked the night shift as an intern. She started to scramble from the bed but Gage reached out and grabbed her hand.

"Stay, linger," he said. "No hurry."

"Bathroom."

"Oh, okay, but then come right back."

"You got it." Giggling helplessly, foolishly, Janet dashed to the bathroom and caught a glimpse of herself in the mirror.

Who was that woman?

Her eyes were bright, her cheeks flushed, her hair sexily mussed. She grinned.

She looked like a woman in love.

Love! *Love?*

Her heart did this crazy, erratic little dance at the notion.

Janet's in love, impish voice sang to the tune of Rickie Lee Jones's *Chuck E's in Love.*

No wrong. She was not in love.

"Jan-et," Gage coaxed in a singsong.

At the sound of him calling her name, goose bumps sprang up her arms. She hurried from the bathroom to find him lying in bed, striking a provocative *GQ*-type pose with the covers thrown back.

Her blood heated.

He crooked a finger at her. "Come here, my sweet."

She went.

He was hard and ready. He reached for her. "My darling," he said, affecting a Latin accent. "It seems years have passed since we were together."

Then they were making love again.

Afterward, Janet lay in the curve in his arm, shaken by the depth of her emotions.

Okay, so they'd had stupendous sex—well, actually, it had been way more than stupendous but the word for it didn't exist, not even in an unabridged dictionary—that didn't mean anything had changed between them. They weren't really engaged, nor were they going to be. They had simply shared a wonderful weekend together. Best to leave it at that.

Right?

But why, why, why? impish voice whined. *I wanna wake up everyday and find him in my bed.*

You should have thought about the consequences before you so freely debased yourself, rational voice sniped, roaring back to life in full bitch-on-wheels mode.

Funny, Janet thought, how rational voice sounded an awful lot like her father. She'd never noticed that before.

It's more than sex and you know it. You're in love with him, admit it, impish voice begged.

She swallowed hard. Could she really be in love?

She turned her head and saw that Gage had been studying her intently.

Oh gosh. He was so handsome.

And hot, impish voice added. *Don't forget he's hotter than all the Hollywood hunks rolled into one.*

He traced a finger down the bridge of her nose. "You're doing some heavy-duty thinking. Wanna talk about it?"

He already knew her so well! It was exciting and flattering and scary.

She shook her head. They'd had a great time but it was over. Finished. Kaput. Their lost weekend had come to an end. The real world of work and responsibilities waited.

Janet started to feel uneasy. The spell Gage had woven over her began to unravel when she thought of facing civilization again. People and their expectations. Her father wanted a famous son-in-law. Her mother wanted grandbabies. CeeCee and Lacy wanted a triple wedding ceremony. Dr. Jackson wanted the paparazzi to go away.

But what did she want?

Janet looked over at Gage lying beside her, propped endearingly up on one elbow.

Her heart tripped.

She wanted him.

And not just sexually. She wanted to laugh with him and cry with him. She wanted to have adventures with him and love him within an inch of her life.

He winked at her, his eyes shining with a sweet, teasing light as he softly brushed his fingertips over her belly button. Involuntarily, she shivered.

Omigod, it was true. You do love him!

Her eyes widened at the realization. But she couldn't. She mustn't be falling in love. Not now. Not with her colleague. She was just starting her career and it meant everything to her. She didn't have time for this. Didn't have room in her life for him.

Fear had her turning away from him, rolling out of bed, searching for her clothes.

"Hey," he whispered, "where you going?"

"It's Sunday afternoon," she croaked.

"So?"

"We've got to be at work in the morning. I've got laundry to wash and it's going to take us a couple of hours to get back to Houston and…"

"Slow down, you're talking ninety to nothing." He spoke soothingly, calmly, as if nothing monumental had changed between them.

His placidity drove her crazy. Couldn't he see what was happening? Didn't he know how awful this was?

They'd sworn they wouldn't hurt each other but no matter how you sliced it, pain was involved.

He reached out to knead her shoulders and she groaned inwardly at his touch. How easy it would be to collapse back into bed with him and lose control all over again.

Lack of control was what had landed her in this mess in the first place.

Ah, but his fingers...

"You're upset," he said perceptively. Too damn perceptively if you asked her. "Talk to me."

"Upset? Who me? I'm fine. Fine," she repeated. She pulled away from those maddening hands that sent fire rampaging through her. "Have you seen my underwear?"

"Janet don't run away from this. From us."

"Running away? Who's running away?" she denied with every ounce of energy she possessed. "I've just got things to do. Places to be. Can't spend my whole life lounging around in bed with you."

She found her panties halfway across the room—she hadn't worn them since Thursday night—and struggled to wriggle into them. Belatedly, she realized she'd slipped her legs through the wrong opening. Darn it. She took a deep breath, stripped off the thong and tried again, totally aware that Gage was watching her every clumsy move.

"What happened?" he demanded, getting out of bed and coming to stand in front of her. At some point he'd slipped on his shorts and a T-shirt. Thank heavens she didn't have the added distraction of his bare bod. "One minute we're enjoying ourselves, getting along famously and the next minute you're running around looking for an exit like your hair's on fire."

What happened? Oh, you simply turned my world inside out, upside down and shook it with the force of a major earthquake, that's all.

"Nothing happened." She didn't look at him, just shrugged into her bra.

He grabbed her chin in his palm and forced her face up to meet his. His dark eyes were troubled. "What?" he demanded.

Something sharp and irrevocable broke loose in her chest, like a glacier caving. Her heart beat faster, her breathing grew shallow, her knees buckled. If Gage hadn't slipped an arm around her waist, she would have sunk to the floor.

"Are you all right?" he asked huskily, nuzzling her neck. He hadn't yet shaved and his stubble scratched her skin. "You look pale."

Damn him for being concerned about her. She twisted from his grasp, took three steps backward and bumped into the wall. She knew what he wanted, but she wasn't ready for this intimacy, this closeness, this loss of herself in the circle of a couple. And she wasn't sure she could become the woman she saw reflected in Gage's eyes.

"I'm scared okay? Chicken as a Rhode Island Red. *Brock, brock, brock,*" she clucked, tucking her hands into her armpits and flapping her arms like wings in a lame poultry imitation. She joked, hoping to lighten the mood. It didn't help.

Gage looked almost grim. "Scared of what?"

She shrugged. "Let's not make a federal case out of it."

"Talk to me, dammit."

She'd never seen him lose his cool. Or act so forcefully. It was thrilling and disconcerting. She really didn't know him at all.

He towered over her, his mouth inches from hers. She looked up at him and gulped. She disliked relying on him. Disliked revealing too much of herself. She had been independent for so long, and completely in charge of her well-planned life. But here he was, shooting those plans all to hell. She hated the fact that when it came to Gage, she could not control her emotions. Terrified, she grasped at straws, saying the one thing she knew would stop him in his tracks.

"I'm scared that you're trying too hard to take care of me. Anticipating my every need, catering to my desires. I won't have it, Gage. I'm too independent for this, for you. The last thing I want is to be some man's pet project."

10

THE LAST THING I want is to be some man's pet project.

Hadn't Pauline uttered similar words when she'd left him? Hadn't he learned one damn thing from that relationship?

I'm too independent for you, he mouthed in imitation of Janet and fiercely shook his head.

Okay. Fine. Terrific. If that's the way she wanted it, then he was out of here. He was through with trying to please women. They just drove a man nuts anyway.

He should never have tried to protect her from her mother's matchmaking or her father's disdain. It had been her problem, not his.

Chump.

So what if they'd just shared the best lovemaking of his life—and he did mean lovemaking and not simply sex. She didn't want him.

Nimrod.

So what if just being near her made his blood heat and his pulse race. Big deal. It sounded like the friggin' flu.

Gooberhead.

Gage jammed his feet in his sneakers, then grabbed

his duffel from where he'd slung it in the corner on the night they'd arrived. He snatched a pair of jeans from the floor and stuffed them in the duffel. He hazarded a glance in her direction.

Janet had her suitcase open on the bed. She pitched her hairspray and makeup bag inside. She was breathing hard, her nostrils flaring.

Great. Now she was having a hissy fit.

He could go her one better. He stalked to the bathroom, retrieved his shaving kit and slammed it into the duffel with an exaggerated flourish.

Janet scooped her clothes from the dresser drawer and flung them in the suitcase. Her face was flushed, her chest heaving. She met his gaze and glared.

But her trembling chin gave her away.

Wait a minute. Janet didn't lose control of her emotions. Not unless she really cared about something.

That thought stopped him cold.

"This isn't about me at all, is it?" he accused, resting his hands on his hips.

"Of course it is." She dropped her gaze. "You feel like you have to take care of everyone. Well, I don't need to be taken care of."

"No, you're just afraid to let yourself love me and you're clinging to any excuse."

When he heard her sharp intake of breath, he knew he'd hit a nerve. "Don't be ridiculous," she declared.

"Yeah, that's right. You fooled me for a minute there, honing in on my weaknesses but this isn't about me taking care of you, this is about you not getting the love you needed from your father. You're scared to death that you inherited his inability to show love.''

''I'm not,'' she whimpered and sank onto the edge of the bed, but in her denial he heard the truth.

Suddenly, he saw it all so clearly. ''That's why you don't believe in true love, that's why you're worried about having children. You don't think you *can* love.''

It was as if he'd cracked open her chest and seen what was inside her heart. Janet gulped. There wasn't enough air in the room. She felt light-headed and confused and...empty.

Biting down on her bottom lip to keep the tears at bay, she got up to finish packing. She jerked her jacket from where she'd slung it over the bedpost. Something fell from the lapel and hit the floor with a soft plunk.

Gracie's Saint Jude pin.

Gage bent down to pick it up. When he stood, their gazes locked. ''Here's the deal, sweetheart,'' he said, dropping the pin into her outstretched palm. ''Until you acknowledge your fears about love and deal with them, you're a lost cause.''

THE DRIVE back to Houston was horrible. Neither of them spoke the entire time. They both stared listlessly at the gray clouds hunkering on the horizon.

They arrived home around eight o'clock that night to discover Peter's getaway vacation had been a success. The paparazzi had disappeared from their front stoop, off to vex someone more happening. According to the radio, a high-profile Hollywood couple had just announced their plans to divorce. Breakups, apparently, were more newsworthy than engagements.

Gage helped her upstairs with her luggage. She thanked him at the door. Without a word, he turned and headed for the elevator.

Janet looked down at the Saint Jude pin she'd clutched in her hand all the way from Lake Travis and her gut wrenched.

Lost cause.

Her heart dragged on the carpet as she shut the door and locked herself inside the empty condo.

Alone.

She fingered the pin.

Lost cause.

No hope for her.

None at all.

Too late for love.

Her bottom lip trembled, and she sank to the floor and pulled her knees to her chest. "But I don't want to be a lost cause," she whispered.

She was helplessly, hopelessly in love with Dr. Gage Gregory. No if, ands or buts about it.

The cold, hard facts hit her like a physical blow.

She wanted to run after him like a forlorn puppy chasing his owner's car. She wanted to go upstairs, knock on his door then fling herself into his arms when he answered. She wanted him to smile that crooked, come-hither grin and lightly tickle her ribs to make her laugh. She wanted to taste him and touch him and take him to bed and make babies with him.

Babies?

Was she nuts? Was she insane? Had Nadine's predictions gripped her common sense and rendered her incognizant the way it had Gracie?

Babies weren't in her immediate future. Nor was marriage. She'd been trying to tell everyone that, but no one had been listening.

Most of all impish voice, who reminded her just how cute a miniature Gage, calling her Mama, would look.

The Baby Predicate had taken control.

No. No. No.

"I'm a sensible woman. I don't act this way. I don't go gaga over men. I don't fall in love after only having known someone a month. I don't. I don't. I don't," she muttered to herself.

This had to be Gracie's doing. Somewhere she and Nadine were performing voodoo magic, making her fall in love with Gage.

Then again, perhaps she should hold her father accountable. If he wasn't so hard to please she wouldn't have ended up on a houseboat with her colleague. Wouldn't have made love to Gage until her head spun and her heart ached with an inexplicable longing.

She had to do something about this. Now.

It was close to ten o'clock when she pulled up outside her father's lavish estate in the Woodlands. Janet sat in the darkness swallowing her fear. Resolutely, she got out of the car, marched up the sidewalk and hammered on the front door.

A few seconds later, her father pulled open the door. He looked rather ridiculous in silk pajamas and a satin bed cap. A man with too much money putting on airs. Funny how she'd never seen him for what he really was. A sad, lonely man who placed wealth and prestige above family and friends.

"Janet," he said. "What are you doing here?"

Not hi, daughter, how are you. Good to see you. Come on in and we'll have Ho Hos and hot chocolate.

He waited, blocking the doorway.

"May I come in?" Why hadn't she ever noticed what a weak chin he had? Why hadn't she ever realized he could stare at you without ever really looking you in the eyes.

"Uh, I was on my way to bed."

"We need to talk. It's important. I'd rather tell you to your face than have you read about it in the newspapers."

He hesitated. Maybe it was the I've-got-this-massive-chip-on-my-shoulder-and-I'm-daring-you-to-knock-it-off expression on her face that quelled him. Or perhaps it was the Rambo way she muscled him aside and entered the house. Either way, Janet didn't care. She was no longer afraid of her father.

Thanks to Gage.

All this time she had thought she was so independent. Autonomous, self-ruling, I-don't-need-anyone-but-me Janet. She'd won scholarships and earned grants to pay her way through medical school. She'd gone to work at age sixteen, waiting tables to help Gracie make ends meet. She'd never followed the crowd, seeing herself as the ultimate maverick because she embraced lofty ideals over having a good time, valued her high standards above relationships, honored inflexible rules over compassion, viewed loving couples as "clingy."

For all her misplaced pride in her sovereignty, it came down to one thing. Anything she'd ever accomplished she'd done to gain the love of this single man.

That wasn't independence. That was neediness of the highest order.

The realization spun her world on its axis.

Filled with anger and remorse, sadness and an odd kind of freedom, Janet trod through the foyer and into the living room. She plunked down in a chair.

"Not that one, Janet!" Her father winced. "That's an authentic Louis the Fourteenth."

"Who cares." She waved a hand. "Why do you buy furniture people can't sit in?"

Her father's mouth dropped. "Wh...what's come over you? Why are you acting like this?" He narrowed his eyes. "Where's Gage? I'm going to call him to come get you."

"I've gotta tell you something and you're not going to like it, so you better sit down."

Eyeing her as if she was a pet poodle that had

suddenly morphed into a Doberman pinscher, Niles eased himself down onto the stiff-backed sofa.

"Here's the deal," she said. "Gage and I are not really engaged. We made the whole thing up. I would have told you the truth, but you were so proud of Gage. Father, you kept telling him how much you wished he was your son. Do you have any idea how that made me feel?"

Her bravado vanished when she reached the core issue. Here it was at last, the confrontation that had been thirty years in the making.

"I...I never thought about it."

"That's right. You've never given me a second thought."

Oh damn. I will not cry, I will not cry, I will not cry.

Her father shifted uncomfortably in his seat, and she had a feeling it wasn't just because the darned sofa was the most uncomfortable piece of furniture under creation.

"You know what, Father? Not one time in my entire life have you ever told me that you loved me."

Crap! Her nose was staring to burn and her eyes filled with unshed tears.

"Do you love me, Father?"

He cleared his throat. "Of course I do."

"Do you? Do you really?"

He clenched his jaw. "I don't understand the point of this conversation."

"And therein lies the problem. Why did you leave

Gracie when I was sick with scarlet fever? Couldn't you have at least waited until I was well?''

He didn't meet her steadfast gaze, instead, he toyed with the hem of his dressing gown. Imagine. What kind of man wore a dressing gown?

"I suppose you have a right to know," he said after a very long pause. "I was married once before your mother."

That came out of left field. Janet pulled herself up straight. "Go on."

"Lillian was my college sweetheart. I loved her with every breath in my body." He was gripping the arm of the sofa as if it was a life raft on the *Titanic*. "We had a son. Benjy. He was the light of my life."

Shocked, Janet could only stare. "I have a brother?" She felt numb. Her father had had a whole other family. His real family. The one that he'd loved.

"Had. Benjy died in a car accident with his mother when he was five."

Janet sucked in her breath. "How awful."

"Yes."

Silence descended. Well, that explained a few things.

"You know that your mother was my secretary. After the car accident I was so grief stricken I could barely function. Your mother took care of everything. And she comforted me in my time of distress. Comforted me in a sexual manner."

Okay. A little more information than I needed.

"She got pregnant with you. I married Gracie because she was a good woman and it was my duty to take care of the two of you. But I never loved her. I couldn't make myself love her.''

"Or me.''

He nodded. "Every time I looked at you I wondered why you were here and Benjy was not.''

Oh, oh, it hurt so much. But she'd asked for truth. She needed to hear what he had to say despite the ice picks jamming their way through her heart.

"Then you got sick. I simply couldn't tolerate the thought of losing another child. I divorced Gracie and distanced myself from you.''

"So you abandoned me before I could abandon you the way Benjy did.''

"Don't you think I've castigated myself for my behavior? Don't you think I know that I was wrong?''

"No, Father, I don't know that. All I ever wanted was for you to love me.''

"I'm sorry I couldn't give you what you needed,'' he said with an exhausted sigh. He looked very old at the moment, drained of energy.

She felt sorry for him. For all the things he'd missed out on. And she felt something else. Understanding, and a calm sense of peace. Niles might not ever be able to fully love her, but that was okay. She had Gracie, a kooky but loving mother. She had Lacy and CeeCee, the two best friends a girl could ever ask for.

And Gage?

A handsome, wealthy doctor with a fabulous sense

of humor. A man who cared deeply for her and showed his feelings in everything he did. A man who shared her passion for medicine. A man with an incredible smile and the patience of Job.

Did he love her as she loved him?

And in that instant, Janet knew it was true. All this time she'd been so wrong, thinking that romantic love was a fairy tale. It did indeed exist.

For she'd seen it simmering in the depths of Gage Gregory's dark eyes.

"JANET!" Peter boomed at her from the doctors' lounge early the next morning.

She turned to find him standing in the hallway behind her, a cup of coffee in his hand.

"Peter, good morning," she forced a smile.

"Is it good, Janet, really? You don't have to put on a happy face for my benefit."

"Er…" She wasn't sure what he was talking about. "Okay."

He moved toward her, placed a comforting hand on her shoulder. "Gage called me last night. He told me everything."

Everything? What did that entail?

"He did?"

Dr. Jackson nodded. "I understand that you two are having problems with your relationship because of the stress of working together."

"He told you that?"

"He also tendered his resignation. Effective immediately. He won't be in today."

"No!"

"I hate losing him, but I understand completely. A great romance only comes along once in a lifetime. A man can't turn his back on love."

"Gage said that?" She felt all trembly and gooey inside.

"Yes. It's a grand gesture. He must love you very much to sacrifice his career for you. Most men wouldn't."

Gage had given up his job for her.

"He can't quit," she said. "This job means everything to him. I'm the one who's leaving."

"But he said the same thing of you. That your work is your life."

She loved her job, yes. And the doctors at the Blanton Street Group were a wonderful bunch of physicians. But she'd struggled to attain this particular position simply to impress her father. Now there was something more important in her life, and she wasn't about to let him get away.

"If you'll excuse me, Peter," she said. "I've got to make a phone call."

HE STOOD in the kitchen listening to the answering machine record the call.

"Gage, it's Janet. Are you there? If you're there, please pick up, we've got to talk."

His heart bumped crazily against his chest at the

sound of her voice, but he didn't pick up the phone. He didn't want to argue with her about quitting his job. Last night he'd realized that he wouldn't be able to keep working with her. Seeing her every day, remembering what they'd shared, wanting her but not being able to have her. Best he pack up and leave now before he'd really gotten his practice established. For the first time in his life, he'd been thinking of his own needs and not those of someone else, and it felt good. He loved Janet, yes, but if she couldn't love him back, then there was no point hanging around.

"I took your advice," she said. "I confronted my father."

He held his breath and waited.

"You were right. Once I found out why he acted the way he did toward me all these years, he lost all power over me. I feel like someone plucked the Empire State Building off my chest."

"Good for you," he murmured under his breath. "I'm so proud of you."

"I've got to see you. I've got to talk to you in person. This is a monumental breakthrough, and I want to share it with you. I'm coming over after I get off work. If you're interested, be there. If you're not, then I'll know it's over between us."

He started to reach for the phone but something held him back.

"Gage," she said. "I love you."

She loved him!

And he loved her. With a calm certainty that didn't

scare him in the least. He loved her with the same unshakable sureness that he loved his parents. This feeling wasn't ever going away.

He grabbed the receiver then, but it was too late. The dial tone buzzed in his ear.

Janet loved him!

He didn't have much time until she got home, but he knew what he must do.

THERE WAS A tuxedoed man on her terrace.

Dr. Janet Hunter froze in midstride, her medical bag and a small flat briefcase tucked underneath one arm. Keys in hand, she'd just returned home from work.

She blinked in disbelief.

Yep. No mirage. A handsome man, resplendent in a black tuxedo with a white cumberbund and red bow tie stood proudly among her wrought iron furniture.

Her table was covered with a white linen cloth. In the middle of the table sat a vase of red roses, two flickering red candles and silver domed serving dishes for two. From a boom box perched on the terrace wall came the strains of Barbra Streisand singing *People Who Need People*.

Okay, Janet thought with a huge grin breaking across her face, two could play this game.

She tossed her briefcase and medical bag on the counter, walked across the floor, threw open the door and hollered, "Hey buddy."

"You talking to me?" he asked, returning her grin.

Her heart was flying, flying, flying. Swooping and dipping, catching the updrafts of her expanding emotions.

"Do you see any other good-looking physicians hanging around here?"

"Yes." His eyes never left her face. "And I'm looking right at her." He held out his arms.

She was across the terrace in nothing flat. Gage wrapped his arm around her and kissed her forehead, her eyelids, her cheeks, her nose. He kissed her as if he hadn't seen her in fifty years and might not see her for another fifty if he dared let her go.

"How did you get in?"

"A little help from Gracie," he murmured, his lips warm against her skin.

"That's what I get for giving her a spare key. Men in tuxedoes turning up unannounced on my terrace."

"What can I say? The woman's crazy about me."

"I can't blame her," she whispered, looking him straight in the eyes as she captured his lips in hers. Enough of that face kissing, her mouth was getting jealous of her nose.

She pulled away after a few of his tongue tricks had her panting. "So, I'm assuming you got my message."

His grin widened. "I did. You said you loved me."

"Did I?" Her stomach tightened. Her knees went weak. She felt so perfectly wonderful, so perfectly beautiful, so perfectly right. She thought she was going to burst.

"Oh yes, you did. No backing out of it. I saved the tape."

"You didn't."

"I did. I'm going to play it for our kids when they ask about the first time Mommy told Daddy that she loved him."

"What are you saying, Dr. Gregory?" She leaned into him, relishing his scent, relishing the wonderful glow of the moment.

"That depends. Are you admitting that you were wrong, that there is such a thing as true love?" His hands, holding hers, were so warm and welcoming, like a snuggly blanket on a cold winter day.

"I might have been mistaken."

"I've got to tell you the truth, Janet. Now don't get scared or anything, but I knew you were the one for me from the moment I met you right here on this very terrace."

"You didn't."

"I did."

"Liar."

"Nonbeliever."

They grinned at each other. He drew her close again and nuzzled her ear. "You're exactly what I need. A woman who knows her own mind and stands up for herself."

"That's me."

"A woman who's not afraid to face her fears."

"Well, it took me a while." She told him then about what had happened with her father, about

Niles's other family. When she was finished, he didn't say a word. He just squeezed her tightly.

"I discovered something else."

"Oh?"

"I realized that you've been there for me from the moment I met you. Not because you considered me a pet project, but because you simply cared. You've taught me the real meaning of love. That's a very precious gift."

They swayed in the twilight, bodies pressed together.

"So," she said, after a long moment of luxuriating in the comfort of his arms. "What's this nonsense about you quitting your job?"

"Well," he said, "that was before you admitted that you loved me."

"You were just going to run off, abandon the position you'd worked so hard to achieve for me?"

"Actually, no. This time I was being a little selfish. I couldn't bear the thought of seeing you day after day, knowing I couldn't have you. Working beside you and knowing that you didn't need me in your life."

"Are you kidding? Gage, I need you so much it's pitiful. Without you, I would never have found the courage to face my father. Like it or not, you've become my pillar of strength."

"Really?"

"What do you think?"

"I'll always be here for you, Janet. In good times and bad. In sickness and in health."

He took her left hand in his and slipped the cubic zirconia off her finger. Then he pulled a small black velvet box from the pocket of his tuxedo.

Her whole body began to shake when she realized his intention. She pressed her right hand to her mouth. "Oh," she whispered, "oh."

"Janet Hunter." He got down on one knee, flicked open the box with his thumb. A two-carat diamond solitaire winked up at her. "Will you do me the honor of becoming my wife?"

"A real engagement."

"Yes."

"Does this mean more paparazzi popping from behind every bush?"

"Probably. Is that a problem?"

"Not on your life," she said.

"Does that mean your answer is yes?"

"Let me just show you." Then slowly, seductively, she began to undo the buttons on his stiff white shirt.

Epilogue

Six months later

LACY CAME DOWN the aisle on her father's arm looking resplendent in her long white wedding gown, her blond hair caught back with a gold clip, a bouquet of old-fashioned tea roses and baby's breath clutched in her hand. Her father left her beside her groom, Dr. Bennett Sheridan, who honestly, looked thunderstruck and was smiling for all he was worth.

Next came CeeCee on the arm of a man who looked exactly like the guy she was going to marry. Zack and Jack were identical twins, Janet had told Gage. CeeCee's wedding dress was short, sleek and modern, her red hair, capped with a short lace veil, fanned out like a flame down her back. She grinned and waved to guests as she went up the aisle. Her groom, Dr. Jack Travis, held out his hand and took her from his brother. Jack looked as if no curse on earth could break the delicious spell of their love.

And last, but most certainly not least, came Gage's bride-to-be.

Gage's heart hung in his chest like a kite on high line wires at the sight of her.

Janet, my love. My one and only. My soul mate. The other half of me. We two are now joined. Not needy but loving freely. Helping, giving, sharing for the rest of our days.

The vows he'd written circled in his head. He would not forget them. Ever.

Janet was absolutely gorgeous in a mid-calf gown with a bodice that showed off her curves. Her black hair was piled loosely atop her head, soft tendrils framing her face the way he liked. Her indigo eyes glistened with joy. Pinned to her shoulder was Saint Jude, a lost cause no more. At last Cupid had coaxed Janet's heart around love.

His heart hammered. His mouth grew dry. He didn't know about Bennett or Jack, but Gage felt as if he were the luckiest man on the face of the earth to be marrying such a fabulous woman. A woman brave enough to face her fears in order to learn that true and lasting love did indeed exist. He loved her beyond measure.

Janet was trembling as she ended her walk beside Gage. He took her hand and squeezed it, giving her strength. She'd thought once that she didn't need him, didn't need love, didn't need anyone. Thank heavens for Gracie, Nadine and that infernal prediction or she might never have overcome her stubbornness long enough to find her one true love.

Taking a deep breath to quiet her pounding heart, she glanced around her. A triple wedding. Three best friends sharing the happiest day of their lives together. Her heart filled to overflowing.

The minister began the ceremony, starting with

Lacy and Bennett. In the pews behind them sat Lacy's huge family and Bennett's parents from Boston.

On the opposite side of the church sat CeeCee and Jack's guests, which included all the single women in CeeCee's family and a group of guys from their sky-diving club.

Janet's mother was in attendance of course. With Sam and his daughters May, Suzie, Jenny, Jenny's husband and brand-new baby Kyle. Gracie was Gracie Pinkerton now. She and Sam had gotten married in a hot air balloon two months ago and spent their honeymoon in Australia. That made her Kyle's grandmother now, successfully averting Nadine's dire prediction. She was a grandmother before fifty-two.

There were coworkers from the hospital, and everyone from the Blanton Street Group had shown up not to mention the paparazzi hanging around outside.

But what pleased Janet the most was that her father had walked her down the aisle, then just before he handed her to Gage, he'd leaned close to whisper, "You're going to be a great wife and mother, Janet. I'm sorry I never told you this when you needed to hear it, but I'm so proud of you."

When the minister reached them, having already pronounced Lacy and Bennett, CeeCee and Jack, man and wife, Gage turned to face her, squeezed her hand again and smiled for all he was worth.

Janet caught her breath. Her heart soared like an eagle. For her deepest held dreams had come true. She'd finally found the love she'd craved for so long.

CALL THE ONES YOU LOVE OVER THE HOLIDAYS!

Save $25 off future book purchases when you buy any four Harlequin® or Silhouette® books in October, November and December 2001,

PLUS

receive a phone card good for 15 minutes of long-distance calls to anyone you want in North America!

WHAT AN INCREDIBLE DEAL!

Just fill out this form and attach 4 proofs of purchase (cash register receipts) from October, November and December 2001 books, and Harlequin Books will send you a coupon booklet worth a total savings of $25 off future purchases of Harlequin® and Silhouette® books, AND a 15-minute phone card to call the ones you love, anywhere in North America.

Please send this form, along with your cash register receipts
as proofs of purchase, to:
In the USA: Harlequin Books, P.O. Box 9057, Buffalo, NY 14269-9057
In Canada: Harlequin Books, P.O. Box 622, Fort Erie, Ontario L2A 5X3
Cash register receipts must be dated no later than December 31, 2001.
Limit of 1 coupon booklet and phone card per household.
Please allow 4-6 weeks for delivery.

**I accept your offer! Enclosed are 4 proofs of purchase.
Please send me my coupon booklet
and a 15-minute phone card:**

Name: _____

Address: _____ City: _____

State/Prov.: _____ Zip/Postal Code: _____

Account Number (if available): _____

---

097 KJB DAGL
PHQ4013

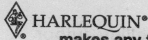

USA Today bestselling author
Jacqueline Diamond really delivers!

"Wonderful humor and
original plot twists and turns...."
–Romantic Times Magazine

"Upbeat, refreshing, and
will tickle your funnybone."
–The Romance Reader

"(Jacqueline Diamond) will make your head spin and
leave you laughing hysterically."
–Rendezvous

And brings two great Harlequin lines together...

The fun starts with Harlequin American Romance®...

SURPRISE, DOC! YOU'RE A DADDY!
On sale September 2001
American Romance® #889

And ends with Harlequin Duets™...

THE DOC'S DOUBLE DELIVERY
On sale December 2001
Duets™ #66

Don't miss a single moment!

Available at your favorite retail outlet.